Praise for the Military Harmless Series

Little Harmless Military Romance Anthology

Volume One

Melissa Schroeder

ISBN-13:
978-1478173083

ISBN-10:
1478173084

Edited by Chloe Vale
Cover by Brandy Walker
Formatting by Chloe Vale

First print publication: July 2012

Table of Contents

To prove her love and save her man, she has to go above and beyond the call of duty.

Infatuation: A Little Military Harmless Romance #1

Francis McKade is a man in lust. He's had a crush on his best friend's little sister for years but he has never acted on it. Besides that fact that she's Malachi's sister, he's a Seal and he learned his lesson with his ex-fiancé. Women do not like being left alone for long months at a time. Still, at a wedding in Hawaii anything can happen—and does. Unfortunately, after the best night of his life, he and Mal are called away to one of their most dangerous missions.

Shannon is blown over by Kade. She's always had a crush on him and after their night together, it starts to feel a little like love. But, after the mission, Kade never calls or writes and she starts to wonder if it was all a dream. Until one night, her brother Mal drags him into her bar and grill and Shannon gets the shock of her life.

Kade isn't the man Shannon knew in Hawaii, or even the last few years. Twelve hours of torture changes a man, especially one who had never felt so vulnerable. He still can't shake the terror that keeps him up at night. Worse, he is realizing that the career he loves just might be over.

Shannon is still mad, but she can't help but hurt for the man she loves. He is darker, a bit more dangerous, but beneath that, he is the Kade she's known for so many years. When he pushes her to her limits in the bedroom, Shannon refuses to back down. One way or another, this military man is going to learn there is no walking away from love—not while she still has breath in her body.

Warning: This book contains two infatuated lovers, a hardheaded military man, a determined woman, some old friends, and a little taste of New Orleans. As always, ice

1

water is suggested while reading. It might be the first military Harmless book, but the only thing that has changed is how hot our hero looks in his uniform—not to mention out of it.

Dedication

To the men and women of the United States Military. Thank you for your sacrifice, your courage, and your commitment to our country.

And to the families and loved ones who keep the home fires burning. You are the heart and soul of the military.

Acknowledgements

I can finish no book without the help of the wonderful support system I have.

Brandy Walker, woman, you know that I would never be able to keep up with everything without. And yes, dammit, I LOVE those lists.

Thanks to Kris Cook, Ali Flores and Joy Harris for the wonderful Harmless in Savannah that gave me the break I needed.

Les, who still hasn't learned how to waltz, but I still love you anyway.

And to the people behind the scenes:

Kendra Egert for her wonderful cover art.

Chloe Vale who worked overtime to get the book edited.

April Martinez for doing the formatting.

I could not have done this without your help. Thank you.

Infatuation

A Little Harmless Military Romance

Melissa Schroeder

Chapter One

The sound of Hawaiian music drifted lightly through the air as Kade took a small sip of his beer. He stood on the side of the dance floor watching the wedding guests. It was one of those days Hawaiians took for granted he was sure, but Kade didn't. The sweet scent of plumeria tickled his nose, and the sound of the ocean just a few hundred yards away combined with the music to ensure that the entire day seemed magical. The groom, Chris Dupree, smiled like a man who had just finished Hell Week with honors, while his new bride, Cynthia, glowed with more than that "happily just married" glow. Her gently rounded tummy was barely visible, but everyone knew she was pregnant.

"Never thought he would settle down," Malachi, Chris' brother, said from beside him. One of Kade's best friends, Mal had dragged him across the Pacific Ocean to make the wedding.

"Really? He's been with her for years. It only took him this long to convince her to marry, right?"

Mal laughed and took a long drink out of his bottle.

"Ain't that the truth," Mal said, New Orleans threading his voice. Their friendship was an odd one, that was for sure. Mal had grown up as part of a huge family in New Orleans, and was half creole. The name Dupree meant something in circles down there, especially in hospitality. Francis McKade grew up the child of Australian immigrants, both scientists recruited to work for the US Military.

"At least there are lots of lovely ladies here for the picking," Mal said, his gaze roaming over the crowd. "There's something about Hawaiian women, you know?"

Kade said nothing but nodded. He wasn't particularly interested in most of the women today. The woman he wanted set off signs of being interested in him, but she had never acted on it.

"Are you two flipping a coin to see who gets what woman?"

The amused female voice slipped down his spine and into his blood. Before turning around, he knew who she was. Shannon Dupree, youngest sister of his best friend, and the woman who had starred in most of his most vivid sex dreams. He turned to face her, thinking he was ready for the impact, but of course he wasn't. As usual, she stole his breath away.

She was dressed in red, the main color of the wedding. The soft material draped over her generous curves. Shannon was built like Kade loved his women. Full hips, abundant breasts, and so many curves his fingers itched to explore. Every time he was near her, he had to count backwards from ten and imagine that he was taking a shower in freezing water. Sometimes that worked.

"What makes you think we're doing that?" Mal asked.

One eyebrow rose as she studied her brother. "I've known you for twenty-eight years, that's how I know."

Shannon turned to Kade expectantly, and he couldn't think. Every damned thought vaporized. It was those eyes. Green with a hint of brown, they were so unusual, and they stood out against her light brown skin. He could just imagine how they would look filled with heat and lust.

He finally cleared his throat and mentally gave himself a shake. Staring at her like a fifteen-year-old with a crush wasn't really cool. "Don't lump me in with your brother, here. He doesn't have any standards."

"Except for that stripper last time you visited?"

There was a beat of silence. "Stripper?"

"Mal ratted you out."

He gave his friend a nasty look. His last visit to New Orleans hadn't gone that well. Shannon had gotten very serious about her current boyfriend, and there had been talk of them moving in together. Kade had done the one thing he could to ignore the pain. He got drunk and went out to strip clubs. And Mal had been the one with the stripper, not him.

"I think your brother had that wrong."

She glanced back and forth between them. "Whatever. Just make sure you stick around for some of the reception before you go sniffing any women."

"Don't worry about me. Your brother has the impulse control problem."

Shannon laughed.

Mal grunted. "Both of you suck."

"They're going to be cutting the cake soon, so at least hold off until then, could you?"

With that she brushed past them, and he could smell her. God, she was exotic. Even with all the scents of Hawaii surrounding him, hers stood out. Spicy, sweet...

He took another pull from his longneck bottle, trying to cool his libido.

"So, who do you have in mind?" Mal asked, pulling him from his thoughts.

"What?"

"Man, it's a wedding. Women are always ripe for seduction at these things. You have to have someone in mind."

His gaze traveled back to Shannon. She walked through the crowd, her hips swaying sensually as she moved from person to person. Her smile enticed everyone she spoke to. As the owner of a bar and grill in New Orleans, she knew how to work a room. And dammit, she had that perfect smile that drew every man to her. His hand started to hurt, and he looked down to find his fist clenched so tight around his bottle his knuckles were white. It took a couple of seconds to calm himself down. He didn't have a right to be jealous. She wasn't his to love, to protect. He'd learned a long time ago that being a Seal and being married just didn't work out.

He noticed Mal looking at him, expecting an answer.

"Not sure, mate, but I have a feeling I'll find someone to occupy my time."

* * * *

Shannon shivered as she took a sip of champagne. She tried not to wince at the taste. What the holy hell was she doing drinking it? She hated the drink. What she needed was two fingers of whiskey. It would clear her head of the sexy Seal that had her pulse skipping.

"What are you doing drinking that?" her sister, Jocelyn, asked.

When Shannon turned, she couldn't fight the smile. Seeing the transformation of her sister in the last year was amazing. Seeing her happily married with Kai added to the joy she felt for Jocelyn. Even if there was a little jolt of envy, Shannon couldn't begrudge her the happiness. After the things she had overcome, Jocelyn deserved it more than anyone she knew.

"I thought it best. You know with the jet lag and all that, I need to keep my wits about me. Champagne should help, right?"

Her sister's eyes danced with barely suppressed amusement. "It couldn't be because of one hot Seal with a hint of an Aussie accent, could it?

Shannon closed her eyes and sighed. "That man gets my temperature up. All he has to do is smile, and I'm ready to strip naked and jump his bones." She opened her eyes. "Is it that obvious?"

Jocelyn shook her head. "Just to someone who knows you like I do."

And no two people knew each other better. As the two girls in a huge family of men, they had depended on each other. Only fifteen months apart in age, they were more like twins than just sisters.

"Are you talking about that hot Seal your brother brought with him?" May Aiona Chambers asked as she stepped up to the two women. After meeting her just months earlier at Jocelyn's wedding, Shannon had instantly liked the sassy Hawaiian. Petite with the most amazing long hair and blue green eyes, she never seemed to have a problem voicing her opinion.

"Oh, May, please, could you join us in the conversation," Jocelyn said with a laugh.

"As my sister-in-law, you should be used to it by now." She dismissed Jocelyn and honed in on Shannon. "He's been watching you."

"What?" she asked, her voice squeaking. "No he hasn't."

"That Seal, he's been watching you all day."

Shannon snorted, trying to hide the way her heart rate jumped. "You're insane. Does this run in the family? You might want to adopt children, Jocelyn."

"No, really, he has. He does it when he thinks you aren't looking."

She turned around and found him easily on the other side of the dance floor. That erect posture made it easy. He always looked like he was standing at attention. Even in civvies, he looked like a Seal. The Hawaiian print polo shirt hugged his shoulders and was tucked neatly into his khaki dress slacks. He wasn't the tallest man in the room, but he stood out. All that hard muscle, not to mention the blond hair and the to-die-for blue eyes, made him a gorgeous package. Everything in her yearned, wanted. Of course, he wasn't looking at them. His attention was on the other side of the room. Probably on some damned stripper. Shannon turned back to her sister and May.

"Are you drunk?" Shannon asked.

May rolled her eyes. "No, really he has. You know what those Seals are like. He can do surveillance without you knowing. It's his job. But you should see the way he looks at you."

She couldn't help herself. "Like how?"

May hummed. "Like he wants to take a big, long bite out of you."

She couldn't stop the shiver that slinked down her spine or the way her body heated at the thought. Since she had met him five years earlier, she had been interested in him. He was quiet, unlike her brothers, and the way he moved…God, she knew for sure he was good in bed. But it was more than that. Kade was sexy, that was for sure, but there was something more to him than just a good-looking man. There was an innate goodness in him, one that made a woman know he would take care of her no matter what.

"If I were you, I would make use of the event to get him in bed."

Shannon snorted again, trying to keep herself from imagining it—and failing. "Please, May, tell me what you really think."

"Believe me, I know about waiting, and it isn't worth it. I waited years for some idiot to notice me. I think of all the time we wasted dancing around like that."

"Did you just call your husband an idiot?" Jocelyn asked.

May rolled her eyes. "He overlooked me for years, then waited forever once he did notice me. Of course he's an idiot. But in this situation, you have to be strategic. I saw Evan almost every day. This guy, he's going to be gone again with that job of his. You have got to take advantage of the wedding and get him into bed. Get a little wedding booty."

She should be mad, but it was hard to be. May looked so innocent with her sweet smile, and her voice sounded like something out of a movie. Shannon just couldn't get irritated with her. Before May could say anything else, they announced the cutting of the cake. She turned to face the banquet table, and as she did, she caught Kade looking at her. It was the briefest moment, just a second, but even across all that space, she saw the heat, the longing, and felt it build inside of her. Her breath backed up in her lungs. In that next instant, he looked away.

It took all her power to turn her attention back to the event at hand, seeing her brother and her sister-in-law beaming at each other, she took another sip of champagne. May was right. She had to take a chance. If he said no, if he ignored her, then she could drink herself in a stupor and have months before she had to face him again.

But there was one thing Shannon Michele Dupree did right, and that was being bold. She chugged the rest of her champagne, set it on the table next to her, and headed off in Kade's direction.

That man wouldn't know what hit him.

Chapter Two

Kade's heart jumped into his throat when he saw Shannon walking determinedly in his direction. She wore her hair up to show off her slender neck and the diamond earrings he knew Mal had bought her. God, she was gorgeous. He liked strong women, and that was definitely Shannon. All the feminine strength in that sexy package, he was having a hard time resisting her. Everything in his body, especially one particular body part, told him to go after her. But his brain wouldn't let him. He couldn't act on his attraction. Mal was his best friend, and one of the things he'd always believed in was you didn't fuck around with your buddy's sister. Since Kade knew he wasn't cut out to be involved for the long haul, he had to ignore the lust that was circling his gut right now.

Damn, as she neared, he saw she was coming after him for something. What had he done? With Shannon, you never knew what would happen. The woman ran a tight ship at work, and no one, not even her trained-to-kill Navy Seal brother, got away with jack shit with her.

"Hey, Kade," she said just as the band started up with a slow country song. Even with the music playing, he could hear her accent. "Do you think you could dance a little two-step with me? I know you have to be one of the only guys here who knows how to do it right."

The way she said it made him think of sex. Who was he fooling? Everything she said made him think of sex. But now, she was smiling, those green eyes sparkling up at him, and he couldn't think again.

"What?"

She laughed. The sound of it sunk into his blood and made his pulse do its own two-step. "Dance. You, me. Two-step. You haven't forgotten how to do it, have you?"

The memory of her teaching him to two-step filtered through his mind. It had felt like purgatory, stuck between heaven and hell. Her body had moved against his, her soft breasts pressed against his chest...he'd almost lost it. The only thing that had saved him was that Mal was on that very same dance floor and probably would have beaten the hell out of him if he had known what Kade was thinking.

"Uh...yeah, I remember."

She didn't wait for a yes or no. She just grabbed his hand and dragged him behind her to the dance floor. She stopped then waited for him to step closer. Kade hesitated, trying to get his brain back into the game. Of course, his little brain wanted to do most of the thinking. His cock twitched as he drew her into his arms. They started to dance, and he tried to keep her further away. She slipped closer.

Oh, shit. Just the little brush of her body against his had his cock hardening. He just hoped she didn't notice.

"I thought you and Mal would be off having a good old time."

He glanced down at her, wondering about the tone. There was a thread of irritation in it. She was smiling up at him as if there was nothing wrong, but he knew there was something she wasn't telling him.

"Apparently your brother had a woman picked out already."

She nodded. "He's a slut."

Kade couldn't help it. He threw back his head and laughed. Shannon had a way of talking about her brothers, especially Mal, that Kade knew was to remind them they were still just her brothers.

"What about you?" she asked.

"I'm not a slut."

She chuckled. "The jury's still out on that one."

"Your brother needs to learn how to be a little more picky."

Her lips curved up at that comment, and he felt the moisture dry up in his mouth. God, he wanted to kiss that smile off her face—then move down her body, exploring every delicious inch of her. He knew her flesh would be sweet.

"I noticed you're pretty picky."

He nodded as he worked her around the dance floor. "I don't fall for every pretty face that comes along."

She said nothing. Instead she laid her head on his shoulder. The gesture was so natural it was as if she did it every day. He knew he should tell her not to. His brain said he should do it. But he couldn't. It was too close to what he wanted, what he yearned for. For five long years he had wanted her, wanted to feel this way with her, her head on his shoulder, her soft, warm body in his arms. He had wanted that for so long, he just couldn't bring himself to stop her.

It was bad enough he would probably have to take a five-hour cold shower when he got back to the room. Sweat slid down his back, and he had to fight the urge to lean down and brush his lips over her forehead.

He had talked himself into not doing more when she sighed and relaxed even more against him. Her breasts were pressed against his chest, and with every breath he drew in that sultry scent that was so unique to her. His head started to spin. His body started to duel with his mind. His brain was starting to lose when the music ended. The band swung into a fast-paced Hawaiian tune. His body protested when he had to pull back.

"Shannon?"

Even to his own ears, his voice sounded gruff. She raised her head and blinked as if coming out of some kind of daze. Her breathing hitched, and her breasts rose above the neckline of her dress. His gaze slipped down, he could see her hardened nipples through the delicate red fabric. He curled his fingers into his palms and counted backwards from ten. If he didn't get away from her soon, he would definitely lose control. There would be nothing to stop him from tearing off her clothes and bending her over a banquet table.

The wind shifted, pulling a few strands of her hair loose from the complicated style.

He cleared his throat. "Well, that was...nice."

Fuck. How lame could he get? She studied him for a second, her expression serious, thoughtful. Then in the next moment, her lips curved.

"You know where my room is, doncha?"

Lust soared. His body reacted at the direct question. Any doubts he had about her interest in him vaporized. She apparently thought there was no reason to hide her attraction to him anymore.

He nodded, unable to form a word.

"Well, then you know where to find me later."

With that, she walked away, and he couldn't help watching her hips and that magnificent ass of hers. He could just imagine having her on all fours in front of him as he took her from behind.

Kade drew in a deep breath. He needed to get a drink. He needed to go away, far away. He could not breach the trust his friend put in him. If another man had thoughts about his sister like he had about Shannon, well, he would kill him. Of course, his sister was married with five kids, so there was a really good chance his brother-in-law had those thoughts.

He headed over to the bar. After ordering another beer, he turned and found himself face to face with Kai Aiona, Shannon's brother-in-law.

"Hey, man. I saw you out there with Shannon."

"Yeah. I've known all the Duprees for a long time."

He nodded. "Those two women, though, they melt a man's brain."

He didn't know what else to say, so he just nodded and took a shallow sip off his bottle.

Kai laughed. "Don't worry, bra. I won't be bugging you about your intentions. The one thing I understand about the Dupree women is that they have their own minds. Just make sure you know what you're about. I'd hate to have to beat the crap out of you to make Jocelyn happy."

"I'm a Seal."

Kai laughed in his face again. "And I've been working on the docks since I was a teen."

They eyed each other, and Kade realized he'd come up against an adversary he might not be able to beat. He wasn't as muscular as Kade, but there was something to be said about a man who knew how to fight dirty.

"Now, speaking of my bride, I need to hunt her up. We have a big suite to use for the night."

He left Kade alone to his thoughts. He didn't have to look for Shannon, he knew where she was. It didn't matter if he tried to ignore her, he could always sense where she was if she was nearby. He could find her in a crowd of a thousand. He watched as she pulled May and Kai's father out onto the dance floor and tried to teach him to two-step. It was silly that his heart turned over just at the sight of her. She was smiling as usual, her joy easy to see. Shannon enjoyed life, every little bit of it, to the fullest extent. Out of all of the Duprees, she was the one who could always find a silver lining in any cloud. And now she had pulled away the barriers he'd thought were there. She had made her interest clear.

As he watched her dance, he felt his resistance melt. He might not have the right, but the lady had given him an invitation, and even if it was for just this one night, he would taste a little bit of paradise.

17

With his job, there were few opportunities for it. Once—just this once—he would take the chance.

* * * *

Shannon looked at herself in the mirror and drew in a deep breath. She looked good. No, correct that. She looked damned hot. The dress Cynthia had picked out for her had been fantastic. Red was definitely her color, and the design suited her fuller figure. Best of all, it was a dress she could wear again. And she would. Either to remind her of a great night, or remind her not to have stupid yearnings that would never come true.

She groaned and grabbed a bottle of water. After taking a swig, she hoped that it helped cool off her raging libido. If history served, nothing would help. Not even her battery-operated boyfriend could relieve the fire that man started in her. She closed her eyes and tried to calm her heart. Just thinking about Kade had her body humming with anticipation. She was already driving herself crazy, and she had only been in her room twenty minutes. It took all of her control not to pace the room. It would be stupid to worry herself over the invitation she'd given Kade. Seriously, she didn't expect him to show. Hoped, but didn't really think it would happen.

Oh, there was no doubt he wanted her. A man didn't get that hard by just dancing unless he wanted a woman or had just had a handful of the blue pills. Shannon was pretty damned sure that Francis McKade didn't need them.

She stepped out onto her balcony and looked out over the water. The scent of salt filled her senses. She loved it in Hawaii. She would never be able to leave New Orleans, but she definitely liked it in Chris's adopted home. While her hometown was always abuzz with activity, something she loved, she did like the slower pace of the islands. She liked to come here and gaze out over the water and just…breathe.

But even that didn't work. Being in the same hotel as Kade, she couldn't think of anything else other than seeing him in her room, preferably naked. She needed something to occupy her time. If she didn't, she would definitely tear into the bag of chocolate macadamia nuts. Her ass didn't need that.

She watched the surf as it rolled in, and she could see why her brother and sister had been drawn to Hawaii. This was a soothing place. Oahu could be a jungle, that was for sure, but there was something so…relaxed. She could never live here. It would take an act of war to get her out of New Orleans. She had rebuilt her bar after Katrina, and she wasn't leaving any time soon. But she needed to find time to return to Hawaii. She had a niece or nephew about to make an appearance, and she was sure Jocelyn and Kai would have children soon.

A little ping hit her heart harder than it ever had before. Thinking of her sister, her confidant, having a baby brought about yearnings she never thought she would have, not now. She thought they would come after marriage, but it was probably because the first Dupree grandchild would be arriving in five months.

Shannon shook herself free of her funk. This wasn't like her. She had men. Not a constant stream of them, and she did have the problem of her career. Her business took up a fair amount of her time, so it had been a long dry spell between men. But for some reason, she hadn't felt the need to scratch the itch. Not until she saw her brother coming down the escalator at the airport with Kade.

She closed her eyes and shivered. Damn, the man got to her. And if he didn't take her up on her offer, she would write him off. His loss. She opened her eyes and glanced at the ABC Drugstore bag. She would throw away the condoms she bought and drink whiskey and eat the chocolate.

There was a knock at the door, pulling her out of thoughts of rebellion by gorging herself. She drew in a deep breath and approached the door. When she looked through the peephole, she sighed. It was an older Asian man. She opened it, and he looked confused.

The door across the hall opened, and a woman who was apparently his wife frowned at him.

"Sorry," he said with a smile.

"No problem," Shannon said, trying to fight the disappointment that now swamped her as she watched his wife usher him into their room. She was closing the door when a hand braced against it and stopped her. She looked up and found Kade staring at her.

"I told you I knew where your room was."

His voice flowed over the words. He had been born in Australia, but his parents had moved to the US when he was younger. That accent still tinged his voice. It sent little tingles of heat racing through her blood.

"You didn't change your mind, did you?"

He actually looked worried. The fact that he would think any woman in her right mind wouldn't beg him to come to her room made him even more attractive.

She smiled and stepped back. "Come on in, Kade."

Chapter Three

As Kade watched Shannon step back, he tried to calm his heart. It was smacking against his chest so hard he was sure she heard it. Lust hummed through his body. He was afraid if he didn't control himself, he would completely lose it, strip her naked, and ride her like she was a mare in heat.

"Kade?" she asked.

He shook himself out of the stupor as he stepped over the threshold and shut the door behind himself. He flipped the deadbolt and took her in his arms. Somewhere in the back of his mind, he realized he was rushing, but he couldn't help it. He couldn't be that controlled when he kissed her. He had waited too long to touch, to taste. She didn't hesitate, but came willingly into his arms and pressed herself against him. *Lord.* His eyes almost crossed at the feel of all that softness against him. Her nipples were hard.

He kissed her then, taking her lips in a hot, open-mouthed kiss. She was better than he dreamed. As he dove into her mouth, she hummed against his tongue. Every hormone in his body screamed, begging for relief, but there was one thing he knew. He might never get to do this again, and if so, he would make sure this would last him a lifetime.

He kissed a path down her neck, enjoying the taste of her flesh. God, she was so sweet. She arched into him, and he swore. He almost came then and there. No woman had ever gotten to him like this. He pulled away.

"Turn around."

His voice was rough, and he saw that her eyes widened slightly. When she did as he ordered, she did it slowly, her hips swaying as she turned. The woman was going to drive him insane. There was no doubt about it.

His hands were shaking when he lifted them to unzip the dress. He was careful not to jerk the delicate fabric, but it was hard. As the fabric spilt, it revealed a black lace corset, stockings, and mother help him, a thong.

She was definitely going to kill him. Blood rushed to his groin, and his head started to spin again. The dress fell away and pooled on the floor at her feet. When she turned around, his eyes almost crossed.

The corset was tight, pushing her generous breasts up to the edge and almost over the top. The stockings were attached by garters. As he allowed his gaze to drift down, he had to sigh. She was made for him. There was no doubt in his mind. He didn't like thin women, disdained them. He liked a handful of a woman. One who knew her worth and who had more curves than he could explore in a lifetime.

"Kade?"

He could barely hear her voice. He lifted his hand and skimmed the tips of his fingers over the delicate flesh above the lace. She shivered then moaned as he slipped his digit between her breasts.

"Kade?"

He looked up at her and the frown she was giving him. "Don't say no now."

She smiled at that. "Not on your life, it's just that...you have a lot of clothes on. I'm almost naked."

He didn't do anything. He couldn't. He was still trying to come to terms with the fact that the woman he had lusted after for so long was standing in front of him in a corset.

He swore then that he was positive there was a God.

Apparently, she got sick of waiting. Shannon stepped forward and took hold of his shirt.

"Arms up, Seal."

He did as ordered, unable to fight the smile curving his lips. He knew it would be like this. Softness,

tenderness, fun, and love. She tossed the shirt behind her
and immediately had her hands on his chest.

"Lord, you Seals know how to build some muscles."

The wonder in her voice shot straight to his dick. She
splayed her hands over his pecs and smoothed them over
his flesh. He was sure she could feel the way his heart
pounded against his chest.

"I like that you aren't all waxed."

He snorted. "No military man would do so, babe."

Her gaze flashed up to his. "Yeah? I bet there are a
few."

"Let me rephrase that. No self-respecting Seal would
wax."

"Ah," she said and nodded as she slipped her hands
up over his shoulders. The lace of her corset scratched
against his skin, and he was amazed he didn't lose
consciousness. There was so much he wanted to do to
her, with her. But he couldn't go into full Dom mode, not
with Shannon. Tonight was more about sharing, caring,
and living in the moment.

He bent his head and kissed her. This time he wasn't
so out of control. Slowly he tasted her, nipping at her lips,
then finally he delved into her mouth. He walked her
back to the bed until her legs hit it. He pulled back and
pushed her a little. She took the hint and fell on the bed, a
laugh bubbling up from within her. That joy was
something he would remember for the rest of his life. He
didn't doubt it.

She was laying on the bed, her hair tousled around
her head now, and that sexy smile inviting him to join
her. He did then, undoing her corset and garters. He
slipped the lace from her body, but he didn't remove the
stockings. Next he worked the tiny thong down her legs.
It was wet with her arousal, the musky scent of it sending
his libido to new heights. He kissed the flesh just above

23

the band of the stocking, then the other leg. He worked his way up to her sex. She was hot, and damn, so wet.

Need crawled through him, urging him to take, to plunder. He couldn't control himself, couldn't wait. He had to have a taste of her. He set his mouth against her pussy and leisurely licked her. She shivered and moaned against him.

He savored her, slipping his tongue inside of her and allowing the flavor of her to dance over his taste buds. God, every little bit of her was exquisite, inside and out. Adding a finger, he enjoyed the way her muscles clamped down on it as he worked in and out of her. He could just imagine sliding inside, having those inner pussy walls tugging on his cock. He sighed against her as he slipped his tongue up and over her clit.

She shivered, moving against him. He sensed her approaching orgasm and pulled away.

She moaned in irritation and gave him a dirty look. He laughed and worked his way up her torso, kissing and licking her sweet skin. When he reached her breasts, he took one hardened nipple into his mouth and sucked—hard. She moaned again, slipping her hands into his hair as he slid his other hand to her breast and teased the nipple.

Little by little, she was killing him. Pleasure took hold of his body, of his mind. At this point, he wasn't sure how much longer he would last. He was a man who loved foreplay. He thought with Shannon he would take hours. He had dreamed of it for years, planned it. Then when she was so out of her mind she was begging for relief, he would take her.

There was no way he would make it. He didn't have the ability to take it slow. If he tried, there was a good chance he would embarrass himself.

She arched up against him, pressing her crotch against his pants. Even through the cotton fabric, he felt her heat. He knew then it was imperative that he got naked ASAP.

He gave her breast one last lick, then he rose to his knees. He was ready to undress, but apparently she was sick of waiting. She sat up and took over the job herself. He didn't wear underwear, so when she unzipped him, his straining cock sprung free. Her eyes widened, and she wrapped her hand around it.

"Oh, Shannon, yeah..."

His words trailed off as he lost the ability to speak. He watched her dip her head and take the tip of his penis into her mouth. The first flick of her tongue pulled a drop of pre-come from him. He shuddered, and he knew he should tell her to stop. There was every chance that he would lose it, lose complete control and come right then in there. But instead, he watched as his cock disappeared between her lips and into the deep recesses of her mouth. It was possibly one of the most erotic things he had ever seen.

She took it slowly at first, just pulling in about half of his cock. But soon he was thrusting in and out of her mouth, and she was humming against his sensitive flesh.

He pulled away right about the time he lost it. It was when he looked down at her that he realized he hadn't brought protection.

Shit.

Before he could say anything, Shannon solved the problem. "In the bag on the table."

He noticed the plastic bag then. He jumped off the bed, got rid of his pants, and pulled out the box of condoms. His hands were shaking with desire, and he could barely get the box open as he crawled back up on the bed. When he did, the condoms went flying all over the bed beside her. She laughed, the joy of it loosening something in his heart. As he looked down at her, he couldn't believe that this woman, with her loving nature and her beauty, wanted him.

"I don't know about you, but that seems pretty ambitious. But you *are* the first Seal I've gone to bed with."

He looked at the condoms and couldn't fight the gurgle of laughter. He grabbed one. "I don't like to waste anything, so we better get started, babe."

He ripped open the condom and had it on in record time. He wanted it fast and hard, but he knew he couldn't push her. He would probably have to leave in the next few hours, knowing his luck. So he decided he would at least try and take it slow.

He slipped his hands over her belly, enjoying the way her muscles quivered beneath his palm. So soft, so silky, her skin amazed him. He would never get enough of her, he knew that much. He slid his hands to her hips and pulled her up. With one hard thrust, he entered her. At first he worried he had been too hard, but the next moment she moaned. The sound of it filled the quiet room and filtered into his soul. He started to move, tried to keep himself in check. He was a man who was known for his control, but where Shannon was concerned, he barely had any.

It didn't take her long. She was coming apart beneath him, and he couldn't stop his own orgasm. Her muscles clamped down hard on his cock, pulling him deeper into her warmth, and he lost himself. With one long, hard thrust, he came, shuddering as he moaned her name.

He collapsed on top of her. She grunted then laughed and wrapped her arms around him. He leaned up and looked down at her. Fuck, there wasn't a more beautiful woman. Oh, physically, plastic surgeons had perfected the female face. But never once had he seen a woman who produced such joy. He had seen some horrible things in his life, and being with her lightened his load.

"You really are too beautiful for me," he said, embarrassed by the way his voice had roughened.

"Oh, really? I will have you know that you and Mal were the topic of discussion among many of the women. Two hot—not my description of Mal, but theirs—Seals… I am the lucky one here."

He couldn't tell her how he felt. There were thoughts in his mind, things that he should say, but he didn't know how to put it into words. Hell, Kade wasn't really sure what he felt. All he knew was that his heart was in his throat and that the man he was an hour ago no longer existed. Not after this. He had known it would be good, but Kade hadn't known exactly how much this would mean to him. He'd had great sex before, but this was something else.

"Kade?"

He heard the worry in her voice and could say nothing to ease them. He knew he had to look too serious for the situation. Instead, he kissed her, pulling her bottom lip between his teeth. She closed her eyes and hummed. After a few minutes of teasing, he rolled off her and went to the bathroom to discard his condom. When he stepped out of the bathroom, he smiled. Shannon was already snuggled under the covers, half asleep. She was notorious for being a heavy sleeper, and someone who could fall asleep at the drop of a hat.

He walked as quietly as possible and slipped into bed. His heart turned over when she shifted closer and snuggled against him. Damn, this was more than he expected, more than he was able to give. But for this night, before the reality of the world returned, he would pretend she was his to keep forever.

Tomorrow would come soon enough.

Chapter Four

Shannon awoke slowly, blinking in the darkness. As usual, the first sense that really took hold was her sense of smell. There was a strange combination of plumeria and musky male that had her confused. It took her a second to remember just where she was.

Hawaii. Chris and Cynthia's wedding. She shifted her weight and came up against a hard wall of muscle.

Kade.

No wonder the bed felt like a heater. The man gave off heat like a steam engine. But she didn't care. She had Francis McKade in her bed.

She smiled. She knew she looked smug, but who wouldn't? The man she had in bed had to be every heterosexual woman's dream come true. As her eyes adjusted to the darkness, she pulled herself up and rested her weight on her elbow. The man was amazing. Never in her life had she had a man that looked like this in her bed. Hard muscles, tattoos on his back, and damn, but he was like a wonderland made just for her. He was as gorgeous on the inside as on the outside.

Her fingers itched to touch, to explore. They were both tired from their trips over the Pacific, but she couldn't stop herself. Without hesitation, she gave into her compulsion to touch him.

The moment she touched him, she felt that connection. It had been there from the first and had grown each time she saw him. Now there was something telling her that this was the man for her, the one that could be forever. But sadly, she didn't think it would happen. His work, her life, it wouldn't work out between the two of them.

She brushed those unhappy thoughts away and slipped her hand down his torso. She shivered at the feel of his warm flesh beneath her fingertips. Could a man be in better shape? She didn't think so. His abs were sculpted, and even without trying, she was pretty sure she could bounce a quarter off his ass.

To get a better look at him, she slipped the sheet away from his body. The moonlight was weak, but she could see him. He was tan everywhere. How did he do that? She knew without a doubt he didn't go to a tanning salon. She looked at the scar on his hip. It was a puckered wound, not very big. She knew a year or so ago, he'd been shot. Mal had told her just that and nothing else.

She grazed her finger over it and then continued down. He had a thin line of hair all the way down to his cock. As she neared it with her hands, it twitched. She glanced up at him and realized she had awakened him. His eyes were barely opened, but he was watching her. The intensity in them was a little scary and very arousing.

"Sorry," she whispered.

His lips curled up on one side. "No problem. Use and abuse me any way you want to."

"Yeah?"

He nodded.

She didn't break eye contact with him as she wrapped her hand around his cock. His eyes closed, and he groaned as she gave it one long stroke. He shifted against the bed as she continued to tease him. Soon, though, that wasn't enough. She wanted a taste. Slipping down the bed, she settled between his legs and took him in her mouth. The first taste of him spurred her arousal. Sweet and salty, with a touch of Kade, so unique, like the man. At first she couldn't fit him in her mouth completely, but soon she didn't care that she gagged once or twice. It didn't seem to bother him. His groans were growing in volume, and he was shifting against her, thrusting into her mouth. She slipped her fingers down to his sac and began to stroke him. Power coursed through her veins as she continued to tease him. She knew he was close. To make him lose control would be the ultimate conquest, but apparently Kade wasn't going to allow it. He pulled her up and switched their positions. She found herself on her back, pinned to the mattress.

"You trying to be naughty, Shannon?" His voice was a guttural whisper, filled with so much arousal she could barely control the lust pouring into her veins. He loomed over her as if he was in charge, and well, it was the truth.

"I thought I was being pretty obvious." Her voice sounded breathless, but it was nothing new. He always did that to her.

His eyes sparkled with a bit of devilment, and she felt her heart skip a beat. "Yeah? Well, I think you deserve some punishment for that."

He rose to his knees, straddling her hips, his cock lying against her sex. Already she was hot, needy, and from the look in his eyes, he was going to make sure she was out of her mind. For a second he looked at her, then shook his head. He reached over to turn on the light.

"No—"

He ignored her. When he had the light on, he returned to his position. "Got a problem with light, babe? You shouldn't, not with a body like this."

He brushed his hands up her stomach, grazing the sides of her breasts, then teasing her nipples with his thumbs. She sucked in a deep breath and moaned as she closed her eyes. She had very sensitive breasts, and just the simple teasing had her pussy dampening.

"Like that, do you?"

He didn't wait for an answer. Instead, he placed a hand on the bed beside her and leaned down to take a nipple in his mouth. The graze of his teeth against the tip sent heat straight to her pussy. Damn, the man was going to kill her. The way he was straddling her, she couldn't move her legs. The pressure built as he continued to suck one, then both nipples. Her body was hot, her heart beating so hard that she wasn't too sure she would survive. When he was done there, he started to move down her body, licking and nipping at her skin. She moved against him, and he stopped.

"Now, naughty girl, you can't move."

She opened her eyes and frowned at him. When she opened her mouth to respond, he placed one finger against her mouth.

"You're the one who awoke the beast, so you get to live with the consequences."

She wanted to tell him to go to hell, but there was something so...sexy about him commanding her, telling her what she could and could not do. Unlike her brother, Chris, she had never been into BDSM, but with Kade, the possibility was titillating. And dammit, arousal deepened his accent. That alone made her toes curl.

He apparently took her silence as agreement. "If you agree, I'll reward you. If not, I'll stop. And you will regret it."

She nodded, not knowing which would be better— the reward or the punishment? Which would be worse?

He traced her lips with his finger. The callus felt odd against her mouth. "No coming unless I say so."

She agreed with another nod. Then he tortured her. Slowly, he worked his way down her body. She had never known a man so skilled with his tongue. Who would have thought that a tongue could arouse her by just flicking over her flesh, dipping into her belly button? By the time he settled between her legs, she was pretty sure he'd touched every inch of her stomach.

He drew in a deep breath, closing his eyes. Then he sighed. When he looked up at her, the need in his gaze had her breath tangling in her chest. In all her encounters, she had never had a man stare at her with such yearning. Tears burned the backs of her eyes as she tried to control her emotions. To know she was that special to him, that this was that special to him, made her want to cry happy tears.

"I'll never get over how you smell. Every bit of you is delicious," he said.

He lowered his head, and without taking his gaze from hers, he set his mouth on her sex. He used his fingers to part her labia and slid his tongue into her. At that moment, she gave into the man, allowing him complete control. She was already halfway there to begin with, but now, he had her body doing whatever he wanted. She would give anything to come, to be allowed to have her release. In and out he worked his tongue, lapping at her as if she were a delicious treat he adored. He slipped two fingers into her as he began to tease her clit. He rolled his tongue over the tiny bundle of nerves, then between his teeth, gently pressing down. Pressure soared, her body shivered with her impending orgasm. She felt the rush of heat flood her sex, but he pulled back. She made a noise that was halfway between a growl and a moan.

"I didn't say you could come."

She wanted to yell at him, but he gently slapped her pussy. The act would get a normal man yelled at, but he had her so aroused, ribbons of lust slipped over her flesh and down into her bones at the action. He did it again, and her body responded even more willingly.

"Damn," he said. Without explanation, he set his mouth against her, slipping his hands beneath her rear end and pulling her up. Relentlessly, he assaulted her senses, pushing her almost to the pinnacle but pulling back just in time to keep her from reaching it. Over and over he teased, pushing her right up to the edge, but not allowing her relief. She moved against him, pressing her cunt as hard as she could against his mouth. The way he was holding her, she really couldn't get leverage.

By the time he lifted his head and set her down on the mattress, she was out of her mind. The only thing she could think of was release. She would do anything to feel the rush of her orgasm.

He slipped his fingers into her sex. "Come for me, baby. Do it."

The order sent her spiraling into her orgasm. Her body convulsed as she screamed as ripples of euphoria washed over her. She could do nothing else. She arched off the bed and allowed the orgasm to take over. Just as she was coming down, he sent her over again as she writhed against his hand.

She was still shivering moments later when he grabbed a condom and donned it. Without any words, he flipped her over onto her stomach, pulled her up to her knees, and entered her from behind. His hands gripped her hips as he thrust in and out of her with such force that the headboard banged against the wall. After her two intense orgasms, she thought another would be impossible, but he smacked her ass. The action sent a mixture of pleasure and pain. He did it again, thrusting even harder into her, and she screamed as another release slammed through her. After a few more thrusts, he shouted her name and followed her.

Several minutes later, he pulled out of her, got rid of the condom, then settled beside her on the bed. He pulled her into his arms, and she cuddled closer.

"Hoo-rah," he said, his voice filled with sleepy satisfaction.

"I have to say I agree, Seal."

He chuckled then kissed her forehead. It was sweet, not sexual at all, but it had a lump filling up her throat. She slipped her hand up to his chest, could feel his heart beat against it. Shannon tried to stay awake, wanting to savor every moment they had together, but soon his even breathing relaxed her, and she drifted into sleep.

* * * *

The sun was barely peeking through the curtains when *Anchors Aweigh* woke Shannon from a dead sleep. She heard Kade curse then grab the phone.

"Yes, sir, McKade here."

He was silent as he listened for a moment or two.

"Understood. Have you talked to Dupree?" He waited. "Okay. Expect us on the next plane we can get out of here."

He turned off the phone and glanced at her. "Gotta go."

She nodded. As the sister of a Seal, she understood. She knew there would be no discussion about where he was going, what he was doing. And he had no control over what would go down and when.

She gave him a kiss. "I understand. Did he talk to Mal?"

Kade studied her for a second. "Yes. So, more than likely, he'll be looking for me."

Again, he was studying her, and she couldn't stand it any longer. "What?"

"I...I thought we might have more time."

She sighed. "You might want to have more time, but you know the military. You get what you can and be happy for that."

She couldn't look at him, not right now. It hurt too much to think of him going away, of being in danger. Shannon had been through this before with both Mal and Kade, but this time was so much different. This time she had so much more to lose.

He slipped his finger under her chin. "Don't be mad."

She frowned. "I'm not mad. I just hate thinking of both of you in danger."

He nodded and gave her a soft, quick kiss. It was really innocent, but she felt the heat, the need behind it. It curled her toes and had her heart turning over. Then it turned hot, his tongue slipping between her lips and stealing into her mouth. Kade started to ease her back, but she stopped him. He pulled back just far enough to talk.

"What?" he asked.

"Don't you have to find a flight?"

"It can wait." His lips curved. "I need one more taste of heaven."

The way he said it had her resistance crumbling. As she allowed him to ease her back onto the bed, she told herself to enjoy the moment. There was time enough to fall to pieces after he left.

Chapter Five

Four months later

"When did he say he was going to be here?" Verna asked as she settled against the barstool.

Shannon looked at her. She saw the expectant look on her employee's face and inwardly cringed. Damn Mal for flirting with her employees. Verna didn't hold a torch for him, but since his last visit, Shannon could tell Verna had been itching to get her hands all over him. If he chased off another employee, she was going to shave his eyebrows off.

"Not sure. He's driving in."

"Kade's not coming?" Verna asked.

Shannon couldn't help but feel the sharp slash at her heart. Verna didn't mean anything because no one, as far as Shannon knew, had guessed she'd spent Kade's last night in Hawaii with him. Almost every time Mal had come into town in the last few years, Kade had come with him.

"Not that I know of."

She finished wiping down the counter and walked back to her office, not wanting to talk anymore about Mal's visit. It was a slow night. Off-season in New Orleans and the weather sucked. A bad storm had hit just thirty minutes earlier, which meant they would probably be left with no customers. Seemed like everyone was staying in. She shut the office door and then collapsed into her desk chair. With a sigh, she indulged in a little pity.

Four months and no word from Kade.

When he had left, he had said he would get in touch. And he had. There had been a few texts, two calls, then nothing. She tried not to panic. After years of Mal in the Seals, she knew exactly how it went. This time was different. Her worry had kept her up at night and rode on her shoulder during the day. Probably because she had no one to talk to about it. She hadn't even told her sister what had happened the night of Chris's wedding.

She had known they were back because Mal had called to tell her both of them had been injured. Mal had played it off, as usual, but she had sensed something had gone wrong. They had lost one member of the team. It had hit them all hard, she was sure. What she didn't understand was why Kade had not called. It wasn't like him at all. Even if it had just been a one-night stand, it wasn't like them to stay away this long. She had worked through the pain and anger, and now...she just wanted an answer. But she apparently wasn't going to get it. Her texts and calls were still being ignored. Whatever she thought they had shared had been an illusion, or possibly just one-sided.

Before she could get too depressed, she heard her brother's voice booming out from the bar area.

"Where is my gorgeous sister?"

Excitement had her jumping up from the chair and running out to see him. He was drenched, but he had a big smile on his face and his arms open wide. She didn't hesitate, didn't think to. The entire family was close, and these last few months had been hard on all of them. She ran to him and jumped into his arms. Tears stung the back of her eyes as he hugged her tight.

"It's so good to see you," she said just loud enough for him to hear. Her voice wavered a bit, and she was afraid she just might start crying.

He gave her one last squeeze and then pulled back. Up close, she could see a new scar on his lip.

"Bad assignment?" she asked and was embarrassed that her voice caught.

He nodded. "But I came out of it with flying colors. Not like the losers I brought with me."

He motioned with his head behind him, and she
followed the direction. There, on the steps leading down
into her bar, stood Kade. A rush of relief came first, her
heart now happier to know that he really was okay. She
knew Mal wouldn't have lied about something major, but
he might have hidden the injuries Kade had suffered.

In the next instant, irritation replaced it. There he
stood in her bar, larger than life, if a little more ragged
around the edge. Dammit, he should look apologetic.
Still, she couldn't say anything. Not with an audience.

"You know Kade, of course," Mal said, his voice
dipping a bit in a threatening way. She glanced at him,
wondering if he had guessed what had gone on, but if he
did, he hid it well. "I don't believe you've met Chief."

She realized that there was another man there beside
Kade. She guessed he was older than both Mal and Kade
by just a few years. Tall, blond, he was assessing the
room like most of the Seals she'd met. His gaze roamed
over her customers. He had his arm in a sling, telling her
more than just Mal and Kade had been injured. When he
focused his attention on her, she felt it to her toes. His
gray eyes were as intense as the man. Damn, these men
were dangerous.

"Chief," she said.

"Deke, ma'am."

She smiled. "Then you must call me Shannon."

He looked at her for a second, then a slow, sexy
smile curled his lips. Dangerous was too simple of a word
for the Viking god standing in front of her.

"Certainly."

Mal made a disgusted sound. "That's enough of
that."

She hadn't truly looked at Kade until now. He hadn't
said a word. Now, though, she turned her attention to
him. If it had not been melodramatic, she would have
gasped. He'd lost weight. He had a fresh scar above his

38

right eye, and his eyes, those beautiful blue eyes, were cold. The sparkle was gone. He offered her no smile. As she allowed her gaze to drop, she noticed he was favoring his right leg.

"Hey, Kade."

He hesitated. "Hey."

She could barely hear him above the noise in the bar. His voice was low and gravelly and very un-Kade-like.

"I was hoping that you had room to spare for us," Mal said.

Shannon tore her attention away from Kade and looked at her brother. He was smiling at her with the same puppy dog eyes that made most women melt. Not his sister. She was ready to say no and send them to her mother. She didn't need to deal with three injured surly men, especially one who had just about broken her heart. But there was something else in Mal's expression, something a little desperate. Their mama could fit them, and she would definitely fatten Kade up and baby the three of them. For some reason, though, Mal wanted to be with her.

She nodded. "Sure. You know my house is big enough for y'all."

Mal kissed her cheek. "Do you have to close up?"

"No, she doesn't," Simon, her bartender said. He was watching her like a hawk, and she knew that he sensed her hesitation. "Go on, boss. I can handle this."

She smiled. "Thanks. I'll just get my things."

Mal nodded.

"You know the way and you have a key. I'll catch up with you in a minute," she said.

He ushered the other two out. She felt Kade give her a look, but she couldn't return it. Her emotions were too raw, too...unbalanced. She didn't know what she would do. If she did, she would surely yell or cry. Or both.

She walked back to her office with Simon on her heels.

"So that's the guy."

She glanced back at one of her best friends and sighed. She should have known that he would figure it out.

"What are you talking about?"

"You've been moping around since you returned from the wedding."

"I have not," she said, lying through her teeth as she pretended to shut down the computer.

"Yeah, sure. This is Simon, child."

She sighed and looked at him. He was a year older than her and ten times prettier. Long brown hair, blue eyes, and a dimple in his chin made him irresistible to both men and women. Being the tramp that he was, Simon had no problem with either of them.

"Simon, how many times do I have to tell you that you're white? *Really* white. When you talk like that, you sound stupid."

He rolled his eyes. "And you're stalling because you don't want to answer me."

"Yes, he's the reason I have been out of sorts."

Simon snorted. "Yeah, sure. 'Out of sorts.'"

"Anyway, we had a little fun in Hawaii. Apparently it meant more to me than to him." She shrugged, trying not to lose her composure. "No big deal."

"Oh, hun, of course it is. I can tell by looking at you. And I really think you're wrong. I know Kade. He's been in here for years mooning over you. A guy that is that infatuated just doesn't have a one-night stand with his brother's best friend. Especially someone like Kade."

She had thought so, but apparently she had been wrong. Very wrong. "Well, I haven't heard from him in months. So I am assuming that the infatuation is over."

He opened his mouth to argue, but she held up her hand. "No more. I don't have time. Could you get Chef to prepare some of that jambalaya to go for me? Enough for the three of them—which will be a lot. Those Seals are going to eat me out of house and home. Oh, and can you handle tomorrow night? I know it's a lot to ask, but I thought maybe I should stick around the house. I feel like Mal has something to tell me."

He wanted to say more. She could tell by the look in his eye, but apparently thought better of it. He left her alone, and she finished shutting down the computer. It would take a few moments to prepare herself to face off with Kade. And they would...have a face off.

But first, she wanted to know what made him look that way, and just why the hell he looked so sickly.

* * * *

"Your sister's a looker," Chief said from the backseat.

Kade barely held back the growl that rumbled in his chest. He couldn't help it. Seeing her had brought about so many emotions that he still didn't have under control. The possessiveness hit him out of left field. And what right did he have to feel that way? Four months had passed. Even if he had reasons for staying away—good reasons—they didn't mean anything right now. She wasn't his, never would be.

Mal laughed. "Hey, watch yourself, Chief. There's a good chance she'd beat you with your injured arm."

"You're not going to warn me off her?" Chief asked.

"Naw, if she doesn't want you, she'll let you know. Right, Kade?"

He glanced at his best friend, trying to figure out if there was another meaning. He had been tossing out strange comments for over a month now. But every time

41

he looked at Mal, he appeared relaxed and gave Kade no hint of any other meaning.

"Sure. After running a bar for a few years, Shannon can handle herself."

Chief sighed. "Not that I can do anything about it tonight. I'm so damned tired from the trip. Damn bones are creaking."

"That's because you're old, Chief," Mal said.

"You got that right," Chief replied. "Although something did smell good in the bar."

"If I know Shannon, she'll be bringing us something home to eat, and I am sure it will be jambalaya."

Kade would normally welcome a bowl, but he hadn't had much of an appetite since returning from their mission. He knew the commander, along with his doctors, were worried about it. Mal pulled up to Shannon's house and parallel parked in front of it. She had one of the historical homes in the Garden District with the iron work fence, the famous balconies, and a garden Kade's mother would definitely kill in two weeks. He had always loved the house, probably almost as much as Shannon did. It always felt like he was coming home when they visited.

"Wow, this is your sister's?"

Mal nodded. "Yeah. It was our grandmother's years ago. She sold it and moved north. Shannon bought it a few years ago after Katrina. She had to repair a little bit here and there, but it is looking pretty good."

They grabbed their gear, and Kade felt the familiar twinge of pain in his knee. After pulling in a few breaths, he followed Mal and Chief up the walkway and into the house. It was dark and panic settled in his chest. He thought after three months, he would be over this stupid fear. Now, though, he felt his heart hammering against his ribs and his throat was closing up.

Mal turned on the lights in the foyer and tossed him a glance. Checking on him again. Like he was some kind of damned invalid. He had never told Mal about his new problem—problems—but he knew his friend sensed it.

"Why don't you take the guest room down here? The stairs are going to be a bitch on your knee."

He nodded and headed off to the room. He needed a shower and a shot of whiskey. Or maybe two whiskeys. He pulled off his clothes with just a few twinges. When he was finally naked, Kade stood there, looking at himself in the mirror. He was a fucking mess. The injuries were healing, but there were still times he was amazed he got through the day without losing it.

He glanced down at his knee and cringed. It was swollen again, but nothing that a little ice wouldn't fix. He didn't need to look at the marks on his back. Even though they had healed, he could still feel them as if he had just been injured. He probably always would.

He heard the front door open just as he stepped into the shower. The house was old, and the wood flooring made it easy to hear movements. He heard her approach the guest room, hesitate, then after a moment or two, she walked away. With a sigh that was half regret and half relief, he picked up the soap and the rag. The hot water pounded on his back, releasing some of the tension that had been keeping him on edge.

He could admit that he'd been worried about facing Shannon. He had avoided it for months, broke off any contact after the total fucked up mess their assignment became. He knew she deserved an explanation, but he'd taken the cowards way out and not called. Hell, he didn't even email her. And there was one thing that he hated being and that was a coward. He would have never thought it would happen to him. He'd taken life in the Seals as one of the greatest adventures. Now, though, he wasn't sure he'd ever be able to put his gear on again.

He closed his eyes, trying to stamp out the feelings that thought brought about, but it didn't help. Every time he did, images from the firefight, of watching one of his best friends get shot, feeling the bullet piercing his skin...

Fuck. People who thought that you didn't remember things like that were fucked in the head. They didn't seem to understand that people would live with the memories the rest of their lives. And fuck, he didn't need to go back there, didn't want to remember how screwed up everything had become and how all of them had come back with more than just a little baggage, including the coffin of one of their own.

He pushed aside the irritation and the damn fucking vulnerability that seemed to choke him constantly and finished his shower.

He might consider himself a coward in a lot of ways now, but it was definitely time to face Shannon.

Chapter Six

Shannon finished pouring the casserole into a pot to warm up when she heard footsteps behind her. She didn't have to turn around to see who it was. She knew it was Kade. Something stirred on the back of her neck anytime he was near.

"It should be warmed up in just a sec."

He hesitated for a second, then he stepped over the threshold. She didn't want to turn around until she was composed. She didn't want to cry, didn't want pity from a man who would probably disdain female tears. The only men who didn't complain about her tears were her gay friends.

When she had herself under control, she turned to face him.

"Do y'all know how long you're going to be in town?"

He studied her for a second. "We have a week off before we have to go back."

She nodded. "Why don't you have a seat at the kitchen table? I'll get some bread cut up."

Before she could do that, he said, "Shannon."

She knew that tone, knew that he was going to try and let her down easy. She wasn't in the mood. Her feelings were too near the surface, a bubbling caldron of irritation, pain and shock.

"Yes?"

"I thought you would want to talk about us."

His normally easy voice sounded strained, as if he were barely holding onto his temper. Why was he mad at her?

"I got the impression there was no 'us.'"

Kade stared at her then with those deep blue eyes of his, as if trying to find out if she were telling the truth.

45

Did he think she would beg him back into her bed? *Fat chance there, buddy.*

"I thought women liked to discuss these things."

"Maybe. Most of the time. But you made it pretty clear by not contacting me. I guess I could beg for a reason, but those are just made up most of the time, right? I mean, when you break up with someone, most of the time it's because they just weren't for you." She forced herself to shrug as if it were nothing big. "It's fine, Kade. You didn't have to pretend it was something it wasn't. I won't bother you."

He muttered something under his breath, and she got a bit of satisfaction over that.

Frustrated? Suck it up, Seal.

"Now, I'm going to get the jambalaya ready for y'all, and then I'm taking a long, hot shower. It's been a bitch of a day."

He stared at her as if she had grown another head.

"It wasn't that I didn't think it was special. It was. Just...things are different now."

She cocked her head to one side and studied him. "How so?"

She knew it was rude, but she didn't give a damn. If he wanted to drag all this shit out, then she wasn't going to make it easy on him.

"Just...things happened. I...," he swallowed, and his breathing increased. "I'm not fit for a relationship right now."

"Okay."

He frowned harder. "Okay?"

"Listen, Kade, I'm not sure what kind of women you usually get involved with, but I'm a sister of a Seal. I know what your life is like. And I know that sometimes you come back a little less stable than before. Don't forget, Mal stays with me most of the time after he comes back from a long mission. The fact you don't want me hurts, of course. I am strong enough to say that."

"I didn't say I didn't want you."

The words seemed to be torn from some place deep inside of him.

"But..."

He swallowed again. "I just can't."

She sighed, regret and pain filling her heart. She wanted to yell, but couldn't. Not with him looking so damned sad, not to mention her other two houseguests.

"Tell you what, Seal. You get your shit together, then you can let me know. But I'm not waiting around forever."

Just then, her brother walked up behind him. "Is that jambalaya I smell?"

She smiled at the happiness in her brother's voice. He always said the smell of jambalaya simmering in the kitchen was the one thing that reminded him of home.

"Sure, and I have some bread too. But first, I have to get changed and de-stress." She walked to the doorway and had to inch past Kade. Dammit, the man wasn't making it easy on her. She could smell him, the soap he had used, and the wild untamed scent that was totally Kade. She inched past him, gave her brother a hug, and then walked to her bedroom.

As soon as she shut the door, she leaned back against it. Her heart was beating a mile a minute, her body a strange mixture of hurt and arousal. How could he still do that to her? Of course, she hadn't really accepted the end, not that there was actually a beginning. Still, there had been that kernel of hope she had held onto. She felt the sharp jab to the chest. Damn the man for getting her tangled up. She knew he still wanted her. Well, she was pretty sure. But something was holding him back. Mal? She figured if Mal knew about them, he wouldn't have brought him here. He played the easygoing brother, but he would kill a man for looking sideways at his sisters.

She closed her eyes and felt the tears slip free. She couldn't do this. *Would* not do this. She had to hold herself together. The three men in her house where all holding on by a very tiny thread. Mal might not have talked to her about it, but she knew the last mission was worse than any of the ones they had been on.

Drawing in a deep breath, she started to undress. She needed to get her emotions under control. They didn't need a blabbering woman crying all over them.

By the time she had changed into comfy clothes and splashed water on her face, her temper had cooled and she had washed away some of the fatigue that was pulling her down. She dried her face and looked at herself in the mirror. She had always been considered the "healthy one." Teenage years being Jocelyn Dupree's sister hadn't been easy, that was for sure. With her tall, athletic body, Jocelyn had always made Shannon feel like a goblin. But in her late teens, she had grown into her body. She was full, curvy, and she thought, happy with what God gave her. Unlike some of her friends who dieted constantly, she never lacked for male companionship. And she had always thought Kade liked her just the way she was.

With a sigh, she decided to clean the rest of her makeup off and get out there. Those Seals needed someone who could hold it together.

And if there was one thing about the Dupree women, they held it together with an iron fist.

* * * *

"So, do you know if your sister is seeing someone?" Deke asked Mal.

Again, Kade had to bite back a growl. Being in her house, being that close to her, had his possessiveness growing.

Mal looked at him then smiled at Deke. "Nope. Not that I know of. There was that one guy...Mike?"

"Jonathon," Kade said.

"Yeah, Mike was the guy before. Well, good old Jon was trying his best to tie her down. Shannon kicked him to the curb. I really thought he would be at the wedding in Hawaii."

"If she cooked this, I think I'm in love."

Mal laughed. "Oh, lord, no. You don't want Shannon's cooking."

"Am I being disparaged in my own kitchen?

He wasn't ready for her. Would he ever get used to being this close? He didn't think so. Before Hawaii, he could control his feelings more easily. Now, he seemed to be completely off. Nothing seemed to work. He felt powerless to do anything about it. Every day he was worried he would freak the hell out.

Before, she had been sexy. There wasn't anything she could wear that would make her look ugly. Shannon personified beauty. Now, though, she looked...cuddly. Due to the cold weather, she had pulled on soft, pink sweats. They shouldn't make her any more attractive, but they did. Just seeing her that way made his body respond. He wanted to do nothing more than pull her into his arms and snuggle. Then fuck her until neither of them remembered their names.

The thought had his brain almost shutting down. From the time he'd been medevac'd out, he had been out of it. Even thinking about Shannon hurt. He had thought that there was a good chance he couldn't be the man for her anymore. He knew he couldn't. Right now, he was desperately trying not to imagine her tied to his bed as he pleasured her.

"Of course I'm making fun of your cooking. It sucks," Mal said, agreeable.

"No pancakes for you," she admonished, but she smiled when she said it.

"Okay, I take that back. Everything Shannon makes sucks, except for her pancakes."

Deke smiled at her. "Cooking isn't that important when a woman can look as beautiful as you do in a pair of sweats."

Shannon laughed and placed her hand on Deke's shoulder in a friendly gesture. Something rumbled in his chest at the sight. She glanced at him, her eyes widening a bit.

"I see y'all definitely left me nothing to eat."

"You don't eat this late," Mal said. "Does she, Kade?"

He was still irritated that her hand was on Chief's shoulder. The contact was far from intimate, but it was driving Kade insane.

"So she claims."

She glanced at him again, her brows now furrowed. But she said nothing to defy his suggestive tone.

"I ate something earlier, before you got here. I would have been home if you would have told me you were bringing guests."

"I had to drag these two along."

She shook her head and went to get herself some water. "What kind of Seal needs to be forced to come to New Orleans? You boys need to have your heads checked out."

"If I had known you would be waiting here, I would have offered to drive," Deke said.

She laughed. It was that sexy little flirty laugh he loved. And she was doing it for some guy. Some other guy, who was looking at her like he had a chance at her.

Dammit, didn't Chief know not to take advantage of Shannon? She was *his*.

He pulled back from that thought. She wasn't his. Never would be again.

Fuck, he needed some rest.

"I think I better get some sleep."

"Do you need anything?" Shannon asked. Her tone was normal, but there was a hint of something else there. He looked over at her, but he couldn't decide if it was wishful thinking.

"No, just some sleep. It was a long drive from Virginia."

She nodded in understanding.

"This old man needs some sleep if he's going to see any of New Orleans tomorrow. Been a while since I've been here," Deke said.

"If you need someone to show you around, let me know. I scheduled myself off the rest of the week to spend time with Mal. I'm sure he will get sick of me within six hours," Shannon said.

Deke smiled at her. "Thanks."

Kade and Deke made their way to their rooms. The guest room was right by the stairs, and Deke stopped him there.

"You don't have a problem if I ask Shannon out while I'm here, do you?"

He wanted to tell him to stay the hell away from Shannon. He wasn't her type. He was too old. And she was his.

But that wasn't true. None of it.

"No problem, mate."

He turned and walked into his room, thinking that for the first time in a week, he would be taking the hard meds.

* * * *

51

"You want to tell me why you brought this motley crew to my house without warning?"

Mal shook his head. "I didn't want to say I was bringing them if I couldn't convince them. Both of them just wanted to spend the week sitting around their quarters. I thought it wasn't a good idea."

"That bad?"

He nodded. "Actually, probably worse. We lost Forrester."

The name brought to mind the young kid that had spent his honeymoon in New Orleans just a year earlier. "Oh, shit."

"Yeah, Amanda is kind of a wreck."

"I can imagine. How are you doing?"

"You can see that my beautiful face is just fine."

She took his hand and tugged on it. "No. I want to know if you are doing okay."

For once, Mal's expression turned serious. "Yeah. A few dreams here and there, but no depression. Seriously, I was knocked unconscious and missed the worst of it."

"I take it Deke and Kade didn't? They looked a little roughed up."

"They look amazing compared to what they looked like a few weeks ago. Kade especially. I understand we almost lost him. He was trying to save Forrester."

Her heart jumped into her throat. "Do Kade's folks know?"

"Probably not. He's shut down. He was quiet before, but now he's damned creepy."

"Mal," she admonished. "That's no way to talk about your best friend."

"Yeah, I know. But it's the truth. You saw. He barely talks now. It's like he's not there. I thought you might be able to help out."

She studied her brother's eyes. "Like how?"

"He's always had a crush on you. You have to know that."

"Yes."

"Well, he always seems so...relaxed around you. He talks to you more than he talks to any woman I've seen him with."

She dropped his hands. "So you want to act as my pimp?"

He rolled his eyes. "Good God, no. I might have to bleach my brain to get that image out of there."

"Why don't you explain what you want from me, Mal?"

"He talks to you. If you could get him to listen, to come back to life, that would be fantastic."

"So a miracle?"

He chuckled. "No, just a sounding board. Not sure if it will work, but I thought maybe you would bring him out of his shell."

"I'll try."

"That's all I ask, sis." He leaned forward and gave her a kiss. "I'm going to go to bed. You need help with the dishes?"

Normally, she would force him to do all the cleaning up. Looking at him though, she saw the dark circles under his eyes and the fatigue weighing him down. He was worried about his friends, and the stress of that and the drive was probably enough to blank any man out, even a Seal.

"Naw, I got it."

She went through the motions as she listened to him walk up the stairs. She couldn't let him see just how much that affected her. He knew it hurt for her to hear, but she also knew her brother. He was worried. Very worried. Kade was usually so self-contained, but now that Mal pointed it out, she realized he was right. Kade had shut down. She rinsed off the dishes and put them in her dishwasher as she thought of his behavior.

He had always been quiet, just as Mal had said, but dammit, he had always been...well, like a guy hiding a secret. A fun secret. His eyes had always sparkled, and he had always been willing to listen and join in when asked. Now, it was as if he saw himself as separate from the world. Even from his closest friend.

She started the washer then began cleaning off the table. Was it as simple as guilt? He hadn't saved Forrester. He had survived. Maybe that was why he was holding back from her, and even Mal?

Did she want to take a chance on helping him? Getting him to talk, trying to draw him out, would hurt. Hurt a lot, that was for sure. Being in the same house as him had her aching from the inside out. Hell, just hearing that funky noise he'd made when she'd touched Deke had sent ribbons of lust streaming through her blood.

She paused and straightened.

He had been cool, at least he'd looked that way. But, in his eyes...her breath caught. "He's jealous."

For a second she thought back, tried to debunk the idea. Why would he be jealous of a simple pat? She understood maybe getting upset if she had slept with Deke, but this was nothing. It had to be that he still had feelings for her, yes? Why else would he have growled?

That had her looking at the situation in a different manner. Did she want to put herself out there, take a chance on being hurt again?

Maybe.

Worse, did she want to take the chance of losing him forever? If he felt guilt for what happened, did he think he wasn't good enough for her? That would make sense. She could at least put out feelers, push him a little. Knowing Mal, he'd been handling his friend with kid gloves. While her brother was a kickass Seal, just like every other Dupree man, he had a gooey, soft center. He hated to see someone he loved hurt and would do anything to protect him or her.

She sat in the chair with a thunk. Well, damn. She had to look at the situation a little differently now. He might be a little rough around the edges now, and she was still pissed at him, but he needed her. He needed more than just a friend, if her suspicions were right.

She would just push some buttons on that damned hardheaded Seal tomorrow and see what happened.

If there was anything worth the pain, it was Francis McKade. And if he was too stupid to realize she was good for him, she'd smack him upside the head and walk away.

She had to try because she didn't want to spend the rest of her life regretting it.

Chapter Seven

Kade opened his eyes to the blinding sun. It felt as if someone had poured acid on them. He slammed his lids shut with a groan. He had been so tired the night before that he'd forgotten to shut the blinds. No wonder he was burning up.

"Fuck," he said.

"Is that any way to talk in my house?"

He was slow to react the moment he heard her voice. He was barely awake, dealing with a blinding pain in his head, and the woman of his dreams was in his room. Her slow, New Orleans accent was threaded with amusement and low enough to send heat racing through his blood. Damn, he was naked but for the sheet over him.

Slowly, he opened his eyes and glanced to the doorway. Damn, the woman was gorgeous. Shit, he didn't need this. He was still dealing with being in her house, being within feet of her, and now she was standing there smiling at him. She was leaning against the doorjamb, a steaming mug of coffee in her hand, and she was wearing some kind of flimsy robe with red flowers all over it.

Of course, without little provocation, his cock went completely hard. What man wouldn't react like that to seeing her there? Her curls were dripping over shoulders, and her face was scrubbed free of makeup. Dammit, he wanted to see her like that every morning. Wanted her in his bed, wanted to wake up beside her, snuggle against her, then love her slowly awake. And that was why he hadn't wanted to come. He knew every minute—every second—of the day he was in New Orleans, his need to touch her would grow. He knew it would be impossible to resist her. Less than twelve hours and he was ready to beg her. Mentally, he chastised himself. He couldn't take her to bed like he wanted, to love her until neither of them knew their names. The man he was in Hawaii had that right. He didn't now, and he couldn't stand hurting her again.

"I'm sure you've heard worse than that with your brothers around."

She smiled as she took a sip. God was not smiling on him, he knew it then and there because she walked into the room. She closed the blinds then leaned against the dresser.

"Do you have any plans today?"

He knew she asked a question, but he couldn't seem to answer. His brain was melting. *Holy fuck.* The robe she was wearing hit her mid-thigh. If she moved just the wrong way, he would find out if she had any panties on. Jesus, what the hell did he ever do to God to deserve this?

"Kade?"

He shook his head, trying to break free of that mesmerizing bit of leg she was showing him and looked up at her face. Those eyes were studying him, and he felt himself shiver. He didn't physically do it, but everything in him trembled as he tried to hold onto his control.

"Not sure."

She took another sip and shifted her weight. Dammit. He couldn't decide if he wanted her to leave or stay. Either one would be bad and good.

"Do you want to come with Deke and me?"

He wanted to. He really wanted to. The idea that Chief was sniffing around her didn't sit well with him. The man had a reputation with women. He might be older than most of the other Seals, but he tended to have more women, if rumors were correct. But even at his age, he didn't seem to be settling down. The last woman Kade had seen him with was younger than Shannon.

Still, Kade knew it wouldn't be a good idea to tag along. He could handle her in small doses, but he needed a break every now and then. And there was a good chance that he might beat the hell out of Chief if he got too handsy.

"Naw. I thought I would hang around the house today."

She frowned. "Your leg's not bothering you, is it?"

"Did Mal tell you I hurt it?"

"No. You were favoring it last night."

He nodded. "It's stiff from the drive. I thought I would take a hot bath, then put it up with some ice."

"Well, if you change your mind, we are leaving at eleven hundred."

He smiled. "Yes ma'am."

She patted him on his leg, and his eyes almost crossed. Just that simple touch had his body heating, his cock jumping. Damn, if the woman wasn't going to have him dead from lack of blood to his brain.

"There are some fresh pastries in the kitchen, and Mal is brewing some coffee."

She left, and he dropped his head back on the pillow. The scent of her was still in the room, and he probably would never smell that spicy perfume again without getting aroused. He knew she was still hoping for something, and dammit, he wanted to give it to her. But he couldn't trust himself. Not with his issues, or with her.

With a grimace, he sat up and stood. He hobbled, ignoring the pain shooting through his leg and the cock stand she had left him with.

* * * *

"Do you want to tell me what's going on between you and Kade?" Deke asked.

Shannon choked on the sip of water she had just taken. She coughed a few times before gaining control.

"Sorry. I'm sometimes a little too blunt for my own good."

She shook her head and patted her lips with her napkin.

"No, really, I grew up with a lot of men in the house. One of them is Mal, who is not much different than you."

She took another sip of water and wiped away a couple of tears.

"Are you going to answer the question?" he asked just as bluntly as before.

She couldn't help but smile. From her experience, military men were always much more tenacious than other men. "Why do you ask?"

He rolled his eyes and took a bite of his sandwich. "He didn't look too happy when we left, and well, I feel like I'm poaching on his goods. We have a good working relationship, and I don't want this to get in the way."

She raised one eyebrow. "Poaching on his goods? I'm not sure I like that phrase."

"Beg your pardon, but I didn't ask."

She threw her head back and laughed. From the moment they had left her house, she had been delighted by Deke. If she wasn't in love with the surly idiot she'd left behind, she definitely would be interested in him.

"That's a pretty sound," he said, his gaze resting on her lips.

"Why thank you."

"So, quit screwing around and trying to avoid the question."

"I'm not sure what we are."

He nodded. "I had a feeling." He sighed. "Well, I was hoping that there would be a chance. I knew he was all moony-eyed over some woman when he returned from that wedding."

She set her elbow on the table then settled her chin on her hand. "I have a feeling you don't really want a chance. And it has nothing to do with me being Mal's sister or the fact that I am somewhat involved with the other idiot my brother brought home. Sure, you'd flirt with me, have a little romance, even take me to bed. But I have a feeling that you'd be out the door and I would be out of your mind before your next mission."

His lips twitched. "Well, why do you think that is, Ms. Dupree?"

"I do love a Georgia accent, Mr. Berg." She took a sip of water. "Well, I think you're carrying a torch for someone."

He looked stunned and blinked at her, those ridiculously long eyelashes catching her attention. It was really a shame both of them were tangled up with someone else. He was a delicious man to look at.

His cheeks turned ruddy and she couldn't believe he was blushing. He cleared his throat. "That's not true."

"Aha, I'm right. You've been here before, yes?"

He nodded. "On my honeymoon."

Her heart did that little dance it did at the romance of it. "So walking around here with me has really bugged you, hasn't it?"

He made a face, and she laughed.

"You still have the hots for your ex?"

He sighed. "God, don't tell her that. We can't be together."

Shannon heard the longing in his voice, and her heart did that little jig again. Who would have thought that the Viking was such a romantic?

"Is she married again?"

"No."

"Had the change?" she asked.

"What?"

"You know, decided she was really a man instead of a woman?"

"Good God, no." He shook his head. "And I thought Mal was bad."

"She's not in jail, I am assuming. What's stopping you, Seal?"

"Just one of those things."

She shook her head. "It isn't 'just one of those things.' Not if walking around here brought your honeymoon back to you. You still want her. I thought Seals had more balls than to sit around and say that it isn't good?"

"We're not good together."

She frowned. "The sex is bad?"

"Lord in heaven, you have a mouth on you."

She laughed again, delighted she'd made him blush. God, was there anything sweeter than a hardened military man who was still in love with his ex-wife? She didn't think so.

"What I mean is we are...combustible. But not just in the bedroom."

"Ah, the temperament. Comes with the passion."

"If I had known I was going to face the inquisition while we were out, I would have made sure to not take the pain pill."

"I guess Mal didn't tell you about me."

"Other than you were single, could handle yourself, and well, that you're pretty."

She narrowed her eyes. "You added that last one in."

He smiled. "Okay, I did."

"I guess Mal didn't tell you the nickname my brothers gave me, did he?"

He shook his head.

"I was known as the informer."

He waited for a second, and when she didn't continue, he asked, "The informer?"

"Yes. We had a big family: four boys, two girls, and a mother who worked by my father's side to get the business going. When my mother worried about the boys, she always let me go with them. And if I didn't, she made sure I got to question them. I can get an answer out of anyone."

"Is that why Mal let you go with me alone?"

She snorted. "First of all, Mal doesn't let me do anything. I stopped answering to a man the day I turned eighteen. Secondly, I don't think so. See, knowing my brother, he's going to go catting around after a few of his lost loves. He's not ready to settle down yet, so I know he will go to the women he knows won't get clingy."

Deke rolled his eyes. "Talk about someone who's carrying a torch."

She zeroed in on that statement. "Do tell."

Deke's eyes widened almost comically. "No. No way. I am not ratting out an officer to his sister. I'll never live it down."

"Spoilsport."

"I would rather be called that than whatever the team would invent to pay me back for telling you something."

"Why don't we go do a little more walking? I need to stop by my bar. I just need to make sure there aren't any problems."

"I think I can handle that."

She nodded. "And maybe we'll stop at a voodoo store, and I'll buy something to make you talk."

"Don't even think about it. I have a healthy respect for that shit."

Laughing, she patted his hand.

"If Kade screws this up with you, I want first dibs at a date."

Amused with him, with the solemn expression on his face, she smiled.

"You're the first man I'd call."

. . . . .

"So, how long you in town for?"

Mal smiled at Verna, and Kade tried not to cuss. He really hadn't wanted to come to the bar, but Mal had insisted, telling him he needed to get out of the house. He knew his friend was right, but it didn't mean he wanted to sit there with the skanky woman wrapped around Mal like he was a life preserver on the Titanic. And he didn't want to be in Shannon's bar.

"We only have a week of leave. So not long. Just needed to get out of Virginia, and I wanted to check on my sister. Has she been seeing anyone?"

Verna shook her head. "That new restaurant owner from down the street has been sniffing around. He's one of the Augustins. But she shut him down. She told me he was just trying to scope out the competition."

"Are we talking about Beau? He has always had a thing for her. When we were in high school, he used to follow her around like she was the goddess of New Orleans."

Verna laughed, and Kade took another quick drink of his water. The woman's laugh was equal to nails on a chalkboard to him.

"I could see that. She said it wasn't that, but man he moons over her. Well, speak of the devil."

He followed the waitress's line of vision, and his heart did that little skip. The bright yellow dress she wore was made of some kind of flimsy fabric that clung to her generous curves. It dipped low between her breasts and stopped just above her knee. She was laughing at something Deke said, and dammit, he couldn't help the way the air backed up in his lungs.

"Looks like they had a good time," Mal said.

Indeed it did. Her face glowed with happiness as she looked up at Deke. He leaned closer and said something to her. She laughed, and although it wasn't loud, he could hear it. It wrapped around his heart and gave a little tug. She was out having the time of her life with one of his buddies. Meanwhile, he had been stuck with Mal and the waitress from hell. He was drinking the damned water because the lazy woman had yet to get him another beer. She spotted them, and he felt her attention stay on him a moment or two longer than it had on Mal. They walked over to the table.

"I had a feeling y'all would be out. Did you do anything more interesting than entertain Verna?" Shannon asked.

"There isn't anything more interesting than that," Mal said, sending the waitress into peals of laughter.

"Verna, you need to get back to work. I have a feeling that both of these Seals need another beer."

She made a face, but she did it all the same.

Shannon settled in the chair next to her brother. Chief took the chair next to her and acted as if he had a right to sit there. Between them. He shot a look at Kade, but then turned his attention to Shannon.

"Really, Mal, the woman is an idiot," Shannon said.

"Why do you keep her around, then?" Mal asked as he scooped up another handful of snack mix.

"When you aren't around, she's a pretty good waitress, and I don't have the patience to train someone else right now. She might not be the brightest bulb, but at least I don't have to work with her anymore."

"She's not stupid," Mal said.

"She went and got a two-for-one tattoo and was amazed that they spelled her name wrong on one of them. Really, who has their name tattooed on their own ass? I'll tell you, an idiot."

Deke chuckled. "It isn't like you couldn't find another woman in this town. It's filled with them."

"Yeah, Deke had a couple of women practically slobbering on him at the voodoo shop. It was embarrassing. I thought they might use a love potion on him."

She leaned back in her chair, and Deke put his arm over the back of it. Like they were a couple. *Fuck*. He told himself for the millionth time that he didn't have a right to get mad, but dammit, Deke wasn't her boyfriend. He wasn't anything to her.

"So, I was trying to talk him into a night on Bourbon Street, but he claims he's an old, tired man," Shannon said.

"I said I would enjoy a nice, relaxing dinner with you. Not some loud bar with a bunch of tourists," Deke said.

His flirtatious tone had Kade grinding his teeth. He read the signs. Chief had shifted his chair closer, leaned into her, as if they were on a date. As if he had a right to touch her. Kade felt his temper rising, but he fought it. He was pretty sure Shannon wouldn't be happy if he embarrassed her by re-breaking Chief's arm.

"What's on the agenda tomorrow?" she asked.

"I plan to follow you around like a puppy dog," Chief said.

Her eyebrows rose slightly, but she didn't say anything. If the red haze of anger and jealousy hadn't blinded him, he would have noticed that she was surprised by Chief's behavior. It was lost on him. All he saw was his friend coming onto the woman he had been in love with for too long. He did the only thing a Seal could do—other than shoot Chief.

Kade stood and walked around the table. Without a word, he grabbed Shannon by the arm and hauled her up.

"That's enough of that," he said.

Kade said nothing else as he dragged her out of the bar. She complained all the way, calling him many names in English and Creole. Some he knew, and he was pretty sure he didn't want to know the others. When they reached the street, he scanned it for her convertible and found it easily. He started to drag her along to it, but she dug in her heels and forced him to stop.

"What in holy hell are you doing?" she asked, loud enough that people passing took notice.

He turned to face her and couldn't think. Right now, he was so damned aroused and irritated, his brain just would not form words. Besides, she was a sight to behold when she was angry. Her face was flushed. Her green eyes were spitting daggers at him, and dammit, she was breathing heavily. With each breath she took, the delicate flesh rose about the flimsy neckline of her dress.

"You do not drag me out of a bar like you own me. I am not into he-men who think they can order me around. Just who the hell do you think you are?"

The darker side he wanted to control came slithering to the top and lashed out at her. He cupped the back of her neck and pulled her to him. He attacked her mouth then, letting all his frustration, his needs, his desires wash over her, over both of them. She resisted at first, but it was futile. He knew she wanted him. He used it to entice her, slipping his tongue between her lips and tasting her.

By the time he pulled back, they were both breathing unsteadily.

"You choose, now. You come back to your place with me, or you tell me to fuck off."

He watched her lashes lower as she sighed. It sounded like regret, and he realized he might have made a big mistake with her. Maybe he had pushed his luck with her, and she had written him off. She wasn't a woman who had to wait around for a man, especially one that had been a jackass.

But in the next instant, she looked up at him, her gaze direct, unwavering. He felt as if she were looking into his soul.

"Let's go."

Chapter Eight

Shannon's nerves were popping with excitement and a little bit of fear by the time she walked into her house. The ride home had been quiet, Kade not saying a word. She didn't live far from her business, but it had seemed to take forever to make it back to her house. Kade shut the door behind him, and she set her purse and keys on the table in the front hallway and faced him.

He looked so different. Fire flamed in his eyes, darkening them with the desire he felt for her. "Last chance, Dupree."

The way he said it sounded scary and thrilling at the same time. She knew he was trying to give her an out. He hadn't spoken of any commitment. At the moment, he wasn't thinking of the future—she was sure of that. Doing this, she was taking a chance on her heart but not her body. Even in his state, she knew that he would never abuse her. He couldn't think beyond today. She understood that. It was the only way he could cope with whatever he was going through. Still, she knew that he would never dally with her if he hadn't felt some kind of connection. She knew he was good, a really good man. And right now, he needed her.

"I don't need any warnings, McKade." She settled her hands on her hips and lifted her chin. He wasn't going to scare her off, not now. "Unless you aren't up to the task, Seal."

He hesitated for a second, as if not believing she had just challenged him. The silence stretched as they stood there staring at each other. For a moment, just a moment, she thought he might walk away. That scared her more than his mood right now. Then, he grabbed her arm again and dragged her back to her room. Not that she was fighting him at all. She wanted this, wanted him in her bed.

He shut the French doors behind him and locked them. When he turned to her, she felt the first little lick of real fear. He masked his emotions, and she couldn't tell what he was thinking. Shannon knew he was a good man, but she wondered at the moment if he realized it himself.

"Strip."

She hesitated, not sure if she heard him right. This was not the playful lover she knew in Hawaii, the one who laughed with her in bed. This man was definitely dangerous. While he did scare her a bit, there was another emotion coursing along with it. *Arousal.*

"Did you hear me, Shannon? Do it now, or I'll punish you."

She shivered at the thought of what he might do. It would definitely be more than last time, she was sure of that. She did as he ordered but slowly. She wanted to make sure that he understood she was giving this to him. It was her choice, not his.

She removed her high-heeled sandals, kicking them to the wall and out of the way. Then, she slowly pulled down the zipper to her dress. She shimmied out of it, letting it fall to the floor. He showed no emotion in his expression. If anything, he looked mad. His lips turned down in a concentrated frown. His eyes, though, told another story. Heat was burning still, even hotter than before.

"Panties and bra too, Shannon."

He didn't raise his voice, but she heard the command. His tone was low and gravelly. It did odd things to her. She liked a little playing in the bedroom, but she had never seen herself as someone who would be into hardcore BDSM. But that low, demanding voice was starting to get to her. In fact, it made her want to make him happy, to please him.

She undid her bra, and he watched. A first for her. She had never stripped for a man. Not that she hadn't thought about it, or didn't have enough confidence in herself to do it. She had just never wanted to do it for a man. Until now.

She shook her shoulders, freeing the fabric and causing her breasts to sway slightly. The cool air hit her nipples, and she drew in a sharp breath. They were already so sensitive. She could not imagine what it would feel like when he touched them. By the time she got it free, she thought he made a sound, but she wasn't sure. He still showed no emotion on his face, and if she hadn't been so tuned in to him, she probably would have missed it.

She held the bra out and then dropped it to the floor. She waited.

"The panties."

Again, not loud, but even more demanding. Shannon got the feeling that Kade was barely holding onto his control, and something in her wanted to push him over the edge. She turned to face the bed, giving him full view of the red thong she wore. Again, as slowly as she could, she skimmed them down her legs, bending over as she did so. Her pussy throbbed, her body ready to be touched, pleasured. She stepped out of them.

"Turn around."

She did, and the man she faced scared her a little bit. She could see the way he was grinding his teeth. His jaw flexed each time he did. And his eyes...they were as dark and dangerous as the man who stood before her.

"Get on the bed, on your back, and spread your legs."

She wanted to tell him not to order her around. A little play was one thing, but being ordered about was different. Everything in her independent nature wanted to rebel. But something deeper, something that yearned to be with Kade, was stronger. It aroused her on some level she had never touched before. Her need spiked. She did as he ordered and waited. Cool air washed over her pussy as she felt it dampen. God, he hadn't even touched her, and she was dripping wet.

He approached the bed, still fully dressed. His blue gaze travelled down her body, and she felt it as if he were touching her. There was no doubt of the bulge in his pants. He was definitely aroused. He apparently wasn't getting rid of his clothes anytime soon. *Dammit.*

He skimmed his hand up the inside of her thigh. Those callused fingers danced over her sensitive skin. She couldn't help the shiver that moved through her body.

"I need a word that tells me I've pushed you too far. Something easy to remember."

"Jazz."

"Do you understand what we are about to do? From this point on, I am in charge. I am the person in control of your pleasure."

She nodded then sucked in a breath as he began to finger her labia. That first little touch had flashes of heat sparking through her blood. It was such a simple touch. It shouldn't have her this close to the edge.

"Rules. No speaking unless I give you permission. Do you understand?"

"Yes."

As if to reward her, he pressed his thumb against her clit, and she almost lost it. She closed her eyes and hummed. God, the pressure pushed her closer, but before she could lift her hips, he slipped his thumb away. She opened her eyes.

"Oh, no, Shannon. You don't come unless I give it to you. I'll make you pay for that little stunt."

She opened her mouth to say she hadn't been that bad when he slapped her pussy. It wasn't hard, just a pat really, but she was already sensitive there, and pleasure rippled out over her.

"I didn't give you permission to speak." He settled on the bed next to her, shaking his head. "You really don't understand yet. Maybe you aren't ready for it."

As he spoke, he skimmed his fingers over her belly up to her breasts. He pinched her nipples. The action had her moaning and closing her eyes again. The man had the most talented fingers.

"Sadly, I can't turn back now, don't want to. It's been a long four months."

He slipped his hand up her neck and then placed his fingers against her mouth.

"Open up, baby."

She opened her eyes again and did as he ordered. He slid his index finger into her mouth. She could taste her arousal. Wanting to be naughty, she slipped her tongue over his finger. He sighed in appreciation then pulled his finger out of her mouth.

Without a word, he stood and pulled off his shirt. She didn't move, didn't want to break the spell he was casting on her.

Holy mother of God. With each inch of flesh he revealed, she became more entranced. Was there a chance he had gotten even more gorgeous? He had lost weight, which emphasized his sculpted physique. She wanted nothing more than to explore that body, but she lay on the bed, waiting for his command. That thrilled her more than the idea of touching him.

There was something wrong with her.

He unzipped his jeans and slipped them off. Of course, he wasn't wearing any underwear. If she had even thought about him walking around commando, she would have probably not been able to concentrate enough to talk. He shucked them off and stood before her, his hand on his cock, stroking it. He had his gaze locked on hers, daring her to watch. She couldn't resist. Watching his hand moving over his hardened cock, seeing the little pearl of pre-come easing out, had her yearning.

As if reading her thoughts, he asked, "Want a little taste, Shannon?"

There was a thread of amusement in his tone. And for a quick moment, he looked lighter than he had since he'd appeared in her bar.

She nodded. He inched closer to the bed. "Up on your knees."

Her eagerness to please had her moving as fast as possible. He pressed his cock against her mouth, and she gladly took him in. With shallow movements, he thrust in and out of her mouth. Just like in Hawaii, the taste of him had her lust surging. She wanted more, wanted him deep within her mouth, to feel him bump against the back of her throat. He did not allow it.

Instead, he continued, giving her just a small taste of him as he slid his hand down her back to her ass. He skimmed the separation between her cheeks and fingered her anus. She hummed against his cock, and he jolted, shoving his penis further into her mouth.

"You like that, huh?"

She figured it was rhetorical and didn't answer him.

"I have a feeling you would like some anal play, but not tonight."

He continued to tease her as he fucked her face, increasing the depth of his thrusts. Soon though, she could tell he was losing control. His movements were not that controlled, and when she slipped her tongue over the tip of his cock, he pulled away with a groan.

"Oh, that was bad, Shannon. Really, bad." He turned from her then, and she was left on her hands and knees, her body needing to be touched. Hell, she needed to touch him, to skim her hands over all that wonderful flesh.

Without turning around, he asked, "Do you have any scarves?"

"Yes, in the top right-hand drawer of the dresser."

He retrieved a couple of scarves and set them on the top of the dresser. Kade turned and smiled at her. It wasn't a huge smile, like the ones she was used to, but it was something. Even as frustrated as she was, it made her heart happy to see it.

"Come on," he said, offering her a hand for support. "Up, off the bed."

She did as ordered, excited to see what he would come up with next. Kade positioned her in front of the mirror.

"Look at you," he said, his voice deepening, and his accent thickening. She did as ordered and was struck by the image of them together. Her light brown skin against his lighter, tanned flesh. He stepped closer, his cock against her ass. He placed his hand against her stomach. She was so tuned in to his touch that the simple gesture had her body reacting. It was hard not to as he moved his hand up to her breasts, caressing the underside of them. Frustration built.

"I can tell from your face that you're not happy with me."

It wasn't a question, so she didn't respond. It was hard to even think at the moment. With each delicate touch, he had her blood pressure rising, her body becoming more and more in tune with him. He slipped his hand down to her pussy. Using his index finger, he traced her labia. She was dripping wet, slick with her desire, but he didn't say anything about that.

"Watch my hand."

She was already doing that, but she understood he wanted to see her expression. He dipped his finger into her pussy, and she sighed.

"What a pretty sound." He was still in control, but she heard the heat simmering in his voice.

As soon as he said it, she pulled her bottom lip between her teeth.

"Don't worry about showing your pleasure. The sweetest sound is hearing you moan my name."

He teased her for just a few more seconds before he pulled away. He took the first of the scarves, a red one with black designs on it, and slid it over her breasts. Her skin was so sensitive to his touch that it almost hurt as the delicate fabric slithered over her nipples. Kade's gaze was glued to the scarf as he moved it over her, his lips curving in satisfaction as she shivered.

He stepped beside her and slipped his finger under her chin and turned her face to him. Bending his head, he gave her a kiss, a soft brush of the lips. It had everything in her yearning for so much more.

When he pulled away, he said, "Spread your legs a little more, then place your hands on the dresser."

She did as ordered, and he slid the scarf between her legs. The slither of silky material against her sex almost sent her over the edge. It was barely a touch. He pulled the material tight against her.

Oh, God. She was going to come. He moved the scarf back and forth slightly as he nuzzled her neck. His cock was hard against her hip, and she knew he wanted her. But he was controlling himself, controlling her. She wasn't an innocent by any standards, but this was beyond what she had ever tried. He tightened the scarf more, the material separating her pussy lips.

She moaned as it rubbed against her clit, pressing ever so slightly but not enough to give her relief. He only gave her so much before he was tugging the scarf away and pulling her to the bed.

"On the bed," he ordered. He had seemed under control, but the deepening of his voice told her more. He was close to the edge, too.

Kade grabbed the second scarf. "Hands over your head."

She complied without thinking. She wanted him to touch her again, wanted his hands on her. He wrapped it around her wrists then threaded it through her iron headboard. After completing the task, he stopped and looked down at her. His gaze slipped down her body, and she felt as if he was touching her everywhere.

In the next instant, he scowled. "Dammit. Condoms."

She smiled. "Bedside table drawer."

If anything, his expression turned darker.

"Oh, good lord, I had to talk."

"It's not that. It's the fact that you had condoms ready. Been seeing someone?"

She rolled her eyes. "They're the ones from Hawaii."

He didn't say anything as he pulled open the drawer. After grabbing one, he ripped open the package and then joined her on the bed. He set the opened package beside him. Then he settled between her legs and leaned down to give her pussy one long lick.

He smiled up at her. "Remember, don't come unless I give you permission."

He drove her crazy. He slipped his hands beneath her rear end and lifted her to his mouth. Then he attacked her. Over and over, he thrust his tongue into her pussy. When he took her clit into his mouth, he hummed against the bundle of nerves.

Damn. The tension that had been simmering now shot to her pussy. She wanted to move, wanted to slip her fingers through that blonde hair and thrust up against his mouth. He held her there, not allowing her any purchase.

Soon, though, he set her down, grabbed the condom. He rolled it on as fast as humanly possible, in her opinion. He lifted her up off the bed again and entered into her in one hard thrust. Without hesitating, he started moving. Each thrust was slow but deep, but not enough to please her. The way she was bound and the way he held her, she could do nothing but allow him to set the pace. Soon his movements were not so measured. He increased his rhythm.

"It's time, baby. Come for me."

He thrust into her hard as he pressed against her clit. She did as he ordered, bowing up against him and screaming out his name. She was still shuddering from her release as he started moving again, squeezing that tiny bundle of nerves between his fingers. She came again, bucking against him. He followed her as she crested again a few seconds later.

A short time later, he rolled off her and reached up to untie her wrists. "You feeling okay?" he asked.

She smiled at him, cupping his cheek. "Okay doesn't describe it."

He smiled, that old crooked smile she knew so well, and her breath caught. In the day he had been back, Kade had been distant and hadn't shown her the boyish grin she was used to.

"What?" he asked, as it started to slip away.

"Nothing. Just, you look good in my bed."

"So do you. How about a little snack?"

Keep it light, Dupree.

"Sure." She started to get out of bed, but he stayed her with his hand.

"No. You stay, I'll find something."

She nodded and watched as he pulled on his jeans. "I'll be right back."

She held her smile until she was alone. She sat up, pulled her knees to her chest and wrapped her arms around her legs. How sad was it that she was so excited to see him smile at her? Sad for both of them. Something was bad. Something had pushed him to his limit while they were gone. He was a strong man, but everyone had their breaking point.

All she could do was support him, let him know she was there for him.

And love him until he left at the end of the week.

Chapter Nine

Shannon settled against the pillows with a sigh that made Kade happier than he thought possible.

"That was a good idea. I didn't realize what an appetite I'd worked up."

He chuckled. "Really? I would have thought you needed a side of beef after that."

"Have you always been into BDSM? I've just never heard you talk about it."

"Does it bother you?"

She shook her head. "I wouldn't have let you touch me like that if I didn't want to. I like sex, but not enough to do something like that if I had issues with it."

He should have known that would be her answer. He had never met a woman so confident and straight up about her sexuality.

"I've always had some interest in it. But it's a little different now."

He could tell by her expression she wanted to ask him more. He was a little surprised by the need to control her. It almost overwhelmed his good senses. Kade just hoped he held himself in check for the week.

"Hm, I need a good night's sleep," she said. The patter of rain hit against the window, and Shannon was snuggled up against Kade as he pulled the sheet up. It was an image he had often dreamed of before his last mission.

He cleared his throat. "You're not the only one."

"And that rain is perfect. It always makes me so drowsy. I love the sound of it."

She was already drifting into sleep. A selfish part of him wanted to stop her, keep her awake. They weren't going to have much time together. Kade wanted to savor every minute, try and draw out his visit.

There was a very good chance he was really screwing up. He had prepared himself to resist her, resist the crazy pull she always had on him. He had thought he could do it.

Inwardly, he snorted. Yeah, he could resist her. He'd been in New Orleans for less than forty-eight hours, and he had already crumbled.

"You're thinking too much."

Her breath tickled his chest. "What?"

She lifted her head and looked up at him. "You're thinking too much. Right now, your head is turning over all the things you're worried about."

"Yeah?"

She nodded. "Don't worry about it. Let it go."

"Aren't women supposed to get all talkative after sex?"

"If you don't do it right. Apparently, you haven't been doing it right."

Her sassy tone made him chuckle. How could he stay out of her bed? The woman had just submitted to him, and now she was messing with him. If a man could resist her, he had to be stupid or gay.

"Or maybe I had the wrong partners."

"I have to agree with that. Listen, I know you've got a lot on your plate. There is no pressure here, not right now. Let's just take it one day at a time. If you can handle that, Seal?"

Her tone was flirtatious, but there was a hint of steel beneath it. He had been preparing for a long, drawn out discussion of why he hadn't contacted her. Instead, she offered him nothing but understanding.

"I am more than up to the task."

"Good." She leaned up and gave him a kiss on the nose then on his mouth. She lingered there, giving him a taste of her, tempting him. She pulled back, a smile curving her lips. In the soft moonlight, there in her room with the rain hitting the window, he knew he was still in love with her. His heart lurched at the thought, but he brushed the worry aside. One day at a time was what she wanted. That was what he would give her.

"You get some sleep," he said, trying to keep a lid on his emotions.

"You betcha." She chuckled, then settled back down and snuggled close to him.

He wanted this, wanted it more than he had ever wanted to be a Seal. It scared him a bit to know that. From the time he entered the Navy, he had wanted to be a Seal. He had questioned that in the last few months, but other than trying to protect her, he had never thought of giving up on Shannon.

Again, he shoved the thoughts aside and decided to do as ordered. A good night's sleep was what he really needed to get his head back on straight.

* * * *

Kade came awake with a shout. His heart was beating out of control, his body slick with sweat. He had been having these nightmares since he got back, but they hadn't been quite this bad. This one had been vivid, almost real to him.

Each time, he saw Forrester's face as he was shot, as the life seeped from him.

With a shake of his head, Kade stood and stretched. Shannon grumbled and settled deeper into the pillows. He brushed her hair from her face and noticed his hand was shaking. He wanted to touch her, to love her again, but he was too raw to handle that now. He needed to get his head out of the dream and back onto the day. He went into the bathroom and splashed his face with some cool water, then found his jeans and pulled them on. Even through the closed blinds, he could see the first stirrings of the sunrise. There was one thing about a good bout of healthy sex. He had finally slept through the night. When he unlocked the door, he heard someone moving around in the kitchen. He had a feeling it was Mal. He didn't want to really deal with his friend without some coffee. Unfortunately, the coffee was, of course, in the kitchen. He could smell it brewing.

Kade squared his shoulders and walked to the kitchen. He found Mal there, frying some bacon.

"About time you emerged from her bedroom," he said without turning around.

He didn't sound mad, but he knew better than to trust that. Mal could be his deadliest when he was cool.

"Look. Mal…"

He trailed off when his friend turned with a smile on his face. "What are you, stupid?"

"Not following you, mate."

"Get some coffee before you fall down."

He did as ordered, watching Mal as he forked up the bacon and put it on a plate. Next, he pulled out some eggs and started cracking them into a bowl.

"See, I know you don't remember after we were evac'd out."

Hell, he could remember up until the moment he was shot. Then nothing until he woke up in the hospital.

Mal nodded. "You were completely out of it there for a while. But I remember. Once I came to, I was by your side."

He had sort of known that. Each time he had surfaced, he had seen him there by the side of his bed. "And?"

"You know the most amazing thing about being out of your mind after an injury? You don't know what you say."

It took Kade a second to figure it out. Then it hit him.

"I said something."

Mal nodded without turning around. "Over and over. You wanted to talk to Shannon."

"Shit."

"I was pretty pissed right then." He glanced back at Kade. "But, then, you were injured, and I couldn't beat the shit out of you. I wanted to, believe me. Especially since I figured out that you might have used the wedding to get her into bed."

"I wouldn't do that."

Mal stopped mixing the eggs and faced him. "Come on, Kade. I know you as well as you know me."

"And you know I'm not a slut like you."

Mal chuckled. "Yeah, you are, but it stopped about a couple of years ago. I realized then how many times you came back to New Orleans with me."

Kade couldn't help the heat that crawled into his face. Damnit, he was blushing.

"I have no idea what you're talking about." The moment he said it, he knew he sounded like an idiot.

Mal shook his head. "Son, you have got to lie better. Anyway, I realized a long time ago you had a crush on her. I ignored it for the most part because, when you have sisters like Jocelyn and Shannon, well, you're used to it. Jocelyn was always so serious, but with Shannon, well, she's got that soft heart of hers. All the guys loved to get her sympathy."

"If that's what you think attracts them and keeps them coming around, you're living in denial."

"Okay, I know it had to do with the way she's built. I'm not blind, but I can pretend. She's my sister." Mal jerked a shoulder. "Anyway, I worked through my anger. It's hard to be pissed at a guy who had his knee all fucked up, and well, knocked stupid. Stupider. I guess I should ask your intentions, but that would get me smacked around by Shannon if she found out."

82

"I'm not truly sure of my intentions."

Mal nodded in understanding. Their job didn't allow for a lot of self-reflection. Any relationship, whether sexual or not, didn't always stand up to the horrible life of the significant other of a Seal.

"I just wanted you to know I will stand clear. Shannon wouldn't have taken you to bed if she didn't want you there."

"Your sister never does anything she doesn't want to." Even Kade could hear the admiration in his own voice. He had always been drawn to strong, capable women.

"You'll get no problems from me unless you hurt her."

Kade sighed and shook his head. "Fuck, Mal, I'm a man. I'm going to hurt her."

"Not intentionally. That's different."

He nodded.

"I decided Chief and I are going out to Mama's. I really don't want to be in a house with you two. Kind of gross."

"I hope you have cheese grated for those eggs," Shannon said from the doorway. He looked in her direction, and his breath caught in his throat. The sun was now streaming in behind her. She was wearing that same little robe she was before, and he couldn't help the heat that poured into his blood at the sight of her.

"Oh, God, you two are disgusting. Can the kitchen be a non-sex part of the house?"

He glanced at his friend. "Get used to it."

Mal chuckled. "And no, I didn't put cheese into the eggs because not everyone wants it."

"My kitchen, my rules."

"But I'm not giving your boyfriend here any issues. And, remember, I am the one cooking. I won't make you any."

"You suck."

"Well, be glad I'm not going to kick your boyfriend's ass. Because he knows I can."

She smiled at her brother then looked at Kade. "He lives in a little world of his own making, doesn't he?"

"Also, be happy I'm leaving you two alone. Chief and I are going to Mama's."

"You'll get more home-cooked meals there."

She walked over to Kade, then as if it was the most natural thing to do, slipped onto his lap. He hesitated, his chest tight at the simple gesture, and slid his arms around her waist. Chief came in next, clean-shaven, looking like he was ready to report to duty.

He gave them a disgusted look. "I still think you would be better off with me."

She laughed at that. "I'm sure you do. I need to get dressed because I have paperwork to get done."

"I thought you had off for the next few days," Kade said.

She nodded. "I forgot I have to get the schedule set up and the time sheets processed. I'll be back and there better be cheese in those eggs."

After she gave him a quick kiss, she said, "You can come with me today, but it would be really boring."

He wanted to go. He wanted to be anywhere she was. For some reason, he felt a desperate need to be in the same room as her.

The moment he thought it, he felt funny, as if something was clutching at his throat. Immediately, he backed up from that thought. They had little time together, but he needed some space. "I think the guys and I are going to go over to your mama's for lunch, or that was the plan yesterday."

Mal nodded. "Mama will be pissed if I don't bring her favorite boy."

She sighed. "Fine, abandon me for an older woman who can cook better than I could ever dream of. See where that gets you."

She slipped off his lap and went to get ready.

He rose to fill his cup when Chief said, "You know if you fuck this up, McKade, there is a good chance that after Dupree finishes with you, I'll kick your ass."

"You could try, Chief," he said cheerfully, feeling somehow lighter. He filled his cup then looked over Mal's shoulder. "Seriously, mate, you better put some cheese in those eggs."

"Shit."

* * * *

"You better get something to drink, Francis," Anna Louise Dupree said. He did as she told him, enjoying the homemade strawberry lemonade more than he would admit. Other than his mother, she was the only person who could get away with calling him by his first name. "And don't you worry. We'll put some meat on you this week."

He loved her as if she was his own mother, and sadly, he had a better relationship with Mal's mother. Closer. Where Jocelyn had taken after their father in looks and temperament, Shannon was her mother through and through. Her mother was average height, delightfully rounded, and so full of joy, you couldn't help but smile at her. She had taken him under her wing the moment he'd shown up with Mal several years earlier. His parents weren't bad people, they were just distant. His sister wasn't much better, not now, especially after her divorce last month. It was their nature. Their work in the field of nuclear energy was important to them, and it was the focus of most of their energy. So, when Anna Louise had hugged him like he was a long lost relative, he had been slightly overwhelmed. And, he had fallen in love with her by the end of the weekend.

"When are you going to run away with me?" he asked as he always did.

She laughed and for a moment, he could hear Shannon. They were so much alike…except for the cooking. Her green eyes danced with merriment.

"Oh, you devil. Don't let Sam hear you, or he'll beat you up."

He snorted. "I can take your husband on."

"Maybe, but I think you might have a little trouble with my little girl, yes?"

Again his face flushed, and dammit, she laughed. It hit him then that this was the most he had spoken in weeks. Shannon and her mother were so much alike. They always drew him out of himself, got him to participate.

"I still can't believe you make this homemade, Mrs. Dupree," Deke said.

"I told you to call me Anna Louise, Deke. No one in the Dupree house stands on formality."

He smiled at her, and Mal made a sound of disgust. "It's bad enough dealing with Shannon and Kade, but do y'all have to flirt with my mother?"

"A beautiful woman like your mother should expect it," Deke said, earning him a knock to the back of the head from Mal.

"Now, you two boys go out and do something. I want to talk to Kade."

Shit. He knew that this was coming, but he hadn't been ready for it. The others agreed mainly because no one, not even Sam Dupree, said no to Anna Louise in her own house.

"Now, you going to tell me why you look like this?" She waved her hand at him.

"Bad assignment?"

She tsked. "More than that, I am sure. You brought some ghosts back with you."

He nodded, knowing there would be no denying to Anna Louise. She wouldn't allow for it.

"I'll not ask you what is bothering you. Not yet. You tell that girl of mine when you're ready."

"How does everyone know about that?"

She rolled her eyes. "What am I, stupid? Seriously, Francis, you follow her around like a puppy dog when you visit. Her brother and his friend are here at my house to stay, but not you. I know my girl has sex."

He cleared his throat. "I really don't want to talk about it."

She made a disgusted sound that he had heard a time or two from Mal. "Oh, the poor little Seal is afraid of his lover's mother." She shook her head. "Don't you talk sex with your mother?"

"Good God, no." He couldn't keep the horror out of his voice.

"Hmm, well, that might be your problem. Either way, know I do not judge. Just be careful, that's all I ask."

He looked into the eyes so similar to Shannon's and nodded. "I will do my best, Anna Louise."

She smiled then and patted his hand. "I promised that boy of mine some cornbread and fried catfish. I need help in the kitchen. You up to the challenge?"

Another thing his parents didn't know about him. He loved to cook. It had come about mainly because his parents would forget to cook. So Kade had taken over. With Anna Louise, though, he had learned so much, and she loved having him in the kitchen.

He nodded. "I'd love to."

* * * *

87

Shannon looked over the schedule for the next two weeks and sighed. She only had three more days, and the guys had to go back to Virginia. She wasn't in the mood to deal with the feelings that brought about, but in the last three days since Kade had returned to her bed, she had been unable to ignore them. She hadn't pushed him, hadn't tried to. It overwhelmed her a bit too much, but it was growing every day. She wanted to ask what he wanted from her other than sex.

She didn't, though. She knew that at the moment, he was doing better, but asking questions like that would be too much. Whatever happened on the mission had really hurt him. She had to give him time to heal, then they could deal with what was going on between them. The nightmares were bad, she knew without being told. And seriously, there was another reason she hadn't pushed him.

She was being a coward.

She could wrap it up in the package of giving him time or the idea that they were living in the moment, but it wasn't that. She didn't push because she didn't want to lose him.

And that was pitiful.

"You going to take the night off again?" Simon asked. She heard the disapproval in his voice.

"Yes. They're leaving tomorrow. I don't have that much time left with Kade."

"What's going on between you two?"

She knew what he wanted but instead she took the chicken's way out. "I don't think I have to explain sex to you, do I? I thought you understood all forms of it."

He frowned and shut the door behind him before sitting down in the chair in front of her desk. "I want to know what the hell is going to happen when he leaves."

"You and me both."

"You haven't discussed it?" he asked.

"We haven't had time to do that. Really."

Simon rolled his eyes. "Really? You're having that much sex?"

She stared at him blankly.

"Oh, now I am jealous." Then he frowned. "Stop trying to get me off the subject.

"You're the one who brought up sex, not me. And just so you know, Kade doesn't swing that way."

"Shannon."

She heard the reprimand in his voice. "What is it you're getting at?"

"I know he needs some help, probably has PTSD from that last mission. He's jumpy, more than usual. But, honey, you need to give yourself the right to ask for more."

"What do you mean?"

"You have always gone for what you wanted. In work, in life, with every man other than this one. You are letting him call the shots."

"Believe me, it's worth it."

"Again, stop trying to distract me with sex. You're trying to help him over what he's dealing with."

She frowned. "I don't know what he's really dealing with."

"You haven't talked about it."

She shook her head "I told you, it's only been a couple of days."

"And you think this is going to help you? Help him? I can tell by looking at him that he needs help."

"Of course he does, but do you think one of those damned Seals have spoken to me?" she asked, her voice rising. "The only thing I got out of Mal was that they lost someone, that Mal was knocked unconscious, and that's it. None of them say anything except that it was a really bad mission."

By the time she finished, she realized how loud she had gotten. The silence was almost deafening.

"Okay, so maybe they aren't ready to talk. You don't know what happened, might never. Remember, my dad was Special Forces. There are just some things they are never going to tell you. But what are you going to ask from Kade?"

Everything.

The word whispered through her mind, but she didn't say it. If she did, it wouldn't come true. She knew she was being a coward, but she had to be careful around him. Pushing him after such a traumatic situation was too much.

She opened her mouth, but Simon shook his head. "Don't say a word. I know. Just make sure that at some point, you tell him what you want. He might be hurting now, but believe me, Kade's a Seal. He can handle a few demands from you. It might be good for both of you."

When Simon finally left her alone, she realized that there was some truth to what he had been saying. She had been holding back, and she normally wouldn't. Yes, he had only been back in her life for less than a week, and their relationship had come out of a friendship. Because she had known him for years, it seemed like a long time, but it wasn't. Their sexual relationship had only been a few nights. Demanding an answer wasn't smart. It wasn't something she even wanted. Shannon knew men, she knew herself even better. She wouldn't be happy to be pushed at a time like this if she were suffering. She would give him what he needed and wait. Someday, she'd make sure he understood he had to make a choice.

She just hoped she could hold out that long.

Chapter Ten

Kade had been feeling antsy all evening. He couldn't really put his finger on it. It was as if something was crawling under his skin, urging him to some kind of action. The docs told him he would have times like this. Kade had been pretty sure the physicians had lost their minds until he came to see Shannon.

He wanted to say it was anything but the woman across the table from him. Shannon had brought home dinner from her bar, and they'd eaten by candlelight. Rain was pattering on the roof again, and there were soft blues filtering through the house. It should have been romantic. It was. Beyond romantic. She was sitting there, a smile on her face, looking like the woman of his dreams. But he couldn't shake the feeling that something really bad was about to happen.

He hated to think it was Shannon. He wanted her so much he thought he would die if he didn't touch her. At the same time, he hated himself for that. It made no sense. Any man would be happy to sit in his place and have this woman across the table smiling at him as if he were the best man on earth. He couldn't face it, didn't want to. It was their last night together, and he didn't want to ruin it with stupid thoughts.

"You done?" she asked, no reprimand in her voice.

He nodded, knowing he had been a bad dinner companion. And that irritated him more. She said nothing as she picked up the plates and took them to her sink. He watched her wash them off, then place them in the dishwasher. He was ruining the little time they had left. He was being a moody ass.

He brushed the thoughts away and rose to follow her to the sink. He stepped up behind her and placed a hand on the counter on either side of her. She stilled then leaned back against him with a purr.

"Are you back with the living?"

"Sorry."

She turned and met his gaze directly.

"Don't be. I told you, I understand. Mal does it sometimes. Dad did, every now and then. He was in Vietnam the last few years we were over there, and when I was younger, I remember he would get quiet every now and then. I realized later it was after he heard from one of his old military buddies." She rose to her tiptoes and kissed his cheek. "Don't worry so much."

The worries he did have disappeared in that kiss. It was not a sexy kiss, one that would tempt him to bed, or it wasn't meant that way. Her reassurance was more than he had expected, more than he deserved. He said nothing but reached over and turned off the water.

"Come on," he said, taking her by the hand. He led her back to her room, ready to make sure that tonight would be a night that neither of them would forget. The only light in the room was the small bedside table lamp on a low setting. Just like the woman, the room was sexy. Cool colors draped the windows, covered her bed, but it was the fabrics, the velvets and satins, that pulled him in. They weren't flowery or even overly feminine, but they were definitely sexy.

He released her and went to the dresser to retrieve the bag he'd hid by it. He'd done some shopping today, and he wanted to play. When he had laid the contents of the bag out, he turned to face her.

"I think you have too many clothes on."

She didn't look at him at first. Her gaze was latched onto the toys.

"Shannon. Look at me." She raised her gaze to his. She was worried, that was for sure. They had talked about anal sex, but had not attempted it. Tonight he wanted to show her just how much she would like it.

She undressed slowly, folding her clothes and placing them on the chair beside her dresser. If he was antsy before, he was downright ready to come undone at the moment. The soft light caressed her curves. That body…it was as if God made her for him. He undressed himself then stepped closer to her, slipping his arms around her and pulling her against him.

He bent his head and brushed his mouth over hers. His entire body reacted to the kiss. His heart sped up, his dick twitched, and his head seemed to float. Shannon would probably always do this to him. He stepped back and cupped her breast, grazing the tip of her nipple with his thumb. She was so fucking responsive.

"You better get on the bed before I lose control."

She smiled as if she didn't believe him but did as he ordered. He removed the toys from the bag and opened the tube of lube and coated the anal plug with it. "We talked about this before, and I bought the smallest one."

When he turned and faced her, he knew she would be wary. She wanted to try it, wanted to let him do what he wanted. In the last three nights, there was one thing he had learned. Shannon loved to let him take control. She was a woman who had complete control in her life, but she wanted someone else to take over in the bedroom. He approached the bed.

"Roll over, baby."

She hesitated, but did as he ordered.

"Remember your safe word if it gets too intense for you."

He slipped the toy between her ass cheeks. She immediately tensed up.

"Take a deep breath and then release it slowly."

She did as he ordered, and he started easing the plug into her. He moved slowly, making sure not to hurt her.

When he finally pressed it past the last ring of muscle, he let go of a breath he hadn't known he was holding.

"How does that feel?"

"Odd."

He smiled. "Turn over, but be careful."

When she was once again on her back, he went to the dresser and picked up the vibrator. "You know the rules. No coming without permission. If you do, I bought a special crop to punish you with."

She shivered, and he knew that excited her. He could just imagine slapping that generous flesh of hers with the butt plug up her ass. It was just too bad he wouldn't have time to fuck her ass. He loved it and knew she would too, but it was too soon for something like that. She wasn't ready.

He turned the vibrator on and slipped it between her legs as he bent his head and took a nipple into his mouth. She gasped when he bit down lightly on the nipple. He did the same to her other breast then rose to his knees. With his free hand, he offered her his cock.

"Take me in, baby. Suck me."

She easily complied. Shannon loved to give head, and holy shit, her mouth should be considered a lethal weapon. She slid her tongue up one side, then over the tip and down again. As she continued to tease him, she caressed his sac. God, he loved that. He usually had tight control on his sexuality, but with Shannon, he barely kept it under control. Part of it was the attraction he felt for her, the almost overwhelming need to succumb to the need that strengthened every day. He couldn't seem to understand just how she did it, how with her, he always had to hold onto his control.

He pulled back as he felt his orgasm approaching. Not yet, not when he wanted to push her to her limits.

"You can be so naughty, Shannon."

She smiled up at him, then it faded when he increased the vibrator's speed one more level, then pressed it into her pussy. The moan she gave him was one of the sweetest sounds he'd heard in a good long time.

"Remember, you aren't allowed to come. Not without my permission. You do, and I can promise you that you'll regret it."

With every word, his voice deepened and his lust was easy to hear. He was sure she heard it too.

"You are such a responsive sub. I wish we had more time to visit a club. I have a feeling you would like a little public play, wouldn't you?"

He could just imagine her there, with people watching them, having him spank her. He adjusted the vibrator, giving himself room to dip his head down between her legs. As he continued to hold the toy firm, he pulled her clit into his mouth. She moaned then, and he could tell she was close, that she was barely holding onto her control. Usually, before her, and mainly before tonight, he would push a submissive to the edge, but not over it. He always wanted to show her that she was under her control. But the punishment he had in mind had him pushing her up and over. Kade knew he was going to send her over the edge, but he wanted her to know that she was his.

He flipped a switch higher and pulled her clit between his teeth. She was fighting it. But one more graze of his teeth, and she screamed through her orgasm. She bucked so hard she pushed him off her.

Moments later, he turned off the vibrator and pulled it from between her legs. He leaned down and pushed damp curls away from her face.

"Like I said, you're a naughty girl. Do you know what I do to naughty women?"

She shook her head.

"You're about to find out. Get up on your knees, put your hands on the headboard and show me that pretty ass of yours."

He moved from the bed and placed the vibrator on the top of the dresser. Joining her back on the bed, he had to hide a smile. She was ready to take him on from the scowl on her face. She wasn't happy with him. He knew he hadn't been fair. His prerogative.

He slid the crop over her flesh, and he felt the desire surging through him. He liked the way she shivered, the way she reacted. In the past, he had subs who tried to hide their emotions from him. She never did. The connection they'd both felt from the first time they met was always there.

"Now, you might not agree with my methods. I know I'm your first Dom, but I've been a little easy on you. Really easy. If…"

He stopped himself. He couldn't talk about the time they wouldn't have. Their agreement had been to live in the moment.

He gave her little pats with the end of the crop. Shannon wiggled her ass at him, and he couldn't help but laugh.

"You really haven't learned how to behave as a sub, have you?"

She turned her head to apparently answer him, but he wasn't waiting for an answer. He pulled back the crop and smacked her. The gasp was loud, quick, and so damned erotic.

He smacked her harder and harder, making sure that no part of her ass was untouched. He skimmed his hand over her ass.

"So pretty. I used to spend hours fantasizing about your ass. If I had truly known what it looked like, I would have never been able to concentrate around you."

He gave her one little smack again, then slipped the crop between her legs, sliding it over her mons before moving away. He needed to get ahold of his control. It was slipping away. Drawing in a few breaths, he counted backwards from ten. Twice. When he finally had control, he grabbed a condom and slipped it on. He'd left her there because he'd liked the way she looked.

Now that he had control, he walked over to the bed. "Come here, honey," he said, easing her down onto the bed and onto her back. For a second, he couldn't think. She was looking up at him with those incredible eyes, her need easy to see. She was so trusting. He wanted to do nothing more than to fuck her until she couldn't remember her name. He barely held onto the savage beast that was clawing at his belly. It wanted complete power. Over her, over him, over the situation. He drew in a breath, pulling his emotions back, trying his best to conceal it from her.

He settled between her legs and then leaned closer, resting a hand on either side of her head. He could smell her arousal. She was so beautiful when she came, so lost in the pleasure. It made him want to do it again and again.

Without closing his eyes, he bent his head and kissed her, slipping his tongue between her lips. When he pulled back, she was smiling, her eyes were sultry, and her face was flush. He rose to his knees and entered her slowly. He wanted to thrust into her with no finesse. But, with the plug in her ass, he couldn't. It might be too much. She groaned in frustration.

"What? You have complaints?"

"Go faster."

He smiled at the impatience in her voice. "I am trying to be gentle."

"Be gentle later."

He should reprimand her, but he couldn't. She shouldn't be telling him what to do. At this time, though, he didn't care. He just wanted to watch her come again. He started thrusting, slowly, shallow, just enough to build her back up again. She arched up against him, and he knew what she was feeling. With the plug inside her ass, it was tighter. Each thrust took her to another level of pleasure.

Soon, she was moaning beneath him, moving in tandem with him.

He leaned down and kissed her. "Come for me, Shannon. Do it."

She was already coming by the time he finished giving her the order. Her muscles clamped down tight on him, pulling him deeper into her pussy. He kept moving, pushing himself to the release he had been needing for what seemed like forever.

She looked up at him then. Those green eyes were heavy-lidded, her lips curved, and she cupped his cheek.

"I love you, Kade."

His heart squeezed as he looked down at her and knew in that moment, she meant every word.

"Come for me," she whispered.

Her voice was so soft, he wasn't sure he heard her, but he could read her lips. He did then, thrusting into her one last time and losing himself to the pleasure.

Chapter Eleven

Darkness surrounded them. It was what they worked best in, the one thing he knew that would make it easier to extract the subject. The plan was in place, and as always, there was a backup. But Kade had a bad feeling about this one. Something in his gut was telling him that they should abort.

"Something's wrong," Mal whispered. "Really wrong."

Mal always knew when something was going down. The fact that Kade was feeling it, too, wasn't a very good sign.

Nothing moved. Not even an animal as they made their way to the rebel camp. It was so fucking hot. He just wanted to get back to Shannon. He wanted to make it out of here alive and go back to the joy he'd shared with her. Then it hit him. It was too quiet. A real base camp would at least have some kind of activity. He held his fist up, telling everyone to halt. It came a second too late. An IED went off several yards in front of them. Mal dropped to the ground and didn't move. Kade's heart was pumping hard, adrenaline coursing through him as chaos exploded around him. They all hit the dirt, and Kade crawled on the floor of the jungle to reach his friend. He was happy to find him unconscious with a steady heartbeat. Then shots were fired. He heard Forrester scream out, and he jumped to his feet. He saw a rebel holding his gun to the kid's head. Kade couldn't get a good shot off. The sound of the other gun going off echoed through the jungle.

Kade came awake screaming. Sweat rolled down his back, and in the coolness of the room, he shivered. His heart was smacking against his ribs.

"Kade? Are you okay?" Shannon asked, her soft voice filled with sleep and worry.

Still feeling the raw from the dream, he said nothing, just rose from the bed and went into the bathroom.

By the time he returned, she had turned on her bedside light and pulled on her robe.

"Do you want to talk about it?"

"Nothing to talk about."

She frowned. "You have nightmares every night. Talking sometimes helps."

"Well, it won't help me. Just forget it."

He settled back in the bed. He didn't want to look at her, couldn't.

"Have you talked to anyone about it?"

"Let it go, Shannon. I'm not in the mood."

He closed his eyes but the light remained on. He sighed and opened his eyes and found her watching him. She was still rumpled from sleep, her hair a tangle of curls down her back. With a smile, he set his hand on her thigh. "I do know what will help me sleep."

Her eyes softened, but she shook her head. "I really do think you need to talk about it. I know having nightmares after a mission is routine, but it's been months. I know when I talk about mine, they don't seem so scary."

He removed his hand from her leg and fought back the panic that rose to his throat. "I'm not scared. Just a messed up dream."

"If you don't face your problem how are you going to fix—"

"Is this about you fixing me?"

Irritated and needing space, he rose from the bed. He pulled on his pants.

"What do you mean by that?"

"I should have known you weren't being truthful. Women are always trying to fix men. You think that you know what's best for us. I don't need any help working through my issues. I'm fine."

The silence in the room had him panicking. When he turned to face her, he was sure he would find her crying, but instead, she was staring at him. Expressionless.

"I was just offering a suggestion, but apparently, I hit a nerve."

He didn't like the way she looked now. As if she had shut down. She was normally so full of life. The contrast was stunning. The fact that it was his fault pissed him off even more. He knew it was wrong. He knew he was digging his grave. Still, he went on.

"No, what you're trying to do is tell me how to live."

She opened her mouth, then snapped it shut. She shut down even more. If she was expressionless before, she was downright icy cold.

"Fine."

She scooted out of bed and moved away from him. His panic increased, and with it, his anger.

"That's what's wrong with women. Always trying to fix us."

"I believe you already mentioned that. I have never tried to fix you, or whatever you're talking about." Her voice was low when she spoke, and he knew her temper was getting the better of her. "In fact, I have walked on eggshells around you since you showed up. It has been only a few days, and I have never asked what was coming up next. Never."

"You were too busy trying to make sure you took care of me."

She stared at him as if he had grown a second head. "You're pissed at me because I cared for you?"

When she said it that way, it made him sound like an ass. He pushed that thought aside. He might only have his pride right now, well not much of it, but some.

"That's not the real problem, though, is it, you stupid Seal? You want to control everything. All the time. Is that why you can't sleep through the night anymore? You went on a mission and things got out of control? So you found out you have no power in a lot of situations. Worse, you can't control me. "

"That has nothing to do with it."

"Because I didn't act like some kind of clinging vine, you had to come up with another reason that I was ruining your life. Fine. Run. Be the coward."

"What did you call me?" he asked. His temper was growing as the panic dissolved.

"You heard me. I'm willing to love you, give you all my love, but you are being such a thickheaded Seal, you can't accept that. Fine. Go. Get out of my house."

"Where the hell am I supposed to go?"

"I have no idea, just get out of my room."

He hesitated, trying to figure out if she was serious. From the fire sparking in her green eyes, he was pretty damned sure she wanted him to leave. He was just glad she didn't believe in owning a handgun. He would worry about what appendage she would shoot off.

"Fine."

Without another word, he walked to the door. Something had his stomach churning, and it wasn't the nightmare. He slammed the door behind him and walked to the guest room. He knew he was probably wrong. What did his father always say? Men are always wrong if there was a woman involved.

Fuck. He had lashed out at her because of his own issues and hurt her. He walked out into the hall again and stopped at her door. He heard her then, the loud sobs piercing his heart. He pressed his hand against the door, wanting nothing more than to go in and hold her. But it would be false. He wasn't truly cut out for this. He would hurt her again. And in the end, she would hate him more than she did now.

Feeling impotent, he turned and walked away. Each step he took hurt him more than his damaged knee. Knowing he loved her with every step was killing him, but a woman like Shannon deserved a whole man.

He would never be able to offer her that again.

* * * *

Shannon went through the motions of saying her goodbyes. She didn't like big emotional scenes, not when no good could come out of them. Kade was going to believe what he wanted, and in the time they'd had, they couldn't work through their problems. And he didn't want to. While she and Kade barely spoke, she did say goodbye.

"You want to tell me what happened there?" Mal asked when they were alone.

"He's a pig-headed fool."

He studied her for a second. "I can beat him up."

"That's sweet." She gave him a kiss. "Your buddy there beats himself up enough. Maybe one day he'll come to his senses. Though, he is a man. So there is a good a chance that he will never come to his senses. You *are* the lesser sex."

He sighed. "Okay, but call me if you change your mind. I can make his life hell."

She nodded. "Stay safe. Please."

He nodded and gave her another kiss on the cheek, and then strode toward the car. Kade refused to look at her. He had mumbled his goodbyes, but she hadn't been truly open to conversation with him, either. She watched as her brother pulled away from the curb and said a little prayer for the three men for their journey, and lord, whatever mission they next went on. She walked back

into her house, shutting the door and walking to the
kitchen. Shannon was cried out. She didn't think she had
another tear left in her.

Her phone rang, and when she saw the eight-oh-eight
area code, she frowned. It was the middle of the night for
her sister.

"What are you doing up?"

"No hello, Jocelyn? I miss you."

Her chest clutched and near tears formed in her eyes.
"I do love you, you know that, you idiot."

Jocelyn sighed. "Malachai called. You need to talk?"

She sniffed. "Yeah, I do."

She heard someone talking in the background and
knew it was Kai.

"Kai said he could beat him up for you."

Shannon chuckled through her tears. "Malachai
already offered, and since they have to spend two days in
the car together, he'll have more of a chance."

"So tell me about it."

She wanted to. She wanted nothing more than to sit
down and talk to the one person she was closest to in the
world. "I will, but I think I want to do it in person. You
up for a guest for a couple of weeks?"

"Always. My father-in-law has been testing out his
two-stepping on the women at the community center, but
he says you are the only one who does it right."

"I would really like that. I would like that a lot."

"You make your plans then let me know."

"Sure. I have to arrange everything at the bar, but I'll
let you know."

"Love you, Shan."

"I love you, Jocey."

When she hung up, she took a deep breath, and
before she could think differently, she pulled out the
phone and called Simon. She needed to get away, and she
needed her sister.

* * * *

Kade cursed the moment he tried to do a roundhouse kick to the punching bag. His knee almost crumbled under his weight.

"Looking good there, Kade," Mal said.

He glanced at his friend who was using the bag next to him. Since they had returned the week before, he hadn't tried to ask Kade anything. Hadn't accused him or tried to kick his ass. It was making him nervous. His friend was mad. He knew that. But he was holding back.

"I could kick your ass any day of the week."

Mal scoffed. "You? You're afraid of a little woman."

The area of the gym where they stood went silent. Kade glanced around at the other Seals. They were watching them as if a show was about to begin.

He turned back to Mal. "What did you say?"

Mal rolled his shoulders. "You're afraid of Shannon."

There were a few whispers as he felt his temper rising. "Did she tell you that?"

"No, but she did call you a pig-headed idiot, or something like that. She didn't have to tell me. I could see you running away from her."

"Go fuck yourself."

"Gladly. If you can stop being a pain in the ass to everyone here."

Kade glanced around at the crowd that had gathered and realized that some of the guys were shaking their heads. He could feel anger whipping through him, crawling into his head and taking control of his better judgment.

"You itching for a fight?" he asked. He was ready for it, needed it, craved it. He took a step toward him.

"McKade! Dupree!"

They both turned around to find the leader of the group staring at them. *Fuck.*

"My office, now."

Without a word between them, they pulled off their gloves and followed the Lieutenant Commander to his office.

"You two want to tell me what the fuck is going on?"

Neither of them said a word.

"I can't have my men fighting like a bunch of idiots. We're still trying to piece the group back together, and you two have to act like ten-year-olds on the playground. I really don't want to do the fucking paperwork involved if I have to discipline. Can you assure me that you will behave like Seals from now on? I would hate to transfer one of you out of here."

Kade knew without a doubt it would be him. He was trying to recover, and Mal was in working order.

They both nodded.

"Dupree, you can go."

His friend tossed him a sympathetic look. When the door shut, Markinson said, "Sit."

Shit, this was going to take a while. They were never offered a seat unless it was going to be a long chat. Still, he did as ordered, fighting the pain that shot through his leg.

"McKade, I know that we don't do the feeling thing. We're men, and worse, we're Seals. But you have got to get the bug that crawled up your ass out of there. From the moment you came back from leave, you have been a pain in the ass. For me, for everyone around you. I thought you would at least be relaxed after a week in New Orleans. You were worse. We'll be on active status again, and I need to know that I can count on you. The men need to know."

"I'll be ready."

He sighed. "I don't want to know what you're feeling, seriously. But, you were closed off for so long, and now you're bitching at everyone. Yes, I used the word bitching. You got in a fight with Smith because he didn't load his weapon right. It's like you've lost your center."

The moment Markinson said it, the image of Shannon came to his mind. She always centered him. Even before they were involved, he could chat with her as a friend and feel his life get back on track. She was the one thing that he needed to make it work, and he had pushed her away. No wonder he'd been acting like a raving lunatic. Without Shannon, he had no compass.

"Are you listening to me?"

He blinked at his commander.

"Uh, yes, sir."

"I understand what it's like to lose someone. I was in Fallujah as you know. So…it was bad. But, you have to work through it. Go see a doctor, get some meds."

Fuck. What a great time to figure out that pushing Shannon away was what had left him screwed up. The mission had been painful, losing his friend bad. It was the worst. Or he thought. Now that he didn't have Shannon, he didn't think straight. He couldn't even work through his emotions.

"Permission to be excused, sir."

Markinson stopped in midsentence and looked up at him.

"I was talking here, McKade."

"I understand. I just figured out what I needed to fix something."

He continued to study Kade. "Okay, but just know I need you one hundred percent by the end of four weeks."

Kade nodded. "Oh, and I need to take off a week."

"What? Another one?" he asked, almost shouting.

"I just figured out what I needed."

"And it takes you a week to fix it?"

"No. It will take me a week to convince her to take me back."

Understanding filled the commander's eyes. "You got it. Good luck."

With more purpose than he'd felt in months, he walked out of the office and walked down the hall. Mal stepped out of the locker room.

"Look, Kade, I'm sorry. I shouldn't have picked that fight with you. Did Markinson bust your ass?"

"No." He started toward the door. "Can you take me to the airport?"

"Wait. What?"

Kade hurried down the stairs and ignored the chill in the air and pain in his knee. Now that he knew what he wanted to do, where he wanted to be, he needed to get to Shannon now.

"I'm flying to New Orleans."

"Why?"

"To get on my knees and beg."

"Shannon isn't there."

He stopped in his tracks and looked up at Mal. "Where is she?"

"Hawaii. She left a couple days ago to spend some time with Jocelyn."

He huffed out a breath. "Okay, I need to move some money around, and then I'm flying to Hawaii."

Mal shook his head. "Do you know what you're doing?"

"Yeah, dammit." He started walking again. "I'm going to get my woman."

Chapter Twelve

Shannon sighed as she picked at her food. Chris had been making all her favorite foods, including the Huli Huli chicken and rice she wasn't eating at the moment. From the moment Kade had left her that morning, she'd hadn't felt like eating. She still didn't have an appetite, which was worrisome.

"You need to eat."

She looked up at her brother, who was studying her as if she were going to fall apart. Okay, so she cried the first three days she was there, but she was done. Sort of. And sure, she hadn't wanted to talk to any men. Not even Evan, whom she adored.

"I'm just not that hungry."

He shook his head. "I told Cynthia that you weren't eating enough."

"And what did she say?"

"She said I was used to being with a woman who ate enough for five people."

Jocelyn laughed. "She looks ready to explode."

"Don't say that around her. I had to help her get her tennis shoes on yesterday. She cried for an hour."

She smiled at her brother. "Aw, and you couldn't take it, you old softie."

He grimaced then he frowned as his attention was drawn to something behind her. "What the fuck is he doing here?"

Her brother didn't cuss that much, at least not in front of her. She turned to follow his line of vision and saw Kade.

Her breath tangled in her throat, and her heart started beating so fast she was amazed she didn't pass out.

He looked wonderful—damn him. He was dressed in his service dress. He freaking looked like freaking

109

Richard Gere. The restaurant had grown quiet. She was sure you didn't see a Navy Seal in full dress whites march into a local business on a regular basis in Honolulu.

He was looking around, and just for a second, she thought about slipping down in the booth and hiding. She wasn't ready to deal with the churning emotions he brought about in her. A moment later, though, he caught sight of her and started in her direction. Lord, he was a sight to see. There was nothing like a Seal on a mission, and apparently, she was his mission.

He strode toward her, every step sending panic racing through her.

"What the hell is he doing here?" she asked more to herself than anyone else.

"I don't give a damn," Chris muttered as he stood. "I'm going to kill him."

She stood up and faced her brother. She loved him with all her heart, but she knew Kade and knew what he could do.

"I can take care of this."

His frown turned darker. "I don't want you to."

"I can handle it. Besides, I do not want to help Cynthia raise that baby because you're in a wheelchair for the rest of your life."

"You don't think I could handle him?" Pure astonishment filled his tone.

"Sure you can. Working behind a stove and running a restaurant gets you in shape to take on a killing machine like a Seal."

He made a face. "Okay, you have a point."

She patted his cheek then turned to face Kade.

He stopped within a few feet of her and stared. The moment got awkward as he continued to gaze at her as if she were his salvation. He looked better, rested, and for a moment, she hated him for that. She hadn't had a good

110

night's sleep in three weeks, and here he was looking like a million bucks.

She could feel everyone still looking at them. Something had to give, so she did what every Dupree knew how to do. She joked.

"Kind of dressed up for the occasion, Kade?'

He didn't say anything, but his lips twitched.

She crossed her arms beneath her breasts. "You flew all the way over here to stare at me?"

He shook his head, but his gaze didn't leave hers. "I came for you."

Her heart did that little happy dance, but she pushed it away. She didn't want this, didn't want to deal with the hurt again. She thought she could, thought she could be patient while he worked himself out, but she realized that she might not be cut out to have a Seal as a lover.

"No."

He frowned.

"No?"

Poor pitiful Seal.

"Yeah, I said no. Just because you put on a uniform and march into my brother's restaurant doesn't mean I'm going to forget everything."

He glanced around at their audience. "Shouldn't we talk about this in private?"

"You picked the setting."

"You tell him, sistah," someone yelled out.

He grimaced. "I thought we would go for a walk."

Oh, he looked miserable. Just so miserable. He might love her, but flying across the Pacific didn't really prove it. She wanted more, she wanted it all. And the only way she could get it was if she knew that he was in it for the long haul, like she was.

"Thinking's overrated."

A few more of the customers started catcalling, and his face started to turn pink. Oh, my. He was embarrassed. And there was a tiny, evil part of her that was happy he was.

"I wanted to talk to you about our future."

"We don't have one."

Up until that moment, he had been what she would call docile—for a Seal. Now his eyes turned hard, his jaw flexed. She had to fight the urge to step back away from him. She had never been scared of him, but at the moment, she could easily see his anger.

"Don't say that."

Even though she could tell he was angry, she could hear a thread of desperation in his voice. It pricked at the already melting ice that encased her heart.

"You're the one who ran away."

He sighed. "I was stupid."

She wanted to punish him, but since he admitted he was stupid, she would at least be cordial. "From the uniform, I assume you're going to stay in the military?"

He nodded.

"So you flew over, and that must have been expensive by the way, dressed up in your little white uniform, to tell me you're staying in the military."

"I came for you."

The declaration had a few of the women sighing, and if she were honest with herself, Shannon's heart did a little flip flop.

"Me? Oh, the person who was trying to fix you?"

His jaw flexed again. "You were right, I was scared. Mainly because my mortality had been in question."

"We're all mortal."

"He *is* a Seal, Shannon," her brother said from behind her.

She glanced over her shoulder with narrowed eyes. "Stay out of this, or I'll tell Cynthia you told me about helping her with her shoes."

He held up his hands in self-defense.

When she turned back to Kade, she was still frowning. She had to stay mad. It was her only safety from falling for the idiot again.

"As I was saying, that last mission was bad. Really bad. I knew it was, and so did Mal, but we didn't act fast enough. I...well, I questioned if I was fit to serve."

Oh, God, he was killing her. He had been like Mal. The only reason he had gotten into the military was to be a Seal. It had been the thing that had driven them, the one thing they identified with the most.

"Just because you had one bad mission doesn't mean that you should quit. You're a good Seal."

He nodded. "Since taking you to bed, I care more about being a good man."

She couldn't take this. Her heart was melting, her better judgment flying out the window with the trade winds. If she gave into him, what would she do?

"You *are* a good man." Her voice was raw with emotion. She might not be able to take him back, but there was one thing she knew. He was good at his core. Always had been.

He nodded, then bent down on one knee. Several of the women gasped, and there was a patter of applause.

"I love you, Shannon. Will you marry me?"

Panic came first. It took her by the throat and would not let go. She couldn't speak, couldn't swallow the lump in her throat. Then on the heels of it came anger. He thought he could propose and everything would be okay.

"No."

"What did you say?"

"You can't just come in here with a ring..." When she noticed him grimace, she realized he wasn't offering her a ring. "You didn't even bring a ring, you idiot." She slapped him on the shoulder and went to move past him, but Kade grabbed her by the wrist.

"I thought you'd want to pick one out."

113

The moment he touched her, her pulse jumped. Fear had her twisting her arm free. She wasn't afraid of him, but of what she would do. She couldn't say yes, deal with the idiot's moods. Months of waiting for him to come home, then have to joke him out of his stupid bad mood and God, hear him laugh as he hugged her.

Tears stung her eyes. She did not want that. No way. "No. Stay away."

He rose to his feet and started after her. She was heading for the door with no idea of where she was going. She left her purse behind, she didn't have a car, but she just needed to get away.

Her hand was inches from the door when he scooped her up off the floor, then positioned her on his shoulder like a freaking sack of potatoes.

"You know, woman, I had to chase you across the Pacific. I came to apologize, to tell you I love you, to tell you I want to spend my life with you, and what do you do? You say no and run away."

"Put. Me. Down."

He apparently heard the threat in her voice and decided to heed the tone. He slowly put her down. She stepped back from him, but put up her hand when he inched closer.

"I promise not to leave. Just…stay there."

If he was close, she would feel his warmth, take in his scent, and she couldn't handle that. Her head was already spinning.

"Why are you running?"

The question had her stomach churning. She *was* running. She wasn't going to admit it to him.

"I just wanted to get away. I needed some space. I don't like public declarations."

He cocked his head, then that slow smile that always melted her bones curved his lips. "You're afraid."

"Go to hell."

She turned to march away, but he caught her and pulled her back against him.

"I'm sorry, baby. So sorry. You didn't take any cheap shots at me, and I shouldn't have been so happy about you being scared."

"I'm not scared." But even as she said it, she knew she was lying.

"Yeah, you are. It's okay. This thing we have is scary."

He turned her gently and cupped her face, wiping away the tears from her cheeks.

"I want to marry you, I want to have babies with you, but know I have to finish my obligation. I have four more years, then I'm out."

"You'll stay in more."

He shook his head. "I love it, really do. But…I love you more. I need you more than I need this. It's a lot to ask. I'll be in Virginia, then out in the field. You'll be in New Orleans. But, we can make this work. I know we can."

She sighed, her heart just falling down at his feet then. It wasn't so much of what he said, but the way he said it, and the soft look in his eyes.

"I have to ask again, because, Shannon, without you, being a Seal means nothing to me. I love you. Please, marry me."

Her vision blurred as another batch of fresh tears filled her eyes. "Oh, Kade, I love you, too. Yes. Yes! I'll marry you."

He pulled her into his arms and kissed her as the sound of customer's applause filled the air.

Epilogue

"What do you have planned?" Shannon asked as Kade took her hand and led her out of the elevator.

"You're the worst about secrets. I thought you were bad at Christmas." She could hear the smile in his voice, but she couldn't see him. He'd blindfolded her downstairs and refused to tell her where they were going. She knew they were still in the hotel where they had their wedding reception, but she wasn't sure where they were going.

"For all I know, you're leading me down the hallway to kill me."

"No, I just have a surprise, and I didn't want you to know about it."

She frowned at that as he stopped her. She opened her mouth to tell him just what she thought, but she heard a woman's delighted squeal in the distance.

"What the hell?" Kade said.

"Was it someone we knew?"

"It looked like Deke with some blonde. Doesn't matter."

She heard him unlock a door, then he guided her inside. The scent of plumeria hit her first along with the sensual scents that she knew to be candles. He stepped behind her, untied her blindfold, and removed it from her eyes.

Candles covered almost every available surface. On the bedside table, the dresser. It was the only light in the room. The bed was covered with plumeria petals. Tears filled her eyes. She recognized the room.

"This was my room for the night of Chris and Cynthia's wedding."

He slid his arms around her waist and pulled her back against him. He brushed his lips against her jaw.

"Yep. I had to pull a few strings to make sure we got it. And Jocelyn helped me. She snuck up here a few minutes ago and got it ready."

She smiled, thinking of her sister and the surprise she had for her husband tonight. She turned in Kade's arms and cupped his face. He had been gorgeous at the ceremony, dressed in the same uniform he'd proposed to her in. But now he was dressed in a Hawaiian shirt and a pair of chinos, and he was just as delicious.

"I am the luckiest woman in the world."

His smile faded as he touched his forehead to hers. "No, love. You can't be with a bloke like me. I put you through some hard times. I'm sorry that I'm going to probably put you through some more. Being a military wife isn't easy."

"No, it's not. But it's the only kind of wife I want to be."

He kissed her then, sweet, hot, and by the time he was finished, they were both breathing heavily. Stepping away, he took her hand. "Come, let me love you."

She followed him to the bed, laying down first. He stood looking at her for a moment.

"You have no idea how amazing you look."

"Yeah?"

"Decadence and innocence all rolled up into one delicious woman."

She didn't think she would ever get used to the way he spoke to her. He might be a quiet one, but when those words flowed over her, they took hold of her heart and would not let go.

"Well, come on, Seal, I think we need to explore that decadent side."

The naughty smile he gave her told Shannon he had more than a little decadence planned for the night.

He joined her on the bed then pulled her into his arms. He rolled them across the mattress so that she was beneath his powerful body.

"Well, Mrs. McKade—"

"I like the sound of that," she said.

"I do too." He brushed his mouth over hers before he slid down her body. "And I am ready to show you just how much I love the fact that you're *my* Mrs. McKade."

"Oh, yeah?"

He inched the hem of her wedding dress up over her thighs, his eyes widening when he saw that she hadn't worn any panties.

She laughed. "Oh, my, I think I shocked you."

He shook his head, his gaze directly on her pussy. He skimmed his fingers over her mons, then dipped two into her sex. She shivered.

"That was very naughty, Shannon."

She heard the change of tone, knew that he was already getting into full Dom mode.

He bent his head and licked her slit then said, "Now, remember, baby. No coming until I say you can."

Then, he set about driving her insane as she lay on a bed of petals in the room where they fell in love.

The End

Loving a military man isn't always easy, and sometimes living with him is impossible.

Possession: A Little Harmless Military Romance Book 2

Deke Berg has been in love with Samantha for ten years. From the moment they met, they could never keep their hands off each other. Their marriage was volatile and short-lived. Now, though, Deke knows what he wants in life, and Samantha is at the center of his plans. Unfortunately, Sam is wary of marriage—especially to a man who broke her heart.

Sam has always loved Deke. Being a former military brat, she thought she'd been prepared for life as a military spouse. But the long separations were hard, especially dealing with the stranger who returned home. She doesn't know if she can handle that pain again, but after spending a night together in Hawaii, it's impossible for her to ignore him.

Old prejudices and painful memories aren't easy to overcome, but there is one thing Deke understands: Samantha is the woman for him, and he will do *anything* to prove his love and win her back.

Warning, this book includes: Another hard-headed military man, a few embarrassing moments, nosey brothers, and two people too stupid to realize they are perfect together. It's Harmless and military, so for your own safety, make sure you have ice water nearby. The author assumes no responsibility for overheating of the reader.

Possession

A Little Harmless Military Romance

Melissa Schroeder

Dedication

To romance readers everywhere. You are a dedicated bunch carving time out to read a , skipping lunch so you can find out just how the book ends, and sharing your love of your favorite book or series with strangers. Because of you, writers are blessed, each and every day.

Acknowledgements

Again, no book is every released without a ton of people behind it. I did this book during a move to a new house and so it was kind of crazy. Thanks to my husband and kids for always believing in me even if they force me to that unhappy place each year. Thanks to Brandy Walker who keeps me on the straight and normal and makes sure I don't kill anyone in the process. Thanks to Jenn Leblanc for the wonderful cover photo and to Kendra Egert for designing it. Another round of thanks to Chloe Vale who did such wonderful editing on the book. Special thanks to Joy Harris who has been a friend and confidant who always understands my mindset because like me, she is a superior CAPPY!

And, lastly, to the Addicts, some who have been with me since the beginning in 2004. It is hard to believe this is the 45th book I have put out and so many more to come! Thank you always for your support.

Chapter One

Deacon Berg drew in a deep breath of the sweet Hawaiian air, enjoying the way it tickled his nose and filled his senses. Soft music played in the background as the wedding guests milled around the expansive buffet, but Deke ignored it for a view of the resort. He couldn't believe he was standing in Honolulu, enjoying the setting sun over the Pacific. Less than a month earlier, he'd been in South America on a rescue mission, and now he was enjoying a Hawaiian sunset.

"Enjoying the view?" Mal asked from behind him.

Deke glanced over his shoulder. "Yeah, I am. Why aren't you living over here with your brother and sister?"

He offered Deke a cocky smile. "You know I live for the Navy and the Seals."

Deke shook his head. He was pretty sure Mal's heart was engaged elsewhere, but Deke didn't comment on it. Malachai Dupree wasn't ready to admit why he couldn't settle down, and pointing it out would just piss Mal off. Deke knew better than to try to get his friend to face his personal fears. As a man who had been avoiding his for years, he was pretty good at knowing that.

Kade, the happy groom, stepped up. "Have you decided what you're going to do?"

"Coming here isn't making the decision any easier. I was pretty sure I was going to move to Coronado. They don't ask just anyone to teach."

"No, but you said you never wanted to do it."

He shrugged and looked out over the beach. It had been a secret desire of his for years, but he had only told one person that. "The job over at Camp Smith is looking more and more attractive. Hard to resist views like this one seven days a week. Maybe I should move to New Orleans and steal Shannon from you?"

124

"I'd have to kill you, Chief."

"She could file for an annulment," Deke said.

Kade gave him a big smile. "Too late for that."

He shook his head. "Sex has to happen after the marriage."

"And your point?"

Deke laughed. "I should have known when you guys disappeared it wasn't about the pictures."

Mal looked from one to the other then made a face. It was at that moment, Deke heard a laugh dance over the air to him. Mal was saying something, but Deke ignored him. He knew that laugh.

He knew it better than he knew his last name.

"Chief?" Mal asked.

"What?" he asked, irritated. Dammit, if Mal didn't shut up, he wouldn't figure out where it was coming from.

"You have an odd look on your face."

He didn't answer Mal. Deke knew she was there. He could feel it in his bones. It always seemed to happen like this. They would finally break free of each other, able to move on to healthier relationships, then by chance they would run into each other. It was as if the universe was bound and determined to keep them together when they both knew it was wrong.

Then he saw her. She was walking with a group of women. God, she was gorgeous. Even ten years later, she still made his temperature rise. She had her hair up, with a few blonde curls trailing down her neck. The blue dress reached her ankles and clung to every luscious curve. She wore a pair of strappy sandals, and he just knew she had painted her toenails.

Damn.

She was still laughing, and he had to, also, in the sight of her. She was never a woman who had one of those tinkling giggles. Her joy was out loud and for everyone to see. The sound was one of the greatest things he had ever heard.

He also knew what she sounded like when she moaned his name.

She spotted him and came to a dead stop. He couldn't help the way his heart turned over when she made eye contact. They were so far away, but he knew the moment she did. Her smile faded. The woman standing next to her said something to her, and she shook her head.

Mal stepped up beside him. "Pretty. But she doesn't look like she thinks you're her type."

Deke drew in a lusty breath and let it release slowly. "Oh, but I am."

"How can you be so sure?" Mal asked.

"She wouldn't have married me if she didn't like me."

With that, he took one last swig on his beer, set it down on the table, and marched in her direction.

* * * *

"Holy Jesus in a skirt," Zoe said beside Sam. "Is that military dude coming over here?"

Sam didn't dare look at her friend. She couldn't tear her gaze from Deke. Something warm unfurled in her belly as she watched him stride down the path that led to her. She wanted to run the other way, screaming, but that would make her a coward. And Samantha Walters wasn't a coward.

"I think he's coming over here," Fiona said from behind her. "I can't see, though, because you're both standing in front of me."

They ignored her until she kicked Zoe in the back of the knee.

"Woman, I am going to smack you upside the head," Zoe said, but she moved out of the way. "I swear to God, one of these days I'm going to leave you in a deep hole you can't get out of."

"Is that a short joke?" Fiona asked.

"No, but you are."

"Shut up. Just shut up," Sam muttered beneath her breath. Usually she took joy in her friends' bickering, but she couldn't today. "What the hell am I going to do when he gets over here?"

"You're going to say, 'This is my friend, Zoe. She would like to meet you and have a one-night stand.'" Zoe took a sip of her drink. "Also mention I like to be spanked."

Sam laughed, but there was no humor in it. "I'm not about to throw you at my ex-husband."

There was a beat of silence, which with her two friends, usually took a miracle. There was one thing she was certain of, Deacon Berg was no miracle. There were times she had thought he was a curse.

"The ex? The one you say drives you crazy? The one who you can't keep your hands off of?" Zoe asked.

She nodded as she watched him walk toward her. As always, people moved out of his path without realizing it. It had always been that way ever since she'd met him years ago in California.

"Oh, mama," Zoe said.

"You let that go?" Fiona asked. "I think you need some help."

"It was do that or one of us was going to kill the other."

She still couldn't look away from him. He was in his mess dress, which meant he had gone to something formal. He could always fill out a uniform so well. The setting sun sparkled off the wealth of medals that crowded his chest.

God, the man never failed to turn her on when he was in his uniform. Of course, he could be wearing a lounge-lizard suit and she would be ready to jump his bones. Or nothing. Yeah, she would really like to see him wearing nothing at all.

She shook her head, trying to clear the image, but she knew it only too well. All those sculpted muscles and that little line of fair hair that bisected his abs. She closed her eyes and took a deep breath. Hell, her panties were damp already and she hadn't even spoken to him.

Sam opened her eyes.

"Who is that tall drink of chocolate next to him?" Zoe asked.

It took her a second to realize that there was another man beside Deke. He was in mess dress also, but the rank on his arm told her he was an officer.

"I have no idea."

He came to a halt in front of Sam. He hadn't looked anywhere else as he had walked to her. Now, he was looking at her as if she might disappear. "Samantha, what are you doing here?"

It took her a second to gather her thoughts. "I live here now."

She had picked it because she had thought never to see him. It wasn't that there weren't a ton of military on the island, but she knew that he never wanted to be assigned to the vehicle teams the Seals had here.

"Sam?" Zoe poked her in the back, and she shot her friend a nasty look before looking back to Deke. He hadn't taken his gaze from her.

"Oh, right, this is Zoe Anderson and Fiona Farelli."

He glanced at her friends and smiled. "Nice to meet you, ladies."

Then he turned his attention right back to her. She could practically hear her friends sighing. She couldn't blame them. Inwardly, she was sighing also. And melting.

When he didn't introduce his friend, she nodded her head in the man's direction. For a second, he didn't react. Then Deke glanced over at his friend.

"Oh, sorry. This is Malachai Dupree."

The other man gave her a smile that normally would have stopped traffic. The fact that Malachai was dressed in mess dress with a chest full of medals also made him impressive. Sam was pretty sure Zoe and Fiona melted beside her. But, as always, when Deacon Berg was in the vicinity, she didn't notice other men.

"What are you doing here?" she asked.

"Wedding. One of our friends got married to Mal's sister, Shannon."

"Ah."

The silence strung out for a few moments while everyone else just stood by. She could hear the music from the wedding reception along with the low murmur of tourists milling around on a Saturday afternoon. She was about to make an excuse to leave, but his friend stopped her before she had a chance.

"Hey, why don't you ladies crash the wedding?" Mal asked.

Before she could say no, Zoe stepped up next to Mal and took his offered arm. "I would love to do that. Come on, Fee."

Fiona glanced at Sam, and she could tell her friend was making sure she was okay. Fiona smiled and took Mal's free arm, and he escorted her two friends off. The traitors.

"I'm not sure your friend knows what he's getting into," she said.

He didn't say anything for a moment, and she had a flashback to the first night she met Deke. He'd had the attention of every woman in the room, but when he'd walked up to her, he'd seemed to lose the ability to talk. It was a stunning thing to make a prime hunk of man tongue-tied. She would have been more impressed with it if she hadn't had the same exact problem.

"Deke?"

He shook himself and seemed to gain his wits again. "Mal's a Seal. He can handle two women."

She let one eyebrow rise. "Is that from experience?"

He chuckled. "Despite Mal's efforts to boast about his escapades, I try my best to ignore them."

"Let me guess, the man talks a little too much?"

He nodded. "Ready for some Scooby Snacks and cake?"

She tried not to be charmed that he remembered their code name for the horrible *hors d'oeuvres* they'd been forced to eat at official functions. It was hard, but she resisted. She knew there was no way out of it. Tearing her friends away from food and beverages—not to mention men in uniform—was going to be hard. And a glance over Deke's shoulder told her there were plenty of both of those things here.

She brought her attention back to Deke. God, he was smiling at her, waiting. It was that smile that always made her heart do that little dance. Right before she threw all her good intentions out the window and gave in to the temptation of Deacon Berg.

But Zoe was her ride, and it was Hawaii. He was probably not going to be there very long, knowing him. She would just be good and she would resist him. It could be done.

"Samantha?"

She blinked and looked at him. "Sure," she said.

His smile widened, causing his dimples to appear and her blood temperature to rise. He was attractive, that's it. This time would be different. She glanced over at him and saw the way the setting sun danced over his skin. Need swelled in her. Her blood heated to dangerous levels, and she felt her head start to spin.

Shit, she was in trouble.

Chapter Two

Deke took a sip of beer as he watched Cynthia Dupree talk to his ex-wife. There was a gaggle of women gathered around Cynthia as she had the newest Dupree to show off at the wedding. No one could resist a baby, especially one dolled up in pink bows for a wedding.

"Looks like your woman has a lot to say to my sister-in-law," Mal remarked. Deke didn't miss the humor in his voice.

"Well, seeing how she left me, there is always a chance Chris could lose his wife."

"Did she tell you what she's doing here now?" Mal asked.

"She's teaching. She wanted a change, and her friends were moving over. She decided to follow them," Deke said.

"She's a teacher?" Mal asked.

He nodded, watching her laugh at something Cynthia said. Something tugged at his heart—not to mention other parts of his body. He couldn't hear her laugh, but he could still hear it from earlier. It never failed to make him feel whole. He wanted to lie in bed and listen to her laugh, feel her body heat next to him. His fingers itched to slip his hands through her silky, blonde hair.

"She teaches middle school math."

"Oh, man, you have got to be kidding me," Mal said. "I don't think I could have concentrated on anything with her teaching me math."

He glanced at the younger man. "Just don't even think about it."

Mal flashed him a smile. "I know better. Besides, I don't think she's interested in me. She's been watching you the whole time."

"Jesus, you sound like a bunch of women over here," Jocelyn, Mal and Shannon's sister, said from behind them.

"Bite me, Joce. Why don't you go bug our brother?"

"You mean Chris? No thanks. He hasn't had sleep in a month, and he's getting mean. And he said he heard me sniffle, so he won't let me hold Jessica. Butthead."

"I don't blame him. Remember how many times you ripped a leg off one of your baby dolls when you were a kid? If I had a kid, I wouldn't let you near him," Mal said.

"So, Seal, what's your plan while on the islands?" Jocelyn asked Deke.

"Why are you questioning my friends like they're criminals?" Mal asked.

Jocelyn sighed. "I'm just asking them questions. The way the women are all making goo-goo eyes at Deke, I have a feeling he won't be around that long."

He laughed, enjoying her. He liked the way the Duprees interacted. They reminded him of his own family. "I'm just here for one more night. I have to get back."

She glanced at her brother, and Deke saw the worry in her eyes.

"No, nothing like that. I have an assignment to decide on. It can't wait. Either way, I am gone from the group within a month, so I have to get back and get that ready."

"But, you're on vacation," she said.

The men shared a smile. Civilians always acted like they had so many choices. "I was asked to teach in California."

"Holy crap, like for Seal training?" she asked. "Like they show in the movies?"

"Yeah, but he might be changing his mind now," Mal said as he nodded in the direction of Samantha.

Jocelyn glanced over at Samantha. Deke followed her gaze just in time to see Nathaniel Dupree, firefighter and a man without morals, slip up to Cynthia and ask to be introduced to Samantha.

Deke frowned.

"I would suggest if you want her, you better go get her, Deke. You know Nat," Jocelyn said.

He took a swig of his beer, shoved it at Mal, and started off in her direction.

* * * *

Sam felt her whole body flush with excitement as Deke crossed the floor to her again. Nathaniel kept talking, as did Cynthia, but their words seemed to dissolve into the background. It was an instant reaction she had almost every time. Even when she was so mad at him that she wanted to do him bodily damage, she couldn't stop the overwhelming need he brought out in her. By now, she should know better. She should have some plan for when she ran into him this way. But she never did. He was the one thing she could always count on in her life. They might be divorced but they knew they would have someone to call on in a time of need. He had been the bane of her existence and the salvation she loved.

He stopped within a few inches of her.

"Wanna dance?" he asked.

She laughed. "Way to romance me, Seal."

His face grew ruddy and she couldn't help allowing her heart to soften just a little more. He was dangerous when he went alpha, but lord, he was irresistible when he was embarrassed.

He cleared his throat, and she was sure that he was as aware of the attention from people surrounding them as she was. "Would you like to dance?"

134

"Not really."

She knew what was going to happen if he touched her. Heck, she knew what was going to happen even if they didn't dance, but she had some pride. She didn't want to embarrass herself in front of his friends and hers.

He looked surprised.

"Why don't we go for a walk?" she asked.

He nodded in agreement and offered his arm. She could feel the stares as they walked out of the area. Once they were free of the attention, she relaxed.

"So, you're teaching here?"

She nodded. "I needed a change. They were cutting our benefits left and right. Pay isn't great here, but there were still as many benefits as in California. And, seriously, how can you not be happy living with this kind of scenery?"

He shook his head. "You make it sound like it's paradise every day."

She chuckled. "No. Just like everywhere else, we have the same issues. But I do like the slower pace here. And you know how I react to long winters."

He nodded, and she knew he remembered her problem with long winters. "Your friends, do they teach, too?"

"No. Fiona is a message therapist and Zoe is a nurse."

"Hmm, does Fiona do house calls?"

She laughed. "She does, but I don't think she would be comfortable with you as a client."

He frowned. "Why is that?"

"She knows a little bit too much about you."

He made a face. "Women."

"What's that supposed to mean?" she asked, feeling more comfortable now. The vibrations between them were still there, but it was easier to concentrate on catching up.

"You tell each other way too much about your sex life."

She stopped and pulled her arm out of his. "Like you don't brag about your conquests to the boys? You just said Mal talked about his women."

"First of all, my friends aren't boys. Mal doesn't count. And second of all, I never brag. Especially when comparing any woman to you is useless."

She sighed and started walking again, trying to keep some distance between them. He didn't say things like that to seduce her. For Deke, it was the truth, and he didn't hold it back. He never did with her. If he did, he might be easier to resist.

"My brother is also stationed here."

He rolled his eyes. "Should have known. So, did he complain until you moved here?"

She smiled. Deke and her brother had a love/hate kind of relationship. "No, actually he's gone a lot because he's on the IG inspecting bases. So, for the Pacific, that means he has to go to Asia a lot."

"Still unmarried?" he asked.

"Of course. You know he never wanted to settle down."

They both knew the state of her parents' marriage. Her father had never been able to adjust to being a civilian, and it had ruined the happiness that usually comes from retirement—not to mention her father had never really taken his marriage vows seriously. Considering how short and turbulent her own marriage to Deke had been, she often wondered if her family wasn't cursed when it came to relationships.

"So, you moved over here with your friends. You didn't tell me."

"I called you to give you my new address. You never responded."

She knew with his job, he was gone a lot. It was something she had never gotten used to. Never would.

"Oh. Yeah, we had a bad mission. Kade was fucked-up pretty bad."

She nodded. "Looks like he recovered."

"Thanks to Shannon."

They walked side by side for a while. It was nice

"I can't believe you moved over here."

"And, I can't believe you seem so interested."

He stopped again and stared at her. "I'm always interested in you, Samantha. You know that."

Seeing him there, with the sun setting behind him and the waves crashing against the rocks, she couldn't fight it, didn't want to. They were wrong for each other. They had bad tempers, they fought too much, and neither of them was ready to negotiate. Compromise wasn't in their vocabulary. But the need that always seemed to ignite when he was near was too strong. She stepped closer and rose to her tiptoes. Slowly, without closing her eyes, she brushed her mouth against his.

"It's the same for me."

He skimmed his fingers up her arms. "We said we wouldn't do this again."

She drew in a deep breath then released it with a sigh of pleasure as he slid his fingers over her pulse. "We always say we won't do it again."

He looked up at her, those gray eyes dark with need. His lips curved slowly. The breath she had been taking tangled in her throat. Her heart did the slow roll it did right before it fell at his feet.

"I have a really nice room with a great view."

She laughed. "Really?"

"Yeah, why don't I show you?" He stepped back and held out his hand. She looked down at it, knew that this was her decision. This time it was all up to her.

She looked at him and smiled. It was insane and it was really stupid, but just like always, she couldn't resist him. All of the barriers she had built crumbled when she saw the curve of his lips. There was something wrong with her—with both of them—but she didn't care.

Without a word, she threw away all her worries and took his hand. He raised it to his mouth. Keeping his gaze on hers, he touched his lips to her fingers.

"Come with me."

Chapter Three

Pleasure crawled through Samantha's body as she
felt Deke's fingers dance over her flesh. He knew just
where to touch her, how to make her feel the greatest
pleasure. He had known from their first night together.
No man before or since could tap into what made her
tick. And the only thing he was doing was trailing his
fingers down her arm.

It wasn't like they could do anything. They were
riding the elevator up to his room with five other people,
and while they always played games, they did not go for
that. Not since they got caught in that hotel in San Diego.

"I want to thank you for your service," an older
woman said to Deke.

Sam shifted her feet, but he pulled her closer. She
had always felt odd when people thanked Deke or her
brother. Both men always seemed to be unfazed by it and,
as usual, Deke handled it.

He nodded. "You're welcome, ma'am."

The doors opened on the twelfth floor, and he led her
out. He hadn't let go of her hand since she had given it to
him. She followed him willingly. By the time they got
inside his room, her body was humming. He shut the door
and crowded her back up against it.

Without waiting, he slammed his mouth down on
hers. The rush of heat that always simmered between
them exploded. It was never different, never easy. His
tongue plunged between her lips, and she reveled in it.
She loved this, loved the way he made her feel when they
ignored the world. When it was only the two of them, it
worked so well.

He tore his mouth away from hers and pressed up
against her. He settled his hands on the door behind her.
As he nuzzled her neck, she took in the scent of him.

139

"Have you been playing with anyone?"

He always asked. It was always the same answer.

"No. You?" she asked. Why did her heart clutch at the idea? Because she loved him, would always love him. And for her, she didn't know if she would ever find another Dom. She never seemed to want to even think about it.

He shook his head. She should have known. They might drive each other crazy, but they had the one thing between them that was essential for a Dom/sub relationship: trust.

"Are you up for play, babe?"

God, she loved that. His voice dipped as he said babe, elongating the vowel. She loved when his dominant streak was allowed to run wild. She was always the beneficiary and happy for it.

"Yes, Sir."

He shuddered. Her heart did a little dance. There was something so delicious about affecting him this way. He stepped back from her.

"Then I expect you to strip out of that dress. Now."

His voice never rose. It stayed steady as he gave the order, as it always did. He took off his jacket and slipped it over the back of a chair. He tugged another chair out and sat down to watch. She hesitated. It had been a year since they'd seen each other, and the move had been stressful. She'd added another ten pounds, and to a woman of her small stature, it definitely showed.

"I'm waiting, Samantha. Unless you'd rather we stop."

She didn't want that. Not in a million years. She pulled the dress over her head then dropped it on the floor beside her.

He glanced down at her feet. "I like those shoes."

Oh, God, he was too sexy. The way those eyes watched her feet. Deke had a thing for feet. Not a freaky

140

thing, but he loved when she wore high heels and had her nails painted.

"Hmm, I really like those pink toes."

His gaze traveled up her body, slowing down at the belly ring she had. "When did you get that?"

She couldn't tell from his voice if he liked it or not.

"I-I got it after I moved here."

His mouth kicked up on one side. "I like it." Then he finally made eye contact. "I like it a lot. But, I think you left a few things on."

She had forgotten her panties and bra. She hadn't done it on purpose, but her brain was kind of frozen. Or melting. Melting was a better description of what her brain was doing right now. He always did this to her when he started giving her orders.

"The bra, Samantha."

She always hated her full name—except when Deke said it in that voice. He rolled his voice over the syllables in a way that made her want to get naked. It didn't matter where they were. And she knew most of the time he didn't do it on purpose.

She slipped her hands up her back and undid her bra. She let it slip down her arms, and with a toss, she added it to her dress on the floor beside her. He rose then. It wasn't common for him. He usually took his time, but there was an energy around him that told her that there was something really new about him tonight.

He stepped up close to her. Again, the musky scent of his aftershave hit her, but there was that hint of him. Deke. She could be blind and know his scent anywhere. It haunted her dreams.

He skimmed his fingers over her breasts and her nipples tightened further.

"Ah, still so responsive. So needy for my mouth."

Gawd, how could a woman resist a man who could talk like that? The one who could had to be a lesbian or dead. And she wasn't so sure in that quarter. He leaned down and took a nipple in his mouth as he teased the other with his fingers. He moved his other hand down her back, slipping it into her panties and pulling her against him. His erection was easy for her to feel. She shuddered.

When he pulled back, he was breathing a little more heavily. He took one step back, then another. "The panties."

She bent down, but he stopped her. "Turn around so I can see your ass."

She did as he ordered, but he said nothing as she stepped out of them.

After she straightened, she waited for the next order. She was already dripping wet.

"Come here, Samantha."

She turned and walked over, reveling in the way his gaze ate her up as if he was starved to look at her. When she stood in front of him with nothing but her heels on, he said, "Take my shirt off."

She should have known. It was one of her favorite things to do, and he would remember that. He always remembered.

With practiced ease, she worked the buttons loose of the dress shirt, pulling it out of his pants. Then, she slipped it off his shoulders.

There was a fresh scar, one on his shoulder, and she looked up at him. He shook his head silently. He would tell her, but now was not the time.

She took the shirt and laid it carefully over the chair where his suit jacket hung.

"Sit down on the chair."

She didn't know what he was thinking, what he was planning. It had been over a year since they had played. When they spent a lot of time together, they worked out the scenarios, but there were times like this one that had no course except the one that he set forth.

She did, feeling especially decadent sitting there naked.

Deke moved in front of her, and not for the first time, she thought of a panther. The man moved with the grace of a male ballerina, with a dash of lethal predator. He wouldn't be happy to hear her description of him. But that was always the way she saw him, from the moment she'd met him.

"Spread your legs."

She did, anticipating. She didn't know what was next, but she knew Deke, and she knew he would give her everything she desired.

He dropped to his knees in front of her and rested his hands on her thighs. The calluses on his fingers rubbed over her flesh, and she closed her eyes. God, that felt so good. He leaned forward and kissed her belly. He traced his tongue over her skin and then she felt his mouth cover the belly ring. He gave it a tug with his teeth before moving down to her pussy.

But, instead of diving in, he took his time, kissing her inner thighs, building the natural heat between them. She wanted to slip her hands into his hair and play with it, but he wouldn't allow for it. Not right now. She knew better. And that was the crux of their issues. They knew each other so well, and what they knew always turned them on. He liked to dominate her, and she loved to be dominated. With every beat of her heart.

He worked his way to her sex and then licked her. She was so sensitive already, dripping with arousal. She would be embarrassed, but they had never had that between them. There was no room for it. He pushed her thighs further apart as he set about to drive her crazy.

He dove into her pussy over and over again. That wicked tongue of his knew just how to push her, just what would get her to the edge, and then he would move away. A few moments later, he pulled back and looked up at her. She opened her eyes to see him licking his lips.

"You always were the tastiest treat, Samantha. There are times when I'm out in the field, when life is really shitty, that I get that memory stuck in my head and the taste comes back to me. It always pulls me through whatever I'm doing." His voice had deepened to a gravelly whisper. She trembled.

He leaned up and kissed her. She tasted herself on his mouth, the need she had for him, the desire. Deke had done it on purpose, of course. He wanted her to know why he craved the taste of her, what drew him to her. He rose to his feet.

"Scoot up."

She was breathing heavily, and her legs barely cooperated. She could hardly move in the chair, and she wondered just what she would do when he asked her to stand.

"Unzip me."

She did, of course, in anticipation. As soon as the pants were undone, his erection sprung free. That was the one thing of his uniform Deke always left out. When he was in mess dress, he hated to wear underwear. She leaned forward, but he stopped her with one word.

"No." She looked up at him with a frown. "You do not anticipate what I will have you do. For that, only your hand."

Damn the man. He knew her too well. She loved oral sex, getting it and giving it. But she did as ordered, moving her hand over his long, hard cock.

"Slowly," he ordered in a not-so-steady voice. She did as he commanded, dragging her thumb over the tip. He shuddered and leaned down for a kiss, cupping her face.

When he pulled back, he asked. "Want a taste of my cock? Huh, baby?"

She nodded, her body already responding to the idea. He straightened. "Suck me, Samantha, and make it good."

She didn't need another invitation. Wrapping her hand around the base, she leaned forward and licked the drop of pre-come that had gathered on the tip. She swallowed and enjoyed the taste of him. Musky, sweet, and so very delectable.

"Quit fucking around, Samantha." He ground out the demand.

She looked up at him, and without taking her gaze from his, she took him fully in her mouth. As she moved his cock in and out, Deke moved his hands through her hair. She gagged a few times, but she didn't care. Samantha had always liked to give oral sex, but she particularly loved to give it to Deke. He'd told her once that he loved the feel of her mouth on him.

She continued to suck him, adding her hand and slipping her tongue over the tip every time she reached the top. Soon he was moving in rhythm with her, his head bent back as he groaned. She wanted to feel him come, have him fill her throat up, but he had other plans. He pulled out of her mouth with a loud growl. He leaned down and kissed her. This time it was like the kiss at the door—no longer measured, no longer in charge. She knew he would get back there, knew he would take charge, but at the moment he wanted her to know what she did to him.

In this, they could always be honest.

"Stand up, babe."

She did, but she needed help. She was so aroused she could barely walk. He apparently knew that because he leaned down and picked her up into his arms.

He took her to the bed and placed her there. "Up on all fours. I think you need a little punishment for that stunt."

She looked at him as he pulled off his pants and placed them on the chair.

"You don't know what I'm talking about?"

She shook her head.

"You were trying to suck me completely off. Admit it."

She hesitated, and he let one brow rise. She nodded.

"You need to be reminded who is in control when we are playing. Apparently, your memory is bad."

He climbed onto the bed, and she waited.

"I wish I had some toys. I would love to take a paddle to your ass. You definitely deserve it. Spread your legs."

She did as ordered, already anticipating what was to come. Her body was throbbing, her pussy so damp. He slipped his hand between her legs, teasing her slit, then her clit. Her heart raced, her body heated, and she could feel her orgasm rushing.

He pulled his hand back and smacked her ass. The sting of the slap filtered out over her body as her pussy contracted.

She needed to press her legs together to gain some kind of relief, but he didn't allow it. Instead, he repeated his actions over and over, teasing her, pushing her closer, and then smacking her. By the time he stopped, her arms were shaking and her legs felt just as unsteady.

He leaned down, and she felt his mouth on the fullest part of her cheek. "So pink. I love the way you get all red when I spank you. You like that, don't you, baby?"

"Yes," she said, but her voice wasn't that steady.

Deke pulled back. "On your back, Samantha."

It took her a second to obey, and she heard him growl. She shot him a look of warning when she finally ended up on her back, but stopped when she saw the look on his face. There was something she couldn't discern there, something that she wasn't sure she had ever seen.

146

Because of that, she broke the rules. "What?"

For a second, he said nothing. He just looked down at her, and then he shook his head. "Nothing, just nothing."

He left the bed and came back with a couple of condoms in his hand. He ripped open one and slipped it over his cock, then joined her back on the bed. He gave her that naughty smile that always undid her. She'd never known another man who could smile at her and almost make her come. Except for Deacon Berg.

He lifted one of her legs and undid her sandal, then took care of the other. She moaned when he kissed the arch of one foot then worked his way up her body, licking, kissing, and nipping at her flesh. Deke fully covered her, kissing her lips with a force that both called to her and scared her at the same time.

She expected him to take her, to just ravish her on the spot, but he had other ideas.

He switched their positions by rolling to his back. She found herself sitting over him, her legs on each side of his hips.

"Take me in."

She looked down at him and realized he was different. He was a bit slower with his commands now, and that made him even sexier.

She lifted up and took hold of his cock. She sunk down on him, enjoying the way he filled her so fully. She started to ride him, slowly at first. He didn't allow her any other way, grabbing hold of her hips and controlling the pace. He increased the rhythm, his fingers digging into her skin as he sped up.

"Come, Samantha, come."

She looked down at him and found him watching her. He pressed his thumb against her clit and then pinched it. Her orgasm exploded through her, racking her body as she bowed back and screamed his name.

She vaguely heard him shout and knew he followed her into bliss seconds later. She collapsed onto him. He grunted and she laughed.

"God, that sounds good."

She shifted to slide down to the mattress, but he kept his arm there to keep her close to him. "What sounds good?"

He looked at her and brushed her curls from her face. "Your laugh. I love the sound, always did."

Her heart did a little jerk. Definitely something was up. "What's wrong?"

"What?"

She rose and settled her weight on her elbows. "There has to be something wrong. You are being way too sweet."

He shook his head. "I didn't do a very good job of showing you affection if a compliment like that makes you think there is something wrong."

"We didn't always have time for it."

And that was the truth. They had fallen together out of lust and found love. But marriage to a Seal was particularly hard. They were never around, and when Deke was around, they were either fighting or making love.

"I should have made time."

Tears burned the backs of her eyes, and her vision started to waver.

"Oh, don't cry." He gave her a quick, sweet kiss. "It's not you. It's me. And we only have tonight, so let's not talk about regrets."

She pulled in a deep breath and nodded.

"Be right back."

He hurried off to the bathroom, probably to toss the condom, then returned, slipped into bed and settled against the pillow. He patted his shoulder. "Come on."

She didn't hesitate. She set her head down, thinking it would take forever to fall asleep.

It was her last thought before she drifted off.

Chapter Four

Deke watched Samantha sleep. It had never been this good between them. They had always had good sex. That had never been a problem, but it had caused others. It was one of the reasons they had found BDSM. They seemed to have no real control around each other, and at least in that, they could control it somewhat.

He brushed a curl back over her shoulder and noticed his hand was shaking. She was unmanning him. The sad thing was she never understood her power over him. He could never really break free, and now that he was ten years older, he didn't want to. Their issues stemmed from their tempers, along with the love. It was hard to be so in love with someone that it hurt.

But Deke didn't want it any other way.

He would have to build their relationship. They knew each other, but they hadn't spent the time to appreciate it before. They would now. Samantha wasn't ready for more than that yet. Not yet. She was a world-class arguer, as he was. Tonight, though, he knew he was right about his plans. They had just shifted to Hawaii instead of Coronado. Not a bad thing.

He traced his hand down her back. She was the prize. From the moment he met her, she was the one for him. He would never be able to find another like her. She drove him crazy, but in these moments, when everything was quiet, he felt at peace. No one had ever given him that but her.

He had fucked it up bad last time. They were both at fault all those years ago, but he knew without a doubt a lot of it was his doing. He'd been older, should have been wiser. With Samantha, though, being wise had never been part of the bargain. He'd been in lust before her, but he'd never been that crazy about a woman. He'd not been able to rest until she was his, and once he'd had her, he'd married her because he wanted to keep her.

But that had fizzled in less than twelve months. Ten years later and they still couldn't walk away. He couldn't. Not now. Now he wanted her, needed her in a way that was almost embarrassing. The mission that had almost done them in had taught him waiting was wrong.

He brushed her hair aside to set his mouth on her back. He kissed her, working his way down her spine. He knew when she woke because she moaned his name. It was reassuring that the first word out of her mouth was his name.

Before was about control and domination. Now, he just wanted to let her know of the love, to make her understand what he felt inside. He pleasured her—and himself—by tasting her flesh. He kissed her ass, rubbing it with his hands. He worked down further, kissing her legs, teasing the back of her knees. He knew it drove her crazy.

By the time he turned her over, her face was flush, her need easy to see. He grabbed a condom and slipped it on, entered her. He pulled her up from the bed, sinking back on his heels. They rode together, looking into each other's eyes. Without words, he showed her, let her feel the love he had for her. They'd never been good at talking anyway.

Samantha leaned down to kiss him. The light touch of her mouth against his was enough to tempt, not enough to satisfy. She slipped her arms around his neck and deepened the kiss. She traced his lips with her tongue then dipped inside. It was almost too sweet, but there was something so hot about it. He tightened his hands on her waist. She came first, her body shuttering with the force of it and pulling him deeper into her wet heat.

He wanted to give in, but he needed to watch her lose herself again. He desired to be there with her.

"Together, come with me." He pulled her lip between his teeth and sucked. She trembled. "Please, baby."

They held each other's gaze as they surrendered to the ecstasy.

* * * *

Sam watched him pack and tried to tell herself that he wasn't breaking her heart. She knew this was part of the job, part of the way he had chosen. And the life she'd given up when it had gotten too hard.

She'd gotten dressed only a few minutes before. They had spent their morning eating room service and pretending that he didn't have a flight to catch. It was all happening too fast. Again.

Deke glanced at her and could read her so well, he stopped. He walked over to sit on the bed with her. "I wish I could stay longer."

"Are you on active?" she asked, afraid of the answer. She didn't want to know, but she knew she needed to.

"No. Actually, I've got a couple of offers for assignments. They want to keep me, but I'm thinking I want to settle down."

She snorted, trying to ignore the way her heart jumped at the idea. He hadn't said that he wanted to settle down with her—with anyone. "Deacon Berg, settle down? Yeah, tell me another tale."

"Seriously." He cupped her face. "I wanted to talk about it with you last night but I couldn't. And now there isn't time."

She sighed and closed her eyes. "There never is."

"We'll find it."

She opened her eyes and found his gaze piercing and demanding.

"I will."

She nodded because she couldn't speak. A lump clogged her throat as she blinked to hold back the tears. Her phone sounded Zoe's ring.

"Hey."

"Almost there. I can meet you upstairs or we can hook up downstairs."

"I can meet you downstairs at reception. Deke has to leave."

"Oh, okay. I'll see you."

Sam hung up then rested her head on Deke's shoulder. "I guess we should go."

He nodded. He stood and offered his hand to her. She took it, and he grabbed his bag as they headed out the door.

It only took a few minutes to get downstairs to the reception area and outside to the circular drive. People were getting ready for their day's activity, the excitement of a Hawaiian vacation.

It made her even sadder.

Sam watched as Zoe sped around the circle in her little convertible. She came to a screeching halt in front of them.

Deke's eyebrows shot up. "Jesus."

She found her first smile of the day. "You said a mouthful, Berg," Sam said.

"She's dangerous."

"In more ways than one." She looked at him then and he looked down at her almost at the same time. "Call me."

He cupped her face and kissed her. It was slow, sensuous, and it broke her heart all over again. He pulled away and rested his forehead against hers.

"You will hear from me. I promise."

She nodded.

"I love you, Samantha. Know that, always."

She did. Even without him saying it, she never doubted it. "Oh, I love you too, Deke."

He gave her a hug, another kiss on her neck, and then he walked her over to Zoe's car.

"Hey, Seal, how you doing this morning?" Zoe asked.

"Pretty good, and yourself?"

"Would have been a lot better if I had gotten my own Seal last night, but I can't complain, I guess."

He gave Sam another kiss and opened the door for her. She hesitated then slipped into the car. Deke shut the door. One last touch of his fingers against her cheek.

"Bye."

She nodded but she couldn't say it. Not this time. Something was different. Zoe waited for him to step back, and for once, she pulled away slowly. When they stopped at the light leading out of the resort, she looked over at Sam. She felt her study.

"How much does it hurt?"

The tears she had been holding back spilled over and she choked. "Like I'm dying."

Zoe reached over and took her hand. "You need to stop?"

"No. Let's just get home. I need to get home."

And maybe there she could think that her world hadn't fallen apart. Again.

Chapter Five

Six weeks later

Sam closed her eyes and breathed through her mouth. Today had been a lesson in keeping her food down. Even the crackers and water were not sitting well. But it grew worse without food or water—it was a sick cycle, and she just wanted to die. She knew for a fact one of her students had given her the flu. Probably on purpose, the little buttheads.

She sat on their lanai and stared out over the hills, wondering what Deke was doing right then. The last time she had heard from him was the day he arrived back on the mainland. He'd called to tell her that he'd made it back safely. It was always like this with the two of them. The times they were together, they couldn't seem to keep their hands off each other. But once they were apart, it was as if they didn't care about each other.

Which was a crock because she had thought about him every day since she had seen him last.

She took a sip of water, wondering if she should call him. It would be the right thing to do since he had been the last person to call, but now she felt vulnerable. Did she want him to know just how much she needed him?

She sniffed back the tears she couldn't seem to control the last few weeks.

"Hey, woman. I just got home," Zoe yelled out. She came out and set a bag from their favorite sushi restaurant on the table. "I know you haven't been doing great, so I thought I would treat you to some sushi."

Just the thought had her stomach revolting. "I'm not sure that is such a good idea."

Zoe looked at her. "What? You never turn down sushi."

155

Bile rose in her throat, and Sam took a sip of water hoping that would keep her from throwing up. "I think I have the stomach flu."

Zoe took a step back. "No. I can't get sick. I hate sickness."

"You're a nurse, and besides you know that the incubation period is pretty long."

"I *will* kill you. You know what kind of patient I am, and you and Fee refuse to help me."

"That's because you call us names."

Zoe pulled out the food. "Well, that means more for me."

She opened the container, and the scent of seafood and seaweed hit Sam. She bolted. She barely made it to the bathroom before losing what little she had in her stomach.

Several minutes later, she returned, and Zoe was no longer looking so jovial. "I promise not to breathe on you."

Zoe shook her head. She didn't even smile. "I have something personal to ask you."

"Don't you always?"

When Zoe didn't laugh, Sam started to get worried. "What?"

"Have you skipped your period since that night with Deke?"

"I…" She started counting back the days. It hit her then. "Oh, shit."

"Exactly."

Sam ran to the calendar they had hanging in the kitchen and counted days. "No. No this can't be. We used a condom."

"Every time?"

She nodded. "Yes."

"There's always a chance that it didn't work. There is a twelve percent fail rate."

156

She stared at Zoe. "That's not right. Is that right?"
Her friend nodded.

"Doesn't matter. It's the stomach flu. I know it. It has to be going around school."

Zoe cocked her head. "How many kids have missed school because of it?"

None.

Zoe read her face. "That's what I thought. And I work at a hospital. Not a lot of stomach flu talked about there."

"I didn't say anything."

"You didn't have to. Let's go get a test and then you can see if you are pregnant or not."

"Don't say it."

Even thinking it had her stomach rolling over again.

Zoe must have been very worried about her, because when she spoke, her voice was especially gentle. Fee and Sam called it her "nurse voice." "We'll call Fiona and have her pick one up on her way home."

She hesitated but then nodded.

An hour later, she stared down at the stick.

Dammit.

"What's the answer?" Zoe asked through the door.

"You're so insensitive, I swear," Fiona said, disgust filling her voice. "You need to give her time."

"What? You want to know, too."

"Yes, but I'm not so insensitive that I would badger her through the door."

Tears filled her eyes. Sam hadn't planned on kids anytime soon, especially not with a man who drove her crazy. And she didn't know if she was ready for it right now, but she had no choice in her mind.

She opened the door.

"Oh, I don't know if those are happy or sad tears," Zoe said.

They spilled down her cheeks. "Happy, sad, scared as shit."

"Oh, so you are pregnant," Fiona said.

"What are you going to do?" Zoe asked.

She sighed and scrubbed her face. "Not sure. First, I have to tell Deke. Then we'll decide from there."

They both nodded. In that split second, the reality came crashing down on her. She was pregnant and had so many things to think about, she couldn't deal with it. Without warning, the tears burning the back of her eyes burst forth. The sob caught her off guard.

"I think you need to calm down," Fiona said.

She opened her mouth to argue, but Zoe nodded. "It's the middle of the night, anyway. You're worn out. That's no way to tell him, if you're going to keep it."

She'd already made the decision. She could afford a baby, and she had decent health care. And even if they weren't a couple anymore, Deke would support her and the baby. He would be a good daddy.

Just thinking that made her go gooey. He was an idiot sometimes. What man wasn't? But he was a good man, one she admired and one she knew would be a good father. He'd had a good example with his father. Deke would give everything he could to a child of his.

"Well, I can see you made your decision," Zoe said.

Sam shook her head. "Keeping it was never in doubt. I've wanted to be a mother, and I'm not sure I'll ever get married again. I just don't know if I'm at a place in my life to do this right now."

"Okay." She expected Zoe the nurse to rear her head, but instead she stepped forward and pulled her into a hug, then handed her off to Fiona, who did the same thing. Sam didn't know what she'd expected, but the acceptance of her friends brought tears to her eyes.

"Oh, I didn't want to make you sad," Fiona said.

"Not sad. Happy."

158

"Why not take a hot bath, relax?"

She nodded. "That sounds good."

They filed out of her room, and she stood by the door and looked at them. They were an odd group, all from different kinds of backgrounds, and they definitely all had varying personalities. But she knew without a doubt whatever she decided or whatever happened, they would be there for her.

"Thanks."

She shut the door, walked over to her dresser and opened her jewelry box. She pulled out the gold chain she wore most days under her shirt. Her engagement and wedding ring dangled from it. The diamond wasn't very big, but it had been so special to her. Running off to the justice of the peace probably wasn't the dream wedding she had wanted as a girl, but it had felt like the right thing to do.

She sat on her bed and held the rings next to her heart. Deke was bigger than life, a man who engaged her on so many levels. He respected her, which she didn't always get from other people. She was so tiny most people took her for granted. Not Deke. He taught her how to protect herself with self-defense. Her father didn't think girls should fight or shoot guns. Deke had taught her both.

She sighed. But they could never stand to be around each other. And when he was gone...she hurt. Sam had thought she would be an excellent military wife, but she had sucked at it. She couldn't pretend it was fun and games. It wasn't romantic spending holidays alone or wondering if he would make it back alive for your anniversary.

She decided to take that bath and let her brain settle. The last few days of barely eating had left her tired and cranky. She set her chain and rings back in the box and went about the process of getting her bath ready. After

slipping below the bubbles, she thought of everything
that needed to be done. She needed to see her doctor first
and foremost. And, lord, she was going to have to tell her
brother, who would freak.

With a sigh, she slipped down until the bubbles hit
her chin and set her hands on her abdomen as she let the
news sink in.

She was having Deke's baby.

Wrong time, wrong place…but something
felt…right.

She shook her head at her silliness. She couldn't
know if it were right. Still, she wanted to at least enjoy
the idea for a few minutes before her worries took hold.
Tomorrow she would worry about everything else,
including Deke.

Chapter Six

Two weeks later

Deke felt his phone vibrate on his belt and pulled it out of its case. When he saw Sam's number, he hit ignore.

"You're going to have to talk to her," Mal said, shaking his head.

He glanced at his friends. Both Mal and Kade had made the trip out to BWI to send him off. He hadn't expected it, but he should have. "I will when I get there."

"Is she meeting you at the airport?" Kade asked.

"She doesn't know I'm coming."

There was a beat of silence as they both stared at Deke.

"What do you mean?" Mal finally asked.

He jerked a shoulder. "I figured it was best that I just showed up."

There was another moment of silence then both men started laughing. They were so loud they gained the attention of some people passing by. Deke could feel his face heating. Damn, he hadn't blushed in he didn't know how long.

"What?" he asked, his irritation getting worse by the moment.

"Chief," Mal said, "I can't believe you're so much older than we are and you still don't know how to handle women. You can't just move over there and not tell her."

It was a good plan. He knew it mainly because he knew Samantha. If she knew, she would have fought him.

"If I called her, she would have figured out a way to talk me out of it."

And she would have. Samantha had a good head on her shoulders, and she would think through the issue and

161

find holes in his plan. He didn't want that. He wanted to just show up and deal with the ramifications. It would all work out in the end.

"So, you think that you need to do this? That not telling her is going to help when you just pop in?" Mal asked.

Now that Mal said it like that, Deke was having second thoughts. *Shit.* She wasn't going to be happy. Not one bit. By his way of thinking, she would just have to deal with it. The news he had been given just two weeks prior had convinced him he had made the right choice.

"Well, too late now," Kade said. "You'll call us?"

"Sure, mommy. Right after you kiss my ass."

When his friend didn't smile, he nodded. He knew that since that one bad mission, the three of them had become the touchstones in each other's lives. Only someone who had been through what they had would understand. Every few days they chatted, even if only by text.

"Make sure you guys get back over there," he said.

"Sure. We both have family there now," Kade said with a grin.

"Plus, I figure they might need someone to identify the body," Mal said.

"Fuck you," Deke said with no heat.

He was hesitating and he knew why. Getting on that plane meant that he was on his mission, and he wasn't sure he could do it. He had made the plans on the way back from Hawaii. There was no need to go to teach in Coronado. Not without Sam there. With her in Hawaii, he had taken what he had called the job from hell. He would have done it without the little tidbit of info he'd found out just two weeks earlier. So, he'd made his plans. Now he was on his way to his new life.

And his woman.

"Well, if she kicks you out, call my brother or sister. They'll put you up. Or that crazy Aiona family will take you in," Mal said.

He gave them both a hug, and then walked into the airport.

An hour later, he was sitting in his seat when his phone vibrated again. She hadn't started calling until two weeks ago, and he had been worried that she had found out about his assignment—or the other information. But now he knew she didn't know. There was no way. Her brother wouldn't have been able to find out, and he knew that Mitchell was her only other connection to the military these days. Still, he turned the phone off. It was too late to have second thoughts.

His new life and the woman he had always loved were in Hawaii. It was all he needed to think about.

He closed his eyes and counted the minutes until the plane took off.

* * * *

Sam was happy she had kept down half a bowl of broth finally. The last few weeks had been horrible. The only thing that had saved her this week was that the kids had been on spring break. Zoe had ordered her to rest, and for once, Sam had listened. It might have been that or the meds the doctor had given her, but Sam was finally feeling a bit better. Keeping a whole bowl of broth down was amazing. Her phone rang. Checking the screen, she saw it was Zoe.

"Hey."

"Aw, you sound horrible. I was hoping you could meet us out."

She pulled the phone out from her ear and looked at it. Being that it wasn't a video call, Zoe couldn't see her nasty look, so she set the phone against her ear.

"Really?"

"I hate that you've spent your entire spring break stuck at the condo."

She snorted. "I think my days of dancing are over at least for the next eight months."

There was a pause, and she could hear the loud music and the people talking in the background. This new Zoe was a little disconcerting. She'd been in full nurse mode for the last two weeks. There were times she really freaked Sam out.

"Still haven't heard from him?"

She sighed. She should have known that Zoe would pick up on that. "Nope. I called three times today. Nothing. Last time went to voice mail. He wasn't supposed to go on a mission, but you never know."

And it might be weeks before he got back. That had panic tickling the back of her throat, but she took a drink of water to keep from choking on it.

"Okay, well, call if you need anything. We'll both keep checking on you."

She smiled. Her friends had turned into perfect mother hens. It might be bothering her that Zoe was being so pleasant, but it had been nice to have two people babying her.

"I will. I'm so tired. I think I might go to bed after I finish this broth."

"Did you take your meds and vitamins?"

"I will after I eat this."

She paused again, and Sam knew she was worried about her. She hated to ruin their night, especially when nothing could be done. She just had to ride out the storm.

"Okay, well, again, call if you need anything."

She hung up and was starting to finish her broth when the doorbell rang. Glancing at the clock and seeing that it was almost eight, she wondered if her brother had decided to stop by. He'd always been protective of her,

164

but he was getting worse by the day. He was using the excuse of her condition to check on her daily. Where she appreciated her friends' attention, her brother was starting to piss her off. She padded barefoot to the door and rose to her tiptoes to check out her visitor. When she looked through the peephole, her stomach started to turn.

Deke.

"I hear you in there, Samantha. Open up."

She breathed through her mouth, trying to keep the little bit of broth she had eaten down.

"If you don't answer, I'll bust down the door."

And wasn't that just like him? He avoids her then shows up in Hawaii and tries to bully her.

"Funny coming from a man who didn't answer his phone for two weeks."

He sighed. "Open up, Sam. I've been flying all day long."

His voice sounded weary, tired. She knew if he had flown from the west coast, he had been at it probably more than twelve hours.

She opened the door. He had his suitcase there beside him. He was dressed in low-riding Wranglers, a pair of running shoes, and a Navy shirt. He looked like he had just gotten out of bed. His hair was a mess and there was a little scruff on his chin.

God, he looked good.

"You going to let me in?"

She nodded and stepped back. She shut the door and leaned back against it.

"Are your roommates here?"

"No. They're out tonight."

He kept looking at her as if she were the only thing in the world. But he always did that, and it never failed to make her feel melty inside.

"I thought you would have called before you came over for a vacation."

"Not here for a vacation, but I guess I should have. I forgot you have to get up in the morning. You look exhausted."

He sounded so damned concerned that it had her stomach flip-flopping. Apparently it was too much for her to take after eating. She swallowed hard.

"No school. Kids are out on spring break here. They always have it the last week of March."

He nodded and opened his mouth.

"I need a second."

He held up his hands, and the determined look on his face warned her that he wasn't going to let things go right now. "Sam, I know you're mad at me, but I knew if I let you call me, you would talk me out of moving here."

Her alarm rose. "Moving here?"

He nodded. "I took a job at PACOM."

That stopped her in her tracks. "A desk job?"

He jerked one shoulder. Samantha knew that it was a definite Berg reaction to life in general. All the guys in his family were like that. "In a way. I'll be doing some work with plans, etc, or whatever."

Sam shook her head. "But you wanted to teach?"

He gave her a smile. "I wanted to be here more."

He stepped closer, and she felt her stomach give way.

"I need to—"

He furrowed his brow. "Sam?"

She shook her head and tried to get away, but he wouldn't let go of her, and she couldn't hold it any longer. She threw up on him.

Chapter Seven

Several minutes and a fresh shirt later, Deke joined
Samantha back in her kitchen, but he kept a respectful
distance. He didn't know exactly what was going on, but
he didn't want to think he was causing her to get sick at
the sight of him. And if she had something, he didn't
want to end up with it.

"Have you been sick for long?"

She gave him a look that told him his question didn't
set well. It was part of that mean look she had always
given him, but there was something else to it, something
that made her look so damned vulnerable.

"No. Why didn't you answer my calls?" she asked.

This was going to be hard to explain. He hadn't
really expected her to think he was dodging her for other
reasons. He could lie and say he was too busy because of
the move, but lying just didn't feel right, even if it was
just a little fib tonight. Samantha always did better when
you told her the truth head-on. Well, most of it.

"Truth is I was afraid I would tell you about moving
here and you would tell me that you didn't want me to do
that."

"But once you had the assignment, the orders were
cut and they wouldn't be able to cancel it."

He shook his head. "They could do anything they
wanted. It's happened before. Truth is they would do
more to keep me in the field if they could, but it's hard to
do at my advanced age."

She gave him a tired smile. "You're not old, Deke."

And why did the way she was looking at him make
him feel soft? There was something different in her gaze.
"Tell that to my back," he said, twisting until it cracked.
"It hasn't been the same for a while."

"I thought you would go teach." It had been his dream for a long time. She was the only person on earth he had told about it.

"Yeah, I did too. Until Kade's wedding." He had known then he had to make it back to her and fast. One thing he had learned in that fucked up mission last year was that he could no longer wait for the right time. He had to make it.

"So, you're going to be working at PACOM?"

He nodded. He knew she was trying to avoid the subject of her illness, but he was worried about her. She looked like she'd dropped weight, and she was pale. It was easy to see the dark circles under her eyes.

Was she really sick and she'd been trying to get a hold of him? Now he felt like a complete ass.

"Are you sure you're okay?" he asked, afraid of the answer.

She nodded and picked up a saltine and nibbled on it. "I tried to call you because I had news for you."

He knew when she had something important to say she would just drag the whole thing out. He resisted the urge to close his eyes. It was bad if she was taking this long to tell him.

"I started getting sick about three weeks ago."

When she didn't continue, he asked, "Have you gone to the doctor?"

She nodded.

"What did he say?"

"He said it would pass in about another month, if I was lucky."

"A month? You've been getting sick like this and he wants you to wait a month? That doesn't sound right. Maybe you need another doctor to look at you. Maybe he has the wrong diagnosis. I think we should get a second opinion."

He would make sure she saw someone. The fact that she looked so sickly worried him. Sam had always been a healthy girl. Curvy, never worrying about her weight, always in excellent shape. Now, though, she looked like she had been through hell.

She gave him a sad smile. "There's no other diagnosis. I've covered my bases on this one."

Fear wrapped its scrawny fingers around his heart, and he had to swallow to rid himself of the lump in his throat. "What is it?"

She apparently realized that he was worried. She reached over to pat his hand, and then she drew away. "It isn't anything life ending. I'm pregnant, Deke."

For a second or two, the comment didn't register. He had been waiting for a cancer diagnosis or something else.

"Pregnant?" he asked, the word seeming weird against his lips. He couldn't seem to wrap his head around the idea that she was carrying a child. Deke was known for his quick thinking, but for once his brain seemed to stop dead in its tracks.

"Yes."

"Ours, of course."

She looked relieved and that angered him. He frowned.

"You can't think that I would think it was someone else's?"

She shrugged, and he hated the defeated attitude. She was a lot of things but his Samantha wasn't someone who accepted defeat. And he didn't like it, not one bit.

"I've been with other men before."

"Yeah, but you wouldn't have slept with me this time if you had been involved with someone else. It's the same for both of us."

"You're right."

"Why didn't you call me? This is a serious situation that I should have known about. Or were you not planning on telling me?"

She looked at him as if he had grown another head. Her face flushed with anger, and he knew he had stepped over the bounds.

"I did call, you jackass. I cannot believe you just accused me of not telling you—like I was hiding it. Maybe if you hadn't been acting like a scared little girl for two weeks and avoiding my calls, you would have known. But, no, Deacon Berg has another of his master plans and he decides he shouldn't tell me. You know, all the calls I've been trying for almost two weeks?"

Usually, this is where she started throwing things. He'd gotten brained with the remote control once for something he said. Instead, she did something very un-Sam-like and started to cry.

He didn't know what to do. He'd dealt with women who cried, but not Sam. Samantha just didn't cry big fat tears, and she definitely didn't sob openly. She was the stereotypical military brat with the stiff upper lip. That woman was apparently gone.

"I called and called and called. When you didn't answer, I thought you might have gone on a mission. I thought about calling your mom, but then I thought she would worry about you, too, or wonder just why I was trying to get ahold of you. And I didn't want to explain, not until I talked to you."

By now, the tears were rolling down her cheeks, and she was sobbing openly. He finally gained his wits and pulled her into his arms. She tried to struggle once or twice, but she settled against him, her head on his chest. Feeling her slight body against his caused some of the tension to ease out of his shoulders. He was still worried, but with her there in his arms, it didn't seem to matter as much.

"I'm sorry, babe. I thought it best I just show up."

She punched his chest half-heartedly. "Well, it wasn't."

He chuckled. "I can see that. First you throw up on me, and then you cry all over me."

She pulled back and looked up at him. Her eyes were still damp, what little makeup she had on was now streaked down her cheeks, and her nose was red. She was a God-awful mess—and the most beautiful woman in the world.

"Tell you what. Why don't you go freshen up and put on some PJs? It might make you feel better. I'll call around and try to find a place for the night."

She shook her head. "You can stay here."

Her immediate offer made him feel a little better. "Are you sure?"

"Yes. I can't kick the father of my baby out on the streets of Hawaii."

He smiled and gave her a kiss on the nose. "Go on."

Once he was alone, he allowed the words she'd said to sink in. *The father of her baby.* Damn, he was hoping for that, had made the decision that he was going to get her to marry him again, but he had planned on that complication after the ceremony.

But now that he knew the situation, he was sure of one damned thing.

The woman was going to have to accept him. There was just no way around it. He sat down at the breakfast bar realizing the ramifications of the news—and what it meant.

His mother was going to flip. She'd been pining for babies, and as every Berg, including Deke's sister, were pretty much married to the military, no one had done anything to that end. Now she would have one, and she would be thrilled. He could call her, but it was a little late, and he figured he needed to get his ducks in a line. If his mother didn't know for a while, it wouldn't hurt. Deke had a plan. It just meant he had to speed it up.

He sighed and scrubbed his hands over his face. This wasn't going the way he had planned, but it never had. From the moment they met, they had never been able to do what normal people would do. It was a hot and fast attraction, marriage, divorce, and there was their inability to keep their hands off each other. He knew her, but he wasn't sure that they knew each other well enough. His plan was to go slowly...

Now, though, he was on a time schedule. He had a baby on the way, and he had to make sure everything was straightened away before the little one came.

Just that thought brought images of a baby, and while most people would think he would want a little boy, a little girl would do him just fine. Especially one with curly blonde hair and big violet eyes like her mama.

He saw something out of the corner of his eye and turned to face her. She was wearing an old T-shirt that hit her mid-thigh. God, how could a woman who looked so horrible look good enough to eat?

In a flash, the answer came to him. She was his other half. It was as simple as that. It had to be why his mouth was dry and his palms damp, not to mention the telltale humming of arousal in his body.

He pushed those needs down and tried to tell himself it was the right thing to do.

"Do you have some blankets for me?"

She shook her head. "I have a queen. Come on, let's go to bed."

He hesitated and she made a face.

"I promise not to throw up on you. Or cry."

He smiled and took her hand. "I just wanted to make sure you were okay with it. You need some rest."

She led him into the bedroom he hadn't paid much attention to. It wasn't girly with lots of flowers. That wasn't Samantha. She was as feminine as could be, but she didn't like things like that. The room was plain, simple, colored with blues and grays, along with all her little knickknacks from all over the world. Her life as a military brat was easy to follow if you paid attention to the various things she had in her bedroom.

"Do you mind if I jump in the shower? That trip was a bad one."

"No problem."

Deke grabbed his gear. "I'll be right out."

He didn't take long in the shower because he didn't want to leave her by herself for too long. He wasn't sure what he could do if she got sick again, but he figured he would at least be there to help.

By the time he slipped out of the bathroom, she was sleeping. He leaned against the doorjamb and just looked at her. She still looked exhausted, but now she appeared serene.

The thought that she was pregnant, carrying a child he knew both of them would love and cherish, had his chest warming. He padded over on bare feet and tried his best not to disturb her. He slipped into bed. The moment he pulled the sheet over him, she rolled over into his arms. Deke looked down and was going to apologize, but he realized she was still sleeping.

He settled against the pillows, the weight of Samantha on his chest, and felt his body relax. Now he was home.

* * * *

Samantha woke the next morning and lay in bed. She realized that she felt rested for the first time in weeks. It had been almost a month since she'd slept through the night. She opened her eyes and noticed she was alone in bed. Knowing from experience to take things slowly, she lay there for a few minutes trying to forget the night before. She covered her eyes. Lord, she couldn't believe she threw up on Deke. The fact that he was still there was a testament to how much he loved her—or, at least, loved this child. She slipped her hands down to her belly. It was hard to believe that in seven months there was going to be a child in her life. Well, other than her brother. And Zoe.

When she thought that her stomach had finally settled enough, she sat up and then slid out of bed. She could hear voices in the kitchen, but she decided to clean up first. Once that was done, she headed out to the kitchen. She needed some toast and a little water. For once it seemed her stomach was behaving.

She found Deke in the kitchen. He was cooking breakfast, and her roommates were sitting at the breakfast bar, soaking in whatever he was talking about. They both were actually drooling. Sam wasn't sure if it was because of the food that she smelled or the man who was preparing it.

"So, she's convinced that she can ride that damned bull."

Oh, God, he was telling *that* story. She couldn't believe he had the nerve to tell it again. Every time he wanted to embarrass her, he started in on it.

"And she isn't taking no for an answer. Granted, most people who get on the bull are drunk, and you know Sam, she doesn't drink much. So, she gets on up there and bets that asshole fifty dollars she can stay on all eight seconds. She didn't last two."

"I lasted four, if I remember correctly."

He was laughing when he turned to her, his dimples in full force and his expression so light and carefree. Her heart squeezed tight right then and there, just like it had done the first night she had seen him.

174

He walked over to her. "How are you feeling this morning? We didn't wake you up, did we?"

She shook her head. "In fact, this is the latest I've slept in weeks."

"Is that medicine working?" Zoe asked. "Dr. Wilcox swears by it."

"Yeah, I think it might be. Waking up and not gagging is a big step."

Deke kissed her forehead. "You want anything? I cooked some eggs, but I wasn't sure if you would be interested in them."

She shook her head.

"Then some toast?" he offered.

"Oh, and I bought some of that tea my friend recommended," Zoe said as she got up and started the kettle. "She's an ob/gyn nurse, so she says it's safe."

Sam sat next to Fiona, who smiled at her. "You missed some fun last night."

"I'm sure I did."

Fiona sipped her tea, then said, "Your brother showed up."

Sam rolled her eyes. "And let me guess, Zoe and he got in a fight."

"Well, everything was fine until this guy started hitting on Zoe."

She looked at Zoe, who was pretending to ignore the conversation, but there was a light pink to her cheeks.

"Really?" Sam asked.

Fiona's hazel eyes danced with undisguised mirth. "Yeah, he was a jerk. Some mainlander here on vacation. You know, the kind who thinks everyone is here for a price? That he paid a huge chunk of money so he gets to dance with the pretty girls. The pretty girl he picked out was Zoe, of course. Your brother let him know otherwise."

She laughed. "Please tell me no fighting. It wouldn't look good on his record."

"Naw, the mainlander took one look at those muscles and he decided Zoe wasn't that much of a catch. And then your brother and one of your best friends got in a fight."

She glanced at Zoe. "Really? How shocking."

She shook her head, her blonde hair sliding over her shoulders. "Your brother needs to learn we aren't all his little sister."

Deke set the plate down in front of Sam. "Eat."

She glanced at him. "Who are you and what did you do with my ex-husband?"

He smiled. "Does your brother know about the baby?"

"Couldn't help it," Zoe said as she handed Sam her tea over the counter. "She was talking to him and started gagging."

"I'm assuming you reserved the throwing up on men for your husband?"

There was a beat of silence, then Fiona asked, "She threw up on you?"

She felt her face heat. "First of all, you're my ex-husband. And you wouldn't listen to me, and then the fact that you decided to just show up..."

"I wouldn't have just shown up if I had known."

"You would have known if you had picked up your phone the last few weeks."

"Are you sure you two are divorced?" Zoe asked.

"I signed the papers, so I know it's true."

Deke said nothing but got the oddest look in his eyes while he stared at Sam. She had to resist the urge to fidget.

"So, you're here working at PACOM? I work over at Tripler," Zoe said. "Do you know where you're looking for a place to live?"

It took him a second to answer Zoe. He tore his gaze from Sam, and she could finally breathe again.

"Not sure yet. I reported in last night, but I will probably head on down today to meet my supervisor in person."

Which wasn't an answer.

Zoe nodded. "That isn't too bad of a drive from here. You just get right on H-3 and drive down. Wouldn't be hard to live over here."

Sam shot Zoe a warning look. She smiled at Sam.

"Do you mind if I use the shower?" he asked.

"No, go ahead."

He walked toward her room but paused by her chair.

"Eat." He softened the order with a kiss on the top of her head.

Once he shut the door, Zoe sighed. "Oh man, oh man. Okay, if you don't want him, I want him. I call dibs on him before Fiona."

Sam sighed. "It isn't a matter of wanting him. That is never a problem. The problem is getting along during the other times."

"If I were you, I would figure out a way. Damn, he is so sweet I want to eat him up." Zoe made smacking noises with her mouth.

"Wait, he will get on your nerves. At some point, he will start barking orders like you're an E-1 who just got in. That was never fun. Think of the way my brother acts."

Zoe's dreamy look dissolved. "Your brother is opinionated."

"And Deke is, too. You just aren't seeing it."

"Does he have a brother?" Fiona asked.

"Two. Jacob and Jonah. Jonah is sort of a black sheep of the family."

"Yeah, what does he do?" Zoe asked.

"Since the family is Navy, being a Marine is bad. They give him crap about it."

Zoe closed her eyes. "Okay, wait, does he look like Deke?"

"Yeah, a little. He has brown eyes, though, like milk chocolate."

"Oh, God. Now, put the two of them together..."

"Ew, I see Jonah as a brother. That is just...ew, no."

Zoe laughed and opened her eyes. "I will happily keep that fantasy to myself."

"What are you going to do, Sam?" Fiona asked.

"Not sure. I think for the most part, I will just play it by ear."

"Wait. You are Samantha Walters, right? The woman who always has a plan? You didn't body snatch her, did you?" Zoe asked.

She smiled and shrugged. "I really don't have a choice, do I?"

"What do you mean by that?" Fiona asked.

"I didn't really plan on getting pregnant."

"No. But there is a bit to that in my way of thinking."

She glanced at Fiona. The most flighty of the three of them, Fiona always seemed to know things before they would happen.

"Well, maybe somewhere in your self-conscious, you wanted to get pregnant. Don't even think of telling us that you didn't want him back here with you."

She sighed. "There was always a part of me that wanted him back with me. Wanted him here, to be married again. I just didn't want it to be like this."

"Is Mitchell still mad at you?" Fiona asked.

"No. Well, sort of. This is not going to go over well."

"What do you mean?"

"Mitch didn't want me to tell him. Which I completely disagreed with, of course. But he thought that maybe Deke could be left out of the picture."

"That doesn't sound like your brother," Zoe said.

Sam and Fiona looked at their friend. Zoe didn't usually worry about defending Mitchell.

"No, don't read anything into it," Zoe continued. "Mitch irritates me on some level I cannot even explain right now. But, that being said, he is a pretty decent guy."

"He always thought that Deke and I should never see each other again. I can't say that I disagreed with that at the time."

"And like a big brother, he wants to protect you," Fiona said. She had a soft heart for brothers since she had lost her own only two years earlier in Iraq.

"So, I have to figure out a way to tell my brother that my ex is here to live. But maybe I don't have to tell him any time soon."

As soon as she said the words, the front doorbell rang.

Sam looked at the door. "No. Karma doesn't hate me this much."

Zoe shook her head. "You knew he was going to get worse with you pregnant."

"Today is a Friday."

"And you should have expected him to be off. He doesn't go out to clubs when he has to work the next day," Zoe said. "You better figure out a way to tell your brother that your ex is here and naked in your bathroom."

Chapter Eight

Deke was shaving when his phone rang. Mal's face popped up to the sound of the *Jersey Shore* theme song.

"Hey, Chief. Recovered from the trip?"

He shaved the last bit of cream off his face. "A bit. Could probably do with a few hours of sleep, though."

"You'll get used to it, and guys your age need extra rebound time."

"Fuck off."

"Are you going into Honolulu today?"

"Might. Not sure. I figured today I would go meet the O-6 I'll be working for. Let him know I have to find a place to live."

"So, you aren't in Honolulu right now?"

He rolled his eyes as he used a towel to scrub the rest of his face free of any traces of shaving cream.

"No." Mal was pussyfooting around the issue.

"Did your lady-love kick you out?"

"Now why would she kick out the father of her child?"

There was a beat of silence.

"Father of her child?"

"Yeah. All those phone calls were because she was trying to tell me."

"Holy shit."

He heard a mumbled voice in the background, and he knew Kade was there. Deke rolled his eyes again. Kade and Mal were getting to be like little old ladies.

"Sam's pregnant."

"That's what I said."

"No, I'm telling Kade. So, it happened at Kade's wedding. Holy shit."

"You already said that."

He couldn't tell from his response what Mal was thinking. Deke didn't know why it mattered so much, but it did. The friendship the three of them had forged through the last few years, and especially after the mission where they lost Forrester, had made these two men like brothers to him.

"What are you going to do?" Mal asked.

"I don't know. We haven't discussed much. Apparently the pregnancy isn't going that well. Sam can't seem to keep any food down and has lost a bunch of weight. So I didn't push her last night."

"You're going to have to talk to her about that."

"I know. I was fucking tired last night and needed time to think."

And he had thought. Now he was pretty sure the plan he had in place before he flew over here would work. It was just that he had to hope that it would work for their sake and the sake of the baby.

He heard voices in the other room. The three women were talking, and there was a man's voice. One he unfortunately recognized.

"Listen, I have to let you go. I'll give you a call tomorrow."

Before Mal could respond, he clicked off the phone. The pounding on the door started. "Open up, dickhead."

"Do not call him a dickhead, you dickhead," Sam said.

Deke rolled his shoulders and opened the door. Mitchell stood in the doorway, anger rolling off him in waves. Sam slipped in between them, but Deke didn't let her talk. He grabbed her and put her behind him. Mitchell wouldn't intentionally hurt her, but he had a wicked temper—especially where Deke was concerned.

"You bastard," he said as he lifted his fist. Being a Seal, he reacted instinctively. He blocked the punch and delivered one of his own. He hit Mitchell square on the nose. The crack of bone filled the room and blood spurted.

"Fucking hell!"

Mitchell stumbled back, and Sam screamed.

"Shit, sorry," Deke said.

"What do you think you were doing?" Mitchell yelled.

"I was defending myself, you asshole. Don't you know better than to try and hit a damn Seal?"

Zoe came forward. "Lean your head back, Mitchell."

He gave her a nasty look. "They say not to do that anymore."

"I know they do. I am an RN, so I kind of know, but you're bleeding on our fucking carpet. Bathroom, now."

She tugged him in the other direction. Once they were alone, he turned to Sam. She had her face covered, and he was worried she was crying.

"Oh, baby, I'm sorry. I didn't even think. I'm not trained to when I'm attacked."

She finally looked up, and she was crying, but it was from laughing. "Oh, Lord, that was funny."

She was snorting.

"You think me breaking your brother's nose is funny?"

"Yeah. He has been a pain in the ass. And I will let you in on a little secret—I did the same thing to him when we were in middle school."

He felt his lips curve. "Is that right?"

She nodded and sat down on her bed. "Mitchell told me that I didn't have the right to play baseball in middle school because I was a girl and girls were weak. So I popped him."

He chuckled. "Of course you did."

"I'm sorry. I didn't have time to tell him you were here."

"Would you have told him?"

She frowned at him. "Of course I would."

"Okay." He grabbed a T-shirt and pulled it on. "I have to talk to your brother, then I have to get dressed to meet my new supervisor. Do you want to go with me?"

She hesitated then shook her head. "I don't have an id card."

"I can sign you on, you know that."

She didn't look too sure. Being an ex-brat, wife, and sister of a military man, she knew the rules, so he knew that she didn't want to do it. Normally, he would push her, but maybe they needed space. But only for a few hours.

"Okay, you stay here. Do you mind going out with me later if you feel up to it?"

She smiled. "Yeah. Just not in the early afternoon. While I am out of school, I've been napping then. I do better if I get a little rest."

He nodded. He quickly finished dressing. "Get some rest and make sure you eat." He gave her a kiss, just a nibble on the lips, but she slipped her hands up his back and he lost himself. Heat exploded between the two of them in an instant. It took him a second to realize he had his fingers slipped under her shirt and was pulling it off her.

With a groan, he pulled back. Her lips were swollen and her eyes heavy lidded. He curled his fingers into his palms. Damn, the woman was dangerous.

"I gotta go."

She smiled at him. "Okay."

His belly clutched. Damn, she looked so sweet, but he knew he had to go check out the new work situation. And he needed to talk to Mitchell at some point today.

"I'll be home—I mean back—before lunch."

She nodded, and he gave her another quick kiss. When he stepped out into the living area, Zoe and

Mitchell were gone. Fiona was cleaning up the kitchen. He realized then he'd left a mess.

"Oh, I'm sorry, Fiona."

She smiled at him and shook her head. "Naw. You cooked. Someone else cleans. And Zoe will bully Mitchell."

He nodded. "Can you be honest with me?"

She turned the water off and faced him. "Yes."

He was struck by just how truthful she was being in that short answer. There was something so direct but otherworldly about Fiona. She was short and round, like a cocoa-skinned Madonna. And he thought for the first time, if his heart wasn't taken, he would definitely ask the woman out. She was downright stunning.

"Sam's doing okay? She isn't lying, right?"

She gave him a maternal smile, which was odd because he was sure he had at least ten years on her. "She's fine. I think the stress of not being able to get ahold of you sort of bothered her a little bit much. And, you have to remember, Samantha loves a plan. This sort of wasn't planned."

He felt his cheeks heat.

"Oh, you have nothing to be embarrassed about. Fate."

He shook his head, wondering if he had missed something. "What?"

"Fate. It has her way with mortals. She wanted you together, and now she has bound you together."

"Uh, okay."

She laughed. "You'll get used to me. Everyone does. Just know I will keep your secret."

That had him frowning.

"What?"

She leaned forward and patted his cheek. "You have secrets, and I know some of them. Just make sure you treat Sam and the love she has for you with respect. It will all work out."

Before he could say anything, she turned and went back to cleaning the dishes.

"She always says stuff like that," Mitchell said from behind him. Deke turned and tried not to wince. Mitch's nose was swollen, and his eyes were already starting to turn black. He deserved it for what he'd done, but it didn't make Deke any happier about doing it. Well, not much.

"Sorry about that."

Mitchell's scowl turned darker. "It's okay."

"Yeah?"

"No, but I'll find a way to pay you back."

It had been three years since he'd seen Samantha's brother, and Mitch had grown into his height. He was over six feet tall and the skinny frame was now what would be termed as lanky. Deke wondered if he even fit in the cockpit of the fighter he flew.

"I have to head out."

"Why don't I take you?"

Deke eyed him suspiciously. "Are you sure you aren't going to dump me somewhere?"

"No. I would be stupid to drop a Seal somewhere and leave him to die."

Deke rolled his shoulders. "Okay."

"Besides, I try to stay on my sister's good side, and leaving you stranded here in Hawaii would set her off."

He eyed his brother-in-law. "Yeah? Since when are you afraid of your sister?"

"These days, there isn't much about her that doesn't frighten me. She's either yelling at me or crying. Either way, I am always the bad guy."

"So, you're ready to let me be the bad guy?"

He grabbed his keys off the counter and smiled at Deke. "Yep. And I am going to love it."

185

* * * *

Samantha stepped out of her room dressed and feeling a bit better. She looked around and didn't see anyone until she spotted Fiona on the lanai. She was sipping her morning tea and taking in nature. Sam wished she could be more like her friend. Fiona had always been a woman who could handle anything life threw her. Sam could, too, and had in more than one way, but Fiona never seemed to deal with the unexpected. Even before Fiona had gotten the word of Brett's death two years ago, she had known. She had called Samantha in tears, and normally she would have brushed it away, but with Fiona, Sam had learned not to do that. She had been at Fiona's little apartment in California when the news arrived of her twin's death.

It was the only time she had seen Fiona fall apart.

She stepped out onto the lanai. The sun was shining, with just a little fog clinging to the mountains.

"Hey."

"Hey, yourself. Feeling better?" Fiona asked.

"Yeah."

"I think we should do some reiki on you later."

She nodded. "Have you seen Mitchell, or did Zoe keep him in her room?"

"He's with Deke."

"What?" Samantha jumped up out of her chair, but Fiona took hold of her hand.

"Sit down. They will be fine. They need to work some things out. These two men are very important in your life—in more ways than the one they are now."

Oh, God, Fee was talking in riddles again. She respected Fiona because she did seem to have an intuition that made Radar on *M*A*S*H* look normal, but sometimes she just would like to ignore her.

"Okay, but they could hurt each other."

"They won't. You need to sit and enjoy, Sam. You have only a few months left for quiet mornings."

She sighed and knew that Fiona was right. She settled into her chair again.

"Did Deke say anything about how he felt about the baby?" Fiona asked.

She shrugged. "I kind of stunned him, then he yelled at me for not telling him sooner."

Fiona nodded. "He felt guilty for not answering."

She shrugged. "I guess."

"I guess you didn't get to talk more about the plans?"

She shook her head. "No. It's the same, though."

"It isn't the same, Sam. There is a baby involved here."

Fiona wasn't admonishing her. That wasn't her way. Her way was to help someone get to where they needed to be emotionally. It was a gift that Sam always wished she had.

"I wish I could tell what he was thinking."

Fee snorted. "Probably that he wants to have sex with you."

"That sounds like something Zoe would say."

She gave her a smile. "The way he looks at you...very sexy. He loves you so much. And I see the same in you. Make sure you don't mess that up."

She chuckled. "Maybe he'll mess it up."

"He could, but he's been warned. I think he will listen." Fee glanced over at her. "What are you afraid of?"

Of course, she knew Sam was afraid. "That he'll leave."

"He won't."

"He's a Seal. He'll leave."

"Being a Seal is his job, but it isn't who he is with you."

She sighed, wishing for once that Fee wasn't so direct. She had Sam thinking of things that were better ignored. "You don't understand."

"I do, but I don't think you do."

She frowned at Fiona. "I'm getting tired again."

Fiona laughed. "Okay, with the rest of the world, he's a Seal. But with you…he's just a man. He might just be figuring that out."

Sam sighed. "We'll just have to wait and see."

Fiona grabbed her hand. "I told Deke it would work out. Don't worry. Now I have to get ready. I have a few clients later and there has been much to muddy my aura today."

With a light squeeze to Sam's hand, Fiona left her to her thoughts. But she couldn't really think. So much was going on, so much turmoil. She pulled her feet up and rested her head on her knees. Life before now was easier, so much easier.

And now that Deacon Berg was with her forever, come hell or high water, she was going to have to figure out just what to do about him.

Chapter Nine

Deke glanced over at Mitchell. "So, you didn't kill me."

Mitchell flashed him an evil smile as he pulled onto H201. It was almost identical to the one Samantha gave when she had a really good hand at poker. He knew to fold as soon as he saw it. Still, Deke hated to admit that he was kind of happy Mitchell had shown him around. He sort of knew his way around the island, but he hadn't spent much time on the bases. It had been much easier to go with his brother-in-law.

"I might have been an ass this morning, but I should have known better than to come at you head-on. You're old, but you are a Seal. If I kill you, it will have to be something really shady."

Deke snorted. "Consider me warned."

Mitchell nodded as they stopped at a light. "Listen, I know I was an ass, like I said. But…you have to understand—"

Deke held up his hand. "Say no more. If it were AJ, I would have the same reaction. I completely understand."

In fact, he had a little more respect for Mitchell. He was a bit overbearing, but he understood that brotherly love a little more since his sister had started dating several years ago. There were quite a few years between his sister and his brothers, being that she was his parents ATMB or After the Military Baby, as they liked to call her. Although Deke wondered if his baby sister would ever tell him she was pregnant until it was much later. Like when the kid was graduating. She had learned to keep things from her brothers being the youngest and the only girl.

"Okay, and I will admit right up front, I told her not to tell you."

Anger had Deke curling his fingers to keep from smacking the major. It probably wouldn't end well for him, though. He outranked Deke, and besides that, Mitchell was driving. And while Samantha might not be too mad eventually, she would initially be upset. That just wasn't something he wanted to do to her. Not right now.

"I will accept the broken nose as punishment for that," Mitchell said.

His nose was a mess, his eyes blackened, and that was going to be hard to explain when he went to work on Monday morning, so Deke let it go.

"I would have found out."

"Yeah, I know, but you have to understand. She...she's fragile. Never in my life have I thought of Sam that way. I might have given her shit before."

"Like when she gave you your first broken nose?"

He snorted then winced. "Fuck that hurt. Yeah, but she has always been sort of the strongest woman I know. She found out she was pregnant and then it was all weeping and hormonal. It brought back memories of her hitting puberty." He shuttered. "It was horrific."

"Sam was weepy." He shrugged. Deke wasn't about to admit that it bothered him.

"No. I mean, I know with the hormones it happens sometimes. I've been working behind a desk since I moved here a year ago, so I have been around women more. We had two women in the office pregnant this year. That was just too much for me to handle."

"I hate to say it, but you are Air Force. I'm a Seal. I'm trained for these kinds of things. I wouldn't freak out just because a woman got a little weepy.

He shot Deke a look. "Yeah? It will be interesting to see what happens when she goes off on you. But you weren't there when she was a teenager. It was bad. Really bad. She took that hormonal imbalance and put it into action. She would spend days devising things to drive me insane. And she's mean."

Deke chuckled, thinking of a teenage Samantha being the bane of her brother's existence. He could just imagine the things she would devise to torture her older and overbearing brother. She would be cute.

"Younger sisters are not the easiest to deal with then. I was lucky that I was out the door before mine hit that age."

"Yeah, well, Sam was nasty. Especially to me. But, now…if I look at her the wrong way, she starts to cry. And, I'll admit, I blamed you."

Deke hated to admit that he could understand Mitchell's point of view. "Then why didn't you contact me so I could deal with it?"

He shrugged as he took the turn off to H-3. "I'm a guy, and according to Zoe, a dumbass."

"Yeah, she said that more than once this morning. She's not too happy with you about last night."

He made a face. "Zoe has been on her own too long. She doesn't understand how to be careful."

Deke heard the proprietary tone in Mitchell's voice, but he figured it wasn't his place to comment.

"So, Deke, are your intentions honorable?"

He looked at her brother. Sam and Mitchell definitely looked like brother and sister. There was no doubt about it. But there was an edgier quality to Mitchell's facial features. His eyes were a little darker, as was his hair.

"The fact that it's taking you so long to answer that is making me kind of nervous."

"Of course my intentions are honorable. I just have to make sure that I don't let Sam know I plan on talking her back into marriage."

There was a beat of silence as Mitchell pulled around a van.

"You're telling me you're scared?"

Like a little boy, but he wasn't about to admit that to his brother-in-law. "I didn't say that."

He snorted. "Listen, son, I don't blame you, but just know this. You better do right by her or all those medals on your chest won't mean a damned thing. I will make sure you're ruined."

For a second, he couldn't believe her brother had just threatened his career.

"You just threatened to ruin my career?"

"Answer me this, Seal. What would you do if AJ was in the same situation?"

He glanced at Samantha's brother. "I would hide the body."

Mitchell chuckled.

"I just want to make sure you keep your nose out of it," Deke said.

"And if I don't?"

Deke shifted in his seat. He didn't know how much to tell Samantha's brother. He wasn't accustomed to sharing things with people. He held back things from Mal and Kade. It was his nature. In a family filled with so many siblings, he'd always been kind of a loner.

"I can't convince her that she should marry me with you hanging around."

The silence lengthened, and Deke started to worry he was going to have to fight both brother and sister.

"I shouldn't. You broke her heart when you left."

He knew, in a way, that was true. It wasn't the whole story, because they were both broken when he left. She had told him to leave, and he had been stupid enough to do it. There wasn't a second that went by in his life that he didn't regret it. Even more now that he'd had a few close calls with death.

"You know that I don't have a choice," Deke said.

Mitchell sighed. "I know, but it doesn't make it any easier to deal with Sam."

Deke nodded. He couldn't argue with her brother. He didn't think he had a right, and if he did, Mitchell would just fight him. Mitchell took the exit that led to the condo the women shared.

"So, you want me to back off, give you space?"

He could almost see the wheels turning in the major's head.

"Yeah. It might work better. If I am always fighting you, I have to divide my energy. It's going to be bad enough dealing with the new job."

"You took it for her, didn't you?"

He nodded. "Yeah. I…well, we had a pretty bad mission about a year ago. Lost a few guys, almost lost a few more. It made me think of what I wanted most in life. I was offered two jobs. One was in Coronado."

"You were offered a job teaching?"

He nodded. "But they wanted me here. They wanted me to be involved in planning. They have some odd idea I can help."

"You gave up the chance to teach to do something you might hate?"

"Yeah."

Mitchell sighed. "And that was for Samantha, of course."

He gave Mitchell a surprised glance. "Yeah."

"Hey, I know you love her. I know she loves you. That doesn't always mean you should be together."

Something in his voice caught Deke's attention.

"Are you speaking from experience?" Deke asked.

"What does that mean?"

He shrugged and went against his earlier thought. "There seems to be a lot of heat between you and Zoe."

"Good lord, no. That woman," he shook his head. "I've been grateful to her and Fiona for helping

193

Samantha, but I definitely don't want anything to do with that woman. She's a pain in the ass."

If it had been a friend, he would have given him crap. There was definitely something there. But he needed Mitchell's help. He pulled into the driveway of the condo.

He turned and faced Deke. "Okay, I will give you some time, but you don't make her happy and I'll make your life a living hell. You might be a Seal, but I will take you down for hurting my sister."

He eyed the younger man and knew without a doubt that Mitchell would follow through.

"You got it."

Because if he failed, he wasn't too sure he wouldn't want Mitchell to kill him.

* * * *

Sam wanted to die. She wanted the world to end, for the earth to crash into the sun, and she didn't give a damn who died with her. It was justified in her opinion. No one should escape. She just wanted to be able to eat a meal and not feel like this. It was definitely another sign to her that God was indeed a man.

"Sam?" Deke asked through the bathroom door.

Oh, God. She hadn't known they'd gotten back. She had hoped to be done with this before they did. Life just wasn't fair. Dammit, couldn't her brother and Deke find something to do?

"Open the door Samantha," her brother ordered.

"Mitchell, leave her alone. I'm her husband. I'll take care of her."

"Ex," she said weakly. She knew they couldn't hear her, but it made her feel a little better.

"Berg, I've had—"

194

"Mitchell, I think you need to allow Deacon to handle this," Fiona's calm voice cut through the rising tension.

Silence lengthened, and she could imagine her brother trying to stare down Fiona. She might be small and she might seem soft, but Fiona wasn't a woman to be messed with.

"Okay," Mitchell said.

A few moments past. "Samantha, open up, love."

She sighed and wished she was stronger, but she wasn't. Not now, and not really ever when it came to Deke. She was just so damned tired of this. Dealing with it alone had been so hard. Worse, when she'd worried that he had been called out on a mission, she had spent more than one night awake. She just wanted someone else to help her, to tell her it was going to be okay.

She crawled over to the door and unlocked it. He opened the door slowly.

He poked his head through the opening. His frown darkened when he saw her.

"Oh, baby."

She wanted to yell at him, because, by God, it was his damned fault she was in this position, but the way his voice rolled over "baby" had the tears gathering in her eyes. He came in slowly and knelt down beside her. It wasn't the most romantic setting, but it made her heart do a little dance.

"Need some help?" he asked, his voice so gentle she felt another rush of tears fill her eyes.

She nodded. He helped her up.

"I need to brush my teeth."

He said nothing. Instead, he led her over to the sink. He waited for her to finish and then cleaned off her mouth with a towel. He placed it on the counter then gave her a sweet kiss. Before she could say anything, he picked her up.

"I can walk."

"I know you can."

He said it as if it were no big deal, as if he picked up women every day.

He set her down on the mattress then tugged off his shirt. For once, he was wearing a pair of boxers. "Do you want some tea?"

She shook her head. "I just want to lie down. I hope this medicine starts working before I have to return to school next week."

He slipped onto the bed next to her and patted his shoulder. He did it all the time with her, and she loved it. "Put your head right there."

She smiled at him and snuggled up against his chest. "So, did you meet your supervisor?"

"No. He's out this week on leave. I don't have to report until a week from Monday, so I have time to find a place to live."

"Oh."

"What?"

"I thought you would just be staying here."

He chuckled. "No. I would love to, because I want to be close to you. But, I don't know if I could live with three women."

She sighed. "I guess so."

"I'd like to find something close by. What are y'all paying here, if you don't mind me asking?"

She told him, and she felt his nod. "I can probably handle that."

She looked up at him. "Really?"

"I've put on some rank the past few years. Add in the hazardous duty pay and the COLA the military gives me here, and I'm doing okay."

She set her head down and wasn't that happy with the situation. And why would she be unhappy with it?

Why did she think that he was going to be living with her and the girls? He was right. It wouldn't work.

"I can hear those wheels turning."

"What do you mean?"

Instead of answering, he asked, "What are you thinking about?"

She shrugged. "I just thought you would stay here. I don't know why. It's silly, really. That wouldn't be very good for either of us."

"You don't have enough space. I don't have a lot of furniture, but I don't want to try and fit it in this room."

She smiled. "There are a few condos for rent in the area."

"I'm sure I can find something. Why don't you get some rest?"

"And you're just going to lay here?"

"Yep. And I might just get some sleep. I've traveled a lot of hours and I got the shock of my life. It is a lot to take for a delicate flower of a man like me."

It was said with enough wry humor that she couldn't help but smile. "How are your mom and dad doing?"

"Pretty good. They were really happy I moved out here. They are kind of sick of having us all so far away."

"Your parents live in Texas. I might teach math but I know geography well enough to know that isn't right next door."

"But I'm not on call now. I can't be called up for an assignment for the three years I'm here. Unless there is a national emergency."

"That's good." And it was. Thinking of the next few years, it would be good to have him around. She might be okay with being a single mother, but she wanted him safe. She wanted him where she could keep an eye on him. And, again, her eyes filled with tears.

"Whoa, I said I wasn't going to be going anywhere anytime soon."

The panic in his voice made her cry more. It was embarrassing to be such an emotional mess.

"Sorry. I didn't mean to cry. I just can't seem to help it these days."

He patted his shoulder again. "Come here."

She did as he ordered and enjoyed the heat of him, the scent that was so familiar to her. She felt her body relaxing. He kissed the top of her head.

"You're going to just have to accept that you can't control this, Samantha."

She sighed. "I know, and it totally pisses me off."

He chuckled, and she felt her eyelids starting to droop.

"I bet it does. You just need some rest. With everything that has been going on, there was extra stress today with me showing up last night and Mitchell being an ass."

It was the last thing she remembered before she drifted off to sleep.

Chapter Ten

Deke woke later, and it took him a second to remember where he was. It wasn't that uncommon for him to be in this position. He opened his eyes and looked around the room.

Hawaii.

Then someone moved beside him, and he looked down. Sam's head was resting on his chest, and she was softly snoring. She still looked exhausted. The bruises beneath her eyes were a testament to the loss of sleep. He could kick his own ass for not contacting her earlier. He shouldn't have avoided her calls for so long, but he couldn't allow her to change the course he had charted.

She hadn't known his plans, and that was the way he liked it.

That thought caught him off guard. Was it some kind of control mechanism that he used? There was a chance it was. So to keep control of the relationship, he didn't tell her things. Okay, that made him even more of an ass. Still, there was a part of him that understood he was doing it for a reason. Telling Samantha everything wasn't always a good idea. He knew that she would often overthink things, and that came from her home life.

Unlike his parents, her folks had a marriage that had never really been a marriage. Her father had been a pilot, and he had taken the saying "what happens on TDY, stays on TDY" to heart. Deke was sure that Samantha knew of her father's affairs. Maybe not at the time, but he sensed she knew what happened by now. And that her mother had suffered for it. Two years into retirement, her father had walked out the door. Seems he didn't like being a regular civilian and hated the idea of just being home with his wife and daughter.

Samantha had been fifteen at the time, and Deke knew without a fact that she often wondered about him. Deke didn't leave because he wanted to. There was always part of him back in the US. His parents, his brother and sister...and Samantha. There wasn't a time that he thought of home, of surviving a mission, that she wasn't there in his mind.

He was just an ass for taking so long to realize she was the center of his world.

Samantha shifted against him, her body warm, and his cock reacted. He would have to do his best to curb that need.

He decided to ease himself away, but when he tried to, she moved closer and started to wake up. She looked up at him with those sleepy blue eyes, and he felt something take hold of his heart and squeeze. He knew now he had made the right decision. Even if she wasn't pregnant, he was supposed to be with her. Always.

He couldn't tell her. He wasn't a man who could always tell people how he felt, but he was usually good at showing them. And telling her would end up in a fight. He had to be careful about what he said.

Her lips curved.

"Hey."

Was it any wonder he loved her? She was beautiful inside and out. She was a dedicated teacher, one who prided herself on her work. She loved each class of kids, and like her mother, believed that everyone should have the best of public education.

"Hey, yourself. Feeling better?"

She nodded and snuggled closer. His body reacted, of course. His cock twitched, and he decided he needed to get out of bed right then and there or he wouldn't be able to resist her.

He dropped a kiss on the top of her head and tried to ease way. She tightened her hold.

"Where you going, Seal?"

He heard the desire in her voice. This was what he was trying to avoid. He wanted her more than he wanted his next breath, always did. No woman had ever tangled him up the way she did. His plan had been to resist her, to try and build the friendship they needed for a good marriage. But as she slipped over him and straddled his body, it was hard to remember why it hadn't been a good idea not to make love.

"You aren't very stealthy for a Seal."

He smiled up at her. "Yeah?"

She nodded as she tugged her shirt over her head, leaving her in a miniscule thong. It was hot pink, which he knew was her favorite color.

"I mean, you've been lying here for what, five minutes, thinking?"

He widened his eyes. "You were awake."

Her lips curved, and her blue eyes sparkled with naughty humor. Was it any wonder that every time he saw her, he lost his mind...and his heart? She was his woman, the one who had always made him feel safe...and loved. He had never known a woman with so much love.

She settled her hands on his bare chest and smiled down at him.

"I've been waiting for you to make the first move. You usually do."

He did. From the first night they met. He had always been the one who pursued. It was that spark, the moment he had seen her across the room. He knew he had to have her. It hadn't changed in all the years he had known her.

There was something different between them now. Maybe it was him. Ever since that bad mission, his view of the world had changed. He'd been in bad situations before that one, but it had affected him as no other had. Part of it was watching his friend Kade fall in love with Shannon. Deke had realized then he hadn't tried hard enough with Samantha. Now, she was staring down at him like she was some kind of predator. There was something so primal about it. His blood drained from his head as his cock hardened even more. If he'd been standing, he wasn't so sure he would have been able to keep from passing out.

"We can't really do much playing during the pregnancy, but I was wondering what it would be like without it?" she asked.

"We didn't always play."

She nodded. "Not at first."

They hadn't. Now they used it to control their urges and to fill that connection. Neither of them played with anyone else. He knew that without asking her—even though he did ask every time. He didn't and she didn't.

"But...what about now? We're older. We're...well, not that smart if I ended up pregnant. But we are a little wiser."

He felt his lips curve. "Yeah."

She moved her hips, and he groaned. He was already hard and getting harder by the minute. It had been six weeks since he'd had her.

She slipped her arms off his chest and onto the mattress as she leaned down to kiss him. He'd expected something ravenous, but instead she brushed her mouth over his without closing her eyes. She licked and nipped at his lips, and her eyes started to close. Then she pulled back.

"Stop thinking, Deke, and just enjoy."

He did just that. She slipped her tongue into his mouth. Then she started to kiss down his body, nipping and licking at his flesh as she had his mouth. When she reached the waistband of his pants, she slowly undid them. He wasn't wearing any underwear, and she was, of course, not surprised. They knew each other well enough.

She drew his cock into her mouth, taking him close, licking him, her tongue driving him crazy.

When he almost lost it, he decided to grab back some of his control. He pulled her up and then rolled them on the bed. He wanted to torture her just as she had done to him. So he kissed down her body, first licking then sucking her nipples. She moaned loudly, and he was hoping that the roomies were gone at that moment—not to mention her brother. He loved hearing her responses, and she might not have shown it with them around. He kissed his way down her stomach, dipping his tongue into her belly button, playing with the piercing there.

Then he slipped down off the mattress, tugging her panties as he went, and pulled her to the edge of the bed. He spread her legs then said, "Sit up."

They might not be able to play games, but he knew just what he wanted, what they both needed. It took her a second, and then without closing his eyes, he set his mouth against her pussy. Fuck, she tasted good. She always did, but now, knowing what he did and where they were going, she was the most delicious of treats to him. Tangy with a hint of sweetness...her essence flowed over his taste buds as he slipped his tongue into her heated core over and over. He pulled her clit into his mouth as he slipped a finger into her pussy. Her muscles clamped down on his digit as he tugged on her clit again. He could feel her orgasm, knew it was close and that she was fighting it. He kept his fingers moving in her but pulled back to talk to her.

"No rules, babe. Just feel."

She looked down at him, her eyes half opened, the very image of a goddess, and he leaned down to pull her clit into his mouth again. She let her head fall back, bracing her weight with her elbows on the mattress, and lost herself. She screamed his name as she came.

God, she was one of the most beautiful things he had ever seen. She had always been sexually in tune with him, but at this moment, he couldn't remember anything that could compete with Samantha as she gave herself over to the orgasm.

When she had finally come down, he pulled her back up on the bed and then settled on top of her. He rose to his knees, pulling her hips up. With one thrust, he entered her to the hilt. She gasped, and he immediately regretted it.

"Oh, I'm sorry, baby. Are you okay?"

She smiled up at him. "I'm more than okay. I'll be a whole lot better when you finish what you started here."

He couldn't stop the laugh that huffed out of him. He gave her a kiss as he started to move. It didn't take him long to build her back up. He took them to the edge and into a free fall.

When he was finished, he collapsed on top of her.

"Hey, Berg, you weigh a ton," she said with a laugh.

He moved to the side, taking most of his weight off her. Resting on his elbow, he brushed away some of her curls. She was flushed and smiling, with her eyes closed. He had never been able to laugh in bed before Samantha. Truthfully, he never did with anyone but her.

She must have felt his study because she asked, "Whatcha looking at?"

He could make a joke, but he didn't want to. When he didn't answer, she opened her eyes. Her smile faded.

"What's wrong?"

He shook his head and brushed away a few more of her curls. "Nothing. Just nothing."

"You have that weird look on your face like when you told me you had to go the first time after we got married."

He kissed her then, soft, sweet, before pulling back. "Just, everything's perfect. You're perfect."

She gave him a look that told him she didn't believe him.

"No. I don't think I told you that enough." She looked like she wanted to cry again, so he pressed his mouth to her forehead. "Don't worry. You feel like you could eat?"

She pulled her lip between her teeth and nodded.

"Why don't I fix us something?"

"That sounds good."

He gave her one last, lingering kiss. After cleaning up and pulling on a pair of pants, he looked back at her on the bed. She snuggled down with one of the pillows and was already falling asleep again. She looked almost innocent except for the fact that she was still naked. That contrast was almost too much to resist, but he had to. She needed rest, and they needed some nourishment. He pulled a sheet up over her and stared at her for a few minutes. He still had calls to make, mainly to his folks, and he had to find a place to live. He grabbed his phone on the way out to the kitchen. The sooner he got everything in order, the sooner he could convince Samantha that they needed to live as husband and wife again.

Chapter Eleven

Samantha sighed as she opened the front door to the condo. It had been a long two weeks since she'd returned to work after spring break, and each day made her wonder if she'd be able to make it through the entire pregnancy. She was so damned tired she barely could keep her eyes open in class.

She shut the door behind her and leaned back against it. She was just thankful the food seemed to be staying down now. In fact, her appetite was starting to come back at the oddest times, like at three am. Deke had been a sweetie about that and had gone out in search of something. On this side of the island, he didn't have much to choose from, but he had found it for her and made sure she ate it.

Sadly, he was moving into his own house at the end of next week. She knew he needed space, needed some privacy, but she was going to miss having him right there with her. His new place was only five minutes away, but she knew it would be different after that. That upset her. Seriously, she thought that maybe it would be intrusive having him there with her, but it had been...nice. They had yet to have a fight, which was really weird and a bit disconcerting.

She heard male voices and realized that there was more than one male in her house. It wasn't her brother because he had a late meeting and was coming over to go out to dinner later.

Then Zoe came around the corner with a wide smile. "There's another Berg in the house and I want him. I want him all for myself. Can I have him?"

"Another Berg?" Her brain was still dead from the long day of middle school mathematics. "Who are you talking about?"

"They say his name is Diablo, but I have a feeling that isn't his real name."

"Oh, Jonah."

"Lord, that is a sexy name. Jonah. Why do they call him Diablo?"

"Has something to do with his temperament as a child, and well, he's kind of a bad boy."

"Oh. Well, I'll call him anything he likes as long as he's naked."

"Diablo's here? You have got to be kidding me."

She brushed Zoe aside and followed the voices. They were sitting on the lanai, drinking a beer. It was odd that she had never seen them calm and joking around. She knew they were like this, had heard Deke say it enough, but she had never spent enough time with the brothers to see it. And how sad was that?

"Did you find a place? Although, I would suggest that you stay here. Three beautiful women...I would take your place."

"Don't even think about it. First, Samantha is off-limits. And you be nice to her friends. They are good girls, and they have been wonderful to Samantha. I'll kick your ass if you even think of treating them like you do the rest of your women."

"What's he mean by that?" Zoe whispered.

"He's a one-night stand kind of guy."

"I can't believe you moved over here. I might have to see if there is some kind of opening for me at Kaneohe, then we can hit the town."

"I'm not really one for the clubs anymore."

"I hear they have a BDSM club here on the island."

"Yeah, Mal's brother knows the owners."

Jonah clapped his hands together. "Hot damn, I'd like to get some of that action. Maybe we can go some night together?"

Anger tinged with jealousy swept through her. She took a deep breath, trying to calm her temper.

"Already planning to corrupt your older brother, Jonah?" she asked.

Both men turned around at the same time, and she couldn't help but smile. They were almost identical in looks except Jonah was...well, a little rougher. Deke, of course, was smiling at her. He had been doing that since he got there, and it was driving her crazy. She would deal with that later. Now, she had to deal with Jonah's bad influence.

"Hey, Sam," he said, coming forward. He pulled her into a huge hug, and she returned it. While she was irritated with him at the moment, he had always been sweet to her. He gave her a kiss on the cheek. "How are you feeling?"

"Tired. All day long with those seventh graders is starting to get really hard to deal with."

"Did you talk to my parents? They are over the moon about the baby."

No, she hadn't talked to them, and she hadn't known how much Deke had told his family. All she had in the world was Mitchell, so it had been no big deal for her.

"No. He didn't tell me," Sam said.

"So, when are you moving over with Deke?" Jonah asked.

"Now, Jonah—" Deke started, but she didn't let him finish.

"Move over?" she asked.

Jonah smiled. "Yeah, he told mom you two were going to be living together."

She looked at Deke and she heard Zoe say, "Oh, shit."

"Living together? Really."

Jonah apparently didn't hear her tone. "Yeah. The house he got should be big enough. You two will be happier near the base anyway, right?"

"Shut up, Jonah," Deke ordered.

"What?" Jonah asked.

"No, please go on, Jonah. Tell me all about it. I need to know exactly what he said," Sam said.

It was then that Deke's brother apparently noticed there was something wrong. "Ahh, I think I'll let my big brother tell you about this."

"Diablo? Why don't you come in and meet Fiona. I just heard her come in the front door," Zoe said.

Sam didn't know if Fiona did or didn't come home. All she knew was that Deke looked guilty, and that told her that what Jonah said was true. When they were finally alone, she settled her hands on her hips. "What was your brother talking about?"

"I don't know what the fuck he was talking about."

"Deacon Berg, don't you dare lie to me."

He sighed as if he were put out by the conversation, then he stood to face her. "I didn't say you were moving in. I mentioned to my mother that it was big enough for you and the baby."

"Really? And so, your mother tells your brother that I'm moving in with you?"

He shifted his weight from one foot to the other, and she knew that was what he did when he was trying to come up with something to get him out of a situation.

"Would it be that bad?"

No, it wouldn't be. In fact, she had wondered if he would ever pose the question. When she had seen the house, she had been amazed at the size and the fact that it would be for him by himself. But he hadn't asked. Apparently he had planned, but he hadn't asked. Again.

"No. That's not the point."

He frowned at her, his expression darkening. Big, bad Seal didn't like anyone questioning his authority— especially not her.

"What's the point, Samantha?"

Oh, she hated that tone, as if she were an imbecile who needed help to even walk upright.

"It's what you were planning, wasn't it?" He didn't have to answer her. She could read his expression. "So, you just come up with a plan, and when were you going to ask me?"

"It's a good plan."

"And what plan is that? One where you decide what we should do and we do it?"

"You're being a little over emotional right now."

"And why do you think that is, Deke? Really, tell me."

He apparently figured out he had stepped over the line. "I think we need to take some time to cool off."

"No, I think there will be no discussing it. I thought you had changed, but you haven't." She turned and stomped back in the house. Damned ignorant man. Just makes plans and expects her to go right along. Like cattle. She didn't say anything to her roommates or Jonah as she marched past them. She turned to shut the door to her room, but a big hand stopped her.

Oh, shit.

He was furious. Those veins in his neck were bulging, and his eyes were narrowed.

"You don't just fucking yell at me and run off."

"I do what I want."

Okay, that was immature, but she didn't care. She was tired from the long day on her feet and from pretending.

"So, what you want to do is run off like a little girl, is that it?"

"What are you trying to say here, Seal?"

"I'm saying that you're being stupid."

Even when her head was telling her to shut up, just to stop arguing, her heart wouldn't let her.

"Really? At least I'm being truthful."

"What's that supposed to mean?"

"You tell me, Deke. Tell me the truth. You come over here to the islands with a plan, being sweet and attentive, and trying to lull me into believing you changed."

"What's that supposed to mean?"

"I can't take the lying, the constant pretending."

"Have you been pretending?"

"Aren't we? In all the years we have been together, have we ever gone two weeks without a fight? No, we haven't. It's unnatural."

"You're whacked."

"I'm not. And just why were you making plans with your brother to go to Rough 'n Ready?"

"I wasn't."

"Well, maybe you should." The moment she said the words, she wanted to call them back. She didn't. She could see the implications of what she said work over his face until it faded.

"Fine." With that, he stormed out of her room. "Come on, Jonah."

She sat on her bed, and Zoe came in. She sat down on the bed beside her and said nothing. Her friend didn't always know when to shut up, but apparently she knew now wasn't a time to talk. A few minutes later, Fiona arrived.

"What happened?" she asked.

"What always happens. We aren't meant to be together," Sam said.

"That's not true," Fiona said.

Zoe rubbed her back. "You've been so happy since he arrived."

211

"I've been waiting for him to tell me what he was planning, and there you have it. He planned for us to move in together."

"The bastard," Zoe said.

She threw Zoe a look. "I know I sound like a spoiled brat, but I can't deal with the orders, the plans, all that stuff. Maybe it's better we aren't together."

"That's just stupid talk," Zoe said.

"You're afraid," Fiona said.

Sam looked at her friend. "I'm not afraid."

Fiona shook her head. "You're afraid to let him be in charge. You think he'll be like your father."

"Deke would never cheat on me."

She knew that without a doubt. When they were together, that was it for Deke and for her. They couldn't play with BDSM if they didn't trust each other.

Fiona waved that away and sat in the chair that faced her bed. "Sex has nothing to do with that."

"I would say with these two, it has a lot to do with everything. Or is it they do a lot of it?" Zoe asked.

She shook her head, knowing Zoe was trying to lessen the tension and found her first smile. Fiona wasn't smiling, though.

"You're not afraid to trust him with your body, that's fine. But if you go along with his plans, you might have to trust that you're strong enough to be his wife."

"That's a lousy thing to say," Zoe said.

But Samantha said nothing. Was Fiona right? She loved Deke, and even though she hadn't planned it this way, she was happy to be pregnant with Deke's baby. So what was holding her back?

Fiona leaned forward and took her hand. "The first time you were together, you were younger and so was he. This time will be different. But you have to apologize, and you have to tell him that you can trust him with your heart."

It hit her then. She had been holding back from him since he arrived…always. She had felt like such a miserable failure when they divorced that she had vowed never to marry again. Because if a woman couldn't make it work with a man like Deacon Berg, she wasn't marrying material. Had she been hoping they would fail?

"Your problem isn't that you don't trust him. You don't trust yourself, Sam. You are his other half. Trust that you are good enough for that and you can trust him with your heart."

"Oh, God, what have I done?" she asked.

"You can fix it," Zoe said.

"I sent him to Rough 'n Ready. Told him to go find someone else."

"He's not going to that club," Fiona said. "Trust me."

With a sigh, she said, "I guess I'll have to."

* * * *

"You have to handle women, bro," Jonah said.

"Bra or bruddah," Deke said.

"What?" Jonah asked.

"It's bra or bruddah."

Jonah rolled his eyes and looked at Mitchell. "What the fuck is he talking about?"

Deke's brother-in-law gave him a drunken smile. "He's talking like a local. That's the term they use for bro."

"Ah, and that is so important to the conversation." His tone suggested he didn't think it was important at all.

Deke didn't really give a flying fuck what his brother or Mitchell thought. All he knew is he fucked things up with Samantha again. He didn't know how things spiraled out of control, but she had been yelling at him and he had reacted. When was he going to learn?

"Back to my point. You don't know how to handle women. You never did. That woman has had you wrapped around her little finger since you met her. I thought you were the Dom?"

"I really don't want to hear about that," Mitchell said as he rose unsteadily and wandered to his kitchen.

"Sorry, man," Jonah said. He leaned forward and slapped Deke on the knee. "Anyway, we can hit all the hot spots while I'm here."

"I'm not interested."

And he wasn't. He wasn't a partier, never had been. He entered the Navy at the tender age of seventeen, and he hadn't even been able to drink. He had a few nights here and there where he blew off steam, but he had never had a need to find the next party, to keep himself occupied. That had been his brother from day one. Diablo was a name his mother had given him years earlier, and Jonah had lived up to it.

"That's just sad. I didn't think you were old. But then, she's had you tied up for years. One of these days, you're gonna have to break loose."

"Yeah, and what the fuck do I do then? Huh? Maybe I can sleep with different women, not remember their names, and hope that none of them find me because I am such a fucking moron I can't even hold onto one of them."

"Oh, I forgot what a nasty drunk you are. I should have stayed over there. That Zoe is a tasty morsel, and I think she likes me."

He opened his mouth to smack his brother down for being disrespectful, but Mitchell was quicker.

"If you want to live, Marine, I would suggest you forget all about Zoe."

The possessive tone in Mitchell's voice didn't surprise Deke. It was said mildly, but Deke knew the feeling.

214

"Christ, back down. I didn't know there was something going on between you two."

Before Mitchell could respond, Jonah stood. "I gotta hit the head. Anyone want another beer?"

Both of them said no, and he was left to deal with his brother-in-law. "I thought you said you were going to make an honest woman out of her."

"Give it a rest, Mitchell. I'm having to deal with a woman who thinks she isn't made for long term."

Mitchell's eyebrows rose. "Yeah? Where did you get that idea?"

He sighed, not in the mood for a one-on-one with him, but Deke didn't have a choice. Samantha wasn't in the mood to talk to him right at the moment.

"Your sister thinks your family can't be married."

Mitchell frowned. "Where did she get such an asinine idea?"

He wondered now if the major knew about his parents. "Your folks?"

Mitchell rolled his eyes. "My parents were whacked."

He took a sip of beer, and Deke waited. When he didn't continue, he asked, "Why do you say that?"

"My mom knew. All those years she had no problem with my father running around. Sam didn't know. Or the idea that my mother, well, she wasn't the most faithful either."

That surprised him. "Really? Sam never said anything."

Mitchell sighed. "She didn't want to see it. Mom wasn't mad when Dad left because he was unfaithful, she was pissed that he ruined the perfect family." It was said with enough scorn that Deke had no doubt of what Mitchell's thoughts were on it. "I had no idea she had thoughts like that. Wait, she was married to you?"

"Yeah, and every chance she got, she fought me. Just like tonight. It makes no sense. She would just go off on me for no reason. I know now what she was doing. She was pushing me away. Then she used the military as the final push, and I was stupid enough to let her."

"And now?"

He gave his brother-in-law a leveled look. "What do you think?"

"You left tonight."

"And somehow I ended up over here. How did that happen?"

Mitchell gave him a drunken smile. "Cuz I saw you coming out of the condo and I thought I'd offer to help to get you as far away from my sister as possible."

"I hate to tell you this, Mitch, but you suck at pushing me away from your sister."

"I know. But then, I didn't realize what a sap you are."

"What?"

"A sap. God, you looked like someone had stolen your puppy when you came out of the condo. First, you looked pissed, but I could tell it was more. It is a bit disconcerting seeing a man so head over heels in love with my sister. So, I figured I would give you a break."

"You should try it, you know."

"What?"

"Love."

He snorted. "There is a little too much truth to what my sister says. I'm not made for long term. Maybe after the military."

Deke opened his mouth, but his brother decided to inject himself into the conversation. "So, you aren't dating Zoe, right? Because I'd like to spend some time with her while I'm here."

"I said you need to watch yourself," Mitchell said as he rose.

"Gentlemen, I think we should avoid arguments when drinking. It only ends up—"

Mitchell threw the first punch before Deke could finish the sentence. With a sigh, he took a sip of beer and waited to see who won the fight. Either way, the women in his life, his mother and Samantha, would be pissed if one of them got hurt. And he would be blamed.

Today was just turning out to be a pisser.

* * * *

The doorbell rang at seven in the morning on Saturday, and Samantha hurried to answer it. The only person she knew who would show up that early was Deke. When she looked through the peephole, she was disappointed to find her brother on the other side. She opened the door and frowned. He looked like hell. His skin was gray, he hadn't brushed his hair, and he was wearing sunglasses.

"What the hell are you doing up so early if you're hung over?"

Even though she couldn't see his eyes, she knew he winced.

"Get in here." She pulled him into the condo. "You're too old for this."

"Blame Deke and that devil of a brother he has."

"Diablo...Deke? What do they have to do with this?"

"We were drinking last night."

Zoe came out wearing her scrubs. "Oh, poor baby. Did you have a little too much to drink last night?"

The last was said loud enough to hurt Sam's head.

"Quit being mean. He said he was with Deke and Diablo last night."

"They're still there."

"At your house?"

217

"Yeah, I left them there. Well, Diablo was passed out on the floor. Deke was probably out running a hundred miles or something."

Deke always could hold his liquor, but she figured pointing that out wasn't going to get her anywhere.

"Did you go out?" Zoe asked as she took Mitchell's arm and walked him into the living room.

"No, we just drank at my house. I think there was an argument. Then we were singing something, then I woke up this morning."

Zoe eased him down on the couch then set her hands on her hips and looked at him. "I'll take pity on you and get you a cure made up. Old Anderson recipe. And some ice for your head."

She gave Sam a look that told her she was giving them some time alone. "What are you doing here?"

"You need to take him back."

That took her back. "Why?"

"He loves you."

She shook her head. "That doesn't matter."

"Could you sit down so I don't have to look up? It's making me kind of sick."

She sat on the ottoman in front of the couch.

"Thank you."

"You're welcome. Now, tell me why I should take him back?"

"He talked a lot last night. About you. About the baby."

"Deke? Talked?"

"Yeah, he adores you, you know? I have never seen a man who wanted a woman more than he does."

"He left."

"Before. Not now."

"He always leaves when it gets hard."

"I am sure he did, but why did he do that? Does Deke strike you as a man who walks away easily?"

"But he does every time."

"And every time it was what you told him you wanted. I'm not saying he didn't make mistakes. He made a lot of them, but the man who talked my ear off last night wasn't giving up on you. I'd say he was just taking a break. Give him a chance. He truly adores you."

"I don't know."

He took off his glasses, and that was when she saw the shiner. "He didn't do that, did he?"

"No, that jackass brother of his did. But we worked it out."

"Men. How does the military entrust you with a million dollar plane?"

"Cuz I'm the best." He frowned. "And stop trying to change the subject. I have a question for you, and I want a straight answer."

"Okay."

"Do you think we aren't marriage material because of our folks?"

She sighed, and she blinked away the tears that burned the backs of her eyes. "I worry about that. I was married once. I screwed it up."

"You both did. I can't believe I am here pleading his case. Seriously, you both were stupid, but do you think you would end up back together over and over if you weren't meant to be together?"

"Fee says the same thing."

"Fiona's right," she said from behind them.

Samantha turned and found her standing just a few feet away. "You usually are."

"Go get him, Sam. For all three of you, do it."

Could she do it? It would mean apologizing, something she hated. And it would mean getting over her insecurities and learning to control her temper. But was it worth it? The image of Deke popped into her head.

"Okay. But I need to get one thing."

"I'll drive you back over."

She looked at her brother and laughed. "No. If I need backup, I'll take Fee. You can sit here and rest." She leaned forward and kissed his forehead. "God, Mitchell. Didn't you bathe or brush your teeth before you came over?"

He opened his mouth but Zoe came in with her vile family recipe for him to drink.

"Have fun, kids."

She ducked into her room and went to her dresser, pulling out the chain with the rings. She looked at them then slipped the chain over her head and hid the rings under her shirt.

She walked to the door and found Fee waiting for her. "Ready to go get your Seal?"

"You're damned straight."

Chapter Twelve

Deke showered and dressed, wondering all the while what had happened to Mitchell. Deke had left early to run but when he returned, the major's car had been missing.

He figured he would show up some time soon. Before he could figure out what to have for breakfast, the door opened. He expected Mitchell, so he was stunned when he saw Samantha and Fiona.

"Samantha?"

She smiled shyly. "I hope it's okay that we came over."

Deke heard something behind him, and he looked over to find his brother sauntering toward them. "Sure it is. As long as you introduce me to your friend," Jonah said.

He wanted to beat his brother. He loved Jonah, but he had one thing on his mind when he was off duty.

"This is Fee..Fiona Farelli. This is Diablo."

Fee smiled and nodded. "The Marine."

Jonah smiled at her, and Deke waited for Fee to melt. When she just continued to stare at him, Deke could tell his brother was a little disconcerted.

"Yes, the Marine."

She nodded. "Well, Diablo, is it? We need to leave these two alone. They have a lot to tell each other. Right, Deacon?"

"Yes, we do."

He was smiling as he watched Fiona herd his brother out to the lanai.

"Your brother fared better than mine."

"Looks can be deceiving. I think Jonah has some bruised ribs."

"What were they fighting over?"

"Not what. Who."

221

She studied him, her eyes clouded with confusion.

"Zoe. Your brother took objection to the idea that my brother was interested."

She chuckled. "I bet he did."

Then silence. It was odd that two people would run out of things to say when there was so much to be discussed.

"I wasn't sure if you would be here."

"Where would I be, Sam?"

"I told you to go out last night."

He looked at her, wondering if she had actually thought he would leave her that way. When he saw the look in her eyes, he damned her parents all over again.

"I love you."

She pulled her bottom lip between her teeth and nodded. "I know. I love you, too, but neither of us have been celibate."

"That's true. But can you tell me something?"

"Yes."

"Did you go out right after we broke things off? Or did you go months thinking you had just lost the most precious thing in your life?"

Tears filled her eyes. "Oh, Deke."

He stepped forward. "It was like that for me. I screwed up by walking out the door so many times. I wanted to take it back. But I figured I would let it go, and that if we were supposed to be together, we would be."

"And then we would run into each other."

He nodded, the lump in his throat making it hard to talk. He swallowed.

"You and I are meant to be together. I know that."

"I want to believe that. I do. But look at last night. Look at what an idiot I was."

"You were an idiot."

She laughed. "I was. And you walked out."

"You told me to leave. I did what you wanted."

She looked away. "I'm always worried you won't come back, but I can't seem to help myself. Every time, I just push."

"And I am going to start pushing right back. Just because we fight doesn't mean I don't love you. Now that I know better, I won't walk. I don't want to, and I refuse to do it anymore."

"How can I know that this isn't just you caring because we are together right now? The baby adds another layer to it, but what if this is just because of that, of the idea that we're starting here together?"

"It was never like that. Never." He walked over to her and took her hand. "Jesus, my whole life I wanted to be a Seal. I dreamed about it, prayed for it."

"I know," she said as she sniffed.

"Do you? Then know this. There is one thing I wanted more than that. It kept me tied up in fucking knots so tight that I couldn't think straight."

"What?"

He knew he had no way around it. He had to tell her what he had been feeling all the years he had known her. He had to or he might lose her.

"You. I was too much of an ass to admit it. Every minute I was gone, every second, you were there. Right here." He pressed their joined hands to his chest. "I should have told you. I should have made you understand."

"Why didn't you?"

"Fear."

She shook her head.

"No, it was fear. What if I told you? What if I said, 'hey honey, you're the one I need forever' and you walked away. You had walked before. It was too much for you, and I wasn't sure if you would want it now, would want to take that chance again."

"And you took a job you hate to be near me."

223

"I thought I would, but I am actually starting to like it. But, I can't say that, at least for the next few years, they won't tap me to go out in the field in case of a national emergency. You know the military. My orders might say no deployment, but if something comes up, they can pull me out. I have the training. What I want to know is if you can do it? Can you handle that if I have to do it?"

He could see her thinking about it, and his heart almost stopped then and there.

"Know that while I want to be with you, there are things bigger than us. I'm not going to do this forever, but…I have a duty. You understand that."

She nodded. "And after. What would you do then?"

"I would come back to you. I always do, babe."

"I liked what I was doing and there are plenty of things for someone like me to do. But know that the military is a duty. I swore an oath, and I have to follow through."

He would. It was one of the things she admired about him.

"But I don't live to work. That was never me. Or it wasn't me after I met you. Everything I do, everything I am, I am because of you. I am a Seal, but in my heart, in my soul, I'm your husband."

Tears welled up in her eyes. "Ex."

He sighed. "About that…"

"What?"

"Answer me one question. Will you marry me?"

"Marry you?"

"Shit, I'm doing this wrong. I want us married again. I want to have ten more kids with you."

"Ten kids?"

"Okay, not ten, but more than just one. What do you say?"

She didn't say anything for a moment and he felt his heart sink just a little.

"Why?" she asked.

He looked at her, his gaze direct. "Because I love you. Without you, I don't even want to be a Seal."

"Oh, Deke." Tears filled her eyes. "Yes."

"Really?"

"Yeah. But, I want a ceremony here, and I want a real dress. And we'll have to do it really soon, before I get big."

"Okay, but about that…"

"And we'll have to apply here for a marriage certificate."

"Sam."

"What?"

"See, before I came to Hawaii, I sort of got some information I didn't share with you."

She frowned. "What?"

Now came the moment of truth. There was probably going to be a fight, but he had her acceptance of marriage, thank God. But she would fight him.

"Uh, apparently the office where we had our divorce finalized has been, well, uh…"

She rolled her eyes. "Good lord, spit it out."

He swallowed. "We're still married. That lawyer who handled the divorced messed up the papers, so they were never really filed correctly."

For a second, she didn't say anything. Her mouth turned down into a frown. "What?"

"We're still married. The divorce didn't go through."

She shook her head. "What do you mean?"

"You are still Samantha Berg."

"Married." She pulled her hand from his and smacked him on the back of the head. "What the hell is wrong with you? Why didn't you tell me?"

225

The slap had his ears ringing and he had to shake his head to clear it. "Because I knew you would get mad and blame me."

"I wouldn't have. I blame you right now for not telling me. Deacon Berg, what the hell were you thinking?"

"That I needed to win you back before I told you."

She paced away, that sassy walk of hers in full force. God, he loved her. She was pissed beyond belief, and for some reason, that turned him on. He was a sick, sick man.

"I should divorce you on principle. No, first, I should shoot you."

She was muttering now, and he knew he had won. He walked up behind her and slipped his arms around her waist. She didn't resist. Instead, she leaned back against him and sighed. He kissed her neck. It felt good to hold her against him. He rested his chin on the top of her head.

"Tell you what. How about we have a big fancy Hawaiian wedding? Your brother can give you away, and we can do it all up right."

She leaned back to look at him. "Yeah?"

"Yeah. Mom would love it. They'd come over. AJ should be able to take some time off, and you can see that Jonah has a lot of time on his hands. Jacob should be able to get some time off the ship, maybe, but most of us will be here."

"And your friends?"

"Mal and Kade? Should be able to, if they haven't been called out."

She turned to face him then. "Can I confess something?"

He nodded and waited. She stepped back then tugged the chain out from beneath her shirt. The two rings that dangled there were familiar.

"You still have them?" he asked, his heart tightening at the sight of them.

226

She waited for him to look at her. "Always. I couldn't get rid of them."

He grabbed her then and pulled her against him. He bent his head and kissed her. It was tender, but soon turned ravenous.

"Get a room, bro," Jonah yelled.

She started laughing against his mouth. "I love you, Deacon Berg."

"I love you too, Samantha Berg. And I promise to get you another ring. Bigger."

"I'm fine with this one."

"Well, how about I take it and incorporate it in a new ring?"

She smiled. "That sounds great."

He tugged her back into his embrace. "Now, Mrs. Berg, how about we start planning that wedding ceremony."

She nodded. "I love you, Deke."

"I love you, too, Samantha."

Epilogue

Almost six months later

Deke smiled down at his daughter in his arms and then looked over at his wife. Samantha was exhausted, but beautiful. Six hours of labor and she still had that radiant glow about her.

"What are you smiling at, you idiot?"

"The most beautiful woman in the world," he responded.

She shook her head. "I think you're delirious from lack of sleep, Seal."

Deke chuckled. "No way. Scared shitless is more like it. I don't think I ever had a man threaten to do bodily harm to my most favored appendages as many times as you did."

One side of her mouth curved as her eyes closed. "I don't remember a thing."

Still cradling their daughter in his arms, Deke rose to lean over and kiss Samantha's forehead.

"We agreed on the name? Anela Dawn?"

She opened her eyes. "It seems appropriate. Angel Dawn."

He heard Mitchell and Zoe arguing in the hallway and knew they were about to be invaded. "Well, our quiet time is over."

Her smile widened as she looked at Anela then up at him. "In more ways than one. I love you, Deacon. I'm so happy you were too hard-headed to give up."

"I love you, too. And you only get until tomorrow to keep calling me names and disparaging my character."

She laughed as he leaned down to give her a kiss. Right before he touched his lips to hers, she said, "Sure thing, Sir."

The End

To claim the woman he loves, he will have to be the Dom she desires.

Surrender: A Little Harmless Military Romance

Navy Seal Malachai Dupree has everything a man could want. Well, not everything. The one woman he wants is too innocent for his Dominant needs, so he plays the role of supportive friend even if it kills him.

Amanda Forrester is tired of being treated as if she were fragile. She might have been through a rough patch losing her husband in the line of duty, but she is not a wimp. Her feelings for Mal have grown and she is more than ready to be the woman he needs in and out of the bedroom.

One night she pushes him too far and the result is more than either of them ever expected. Mal wants forever, but after losing one husband, commitment isn't in Amanda's vocabulary. What she doesn't realize is that Mal is one Seal who isn't backing down until he gets exactly what he wants: Amanda's total submission.

WARNING, the following book contains: Sexy Navy Seals, a stubborn woman, and a little submission. This book has one of those hot Duprees, so you know that you will need a glass of water to cool off. Every *Addict* will tell you that reading a Harmless book is anything BUT harmless—so read at your own risk.

Surrender

A Little Harmless Military Romance

Melissa Schroeder

Dedication

To my husband Les. After twenty years of marriage you still make my knees go weak with just a kiss. Thank you for loving me the way I am.

Acknowledgements

Again, seriously, you all know I could not do any of this without help. This marks the sixth new book from Melissa Schroeder Publishing and I am pleased that so many readers have continued on the journey with me. Thank you for your support and especially to the Harmless Addicts who continually make me laugh on a daily basis. Thanks to my personal assistant Brandy Walker who keeps me on the straight and narrow as much at possible. Thanks to Joy Harris who understands me as only another Capricorn can. And special thanks to my family. I finished off the last three Harmless books while in the middle of a move and a health crisis and without them, I am not sure I could have done it. Thanks to Kendra Egert for the wonderful cover, Jenn Leblanc for the kick ass photography, and to Chloe Vale for her hard work on editing and formatting.

Chapter One

Malachai Dupree shook his head as he turned down the aisle of freezer cases. He'd sunk so low that he was spending Friday night at Wegmans grocery store. A box of wings caught his eye, and he slowed down the cart. He should have just stopped by some fast food joint on the way back to the hotel, but he hadn't been in the mood for another meal like that. Mal studied the selection in the freezer case. Okay, this might not be much better, but at least it was different than what he'd been doing. He was still pathetic but at least he wasn't eating another burger. Friday night at Wegmans was no way for a single man to live.

After his third week at the Pentagon, he just wasn't in the mood to give a damn. Early mornings and late nights had worn old. *No.* Monotonous. That was a better word for the crap he was dealing with while on special assignment. Why anyone would choose to do the job was beyond him. He missed being out in the field, training…damn, he missed blowing shit up.

"A man like you should eat better, Dupree," the sultry southern voice said from behind Mal. He knew without turning around who it was. The voice was imprinted on his mind…and haunted his dreams.

He turned around to face Amanda Forrester smiling at him, looking just as gorgeous as the first day he'd met her. She was petite and a little more rounded on the bottom than on the top. The green, long-sleeved knit shirt matched her eyes, and she was wearing her regular faded blue jeans that hugged her full hips. The moment he heard her voice, his heart had started doing a tap dance, but seeing her had his body heating. Even the cold air from the freezer case wouldn't help.

Friend.

If he repeated the word enough times, he might remember that she was *just* a friend. His brain knew it, but his body tended to ignore any sane thoughts when Amanda was around. He reminded himself that she'd been married to one of his best friends and only been a widow for eighteen months.

"Hey, Amanda."

She glanced into his cart, making a tsking sound. He couldn't fight the smile that curved his lips when he saw the amusement dancing in her eyes. Amanda had a wicked sense of humor, and with three older brothers, she knew just how to mess with him.

"Are you going to a frat party?"

When he looked down in the buggy, he realized that it did look like a party. Beer, hot wings, and chips. Boredom had driven him to shop for food, and it was a mistake to do that after skipping lunch.

But a man couldn't admit it, especially to a woman.

"Look, woman, I live in a man house, and we eat the way we want to. And what are you doing here on a Friday night?"

She leaned her arm against the hand rest of her own shopping cart. The grin she gave him had his body heating more and his palms sweating.

"I have a morning wedding, so I figured I'd pick up something to eat."

Amanda owned her own floral shop in the Woodbridge area, not too far from the grocery store. And, dammit, he realized he drove out there for a reason. It wasn't until that moment he realized there was a Wegmans closer to the hotel he was bunking at.

"Ah. So what were you doing in this section if you think the choices are so bad?"

She let one eyebrow rise and damned if that didn't turn him on more. "First, I wasn't in this section. I was down there," she motioned with her head, "looking for a good bottle of wine when I saw you. Oh, and secondly, I'm *much* younger and I can eat this stuff. Although I don't. My mother would have a heart attack if she found out."

"I thought your parents were living in Texas?"

She laughed. "Yes, but my mother always knows."

He smiled. "Your mother and my mother have a lot in common."

Then, silence. It had been happening a lot lately. They used to have such a comfortable relationship. It had been the reason he'd taken on the task of checking up on her. Most of the guys on his Seal team were married or involved with someone. He was one of the few left that was not in a committed relationship, so he had taken to looking in on her. She had been so young, widowed, and vulnerable. Their friendship had been natural...until the last couple of months. Now, they couldn't seem to have a conversation without an awkward pause. It might have to do with the fact that he wanted nothing more than to strip her down and feast on her flesh.

Damn, he needed to escape. The more time he spent with her, the more those thoughts popped up in his head.

"Well...I guess—"

"Tell you what, Dupree. Why don't we have dinner together?"

They had done it before. Since Kyle Forrester, her husband of less than a year, had been killed on a mission, he had been there for her, as had many of the guys on the team. But now...it seemed weird.

"I was looking forward to a quiet night at home."

She laughed and patted his hand, which he tightened on the buggy to keep from reaching for her. His fingers were freaking itching to reach over and touch.

"Why not a light dinner, some good conversation, and then we can get to bed early."

He knew what she meant, but it didn't keep the image from popping into his head. Mal would like nothing better than to slip into her bed and pull her against him as they slept. She always smelled of roses. Until he met her, he had always hated flowery perfume, but hers was natural. He knew her scent came from the flowers she worked with all day long.

"Mal?" she asked.

He shook his head, trying to clear it. It was hard because the images of her wearing nothing but rose petals came into his head more often these days, and at the most inappropriate times. Like now.

"Is that a no?" she asked.

He gave his head one last hard shake and finally knocked enough brain cells loose to form words. "No, that's a yes. I mean…" He drew in a deep breath, trying to get his brain to work. "I know what a good cook you are, so I would be an idiot to turn you down."

She smiled. Not one of her little smiles, but one that lit up her whole face and brought out her dimples. He felt as if he had won the lottery. Damn, he was in trouble if that was all it took for him to get hot.

"I buy the food, you cook?" he offered.

She shook her head. "Why don't you pay for the wine, and I'll do the food?"

He cocked his head to one side. "That doesn't seem fair."

"You haven't seen the price of the wine I wanted to get. It's fair."

He laughed. "Okay, but you better fix me something good."

"You bet," she said and turned her cart around. "Come on."

He tried his best to ignore the way her hips swayed as she walked down the aisle, but it was more that a little difficult. Until he notice one or two men having the same reaction. He tossed them mean looks and hurried up to follow after her. The woman was completely oblivious, but it didn't keep them from ogling her. Mal tossed a few of them death looks and then caught up to her. If there was one thing he could do for Kyle Forrester, it was protect her from men like that.

Even himself.

* * * *

Amanda silently swore when she dropped the tongs for the third time in five minutes. Closing her eyes, she drew in a deep breath and tried to control her heartbeat. Malachai Dupree in her house. God, it was something she hadn't really thought would happen.

Well, it had before but this was different. She was different. The past six weeks she had been having daydreams about him, night dreams about him, and the stray thought about him had her brain scrambling and her body overheating. She had been acting more like a sixteen-year-old with a crush than a twenty-three-year-old widow.

"Did you need some help there?" he asked.

She glanced at him, and she found herself at a loss for words. He was leaning against the counter drinking a glass of water. The red polo shirt he wore stretched over his massive chest. He was beyond gorgeous. Sculpted muscles, dark mocha skin...and all that control. Amanda knew without a doubt he would be amazing in bed

That little quiver in her stomach happened again. Dammit.

"Amanda?"

God, she loved his voice. The hint of New Orleans threaded his deep baritone. Worse, any time he talked, she would watch his mouth. It was impossible not to look at it and wonder how it would feel as he moved it over her skin.

"Amanda?" he asked, the worry in his voice finally getting through to her.

She shook her head when he stepped toward her. No good would come of him touching her. Right now, she was barely keeping herself in check. "No, I've been dropping things a lot. Just one of those days."

He relaxed against the counter again and smiled. "Doesn't bode well for your wedding tomorrow."

"Well, there is that. But I have some helpers." And Malachai Dupree wouldn't be staring at her. Like he was now. She glanced at him as she rinsed off the asparagus. "If you want to earn your food tonight, you need to dry these off, then wrap the bacon around them."

He gave her a look that told Amanda he wasn't accustomed to a woman telling him to work in the kitchen. But he still did what she ordered.

"How did you get to be such a good cook?"

She shrugged. "Mama loved to cook. It's a family thing."

"It's hard to see General Simmons hanging around the kitchen."

She shrugged. "Mama didn't think having stars made him the commander of the household."

Mal chuckled, and her heart danced along with the tune. It was worse, much worse, with each passing day, but there was something about him, something that made her so danged happy she couldn't help being around him.

When she realized she was just standing there staring at him, she shook herself and pulled out a cutting board.

"Your family is very culinary. What happened to you?" she asked.

"What, you think I can't cook?" his voice was filled with mock disbelief. "Personally, I am offended."

She shook her head. "You were buying hot wings for dinner."

"Doesn't mean I don't like to cook or can't. Just didn't feel like it tonight. And my room doesn't really allow for it."

She sensed something in his voice and glanced over at him. "Not liking the new job?"

He shrugged. "It's temporary, only until this other person gets back. I have figured out one thing from my three weeks so far at the Pentagon."

"What's that?"

"They're all fucking crazy there."

She laughed. "Dad always called it a necessary evil for his career, but he didn't like it much either. It's why he was happy to get out with two stars. He was ready to spend time at home."

"It couldn't have been easy growing up military like that."

"There are privileges to it, too, and I'm not talking about being a general's brat, but being just a military brat. Crappy having to move every two years, but I've lived all over the world, and I speak four languages."

"There is that. I guess it isn't something I thought about before my sister got married to Kade. Then with Samantha pregnant, sort of brings it all home."

"I can assure you, it isn't always fun. It sucks a lot of the time, but I don't think I would have wanted to grow up any other way." She glanced over at his bundles. "You're pretty good with your hands, Mal."

He paused in wrapping the last bundle and then her face flushed when she realized what she had just said. Hell, she was acting like an idiot. Worse, she wanted to keep this relationship. No, not relationship. Friendship. That's all it was. All it ever would be.

She decided it was better to just pretend that she hadn't said a thing. "W-why don't you pop those into the oven? I'll get the scallops started."

It took him a second to act, and that was when she realized she was ordering him around the kitchen. Amanda knew from rumors that he was a Dom and was a member of Capital Punishment in DC. He probably wasn't accustomed to women telling him what to do.

"Do you mind?" he asked.

She noticed he'd snagged a beer. "Not at all, as long as you pour me some of that wine."

She finished mincing the garlic, then grabbed the flour and scallops. Pouring a couple of tablespoons of olive oil in the skillet, she set it to medium heat and started to prepare the scallops.

"I was surprised that you decided to stay in the area," he said.

"You've said that before, but I do like the DC area. Not so much DC, although I like being near all the touristy things, but I like the weather here, the people. I like the idea that I can walk down the street and hear five languages in just a matter of minutes. Even out here in the burbs."

"I guess that appeals to the military brat in you."

She nodded. "What about you? With Berg over there in Hawaii, and a sister and brother there also, have you thought about going for one of those teams over there?"

Even as she said it, she felt her heart sink a little. The idea he would be so far away made her sad. She had no rights to him, being only his friend, but she knew if he moved away from the DC area, she would probably not hear much from him.

"I thought about it. I like Hawaii. I like it here, though."

"Ah, you might change your mind after spending a few more days at the Pentagon."

"There is that. But as I said, it's temporary. Since the days are lean with officers, when one of us gets deployed, they grab someone else to fill in. Of course, it's odd that they picked me, being a Seal."

"What do you mean?"

"Usually, it's a last resort that they would pull someone in a career field like mine. They spend a fortune to train us, so it isn't something they like to do. But we aren't on the schedule to be active for another three months, so I guess a couple of months of me doing this will make me happy to go back out in the field."

She knew better. They didn't just pick him. She had been around the military long enough to understand that the man was being prepped for some kind of higher-up position. They wanted him to move up out of the Seals. But she wasn't going to deal with that. Most active duty people ignored her comments. Even her husband had.

She brushed that thought aside and dropped the first of the scallops into the pan. She had let the oil get too hot and it popped up onto her hand.

"Dammit."

Mal grabbed it. "Are you okay?"

"Yeah, just a little burn, nothing big."

He pulled her over to the sink. "You should be more careful."

His brow was furrowed as he studied her flesh before turning on the cold water and thrusting her hand under it.

"Mal, it's okay."

He looked up at her, and she realized that she was only inches away from him.

"Uh..."

He didn't finish. She didn't blame him. Her brain wasn't working too well, either. She could smell that unique musky scent of him as she drew in a big breath. Her breast brushed against his arm, and he shuddered.

He dropped her hand like she had a disease then turned off the water.

"You should put some cream on that hand."

Her body was still throbbing, her nipples tightened almost to the point of pain, and he was asking her to do something. Her brain would just not allow it. Not right now. It seemed to have stalled on the way his fingers had felt gliding over hers as he'd slipped her hand under the water.

She grabbed a towel and pressed it against her skin. She didn't really think she needed first aid cream, but she did need space.

"Could you keep an eye on those scallops. Turn down the heat to low while I get some cream."

He nodded and stepped out of her way. By the time she reached the bathroom, her heart was almost beating normally again. She closed the door, then leaned back against it. Holy mother of God. What the hell was that? She'd had a crush on him that she'd kept under wraps for a while. Mal was a military man, and since she'd lost her husband, she had made sure that she'd steered clear of them. It wasn't something she ever wanted to go through again.

She pulled herself together and pushed away from the door, rummaging through her medicine cabinet to find the cream. She shut the mirrored door and looked up at herself. Her face was flushed, and she could even see her pulse fluttering in her neck.

Dammit! She needed to keep away from him from now on.

But even the thought had her heart breaking. She couldn't think of being far away from him even if she wasn't romantically involved with him. She knew women who liked the thrill and would jump from military man to military man. Some even specialized in career fields like pilots or Seals. She had never been that kind of woman.

In fact, even with her husband, she had avoided it. Kyle had been military through and through, and not in the best of ways. To this day, she hadn't told a soul about what she had discovered while he had been away on that last mission. She had been too embarrassed. After that experience, she wanted nothing to do with military in the romantic way. It was hard to avoid altogether when she still had two active duty brothers and a retired general father.

She splashed some water on her face and then blotted it dry. This was just one night, one dinner. She owed Mal this home cooked meal after all he had done for her. She could get through this night and then maybe all this sexual tension she felt would disappear.

She opened the door and walked down the hall. When she turned the corner into the kitchen, the scene caught her completely off guard. Mal was standing at the stove, expertly flipping over the scallops. It shouldn't turn her on so much, but seeing him do something so mundane, so…normal, was arousing. He glanced at her and smiled, and her stomach didn't just quiver, it did a somersault.

Oh, mama, she was in trouble.

Chapter Two

Mal was happy when dinner went by without incident. It was easy to concentrate just on the food. For a guy who grew up in a family of chefs, it was hard to be impressed by others' cooking.

"So you aren't liking the Pentagon work?"

He shrugged. He'd been asked that enough from friends and family. It was as if they expected him to either say he loved it or hated it. At the moment, other than the usual problems, he just missed being in the field training.

"Too many people, too much drama. They run on a forty-eight hour day, or it seems that way."

She laughed, and he felt his heart soften. She was a woman who should always laugh. It made her eyes sparkle and her whole body shine.

And he was not supposed to be thinking about that.

"Dad talked about his first day there. He was walking in from the metro station and some guy fell down, had a heart attack. Dad and one other guy stopped. Everyone else just kept on walking."

"But he stayed at the Pentagon for a long time."

Now she shrugged. "He wanted a star. He wanted all four at one time."

"What happened?"

She took a sip of wine then set the glass down on the table. "Once he got his first star, the gold lost its shine. He had his second when mom was diagnosed with breast cancer. He said it made him realize that the next two stars didn't mean crap without her by his side, so he resigned his commission and retired."

"Oh, I didn't know your mother had been sick."

She gave him a surprised look. "How could you? I was in high school."

"She's doing fine now?"

She smiled. "Yeah, remission for years, but their slower pace life has something to do with it, I'm sure. So what are you going to do when they give you a permanent job at the Pentagon?"

He shook his head. He wasn't sure he was cut out for the Pentagon, but he had seen the knowing looks from others.

"This job is only temporary."

She snorted and picked up her glass again.

"What?" he asked.

"Take your head out of the sand, Seal. They're grooming you."

He felt his belly tighten. Mal had been worried about that. Especially after he talked to his supervisor.

"I don't think so."

"You made O-4 early, right? And no offense, but you have an excellent record, a masters, and the big thing, you're an African-American. You are too much for all those stars to resist in the Pentagon."

"So, you're telling me I should become a fuck up?"

She laughed like he'd hoped. He didn't want to worry about the future, about whatever plans they might have for him. Right now, all he cared about was keeping her happy. Forever.

Whoa, buddy, back the hell up. That wasn't his job. That was some other nameless, faceless asshole's job.

Dammit. He shoved those thoughts aside and tried to change the subject.

"How are your brothers doing?"

"Fine. Dylan is enjoying his time at the Pentagon, which I think makes him crazy. Brent is at Fort Jackson now. And our black sheep, Seth the chef, is living down in Atlanta. He's opening his new place in a couple of weeks. How's everything going with yours? I haven't heard from Nate in a while."

That caused him to pause, the beer bottle halfway to his mouth. "Nate? As in my brother Nate?"

She nodded. "I was down in New Orleans, and we went out."

He was trying to come to terms with the fact that Amanda had gone out with his younger brother Nathaniel, self-described confirmed bachelor who slept with every pretty woman he could talk into bed. And he could talk a lot of them into bed.

"Why wasn't I told?"

Her brow furrowed. "What do you mean? What was I supposed to tell you? I was in town, looked Shannon up, and the three of them were going out to eat. I went with them when they invited me."

"Oh." That sounded okay.

"The next night we did the town up right."

That had his temper boiling. "Really?"

She nodded, apparently completely oblivious to his reaction. Hell, he didn't know what his reaction was. It was...uncomfortable. He was sure the death grip he had on the bottle might break it, so he set it down.

"Yeah. You know when Kyle and I went there for our honeymoon, we couldn't do a lot of bars. I wasn't old enough, and well, you know that we didn't have enough money for stuff like that."

Of course they hadn't. Kyle had just come into the military, barely an O-2, and they didn't make a lot of money.

"I had no idea there were so many bars. I mean, definitely, it's New Orleans, so I expected a lot, but they are all packed in there tight." She laughed. "And they all knew Nate. But I bet a lot of them know all of the Duprees. The funniest part of the night was running into one of his old girlfriends. Your brother really doesn't know how to handle a woman who confronts him about being a mimbo."

"A mimbo?" he asked, his brain trying to keep up with her rundown. He was still trying to come to grips with the thought that she had spent so much time with his brother and no one had thought fit to tell him.

"You know, he sleeps around a lot. He's like the male version of a bimbo."

He chuckled and something loosened in his chest—something he knew was embarrassingly close to jealousy. It was stupid the way he was behaving. He knew they were emotions and most people would dismiss them. For him, though, it was unusual.

"That's Nathaniel."

"Well, the girl was so upset with him because apparently he said he'd call as soon as he got into town, and of course he didn't. He claimed he forgot."

She stood and started to clear the table. He watched the way her chestnut hair fell forward. It looked so soft he wanted to touch it, to feel it slip through his fingers.

Instead, he stood and helped her with the dishes.

"You staying somewhere in town, I take it?"

He shrugged. "They actually gave me a room over in Crystal City at a hotel. It's considered a Temporary Duty."

She shook her head. "Fraud, waste, and abuse."

He laughed. "It was cheaper than moving someone here."

"That's true," she said, finishing off their plates. He went back to the table and brought the rest of the dishes. He returned just in time to see her bend over the dishwasher. He almost dropped the dishes he was carrying. Lord, the woman had an ass on her. Full, but not too full, and he knew she was a walker, someone who exercised on a regular basis. He could just imagine what it would feel like to smack his hand against the firm flesh.

Take a step back, Dupree. Not yours. Too young, too innocent, too many problems.

248

He set the dishes down on the counter with a clatter. She jumped and turned around.

"Sorry," he mumbled and took a step back.

"No worries."

She apparently hadn't noticed his reaction. He rolled his shoulders, trying to get his mind off her and the way she would look if he bent her over the table to flog her.

Shit. His cock twitched at the thought, his brain draining of any remaining blood.

"I better head off."

She glanced up. Her eyes were filled with surprise then resignation, which he didn't understand.

"Of course." She shut the dishwasher and dried off her hands. He wanted to say something more, something to ease the tension that now rose between them. It had never been like this, and hell, he would rather have the sexual tension back. Now, though, he could feel something else in the air, something that felt like disgust. He wanted to do something to change it, but he didn't know how. Hell, he didn't even know what he did wrong.

He couldn't let the evening end this way. "Is there something wrong?"

She shook her head and sighed. "Just a million things on my mind for tomorrow. She's kind of a bridezilla, so I'll have my hands full."

Of course, it had nothing to do with him. She was a woman with a full life, one that didn't include a man who was too old for her and had sexual needs a woman like her would never understand.

She walked him to the door in silence, and he hated it. They had never had this issue before. She opened the door and offered him a soft, tired smile. It was then that he saw the violet smudges under her eyes and realized she hadn't been getting sleep.

"Are you getting enough rest? The insomnia isn't back, is it?"

She looked surprised and shook her head. "No. Just been a long week. Once this wedding is over, I'm going to sleep all day on Sunday."

He nodded. He moved closer, then realized he was going to kiss her. He stopped himself just short of embarrassment.

"Goodnight, Amanda."

"Night, Mal."

She shut the door, and he waited until he heard the locks slide into place. With more than just a few regrets, he headed to his car.

* * * *

Amanda sighed as she watched the bride and father walk down the aisle together.

"Feeling melancholy?" Addy asked from beside her.

She glanced at her business partner and shook her head. "Naw. Well, a little. This time there is more relief."

Addy slung her arm over Amanda's shoulders. "Don't be sad. You'll have a real wedding one of these days."

But she wouldn't. She knew it better than anyone, but she never argued with Addison Mahler. Amanda knew she wouldn't win.

"What do you say we clean up right now so when the ceremony is done, we can run away?" Addy said.

Amanda nodded and followed her back to the bride's room. They were an odd couple of friends. Addison had grown up in the wealth of DC, a daughter of a federal judge and the niece of a former attorney general. You would never know it by looking at her. From the top of her spikey purple hair—that was the color this week—down to the grunge clothing, she was the antithesis of DC upper class.

"She wasn't so bad today," Addy said. "I thought it was going to be horrible after the way she was all the way up to the wedding."

"There was a little stress inside the family."

Addy nodded. "I know. We both understand having a mother diagnosed with breast cancer, but still. She attacked my choice of hair color a few weeks ago."

"It was green. And not just green, but neon green." Amanda picked up some of the boxes they had brought the flowers over in. "Plus, I think she was worried her mother wouldn't be here for the ceremony. She lost an aunt just two years ago to breast cancer."

Addy stopped in gathering up the equipment. "Oh, I didn't know that. Well, that makes sense. Still, there was nothing wrong with my green hair. And, to be nice, I dyed it purple to match her bridesmaid dresses."

Amanda chuckled. "She did thank you."

"Not our worse, huh? I think our worst would be that Denise Charles. It was hard not to run down the aisle and rescue the groom."

"They just got divorced."

She smiled. "Oh, see, I could have saved him a lot of money."

They finished packing away their supplies and headed out to the van. "What do you have on tap tonight? Why don't we go clubbing?"

"Addy, I don't know how you do it. All day at work and out at night. And worse, I'm five years younger than you."

"So that's a no, right?" she asked. "You have no social life."

They were walking up the path to the church. "I have a social life."

"You can't count these functions as a social life, even if you go to the reception afterward. Are we going to this one?"

She hadn't thought about it. They'd made the arrangements and they usually went and checked, but they had worked with the reception hall before, and it wasn't part of the contract. Amanda had thought a hot soak in the tub sounded heavenly, but now going back to her little apartment didn't hold the same appeal.

"I heard they were going to have shrimp."

Addy glanced at her. Four inches taller than Amanda, her best friend could eat just about anything. It was disgusting, and if she didn't love her like the sister she never had, she would hate her.

"You don't say."

Amanda shrugged. "Yeah."

"Is there some reason you don't want to go home?"

Addy was a little too smart for her own good. From the moment they met in a survivor's support group, they had hit it off. Addison's older brother had been killed by a roadside bomb in Iraq, and Amanda had been dealing with the repercussions of the death of her husband and the lies he left behind.

"Nope. I just think a nice big meal, then a relaxing night in is just what I need."

"You did that last night. I know you went to bed before ten."

Of course she had. She hadn't had much sleep because images of Mal looking at her with heat in his eyes had kept her awake all night. She had never seen that look on his face before and it made her...burn.

"Ohhhh, what's his name?"

She glanced at Addy and saw the interested look in her eyes. Dammit. "What do you mean by that?"

"You got a dreamy look on your face, and I have never seen that look on your face. Well, except when you talked about going to the Netherlands for the tulip shows. Did you hook up? Come on, tell me."

She sighed. "I did not hook up and there was no dreamy look on my face. Mal was over last night for dinner."

"Dupree? You had him over for dinner? And you didn't invite me?"

She chuckled. "It was by accident. We bumped into each other at Wegmans."

Addy let out a little sigh of pleasure. "Wegmans. Wait, let me think about that place for a sec." She stopped walking, closed her eyes and hummed. "I love that place."

"Yes, I know you have an abnormal attachment to Wegmans."

"There is nothing abnormal about it. So you bumped into him, and then how did he end up sponging a meal off you?"

"I invited him."

There was a beat of silence. "You invited him over on a Friday night?"

"Yeah. You should have seen what he was eating. Some kind of wings or something, it was disgusting. And I was in the mood for scallops--"

"You made your pan seared scallops and didn't invite me?" Addy asked, pouting again. "I can't believe you did that."

"You had a date last night."

"Oh yeah, he was boring. And definitely not a Seal I have a crush on."

"You have a crush on Mal?"

She rolled her eyes. "No, you do, Amanda."

She sat down in one of the chairs lining the hallway in the back of the church. Since there was a row of windows and a door that separated them from the wedding guests, she felt free to talk. "I do not."

"Yes, you do. Remember, I've seen you with him. You get all goo-goo over him, and I say about time."

253

She sat down next to Amanda with a satisfied smile on her face.

"I do not, and if I was ready for another relationship, I would definitely not pick a Seal. There is only heartbreak with those guys."

She could feel Addison's study of her, but she said nothing else. Amanda told Addison just about everything, but she hadn't told her about the worst part of her marriage. Even being a smart woman and knowing her husband's infidelity had nothing to do with her but was a default in his personality, Amanda couldn't help but be embarrassed by it. It was the one thing that she would keep to her grave.

"Let's just get through this, get some good food, and then I am spending all day in bed tomorrow with a book. In fact, I might just move only for food."

"That sounds like an excellent plan. I can't do it myself because I have been summoned to the family estate for brunch. Wanna come protect me?"

"No. First of all, your father has a big house, not an estate. And secondly, you don't need my protection. You have your father wrapped around your finger."

There was a look in Addy's eyes that had Amanda pausing. There was a vulnerable quality to her, then it disappeared in an instant. "Dad said something about ham."

"No. I am going to be completely selfish for one day."

"Fine, but I will tell Dad that you refused to come."

Amanda rolled her eyes. "I'm sure he'll really care about that."

"He likes you."

"I didn't say that, but he wants to see you."

Addy sighed. "Yeah, I know. I just hate that there will probably be another lawyer there he tries to fix me up with. That lawyer will take one look at my purple hair and freak out."

Amanda slipped her arm over her friend's shoulders. "But he loves you."

Addy sighed. "Yeah. So you won't help me?"

"You're on your own there, kid. I'm going to vegetate."

Chapter Three

The next morning, bright and early, Amanda was putting on her walking shoes and complaining about her damned fantasies. All night long, she had been dreaming of the man she shouldn't even be thinking about that way. Malachai Dupree.

Her plans of being lazy had dissolved ten minutes into her lazifest. She cursed her imagination and pulled her hair up into a ponytail. Her brain would not let her just vegetate. Instead, Mal was there, laughing with her, letting her cry on his shoulder, silently holding her hand the first time she went to her husband's grave in Arlington.

Dammit. Tears burned the back of her eyes, and she scrubbed her hands over her face. As she had learned before, the best way to deal with her feelings was to go out for a walk, think, and let the exercise work its magic on her negative mood.

Ten minutes later, she was walking on the path near her house, enjoying the day. It was cloudy, the hint of rain in the air, and cool enough not to cause her to sweat too much. She loved the DC area for just these kinds of things. She loved seasons, loved the fall, the winters, the springs and summers, and especially liked that she could find a good place to walk or run even out in the boonies. The hot summers in Texas were too much for her to take, and she wasn't sure she could ever give up the mixture of culture in the DC area.

She was just getting into her walk, listening to the latest Nora Roberts book on her iPod, when she heard someone yelling. She turned just in time to have a biker run into her. She fell back and had no time to brace herself. Her butt hit first, her back, and then her head conked hard against the pavement.

"Oh my goodness, I am so sorry," an older woman said. She was leaning over Amanda, her face creased with concern.

"Mildred, I told you we should do this at home," said someone else, a man, but it was hard for her to tell. She was still seeing stars and her ears were ringing.

"I didn't want our neighbors to see me try to learn how to ride a bike."

"Yes, injuring a stranger is even better." Even with her head spinning, she could hear the sarcasm in the old man's voice.

"Dear, are you okay? Do you need help up?"

They each took an arm, and she tried to stand, but the world around her started to spin. The colors of the surrounding landscape blurred.

"Oh, that's not good," she said weakly as her spinning world went to complete black.

* * * *

Mal's heart was pounding so damn hard as he hurried into the Potomac ER. He rushed to the information desk. "I'm the POC for Amanda Forrester."

"Are you her husband?" the woman asked.

"No. I'm...was a friend of her husband's. The ER called me and said she had been injured."

The woman nodded to the people behind the counter. "This one's here for Forrester." She turned back to Mal. They'll let you in."

There was a buzz and he strode over to the doors. A round, happy nurse smiled at him. "She's right down here in room 5F."

"How is she doing?"

"Fine. She hit her head, and they are talking of admitting her for that reason. But I'm not too sure Ms. Forrester agrees."

She opened the door, and he felt his heart slide down into his stomach. She looked so damned pale. She had bandages on both hands. There were dark circles beneath her eyes and at that moment, she looked so still.

"We're keeping the lights dimmed because they hurt her eyes."

"Concussion?"

"Slight. Not anything major."

"I hear you whispering over there," she said, a smile playing about her mouth. "I didn't lose my hearing, Nurse Brady."

The nurse chuckled. "If I thought you were sleeping, I would have had to wake you up."

She slowly opened her eyes. "Mal, they called you."

"I'll leave you two alone. Ms. Forrester, just so you know, the doctor is not giving up on you being here overnight."

"Tell him to stick it."

The nurse giggled and left them alone.

"I see you're already making friends," he said. He tried to keep his tone light, but it was hard. His throat was still tight. He had never known terror like what he felt getting that call.

"Come on in. I don't bite, Malachai."

He collected himself and walked to the side of her bed. "How are you doing?"

"I've had better days. You?"

"Well, I was having a great day until they called me."

"You can go now."

He heard the amusement in her voice, and he smiled. "Not a chance. I didn't know I was on your list of contacts."

She shook her head, and he thought it was more about clearing it than it was to deny what he was saying.

258

"Remember, you said to put you on there after Kyle died, that I was to put you on there."

He had, but it had been over a year and her brother had moved to the area. He was trying not to let the fact she left him on her contact list get to him, but it was hard. And he was in big trouble if just a simple thing like that was getting him excited.

"I thought they would call your brother."

"They did before I was coherent enough to tell them he was still on TDY in San Antonio. Addy is out at her father's, so I didn't want to bother her."

"Nothing like being a woman's last resort to make a guy feel good about himself."

One side of her mouth curved, and he felt the flutter in his chest that he hated. The one that kept him up at nights, and the one that was making it damned hard to find another woman.

Pushing that thought aside, he moved to sit in the chair beside her. She looked so small lying there on the bed. Mal knew she hated being considered fragile. She was a tough woman, but at the moment she didn't look that way. It was damned hard not to gather her in his arms to hold.

"I thought you said you were going to just rest today?" he asked.

She pouted, and he had to resist the urge to kiss it away.

"I was, but I just couldn't settle."

"Really?" he asked, not trying to hide the disbelief in his voice. She never did settle that he had seen. Amanda always had something going on, as if she never slowed down.

"*Really*. Sometimes when I have a big job like yesterday, I get too caught up in the work, and it's hard to just be still. My mind jumps from one thing to another. Concentration gets hard."

"So you decided to run?"

"No, I decided to go out for a walk. It was hard to ignore such a pretty day."

"Only you would think today was a pretty day."

"I like fall. No, I love fall, especially when we have those storms move through."

Before he could berate her for not taking care of herself, the doctor slipped into the room. He was wearing scrubs. He strode toward Mal with his hand outstretched. "I'm Dr. Franklin. You must be Mr. Forrester."

"Ah, no. I'm a good friend." He leaned forward and lowered his voice. "Her husband was killed in the line of duty."

The doctor nodded in understanding.

"I didn't lose my hearing. You can say my husband is dead. I can take it."

She had that grumpy voice he recognized. She didn't feel well, and now she was going to take it out on everyone. Amanda could usually smile through anything, but when she was irritable, she couldn't hide it. But that was one thing he loved about Amanda. She never tried to hide her emotions.

"Well, Ms. Forrester, you're going to have to stay overnight. You have a slight concussion."

Her eyelids lifted slightly, and he could read the irritation.

"I don't want to." She sounded like a toddler denied a treat, but he understood. Mal wasn't the best patient either. He really hated hospitals and could never feel comfortable in one.

"You live alone according to your chart. When I saw…"

"Malachai Dupree."

The doctor nodded. "I thought he was your husband and someone would be with you through the night. But since you do live alone, you're going to need to stay here. You need someone to keep an eye on you."

"What about your brother?" Mal asked

"I told you, he's TDY."

Malachai nodded. Her brother had been assigned to the Pentagon like him, but he was working in some kind of job that had him out of town a lot. "I can do it."

The moment he said the words, he wanted to pull them back. It wasn't a good idea for him to stay the night at her place. But the grateful look she gave him was a little too much to resist. He knew she hated the idea of being stuck in the hospital, and if they couldn't get a hold of Addy, Amanda would be stuck there all night. The doctor looked between them. "You'll have to stay through tomorrow."

He filtered through what he needed to do tomorrow, then nodded. "I have to make a few phone calls, but I can swing it."

"Okay."

"I don't need to be taken care of," she said, her voice filled with irritation. She was going to give him issues if he didn't nip this attitude in the bud.

Mal saw the doctor open his mouth, but he stopped him.

"Stop being a whiner, Forrester. Do what the doctor wants or I'll call your folks."

Her eyes sparked with anger. "Not fair."

"Most of life isn't. Get used to it."

With that comment, he stepped out of the room and into the lobby. He had some things to move around at work. He pulled up his supervisor's number on his cell and tapped it. He would definitely have to summon all his legendary control to keep himself in check.

* * * *

261

Amanda came awake slowly. For a moment, she couldn't figure out where she was but then she realized she was home in her bed. The faint light peeking out from behind the blinds told her it was morning. She didn't move. Instead, she lay motionless, assessing her bodily injuries. Lifting her hands, she inspected the bandages on them. Her palms no longer stung from the fall to the pavement but her body still ached from the bumps and bruises created by the impact.

She tried to sit up, pulling herself up with her arms, being careful of her palms. The room spun and her stomach started to revolt. Oh, not good. Her head might not hurt, but she wasn't so sure that she could move at the moment. Swallowing, she lay back down and closed her eyes.

She still felt as if she'd been hit by a bus. Along with the pain of the injury, she hadn't had much rest. Just knowing that Mal was in her apartment had her itching. Sure it wasn't romantic, but she hadn't had a man spend the night since Kyle had left—except one of her brothers. And they didn't count as men.

After a few moments, she couldn't ignore the fact that it had been hours since her last trip to the bathroom. As carefully as she could, she sat up again, then slipped out of bed. It only took her a few moments to finish her task. She looked down at her shorts and T-shirt. She really didn't feel like changing, but she couldn't walk out into the living room like this. She tugged off her shorts and grabbed a pair of PJ bottoms, then made her way to the living room.

It was then that she heard the low murmur of voices. She saw the couch was empty and followed the voices she heard into the kitchen.

Mal stood there cooking, with Addy leaning against the counter drinking a large mug of coffee.

"You said the doctor said she was okay, right? We don't have much going on this week other than normal orders. After this weekend, Amanda wanted to take it easy."

"I think you should try and keep her from being at work this week."

She saw Addy nod. "I can do that."

Irritation slinked down Amanda's spine. She hadn't let anyone rearrange her life in a good long while, and she wasn't about to start letting people take over now.

"I think I can handle my own schedule."

Addy jumped a little bit and looked guilty. Mal, damn him, just kept working on whatever he was cooking. He had probably known she was there the entire time. Freaking Seal.

"What are you doing out of bed?" Addy asked as she approached Amanda with concern darkening her large blue eyes.

"I..." She didn't want to say she had to pee in front of Mal. "I was sick of being in bed."

"You haven't been there that long," Mal said conversationally. "You have two choices. Go back to bed or lay down on the couch. Doc said to rest today."

She frowned at his back. "I don't think I put you in charge, Dupree."

"Call me a natural leader then. You go, or I put you there."

He hadn't raised his voice, not even when he'd issued his threat. Amanda hated it just as much as she hated how her body reacted to it. Heat feathered over her flesh as she thought of the way his voice easily rolled over the words. She didn't like it, not one bit. Somehow she needed some space. She opened her mouth to argue with him, but Addy slipped her arm around her waist.

"Come on. He's making omelets that look as good as they smell. And you know how you like them."

"Okay, but just so you know, I don't have to spend the day in bed."

Again, without turning around, Mal answered. "I think you'll do what I tell you to do."

Why did that turn her on so much? Probably because she had a concussion. Before she could answer him, Addy led her away to the couch. "I know you want to blast him. Save your energy for arguing later."

"I don't want to be treated like an invalid."

"Ah, except for the fact that you are an invalid. A concussion is nothing to play fast and easy with."

Amanda allowed Addy to sit her on the couch and then fuss over her. She knew it was her way, especially with someone who had been injured.

"I guess you decided not to call me because you hate me?"

Amanda recognized the sardonic humor in her friend's voice.

"So, the visit with your father was bad?"

Addy set her hands on her hips. "He invited that guy again."

Amanda chuckled. "The lawyer."

"Yep. It's like, I couldn't make you a lawyer, so I'll hook you up with one and hope that we succeed in getting grandbabies who don't embarrass us."

"Oh, Addy, he isn't embarrassed by you."

"You didn't see the look on his face when he saw my hair."

Amanda glanced up at the bright purple. "It is a bit shocking. How did Larry take it?"

"Larry?"

"The lawyer?"

Addy laughed. "His name isn't Larry. I just called him Larry the Lawyer because, well, because."

There was something in her voice that caught Amanda's attention. "You like him."

264

She pouted. "No, I don't. "

"Yeah, you do. Well, you're attracted."

"It's hard not to be. He reminds me of Channing Tatum. So there's that. But his personality is just not what I look for in a guy."

"And, considering I have met some of those guys, what are you looking for? They all seem to be…different."

Addy's eyes narrowed. "May I ask what you are implying?"

Amanda shrugged. "Nothing really, just that there is a thin line between love and hate."

"Really? And that line is there between you and Mr. Hunky Seal?"

The snort escaped before she could stop it. "I would love to see his face if he heard you say that."

"All I know is I get a phone call this morning, before six a.m. I might add, telling me you had been hurt and that you were taking the day off. When I said I wanted to see you, he refused at first."

"He refused?" Amanda asked, her temper bubbling a bit. The man had nerve trying to order her friends not to come.

"I got the feeling that he wanted to make sure I wouldn't bother you." Addy crossed her arms and snorted. "As if."

"You're too old to use the term 'as if.'"

Addy ignored the comment. "I was ready to blast him when I got here. Telling me what I can do, and before six a.m. and decaffeinated. But I got here and he looked so grumpy that I couldn't help but ignore it."

"I am sure it has nothing to do with the fact that he is gorgeous."

"Like that would matter. The vibe I got from him tells me that he could care less about me."

"What kind of vibe? And since you mentioned you don't like guys telling you what to do, I would suggest that you rethink that. He's not only military and a Seal at that, but he's a Dom."

Addy rolled her eyes again. "Not that kind, although for him, I might forgo that worry. No, I would say it was more a vibe toward you."

It was Amanda's turn to roll her eyes. "If there is any kind of vibe, it's a brotherly one."

"Uh, you have been without a man too long. Men do not, *repeat*, do not read me the riot act for not being reachable to you. Not the way he did it."

Amanda didn't like the way her heart jumped at the description. She shouldn't be so damned happy that a man called her best friend and yelled at her in the morning. And it didn't prove anything. Maybe he was just irritated and tired. Her couch couldn't have been that comfortable.

Amanda shrugged. "You have a lousy track record with men, so I'm not listening to you."

"I know enough to know that man has a thing for you. Guys like that don't play nursemaid for nothin'."

She opened her mouth to refute it again, but Addy popped up. "I have to go open the shop. You know we have nothing scheduled today other than regular shop hours."

Before Amanda could stop her, Mal stepped into the room. "Doc said Amanda should stay home for the next couple of days."

She shook her head and had to fight wincing. "Now, I can stay home today, but I need to go in tomorrow."

The look Mal shot her told Amanda that she was in for a fight.

Again, before she could say anything, Addy agreed. "No problem. See, the boss here didn't schedule anything big this week after the Washington and Michelson wedding."

"Boss?" Mal asked. "I thought you were partners."

"Yes, but Amanda runs the schedule. You don't even think of changing anything without an hour conference with her. I mean, she schedules everything down to the minute. Then, throw a kink into the schedule and she will hunt you down and kill you."

"Really?" Mal asked, and she could feel his gaze resting on her. Her face started to burn.

"Yes. You know, one time there was this groom who was military, and he was late to his wedding and she lost it on him. He wasn't fully dressed when she burst into the groom's room at the church and gave him a dressing down that would have frightened even the scariest of drill sergeants."

"I thought you were leaving to open the shop?" she asked and winced inwardly at the prim tone in her voice.

"Right, *boss*," Addy said with a smile. She leaned down, gave Amanda a kiss, then abandoned her.

She looked at Mal, who was still standing and watching her as if he were on a security mission and she was his detail.

"Eat."

She frowned at him, but she wasn't going to say no. She could already smell the gooey cheese and eggs, and her stomach rumbled. Mal watched her as she picked up the plate and started to eat.

"If you stare at me, it's going to make me nervous." He didn't stop looking at her. "At least get yourself something to eat and sit down."

He sat. "I ate earlier."

She nodded as she gobbled up the eggs. She knew he would have been up at dawn, especially considering he slept on the couch. There had been enough room in her bed for him. Waking up next to him would have been much better than waking up alone.

Oh Lord, that wasn't where her mind should be going. Thinking about Mal in her bed was not a good idea. It led to thinking about all kinds of silly things like…would her sheets smell like him when he left?

She cleared her throat. "Don't you have to go in to work today?"

"I took the day off."

"Oh, Mal, I didn't mean for you to do that. I didn't even know that you could take time off during a deployment."

He shook his head and leaned back in the chair, stretching out his long legs. "No problem. I always have 'use or lose' leave come September, so it never hurts to take a few days here and there. And when I explained who you were, there was no problem."

She nodded and took the last bite of omelet. Of course it was because she was Kyle's wife. It was something she admired in the military. Whether you liked each other or not, you were a family of sorts, and especially with the Seals and other special forces. The constant deployments made it hard for many of the families to cope. A little help from other people in the group was usually normal. She just hadn't expected it to last so long after Kyle's death, but then Mal was different.

She swallowed the last bite and tried to ignore him. It was hard because he was staring at her as if he were worried she would pass out.

"What?"

"Just making sure you keep it down."

She snorted. "No nausea here. I know the warning signs of a concussion."

He cocked his head to watch her. "Had experience with it?"

"Two brothers who played football. And all three of those idiots used to beat the hell out of each other."

He nodded as he stood and took the plate from her.

"I thought you should take it easy today. If you have some pain, the doc said it was okay to take the meds we got last night."

She was about to refuse, but when she shook her head, pain radiated through it. "Maybe I'll take you up on that."

He nodded again and then left her alone to her thoughts. Which, with Malachai Dupree, was a problem. Now that Addy had put it in her head that he was somehow attracted to her, she couldn't get the idea off her mind.

She thought back over the last eighteen months and his support. Her folks had been great. Her brothers...not so much, but they were guys who had never handled her tears well. There had been a part of her that thought of moving back to the safety of Texas. Her parents were there, and that's where she went to high school. They had made no concrete plans about the business, so if she had decided to run back to Texas, Addy would have understood.

But there was one thing Amanda realized about herself in that year after Kyle died. She was too much like her father, which meant she was too damned stubborn to give up. Addy had helped, but the big part of her recovery had been through help from Mal. He had always been there when he could. Being a Seal, he was gone a lot, but he always checked on her when he was in town. And there were those pics from his travels and the Hawaiian weddings.

"Here you go," he said as he approached her with a pill and some water. "The doc said these might make you sleepy, so he wanted to wait at least twelve hours past the time of the accident."

She nodded as she downed the water.

"So what are your plans for me today?"

For a moment, he didn't say anything. He got a really weird look on his face. Heat swept through her body in embarrassment, tinged with arousal.

"What I mean is what am I allowed to do today?"

He rolled his shoulders and took the glass from her. "Not much. They wanted you to rest."

"Mal, I can really take care of myself if you need to check in."

"What do you mean?"

"My dad was at the Pentagon, so I know what they expect of you. You can go to work."

He pursed his lips then rolled his shoulders again. She got the distinct feeling he was irritated, but she didn't know why. "Trying to get rid of me, Forrester?"

She snorted. "No. It just makes me feel weird getting waited on."

"Something wrong with that?" he asked.

"I'm just not used to it."

"Are you telling me Kyle never pampered you?"

She snorted again, but this time it was to hide the pain. "No. No, he wasn't into romance that much."

Not with her, anyway. He apparently ran up a bunch of bills sending someone flowers. There was also a weekend in New York. She was so happy to pay those off for him after he died. She noticed that Mal was watching her, and she decided it best to think about something else. Kyle's cheating had been something she refused to let anyone know about.

"Why don't we watch one of those SyFy movies?"

He smiled like she knew he would. "Sounds good. Did you record the newest one?"

She nodded and snuggled down on the couch. "Sure did."

Their mutual love of the campy movies had been a surprise and a delight. They had spent many nights sharing popcorn and laughing at the crazy antics on the TV.

He sat back down and grabbed the remote to start the movie, and Amanda settled back against the pillows. If this was all she was going to have, it would be enough.

Chapter Four

Mal watched her sleep. It wasn't hard to do. She had tried to stay awake, but she'd only made it through the first fifteen minutes of the movie.

She looked good. The color was back in her face, and she no longer looked that fragile. Still, he was worried. A hit like that wasn't the best thing in the world. He knew he was overreacting, but there were things he couldn't handle and this was one of them.

He needed to know she was okay. It was the same with his family. He couldn't even fathom one of them getting hurt. Chris knew it and had ordered the family to keep quiet about Jocelyn's problems a few years back. They had eventually told him, but he had been going through Hell Week at the time. Mal had been pissed, but he had understood. He knew his brothers in the Seals would be under fire, that there was always a chance he would lose one of them. One thing he needed was to know those he cared about were safe.

He leaned back in the chair and thought about getting a little catnap in. He hadn't slept much the night before. The doc had said Amanda would be okay, that the concussion wasn't that bad, but Mal couldn't keep from peeking into her room every thirty minutes to make sure she was still okay. It had been almost too tempting. She had a huge bed, and seeing her lay there snuggled against her pillows had made him want to slip in beside her, pull her close, and snuggle there with her.

But he didn't have that right. The need had been almost overwhelming, but Mal knew that his role was as a friend and nothing more.

He was dozing off when the front door buzzed. He glanced over at Amanda and noticed she hadn't budged.

He padded to the door and looked out the peephole. Dylan, her brother.

Mal opened the door.

"She's okay?" he asked without saying anything else. Mal moved out of his way as Dylan stepped over the threshold of the apartment. The worry in his expression was easy to see. "Mom and Dad said it wasn't that bad."

Mal nodded toward the couch. He saw the man's shoulders relax.

"Let's talk in her bedroom so we don't wake her up," Mal said.

The major followed him in, and Mal closed the door.

"The doc said a mild concussion, although she lost consciousness for a few seconds after it happened. He took an MRI and everything looked okay other than that, but she needs to see her doctor next week. She rested all night."

"I appreciate it. Mom was going to fly up here, and Dad and I talked her down."

"You were in San Antonio?"

He nodded. "I had TDY at Fort Sam that I extended a few days so that I could spend some time with the folks. They've been complaining none of us come down there anymore, so I thought this would be perfect. Of course, I should have known something like this would happen. Amanda always did have the worst timing."

"Amanda didn't cause this," he said.

It wasn't until Dylan gave him an odd look that he realized how mean he had sounded. He didn't have the right to get pissed at her brother, but the thought that she had no one here to watch out for her when he was gone was irritating Mal. He had thought he could count on Dylan, but apparently his support was sketchy at best.

"No, she didn't. You're sounding like it's worse than you let on."

It wasn't. It was a bump on the head. It was just the idea that if he had been deployed, she wouldn't have had any kind of backup apparently. Amanda was the kind of woman who was always there for people, but when she needed someone, she hadn't had anyone to call.

He pulled back his temper. She wasn't his so he shouldn't be getting so damned angry on her behalf.

"She's fine. She has some meds," Mal said as he slipped into the bathroom and then returned with a bottle of painkillers. "I gave her one about thirty minutes ago, so she should be good to go."

"Mom and Dad really appreciate you taking care of her. She thinks she doesn't need anyone, but she does."

He studied her brother for a moment, and then it hit him. "You took that horrible job because of her, didn't you?"

Dylan sighed and settled on the bed. "Yeah. Don't get me wrong. It will help my career, but I still would have taken the job if it ruined it. Amanda's...well you have to know how she keeps everything beneath the surface."

"Yeah," Mal said.

"Mom wanted to move up here, but then they were worried that if they did, Dad would be lured back in to the Pentagon and politics. He just can't resist it, and it isn't what they want now. So this job popped up and I got it."

"Amanda's doing fine."

"You think?" Dylan shook his head. "Then you don't know everything about her."

"Explain."

He rolled his shoulders. "Amanda had it tough being the youngest and a girl. We terrorized her so much. She just wanted to be one of the boys, and she thought by doing what we did, she would fit in. By the time she was seven, she rarely cried. I mean, what little girl doesn't cry when she breaks her arm climbing up a tree?"

"A tomboy."

Dylan snorted. "Yeah, and then some. Of course, Seth and I got in a lot of trouble for it, which she enjoyed."

"Why did you get in trouble?"

He smiled, and Mal saw even more of the resemblance between Dylan and his sister. The quick grin, the sparkling green eyes—he was the male version of Amanda. "We dared her."

Mal chuckled. "And Amanda can't deal with anyone daring her."

Dylan gave him an odd look and then nodded. "You do know her well. Anyway, she fell, we panicked, and during all the yelling and screaming, not to mention the smacks to the back of our heads, she never cried. Not once did she shed a tear in front of us. So I had to get the next flight back or you would have been dealing with my mother, and believe me, the no crying doesn't extend to Mom."

Mal smiled. "If you want to go back to your place and clean up, I can wait."

He shook his head. "I'll take care of that later. Maybe I can talk her into staying at my house in Arlington."

"Yeah, good luck with that, Major."

"Just what are you two plotting in here?" Amanda asked sleepily.

Both of them turned at the same time, but Mal knew Dylan's heart didn't turn over at the sight of her. Her hair was a mess, a tangle of silky locks tumbling over her shoulders. She was rubbing her eyes as if trying to wake herself up, and he could imagine she was having a hard time doing so. The pain killers were strong.

"What are you doing up?" he asked.

She frowned. "You guys aren't really quiet."

"Yeah, like you can talk," her brother said as he rose from the bed and hugged her. "Mom wants to talk to you today. And I'll warn you, unless you want both of them here, you will make sure to ease her worries. She was halfway packed before Dad and I convinced her to stay in San Antonio."

She smiled as she kept her arms locked around her brother. They had a family much like Mal's. They were close, closer than most families, and he knew that came from being a military family, but there was more there. The love they felt for each other was never hidden.

"I can take care of her now, Dupree," Dylan said. "I was already scheduled for a few days after the TDY, so I'll stay here and take care of the invalid."

That earned him a punch from Amanda. "Suck it, Dylan."

He studied her for a second, a frown marring those movie star looks of his. "Get in bed or I will call Mom and tell her you want her here."

Amanda matched the frown. "You fight mean."

"You should know that by now."

She smiled at him. "Thanks again, Mal, for taking care of me."

"Anytime," he said. "Call if you need anything."

He didn't want to leave. He wanted to stay and make sure she was cared for. He knew that Dylan would look out for her. Still, there was a part of him that wanted to make sure that everything was taken care of, and for some reason, he was the only one who had the right to watch over her.

He said nothing else as he stepped around the brother and sister. He just needed to remember the woman wasn't his for the taking and he would be fine.

But as he was driving back to his room, he wondered just when his body would start listening to him.

* * * *

"What's going on with you and Dupree?" Dylan asked her.

Amanda had just taken a sip of water and choked on it.

"What?" she asked and tried to cover her dismay by patting her lips with a napkin. She didn't need her brother embarrassing her with Mal. Sure, she had a little crush on him, but it was no big deal. Really.

Dylan was studying her like he was trying to put a puzzle together. And that was bad. Really bad. Dylan loved puzzles. "There's something going on there, and I'm not too sure I'm that happy with it."

"All those slaps to the back of your head Dad gave you must have knocked something loose. There's nothing going on. Mal thinks he needs to take care of me."

"No. Well, okay he does, but it has more to do with the fact that he wants to be here. When I told him he could go, you should have seen the look on his face."

She frowned. "What do you mean?"

"He was going to argue. I could sense it."

She shook her head and was happy that for once that day, it didn't send the room spinning around her. It meant that she should be able to handle work tomorrow.

"He wasn't going to argue. He just disagrees with me that I can go back to the shop tomorrow."

Dylan crossed his arms. "No."

"What?"

"You are not going back to work until at least Wednesday. Addy's orders."

She made a face.

"And let's get back to Dupree. I thought you swore off military men."

She had. While her brothers and her father had always been faithful to their women, she knew a lot of them weren't. She knew that the faithfulness of men in the military wasn't any different than civilians. She had proven that with a long line of cheating exes. But with the military, there had to be trust. More trust than civilian marriages. People outside of it just didn't understand that. She had promised herself not to ever marry, but especially not military. Well, except for Mal.

She choked on her sip of water again. Oh, no. Dammit. She was losing her grip on reality.

"You're not getting sick are you?" her brother asked, panic threading his voice.

"What?"

"You look a little green around the gills there."

She shook her head but it didn't really dislodge the thought of having Mal as a husband. Hell, what was she thinking? She couldn't even handle someone like Kyle, keep him happy. Granted, he wasn't Malachai Dupree, but he had been sexy as hell, and she had wanted him like no one before. Until Mal.

Dammit.

"He's a member of Capital Punishment," her brother said.

That caught her attention. "What?"

"Capital Punishment, that BDSM club."

"Hmm." Then it hit her that her brother knew of Mal's membership. "How do you know that? You didn't go through his records, did you?"

He shook his head. "No. Even if I wanted to, I'm not sure I could get into them. He has one level higher security clearance than I do. It would raise too many flags."

"That means you thought about doing it." She slapped his thigh. "Then how did you find out?"

He frowned, and she knew that he was unhappy with the direction of the conversation. He sighed. "Think about it, Mandy."

The only way he would know about Mal being a
member was…"You're a member? Really?"

"No. Well, I am, but lately I haven't been able to get
in there and away from work. I know the owner so I get
in easily."

"Really?" she asked, unable to fight the excitement.

"No. I don't think so. I am not about to get my kid
sister a complimentary membership."

She pouted at him, but she knew it wouldn't get her
anywhere. "Spoilsport."

He shrugged. "Either way, I don't think your Seal is
looking for a Domme."

"He's not my Seal. And why do you think I'm a
Domme?""

"Really? I mean, Mandy, you run everything. You
run my life, Addy's life, the business…you always like to
be in control."

That was true, but there had been a part of her that
knew something was missing in the bedroom. Guys
always expected her to take charge, and it was something
that didn't always sit well.

"I'm going to call in and make sure the colonel
knows I'm here in DC again. I left a message, but just to
check in."

She nodded but barely noticed when he rose to leave
her alone. Her mind was turning over the idea of herself
as a Domme. She wasn't. Okay, maybe in the real world
she was, but she had always wanted someone to take
charge in the bedroom. Kyle had called her cold. She
would get aroused but she couldn't seem to be that into
what they were doing. And it had been because he
wanted her to take charge.

The thought of Mal being in charge of her, of taking
charge of the situation, had her pulse skipping a beat.
Was that the important factor that had been missing in her
marriage? There had been little time for them to figure it

out. They met while she was in California, married in Vegas, and he was gone before she had unpacked from the trip. The few months they had spent together before that ill-fated mission had been…stressful. They barely knew each other, and even then they both knew it had been a mistake. But then he got called back for that last mission.

And maybe he expected more out of her in the bedroom. She guessed she had wanted someone who took charge, and marrying a Seal, she thought she had.

"Hey, you okay?"

She shook her head to clear it of the tainted memories of her marriage.

"Fine. Just a little woo woo because of my meds. I think I'll take a nap."

He nodded and gave her a kiss. "I'm going to hang out on the couch. Call if you need me."

She snuggled down in her bed. Thoughts that Mal would never be interested in someone like her would normally keep her awake, but she hadn't been lying. The meds were strong, and she wasn't accustomed to taking anything more than aspirin.

The last though in her head before she fell asleep was that it would be much better with Mal in her bed with her.

* * * *

Friday, Mal was still playing catch up. It seemed that everything ran on a forty-eight hour cycle at the Pentagon, and the punishment for taking that one day resulted in a week of living hell. He still hadn't caught up on his email over the last four days. He didn't regret the decision, and he knew he wouldn't hesitate to do it again.

He glanced at the clock. By the time seven rolled around that evening, he had been at work for thirteen hours, and all he wanted was a break. He had fought his need to call more than once a day to check on Amanda. Taking care of a sick friend was one thing, being obsessed with her health was a little off the mark. Mal knew that her brother was already more than a little curious about his fixation on her. If he called more often, there was a good chance Dylan would figure it out.

He was shutting down for the night when his phone rang. He didn't recognize the number, but it was a two one zero, which meant San Antonio, which could be anything since it was the headquarters for the Air Force.

"Lieutenant Commander Dupree, how may I help you?"

"Dupree, this is General Simmons, Mandy's father. I understand you helped her this weekend?"

For a second, he couldn't think. Who was Mandy? Then it hit him.

"Oh, Amanda. Yes, I was still on the roster to be called in case of an emergency."

"What is your interest in my daughter?"

His brain stopped functioning. Mal was accustomed to being ordered to do things. From the time he entered Annapolis, he had thrived on it, but now…well, he was being asked about something he couldn't figure out himself. And by the father of the woman he had been lusting after.

He cleared his throat. "Excuse me, sir?"

There was a pause. "I asked what your interest in my daughter was. Are you dating?"

"No."

"Then why did she call you?"

"Who are you talking to?" a faint voice said from the background.

"I'm talking to this Dupree."

"Oh, for goodness sake. You know him. He was at Kyle's funeral."

There was some noise of the phone being jostled around and then a soft, southern voice said, "Malachai, this is Francine, Amanda's mother. How are you doing?"

"I'm fine."

"I am very sorry for my husband. He seemed to have the wrong idea and wanted to call you on the carpet. He's forgotten he isn't in the military anymore, and no one has to listen to his orders."

He didn't know what to say to that.

"Dylan called and said Amanda was okay and you took good care of her. I want to thank you so much. She's our baby, so we worry."

"She's fine, Mrs. Simmons. She just needs a little rest, and Addy has ensured me that she was going to make sure she took it easy this week."

"Good. She doesn't always rest like she should. I am so thankful you were there to take care of her. She won't admit it, but she likes to be pampered every now and then. She doesn't allow for it unless she's really sick."

"I talked to Addy yesterday, and she assured me Amanda was fine."

"Yes, but I wanted to thank you personally. Frank and I come into town every now and then, so we would love to meet with you when we come there next month."

"Uh…"

"That is if you aren't called out to duty. I completely understand."

There was going to be no way out of it, he knew. She might speak softly, but he knew any military wife of twenty-five years was not to be taken lightly. They usually had nerves of steel and their word was final. And his mama, well, he had been schooled on how to treat mothers with respect.

"No, I am actually working at the Pentagon for someone deployed. Unless we are attacked, I'm pretty much stuck here until she comes back."

"Excellent. Again, I am sorry that Frank bothered you. Goodnight, Malachai."

"Goodnight, Mrs. Simmons."

The phone went dead, and he sat there for a second. How the hell had Amanda's dad gotten his number at the Pentagon? He rolled his eyes. "The man's a retired major general. He has connections everywhere."

"Talking to yourself, Dupree?"

He glanced up and found Veronica Paul at the doorway. The sexy Air Force Major had been popping by unannounced, dropping not too subtle hints that she was in the mood for a bit of play. They had played in the past, and she was considered a favorite sub at Capital Punishment. Hell, at one time she was one of his favorite subs. But now, he wasn't interested.

"Too many hours. How you pencil pushers take this crap all the time, I don't know."

"Too many hours? From a Seal? Please, you just can't handle the things we do because you aren't grabbing glory," she said, her smile telling him she was joking. She was a gorgeous woman, tall, athletic, with the most amazing green eyes and the silkiest of red hair he knew reached the small of her back. And still, he wasn't the least bit interested.

That should scare the hell out of him, but for some reason, it didn't. In fact, it felt right.

"Whatcha up to tonight, Roni?"

She shrugged and walked into his office. "I was going to ask if you're up for a little play, but I have a feeling that you aren't."

He frowned. "What makes you think that?"

"You've checked the clock three times in the last two minutes. You're off to see someone."

He shook his head. He wished. "No, not really."

She smiled at him but there was no seduction in it. "Well, your mind is on someone. Someone you would rather play with." He opened his mouth to deny it, but she stopped him by raising her hand. "Mal, let's not lie to each other. We both know we weren't looking for anything but some fun. It allows us to be friends."

He nodded. "She's not...into play. And she's completely off limits."

She frowned. "Really? How odd. I mean, why would you get all tangled up over some woman who isn't interested in you?"

Why indeed. That was the question that had been plaguing him for months. He knew that his round of one-night stands six months ago had more to do with trying to ignore his feelings for Amanda than anything else. Even when he tried to tell himself it was the fact that it had been his friends getting married, he knew it had been wrong. And at the end of his few weeks of acting like an ass, he realized he wasn't any happier. He'd been living like a monk the last few months.

He brushed away those worries. "Are you going to CP tonight?"

"I wasn't going to but since you are otherwise engaged, I probably will."

"I might just have to join you."

She hesitated.

"What?" he asked.

"Please don't do the big brother routine you did with me when we were there last time. I want to actually find a Dom tonight, okay?"

He chuckled. "I promise."

With that, he pulled out his CAC card that gave him access to the computer and stood.

"I need to get out and do...something."

284

As he followed Roni out the office door, he realized he was in real trouble if he was having to manufacture interest in going to CP. Hopefully when he got there, he would be able to ignore thoughts about Amanda and find a woman for the night.

Chapter Five

Amanda glanced around the club and frowned. How had she ended up at the most notorious BDSM club in the DC area?

Addy. Her best friend had talked her into coming. It was her fault, really. Amanda knew the painkillers made her loopy, and on Wednesday night, she admitted to Addy that she was lusting after Mal and that he was a member of the club. That had been a mistake bigger than Amanda had ever imagined.

"Why are we here?" she asked.

"Because you finally admitted you wanted Malachai and your brother said he comes here. I have a feeling that he will not act unless you get right up in his face. And I want to be an auntee, and that won't happen if I can't get you off your ass."

"Why not have your own children?"

"Because being an aunt is ten times better. I don't want them in my house all the time. Plus, I think you and Dupree will make some gorgeous babies together."

"I don't want to get married. I...I wasn't good at it."

Addy shook her head and rolled her eyes. There was no use trying to convince her best friend she wasn't a woman men wanted to keep. Kyle had proven that.

"How did you get us in here?"

She didn't answer. Instead, she took a drink of her soda and looked around the club.

"Addison!"

She sighed. "Well, I know the owner."

Amanda looked at her. "Really? Who is that?"

Addy shrugged.

"No, you tell me. I told you my secret, you tell me yours."

"Remember that guy the other night my dad tried to fix me up with?"

"The lawyer?"

"Yeah, well, I did some research and found out that he is part owner of the club. So..."

Amanda shut her eyes. "You blackmailed him. Oh my God. You blackmailed a lawyer."

"It wasn't that hard, really. I mean, he did try to lie about it, but then I gave him the proof."

Amanda opened her eyes and looked at her friend. "What?"

Addy shrugged. "Nothing."

"No, there is something there again."

"Okay, well, he is much more attractive to me now that I know this."

"You aren't into BDSM. You said you didn't like it at all."

"I'm not. Really. I'm more into the fact that he has this kind of double life. One he shows everyone else, and one I know. Sort of like a sexual superhero."

Amanda snorted then started laughing. "Oh my God. You never fail to surprise me."

"I know, right? I'm damned astonished at myself. He's so damned rigid. I hate men like that."

"And it's been working out so well with the 'go with the flow' guys?"

Addy opened her mouth to answer then snapped it shut as she looked across the floor. "Your Seal just showed up."

She followed Addy's gaze across the floor to the door and found she was right. Mal was walking in the room dressed in black leather, but he wasn't alone. A tall, skinny redhead was with him.

"Shit, I knew this was a bad idea."

She set her glass down and turned to leave. Addy stopped her. "No, they aren't together."

"What?"

She looked up and saw the redhead give Mal a kiss on the cheek, then she left him.

"Looks like they just walked in together. They apparently aren't here together, as in for public play."

"Dupree doesn't really do public play," said a deep voice, rich with a Boston accent. She turned and found herself face to face with probably the prettiest man she had ever seen.

He was tall, even taller than her brothers, who were over six feet. He had wavy dark blond hair that danced over the edge of the collar of his shirt. Piercing green eyes had her pulling in a deep breath. The strong jawline and slightly crooked nose kept him from looking too feminine.

"I didn't say we wanted to spend time with you, Walton," Addy said, her usual cool exterior now flashing with irritation.

"I don't think I asked. I wanted to see the woman you wanted to get in this club so badly that you blackmailed me."

"I didn't blackmail you. I let you know that I had information on you."

His lips twitched. "And when you told me that you would let people know about it, you turned it into blackmail. Why don't you introduce me to your friend?"

Addy's usual unflappable personality was in direct contrast to her behavior with this guy. And she was acting like a snot, which wasn't like her. Amanda's interest in the lawyer increased tenfold.

Addy crossed her arms beneath her breasts. "You know her name."

"Addison."

There was steel in his voice that usually would have sent Addy into doing something deliberately bad, but instead she responded to it.

"Okay, Amanda this is Walton. Vic Walton, this is my business partner, Amanda."

Amanda gave her friend a look then offered her hand. She didn't expect him to take it and kiss it.

He released her hand and smiled at Addy. "You didn't tell me she was so cute."

"And she isn't interested."

"No, she likes Dupree over there and she wants his attention."

"We don't need help with that," Addy countered.

"What better way to grab the attention of a man than to be seen with one of the owners of a very infamous club?"

Amanda glanced at Addy, waiting for her to counter. She also wondered if her friend knew that Walton was doing this all for Addy. The calculating look in Addy's eyes told Amanda that she was definitely listening to the club owner.

"I have my own table up here and everyone watches it. Why don't you ladies come with me? Dupree will be over there the minute he sees me with you."

Amanda wasn't so sure, but there was something alluring about the man that made her want to follow him anywhere. "Okay."

He took her hand and then pulled Addy closer with his free hand. "Come along with me, Addison."

Amanda followed him along, wondering if this was actually going to work. She settled in her chair. Walton waited for Addy to sit, then he took his own seat. He had pretty manners, and she was enough of a girl to be impressed by them. Granted, she liked being her own woman, but she didn't mind a little attention from a man now and then.

"So, Amanda, you and Addison own a flower shop?"

She nodded but Addy interrupted her. "Don't use that tone, Walton"

"Do you notice she uses my last name?"

Amanda had to bite her lip to keep from laughing. Addy was acting so out of character.

"Yes."

"I think it's a way for her to keep me at a distance. Can I let you in on a secret?"

Amanda looked at her friend, who was pretending to ignore them.

She smiled at him. "Sure."

He leaned closer to whisper in her ear. "I am a very patient man."

She couldn't stop the bubble of laughter. "Oh my, I think she might be in trouble."

He sat back and smiled at her. Before he could respond, another deep voice, ripe with New Orleans and filled with irritation, interrupted them.

"Well, isn't this cozy?"

She turned and found a very angry Malachai Dupree standing beside their table.

Chapter Six

Mal had been grabbing a bottle of water when he saw Amanda. He'd shaken his head, trying to figure out if he was delirious from too many hours of paperwork. But of course, he wasn't. She was there, walking along as if she came to a BDSM club every day. What the hell was she wearing? It was black, tight, and barely there. He noticed that Addy was with her, and they were following Walton to his table.

Now he was at the table, and he had to figure out a way to get her out of there. Of course, it was going to be hard to do since Walton had taken an interest in her. He was known for his tenacity when it came to subs, and many of them clamored to be his.

"Dupree, why don't you join us?" he said conversationally. "We were just getting acquainted."

"Amanda, I would like to speak with you privately."

She glanced up at him. "I don't think I want to speak privately with you."

For a moment, he couldn't believe she had just said that to him. "Yes, you do."

"I think the lady said no," Walton said, even though he hadn't risen. There was enough of a threat in his voice to gain the attention of the nearby patrons.

"Well, since you seem to be speaking for her, ask her what her father would think if she were in a place like this?"

"And just how are you going to do that?" Amanda asked.

"He called me tonight, so I have his number."

Her eyes widened. "What?"

"I had a long chat with old Frank, so you might want to tread lightly here. Talk, now."

He waited for her to stand, and he was mildly surprised that Walton didn't object. He was known for being very territorial when it came to subs, but he smiled. "You let one of the bouncers know if you need help."

She shot Mal a nasty look but started to walk. Shit, the dress she was wearing was barely there. It stopped just a few inches below that wonderfully full ass. God, she was either wearing a thong or nothing. Just the thought had his cock twitching and his hands itching to touch.

"Down the hallway."

He waited for her to obey his order. When she did, he had to remind himself it had nothing to do with sexual play. It was just a means to an end for her. She was trying to get him the hell out of there so she could do what she wanted. The hell with that.

Once they passed by most of the people and they had some privacy, he grabbed her arm and stopped her.

"Just what the hell are you doing here?"

"Addy wanted to come, and she knows Walton, so he got us in."

"You aren't supposed to be here," he said more for himself. He was trying to convince himself that she shouldn't, but now that she was, he couldn't get the idea of spanking her for being so bad out of his head.

Shit.

"What the hell is that supposed to mean?"

Mal took a step closer, enjoying the scent of her. Amanda didn't wear perfume, but he could smell the soap she used and that basic primal aroma that always called to him.

"I think you need to watch yourself, Amanda. You're a little out of your depth here."

She blinked up at him, those luminous green eyes shining with arousal he knew she didn't understand. She wasn't a virgin, of course. She'd been married almost a year before her husband had been KIA. But being a sub was something different, something he knew she didn't comprehend.

"I think you don't know me that well, Malachai."

Damn, he loved the way she talked. She was a military brat who'd lived in five different countries, but that deep Georgia accent clung to every one of her words, drawing out his name. He could only imagine the way it would sound when she moaned.

Shaking his head, he tried to step away. At least he told his feet to move, but another part of his anatomy seemed to be controlling his actions.

She reached up and brushed her fingers over his jaw. He growled and she smiled.

"I'm not a little girl."

"No, but you don't know what goes on here or what a Dom will expect from you."

She cocked her head, the silky strands of her chestnut hair sliding over her bare shoulder. "The question is, are you Dom enough to show me?"

He heard the defiance in her voice, and he knew what she wanted—what she thought she wanted. Settling a hand against the wall on either side of her head, he leaned even closer. Her breath caught, and he could see her pulse flutter in her neck.

"Is that a dare, Amanda? Because there is one thing you should never do and that is taunt a Dom."

She looked down for a moment, pulling her bottom lip between her teeth. His breath seemed to clog in his throat as he thought that maybe he had convinced her she was wrong. Part of him was happy, but a bigger part of him, the one that dreamed of her every night, thought of her every day, was crushed.

She slowly raised her gaze to his and one side of her mouth curved.

"Yeah, Mal, I think I am taunting you." Her tongue darted out over her lips, and her eyes shone with challenge. "Whatcha gonna do about it?"

For a moment he stared at her, trying to convince himself again that she wasn't for him. He knew that. Everyone knew that. She was too innocent for this. When she sighed and started to look down, he grabbed her chin.

"We do this, you have to agree to what I want or I walk away. I won't force you, but if you're going to try this out, I'll help you."

She nodded.

"Okay, let's go."

He grabbed her hand and dragged her out of the club and into the night. If he was going to have this one taste of heaven, he would make sure that what they did was private.

And he would walk away in the morning.

Chapter Seven

After a quick call to Addy to let her know that she
was going home with Mal, Amanda allowed Mal to lead
her to his car. Her body was throbbing when they got to
her apartment. Every inch of her skin was sensitive to the
touch. Even the flimsy outfit she'd worn felt constricting.
She was still amazed that he'd risen to the challenge. She
had hoped, prayed, that if she ever had the nerve, he
would. There was still part of her that thought he just did
it to get her out of the club. Now, though, she knew that
he was attracted to her. If there was one thing she had
learned from the horrible experiment of her marriage, it
was never to second-guess anything. Life was too short to
worry about regrets.

Amanda pulled her keys out of her purse, but Mal
took them from her and unlocked the door, waiting for
her to enter.

She looked at him. "I can unlock my own door."

He said nothing, but waited patiently as she stepped
over the threshold. She didn't like the way he was
looking at her. It was distant and…cold. It was as if she
were with a totally different person than the Mal she had
grown to love.

Whoa, back up, she ordered herself. She wasn't in
love with the man. Lust, that was okay, but love wasn't
something she could handle at the moment.

She needed something to be on even ground again.
The feeling that he had all the control didn't go over well
with her.

"If you're just dropping me off, I'm going to go back
to the club. I don't need someone telling me what to do."

He flipped the deadbolt on the door and then turned
around and looked at her.

"I think you're done flaunting yourself at the club for the night."

She did not like that tone. Okay, she did a bit. It lit a fire that roared over her. She always liked commanding men, but she had never experienced this. No man had ordered her around like this. There was still a small part of her that wanted to oppose it. She was a woman who knew her own worth, who was independent and didn't need a man. But dammit, he had her body yearning to be touched with just that one touch.

"I don't think I asked your opinion."

His nostrils flared, and she felt herself shiver. Oh God, now *that* was sexy. He might look calm, but she could feel the power within him, shimmering just beneath the surface.

"You will learn to mind that tongue of yours, Amanda. You wanted this, and now you're going to get a taste."

She opened her mouth to disagree, but he held up his hand.

"Before you tell me how it's going to go, there are things you have to understand about tonight. When we start, *I* am in control. Of when you can talk, what you can do, and just how much I will spank that ass of yours for pulling a stunt like this."

Her nipples hardened further. Oh lord, that was sexy.

"If you can't give that to me, we better stop right now."

He waited for her to answer, and she could feel the weight of his question. She knew he was asking for more. She had to understand what they were getting into, and Mal being the kind of guy he was, wanted to make sure she understood what was going on.

She nodded.

"We aren't going to go full force with the submission tonight, but I want to give you a taste of it, let you know exactly what you are getting into. You will not speak unless I ask a question or you give me your safe word. Do you have one?"

She shook her head.

"Well, pick one."

His words lashed out at her, and she didn't like that he was getting so pissed at her. But then there was something in those chocolate eyes of his that had her stopping. He was doing everything he could to control himself, and for a Dom, that had to be a problem. A pretty big problem.

"Flowers."

He nodded in understanding. "You use it if I push you too far, if I hurt you beyond what you can handle. Part of the pain will be...arousing. Every sub has their limits, though. Like I said, we will keep it light tonight, but I want the understanding between us from the start that I will stop if you say that word. I will never push you past that point. But understand that you shouldn't let it loose unless you are willing to stop." He stepped closer and cupped her face with his hand. She could smell him, the scent of the night lying heavily on his clothes, but there was something else there, something that she would recognize until the day she died. Deep, dark, musky. The natural scent of Mal made her stomach muscles quiver. It was as if she had caught the scent of his arousal and her body just took over.

He brushed his thumb over her mouth then slipped it between her lips. "Suck, baby."

She did as he directed, not closing her eyes. She knew without him ordering her that he wanted her to be looking at him.

"I can't wait to slip my cock between those pretty lips. You like that idea, don'tcha, Amanda."

She nodded as he pulled his hand away.

"I like those shoes you have on." He was talking as if they were having a regular conversation. He turned and walked to the kitchenette area. He grabbed a chair and dragged it back over to where she was standing. He turned it and straddled it backwards, leaning his chest against it.

"Take that shirt off for me."

Her fingers were shaking so badly, she wasn't sure if she could get the buttons undone. Drawing in a deep breath, she slipped each button free of the fabric then let the shirt fall to the ground.

Even in the dim light, she could see heat flare in his eyes. One side of his mouth curved. "Nice. I like that bra."

She didn't. Not now. The demi bra was all lace, and each time she moved, her nipples ached.

"What has you frowning, Amanda?"

She was embarrassed and didn't want to answer. It was insane that she was standing there half-dressed and had agreed to bed games with a freaking Seal, but she was mortified to tell him her nipples hurt.

"If you can't answer when I ask you a question, I can leave now."

That thought had panic settling in her chest.

"The lace, it rubs against my nipples."

"Ah," he said with a nod. He rose, then walked over to her. "I can see them peeking through the fabric."

Mal lifted his hand to rub his thumb over the tip. It sent a shaft of heat straight to her sex. Damn.

"Does that hurt, *chéri*?"

She drew in a shuddering breath. "A little. But..."

"Go on."

"It also feels good."

She felt her face heat at the admission, but he didn't laugh.

"Yeah, I can see that. And there will be more of that. There's a thin line between pleasure and pain. We will skirt it, allowing the little lash of pain to increase your arousal."

She frowned, and he smiled as he brushed his mouth against hers. While he was kissing her, he pinched her nipple.

Damn.

"Yeah, you like that. So I think since it's bothering you, we will leave that bra on. Nipple clamps might be something we play with later. You might really respond to them."

Then he turned and walked to the chair. When he straddled it this time, she could see his erection, and her eyes widened. He was definitely aroused...and well...big.

He chuckled, drawing her attention. She looked at his face. "Yeah, there is something I want to do more than take you back there and fuck you until you can't walk. But there is this part of me that enjoys this, that needs it on a level that is almost unexplainable. And watching your surrender is going to be the ultimate prize for my control."

Every word was threaded with the taste of his New Orleans' accent. It thickened the more aroused he got.

"Now, let's take off that skirt."

She reached behind her and unzipped it. He stopped her.

"Turn around. I want to see that ass when you bend over."

She did as ordered and sighed when she felt the cool air against her bare bottom.

"Nice," he said, and his voice deepened. "I love a woman who wears a thong. Of course, next time you wear that outfit around me, I'm going to expect you to be without any underwear. That makes it so much easier to touch you."

The thought had her heart thumping hard against her chest. Just how would he touch her? And, oh God, would he do it in public?

"Turn around."

She did and felt heat flare in her belly. His eyes were narrowed in concentration, and for once in her life, she felt as if she were the most important woman in the world.

"Come here."

She moved without thinking, stopping in front of him. He slid his hands to her hips, his thumbs moving against her stomach. Then he leaned forward and sniffed.

"Damn, you smell good. And you're beyond aroused. I bet you taste like heaven."

Again, her stomach muscles clenched. Her sex was wet, her panties dripping with the evidence of her arousal. He set the flat of his tongue against her belly. He licked her then started to nip and kiss her flesh. It wasn't especially arousing but for some reason, her body reacted more to that than anything else that had ever been done to her. It was like they had some kind of connection on another level. Which was silly, but when he dipped his tongue into her belly button, she groaned.

"Yeah, I like that sound," he said before giving her one last nip and pulling back. "I see it as my duty to get you to scream before the end of the night."

She had no doubt he would.

"Turn around."

She did, and she heard him sigh. It was the barest of sounds, but it feathered over her skin.

"I've been wondering what your ass looked like. God."

He took a cheek in each hand and squeezed, then slapped her lightly. Amanda felt the smack feather over her skin. Her pussy tightened.

"Yeah, you like that. That's good because I like to give a sub a good spanking."

He gave her another slap before letting go.

"Now, take that thong off and give it to me."

She wasted no time pulling the small bit of fabric off and handing it to him. He captured her gaze as she pressed the panties in his hand.

"Damn, woman, soaking wet. I can imagine what that pussy is going to feel like while I fuck you." He rose, and now there was no way anyone could mistake his condition. He was beyond aroused, and for some reason, she felt her heart jump in anticipation. She wasn't a virgin, and while she hadn't been overly slutty, she had been with men. She had never been this turned on by her partner's arousal before.

"Yeah, you got me harder than a fucking spike. What I'm trying to decide right now is if I should let you suck me off first or not."

Her mouth went dry at the thought. She loved oral sex, especially giving it. She licked her lips.

Mal smiled as he noticed her interest in it. "Oh, so Amanda likes to have her mouth fucked?"

"I...yes."

She should feel ashamed, and Kyle had made her feel that way. She loved to suck a man off until he came. She was one of the few women she knew who actually wanted to do that first and foremost. It was a turn-on for her.

"Well, hmm, how much do you want my cock in your mouth? What would you do for it?"

She knew he was asking a rhetorical question.

He walked around her, smacking her as he got behind her.

"Have you ever had anal sex before?"

She shook her head.

"Shame, I'd like to fuck that pretty ass, too."

She shivered. Oh God, he was like a wet dream she had created for herself

"Oh, better and better, but we can't do that the first night. You can't do anal if you aren't prepared. Turn around, baby."

She did.

"Unbutton and unzip my pants."

She didn't hesitate. Of course, he wasn't wearing underwear, and his cock sprang free once she slipped the zipper down.

"Wrap your hand around it. Nice and easy, stroke me."

As she moved her hand over his hard flesh, he cupped her face with both his hands and exposed her neck to him. He nipped at her throat.

"Oh yeah, baby, that's good. You're going to be the best sub. You like making me happy, don't you?"

"Yes," she said and immediately felt guilty.

"No. Don't look that way." He made her look at him. "This isn't about anybody but us. What makes us happy, what makes us hot, and what ultimately will make you come. There is nothing to feel guilty about and nothing to be embarrassed about. Get out of your head and just feel."

She nodded but adhered to the rules.

"Good, now let go of my cock."

She didn't want to but she did. He slipped his hands to her breasts and pinched her nipples hard. It hurt because they were so sensitive, but it still felt good.

"Now, get on your knees and suck me like a good submissive does."

She did as he ordered. She lifted her hand, but he stopped her.

"Put your hands behind your back."

It wasn't easy, but she did it. He took his dick in his hand and stroked it. God, he was gorgeous. She watched avidly as his fingers moved over his hard flesh, and he groaned. She looked up at him.

"You are like a treat, and unwrapping you is probably going to kill me. Open up that mouth and just take the tip in."

When she did, he shuddered and she loved it. She wanted more, wanted to taste his come, feel him lose control. But she couldn't move very far on her knees with her hands behind her back. Mal wasn't letting her have any more than the broad head. The taste of him was enough at the moment. Salty sweet, she sucked hard, pulling a bit of his pre-come into her mouth. She swallowed it and hummed against his cock.

"Yeah, that's nice."

He lifted his cock. "Lick it, from the base on up."

She couldn't deny him that. At that moment, she would give him anything. Seeing the pleasure move over his face as she licked the shaft was almost mesmerizing. Knowing she was giving him pleasure was enough to make her come right then and there.

Soon though, he stepped back.

"Maybe we'll let you suck me dry a little later, but I think we need to move into the bedroom for what I have planned next."

She wanted to disagree, but she didn't. The excitement of not knowing what he had planned for her next had her rising from her kneeling position.

He guided her into the bedroom. Each step was excruciating. Her sex was so sensitive, and each time she moved it was like she lit up like Christmas lights.

By the time they reached her bed, she wanted to cry. She had never been this aroused before, and they had hardly scratched the surface.

He left her standing. He undressed fast, toeing off his shoes, shimmying off his pants, and slipping his shirt up and over his head. Then, apparently comfortable with his nudity, he sat down on the bed.

"Come here."

As before, she did just as he ordered. After she had been given pleasure, she was sure she would think better of it, but right now, she didn't care. She wanted what he did because she knew in the end, he would give her pleasure.

She stopped between his legs. He gripped her waist, then slipped his hand up her torso and behind her back. Finally, he undid her bra and she sighed. More than anything she wanted to press her palms against her nipples to give them some release, but he stopped her.

"Don't touch yourself unless I tell you to. I will make sure you regret it if you go against my command."

She wanted to pout, but he didn't give her a chance. He pulled her closer and took one of her nipples into his mouth. He sucked hard. The combination of pleasure and pain had her moaning his name.

"Yeah, like that, baby."

He teased her other nipple, patting it lightly, then rolling it between his fingers. All the while he sucked her other. She had never been that sensitive to someone playing with her nipples, but for some reason, this was more arousing than anything any other man had done to her. She was standing in front of him with nothing on but a pair of fuck-me heels. He was doing nothing more than teasing her nipples and she could feel her pussy dripping with need.

He leaned back and smiled at her. "You have very sensitive nipples. Have they always been that sensitive?"

She shook her head.

"I take that as a good sign. And it's a very good sign that you understand who is in charge here." He shifted his gaze to her sex. "Spread your legs. I want a taste."

304

She did, although it was hard to give up the sensation of having her legs against each other. He slipped a finger in first, teasing her clitoris with his thumb. Slowly, he brushed it against her, and she bit her lip to keep from coming.

Then he pulled his fingers out. "Look at me."

She lifted her eyelids and watched as he lifted his fingers to his mouth. Oh holy mother of God, he slid his tongue up and over his fingers. Then he hummed. He was no longer touching her, but she could have sworn she felt the vibrations in her pussy.

"I was right. You do taste like heaven." Then he rose, and his cock pressed against her stomach. "I think I want you on the bed. I want to feast on you."

He changed positions with her, placing her on the bed then pressing her legs apart as far as they could go. He kissed up her right thigh and she quivered. God, she couldn't wait to feel his mouth on her. Then he was there, his tongue gliding over her slit, then her labia. He sucked and teased her with his tongue, mouth, and teeth. All the quivering muscles in her stomach tightened, her body preparing for a release. Each time she felt near the edge, he pulled back. She lost track of how many times he did it to her before he moved back.

He pulled her down and devoured her mouth. And there she could taste the pungent flavor of her own arousal.

Then he slipped off her shoes and grabbed up his pants. He searched his pockets before pulling out his wallet and retrieving a condom. He ripped the package open then slowly slipped the condom over his cock. She noticed that his hands were shaking when he did it, so she felt a little satisfied that he was as affected by this as she was.

He joined her on the bed, then covered her with his body. Without hesitation, he pulled her legs apart and

entered her in one swift move. She groaned. Even as
aroused as she was, he was big and it had been over a
year since she'd had sex.

"Amanda, baby, are you okay?"

She nodded and reached for him. He might be the
one in charge, but she wanted a kiss. She wanted to feel
this connection with him. He did as she bid, apparently
sensing her need. He kissed her, but it wasn't the
ravenous kiss from before. Instead it was slow, sweet,
and it had her heart flip-flopping with the way it warmed
her from the inside out.

He pulled back and lifted her legs to his waist,
settling on his knees. Then he started to move. It was
slow, like the kiss, and just as earth shattering. He locked
his gaze with her as he moved in and out of her sex, her
body quivering close to the edge.

She wanted to look away, but she knew even without
any order that this was the connection he needed, just as
she had needed hers earlier. Soon, though, his fingers
were digging into her flesh as he started to increase the
tempo of his thrusts.

"Now, Amanda, come with me."

She was close, but not close enough. He doubled his
efforts, the headboard slamming against the wall behind
her.

"Come now. I want to feel it. Do it."

The last of the order apparently got her body to
respond. In that next instant, her orgasm hit, her body
jolting from the release. She bowed up and screamed his
name as wave after wave of sensation moved over her
body. Just as she was coming down, he started pushing
again, and unbelievably, she felt another orgasm
approaching.

"With me this time, baby. Come now, *chéri*. Come
with me."

She couldn't deny him anything. The tidal wave of pleasure shifted over her, flowing over her, more powerful than the first.

"Yes, that's it," he groaned, then he slammed into her one more time before he shuddered.

Moments later, he released her legs, then collapsed on top of her. She smiled and wrapped her arms and legs around him.

"I am too old for this."

She laughed. "I think you kept up pretty good for an old man."

He chuckled and pulled himself up to look down at her. His smile dissolved, and he kept staring at her. When he said nothing, she let her arms fall to the side.

"What?"

"Nothing, just...I imagined this so many different ways, I just never thought it would happen."

The straightforward way he said it made her believe he was telling her the truth.

"You imagined this?"

He nodded.

"For how long?"

"At least six months now."

She frowned. "What took you so long?"

For a second he said nothing, then his lips curved. "I can't remember now."

He leaned down and gave her a soft kiss. This one meant more to her, and she thought maybe it did to him, too. "I didn't hurt you, did I?"

"Naw."

He nodded. "Be right back."

She waited while he went into the bathroom. Once he was out of site, she did a little jig. She had Malachai Dupree in her bed. And apparently he'd been wanting it as much as she had. Which meant she would get him more than once.

Thankfully she was done before he returned. He slipped into her bed then pulled her close.

"Is there anything you want to talk about?" he asked.

She looked up at him with a frown. "Like what?"

"Like the ramifications of this?"

She shook her head. "No, I just want to live in the moment. I want to enjoy the fact I bagged myself the sexiest Dom in CP tonight and that he's sleeping in my bed." He opened his mouth but she pressed her fingers to his lips. "No. Let's just enjoy tonight. We'll deal with all the other stuff later."

She could tell he wavered, then he nodded. She leaned up and kissed him.

As she snuggled against him, she enjoyed the warmth of his body and the fact that for the first time in a long time, she was thankful there was someone there, someone who apparently accepted her the way she was.

It was her last thought before she drifted off to sleep.

Chapter Eight

Mal woke the next morning. It was early, of course.
Since he'd been at Annapolis, he had been an early riser.
He'd had no choice. Now, though, it gave him a chance
to watch her sleep. He couldn't help but be mesmerized
by her. Hell, he couldn't believe he had spent the night in
her bed or that he was still there. The sun was peeking
through the blinds, and he realized they had left her
curtains open. Thank goodness the blinds were closed.

She was lying on her stomach facing him. She was
always so animated, so seeing her like this was different.
When she'd been sick, he had watched over her. Now,
though, Mal knew her sleep was peaceful. The morning
light added an extra glow to her skin. He knew her
mother had a little Native American in her which gave
her the most amazing tone, but in the morning light, it
was stunning. He was afraid to touch her, but not because
he might wake her. There was a part of him that worried
if he touched her, she would dissolve and he would find
out this was all a dream.

He took a chance and skimmed his fingers down her
spine, moving the sheet down, exposing more flesh.

She sighed, and he looked up. Her eyes were still
closed but her lips curved. And just like that his heart
exploded.

"Good morning, *chéri*" he said. Even to his own ears
his voice sounded rough.

"Morning." Her voice was filled with drowsy
happiness.

"Didn't mean to wake you."

Amanda opened her eyes, barely. He could just make
out the green in them.

"Yeah? Then why have you been staring at me
forever?"

He chuckled. "You play a good possum."

"I had to have something to guard against my brothers. They were constantly devising ways to make my life hell."

"Hmm," he said, leaning down to kiss her shoulder.

"I guess y'all weren't too nice to Jocelyn and Shannon, were you?"

"I plead the fifth."

She turned over, allowing the sheet to slip even further down. God, she was exquisite. Her breasts weren't huge, but they were just the size of his palms. The golden undertone to her flesh along with her hardened nipples was making his mouth dry. He wanted to touch, to taste.

"I can just imagine you guys being mean to them."

"Aww, no, you got it wrong, darlin'. Those two banshees are demon spawns."

Her smile widened. "Really?"

"Swear to God."

"You better be careful lying."

He frowned and crossed his heart. "Cross my heart."

She rolled her eyes. "So, if I call Shannon and ask her if she knows you call her a banshee, she's going to agree?"

"Don't use the word banshee. She does know some voodoo."

Amanda laughed, and he couldn't stop himself from leaning in to taste her. It started simple, just a brush of his lips over hers, but soon he couldn't resist dipping his tongue into the warmth of her mouth.

He was already hard, but he grew harder. He wanted her with a need that almost scared him. And amazingly, while the Dom in him wanted to bust loose, to grab the control completely from her and make her submit, Mal wanted something else, something...just for them.

He kissed his way down her neck, then glided his mouth over her full breast. She arched up against him, a moan escaping from her. He continued his path down to her pussy. She opened easily for him. The flavor of her arousal exploded across his taste buds.

He pulled her clit into his mouth, sucking it slowly. She arched up, urging him to take more, to give her release. He wasn't ready for that.

Instead, he moved away and without saying anything, he turned her over on her stomach. She giggled before she hit the mattress. He loved that sound. He hadn't heard something like that from her in over a year.

She looked back over her shoulder at him, a slow smile curving her full lips. Just like the night before, he felt his heart roll over in his chest. Never before had a woman been able to undo him with only a smile.

"What do you think you're doing?" she asked, but he heard the thread of amusement in her voice.

"I think I promised you a spanking."

She lowered her eyes, but not before he saw the excitement. He raised his hand and smacked her once, enjoying the sound of his skin against hers. He knew what it did to women who were spanked, knew the way the sting of the slap would filter over her body. He raised his hand over and over, leaving her full, heart-shaped ass pink. She was squirming against the bed.

Her arousal spurred his. Hell, the fact that she was in bed with him left him aroused. Now he was losing the last of his control.

He reached for a condom, ripped it open, and had it on in record time. Mal reached for her then. He flipped her back over and pulled her on top of him. The gasp that filled the room was one of the most erotic sounds he had ever heard.

"Take me in."

311

He wanted to watch her, to see her pleasure with the sunshine filling the room.

She did, slowly slipping down onto his cock. She leaned her head back as she started to ride him. Slowly at first, then she increased her rhythm. He was near his orgasm, but he didn't want to be there alone.

"Amanda, baby, look at me."

She did, without question. One night and just the tip of the iceberg of their D/s relationship, but her immediate response told him they were already in sync.

Her hair fell forward as she looked down at him. Mal gathered what control he had and slid his hand down to her sex.

"Come with me," he said as he pressed against her clit. He watched in awe as the orgasm swept over her. Her inner muscles clamped down hard on his cock. The pressure pulled his own release from him. He shouted her name as he thrust up into her one last time.

Moments later, she collapsed on top of him. He groaned.

She lifted herself up and looked down at him. "I'm sorry."

She was grinning at him, so he knew she really wasn't. "You don't look very sorry."

"Well, I'm not. I think this is the best morning I've had in a long while."

He smiled, but while he was looking at her, he felt his smile fade. He didn't regret last night. It was hard to regret something like that. But he did worry about her, and if she was attracted to him or the fact he was a Dom.

"Stop it," she ordered.

"What?"

"I can see your mind churning up all kinds of excuses that maybe we shouldn't be together."

"No, not that." He picked up her hair and started playing with it. It was soft and silky. He loved the way it felt against his skin. "It's just that I wonder if you're ready for this."

"I wasn't a virgin."

She said it so sincerely, he laughed. "I know. You had never submitted, and we didn't talk much about it beforehand."

"I've researched it."

"There's more to it than just reading books and articles."

She nodded. "And that's what you can teach me."

He opened his mouth but she stopped him.

"Let it go, Malachai. Everything will be okay."

She kissed him then slipped out of bed. She picked up a tiny pink robe. "What would you like for breakfast? French toast?"

"You're going to cook for me again?"

"Yep. And you can handle our next meal. How does that sound?"

He nodded, and she leaned down to give him a quick kiss.

"Stop thinking, Dupree. If there is one thing I have learned over the last two years, it is to live in the moment. No regrets."

With that she went into the bathroom, closing the door. He lay there thinking of her words. She had been a woman who had led a charmed life, the daughter of a general. But she had heartache early in life losing Kyle the way she did. It had broken her in some way, and there was a point he knew her family had been seriously worried about her mental state. Amanda was strong, though, and she pushed through the pain and moved ahead with her life plans. Her friendship with Addison had helped, both of them dealing with grief in different ways, he thought with a smile. Well, they approached it differently but came up with Double A Floral Design. Amanda rearranged her life to work toward the goal, and

Addison, well, she let her creative side go crazy. He always wondered what color her hair would be.

So, live in the moment? He could do it for a while, but not long. He didn't know what it meant to her, but he was playing for keeps. He knew she might not be ready right now, but he would move her into the direction he wanted.

She came out of the bathroom with a smile. "Get your ass out of bed, Seal. I need some help cutting up the strawberries."

She practically danced out of the room. Slowly, he let his lips curve as the warmth of his happiness filled him. She wanted to learn how to be a sub…although she was pretty good the night before. He was okay with that, moving slowly. Being the man who would give her the first taste of submission was enough for him right now. He would live in the moment, that's for damned sure.

Because at the end of the day, all that mattered was that she was with him. For now.

* * * *

"So, how are things going with Malachai?" Addy asked.

Amanda glanced at her friend and wondered how much she should tell her. That she was afraid she was falling in love with the man?

"That good, huh?"

Amanda sighed and stabbed a piece of lettuce with her fork. "I'm not sure. It's been a week. And we were both busy most of the time."

Except the nights. Each night he would come over, tease her, push her to her limits.

But they hadn't done much talking beyond that. She had been expecting some kind of discussion, something that would tell her where he expected their relationship to go.

"So, you're not going to dish about what kind of Dom he is?"

"Do I really have to tell you?"

"No, but I like the idea of you telling me so I can picture it."

"Ew. You would picture us having sex? That's gross."

"Oh, no. I can imagine him doing it to me."

"You have a Dom interested in you."

Now it was Addy's turn to blush. "I really don't know what you are talking about."

She tried not to laugh. Addy could hide her feelings from a lot of people but not from Amanda. They had been through too much together for either one of them to be able to mask their true feelings.

"Really? Well, he seemed very interested in you the other night, and I don't think he did all that stuff for me. He did it to impress you."

Addy didn't say anything for a second, but Amanda knew better. Her best friend was simmering beneath the surface.

"Fine, he's attractive, sort of, but seriously, it has nothing to do with me."

"Yeah, so if I call up that one chick who was eyeing him the other night, you would be okay with that?" she asked with her tongue in her cheek.

"Sure." Then Addy frowned. "Wait, what woman?"

"Some little blonde. The one dressed in fire-engine red."

"Well, I don't care." Addy sniffed. The prissy tone was so unlike her best friend, Amanda knew she was lying. Amanda was quiet again. It was better to just wait things out with Addy. Her friend was a horrible liar and couldn't stand anyone lying, let alone herself.

"Okay, fine. I want him."

"Really?" Amanda shook her head. "Hard to tell."

Addy sighed. "But he's not for me. You know how I am about domination."

After experiencing it with Mal, Amanda wondered why anyone wouldn't want to be dominated. She knew they had only brushed the surface, but she had never been this satisfied. From her own reading, there was so much more to learn. Of course, she also knew that not everyone was programed that way. Her need to be dominated was probably as great as Mal's need to dominate.

"You don't know until you try."

She made a face. "I'm not sure I could trust him enough."

Amanda wanted to argue with her, but she knew better. Besides, what did she know about the man in question? She wasn't a good judge of character when it came to men. Except for Mal.

She loved the sex. Any woman with half an ounce of brains would love what he did to her. But there were those other moments...the ones that had her heart turning over. He would look at her a certain way and everything just stopped.

"Oh God, you got that look again." Addy shook her head as she shut down her computer for the day.

"What look?"

"For the past few days, I'll see you working on something and then...you just get this goofy look on your face. Admit it. You're in love."

Panic had the air clogging up the back of her throat. "I never said that."

"Hey, I call it like I see it, and you are in love."

She could lie. It would be easy to do to anyone else but Addy. That not being able to hide anything was a two-way street.

Amanda sighed. "I don't want to be in love."

Addy studied her for a second as Amanda started to put up her tools.

"You haven't told me everything that went on between you and Kyle."

She glanced at Addy but said nothing.

"And I am not going to pry, but whatever it is, you need to let it go."

She knew that. More than anything she wanted to be the kind of person who could walk away from the pain of her crappy marriage. If there was a man who would be worth it, it would be Malachai Dupree. But there was still part of her that couldn't. "I'm not sure I can, and it scares me so much."

"Because you can't let it go, or that you might lose Mal because of it?"

Even thinking about him gone, of not seeing him on a regular basis, talking to him late at night…it made her hurt.

"Well, I guess that answers the question."

She looked at her friend as pain twisted in her heart. "I just don't know what to do about it."

"You don't have to figure it out tonight."

She nodded even as she felt the tears burn the back of her eyes. Addy pulled Amanda into her arms for a hug.

"It will all work itself out," Addy said.

Amanda pulled back with a laugh and looked at her friend. "And when did you become the person of wise antidotes?"

"Since you fell in love with a Seal. Let's go have some sushi at Wegmans."

"Sounds good."

"I'll lock up the back door and meet you out front."

With a nod, she watched Addy practically skip out the door. Amanda smiled but it faded the moment she thought of Mal. She just hoped that her friend was right, because something was telling her that sooner rather than later, Mal was going to push her. And she hoped she was ready.

Chapter Nine

"So, I understand there's a rumor you might be stuck here for life," Kade said from the doorway.

Mal smiled at his brother-in-law. "When did you get back from New Orleans?"

Mal's sister Shannon still lived in their home city. It had been tough, but they seemed to be making it work.

"Last night, late. I called you, but you didn't pick up."

He had been over at Amanda's of course—as he had every night since that first night.

"I was busy."

"You don't say. Since I am married to your sister, and I could get smacked for not asking, is it someone I know?"

"Amanda Forrester."

He nodded. "Okay."

"You don't sound surprised."

He walked into the office with a smile. "Give me a break, Mal. You've been mooning over the woman for months. About time you got together. How did that happen?"

"She showed up at CP."

Kade didn't say anything for a second, then he grinned. "Well, I'll be damned. The woman knows you better than any of us. How long has this been going on?"

"I take it that you're going to carry tales back to my mama."

"You make me sound like some kind of spy for the women in your family."

He shrugged. "I call it like I see it."

"So, will I get in too much trouble if Mama Dupree finds out?"

He shook his head. "No, actually, I found a house over by Amanda's shop."

There was a beat of silence. "And?"

"I figured it would be good, especially if I end up here at the Pentagon."

Kade said nothing for a second, which made Mal a little itchy. Kade was rarely quiet with him. "And you haven't talked to her about it at all?"

"I have a feeling she isn't really into the whole idea of marriage. So I thought maybe I could get the house, ease her in. It'll work."

Another beat of silence, then Kade's mouth opened and shut...twice. "Holy shit, Dupree, you're scared."

That hit too close to home for him. "I am not scared of a woman."

"Then you're not that smart."

He gave his friend an annoyed look. "Talking riddles again?"

"No, just letting you know that when a man says he isn't scared of a woman, he usually gets his ass handed to him."

* * * *

Mal pulled to a stop and turned off the engine.

"What do you think?"

Amanda blinked at the townhouse. She had been so tired from the wedding she had worked on that morning that she hadn't been paying attention to where he was driving.

"Of what?"

"The house. I just signed a lease on it."

She glanced around at the neighborhood. It was nice, neat, a little bit of yard. "Oh, isn't it kind of far from Annapolis?"

"We'll talk about it. Let's take a look."

The normally smooth Mal was rushing. She could feel it in the way he was talking, and if she didn't know better, she would think he was nervous. He stepped out of his car and then rounded the hood. She pulled together the strength to step out of the car herself when he pulled the door open.

It wasn't big. In fact, it was just the right size. The yard wouldn't take that long to work, and the porch had just enough space to put some potted plants on it in the spring.

"I moved on it because it's an end unit. I don't mind sharing one wall, but I need some space."

"Yeah. I understand that."

He unlocked the door and then pushed it open. He waited for her to step over the threshold. She hesitated for a second, then entered the house. It was beautiful of course. The wooden floor gleamed, and the pale gold paint warmed the room.

"This is the living room. I figured I could put my TV over the fireplace. I can toss out my couch in favor of yours."

That stopped her.

"What did you just say?"

His expression blanked. "What?"

"You just said that you could use my couch. I'm not moving in with you."

He sighed. "Okay, I wasn't planning on springing this on you right now."

Dread filled her stomach as the dinner she had just eaten started to sour. "What were you planning on springing on me, Mal."

"That we could move in together. I know that you have a few more months left on your apartment, but then we could get you moved over here."

"No."

"What?"

"No."

He smiled. "I don't mean now."

"It doesn't matter when. It will always be no."

His smile faded. "I thought—"

She shook her head. "You thought wrong."

He studied her for a second. She knew she probably looked madder than a pissed off hornet. But she needed to get out of there before she freaked out. Well, before he knew she was freaking out.

"What is it you think we're doing here together?"

She stared at him, wondering at the tone.

"We're seeing each other."

She could tell that he wasn't happy with her answer. She didn't understand his issue.

"So, we're just playing around? No commitment."

Her heart was starting to sink. That was what she wanted. Why did the thought of not having forever with Malachai seem wrong now? She had been ready to walk away at the end of the relationship. She couldn't trust another man with her heart…right?

"I just told you I'm not marrying again."

He crossed his arms over his chest. "That's stupid."

"Don't you call me stupid. I'm not stupid."

He paused for a second, probably because she sounded like she was ready to kill. That and she was shrieking now.

"I didn't say you were stupid. I said that idea was stupid. I don't know why you're letting what happened with Kyle color your feelings toward marriage."

The word had panic clogging her throat. "Marriage?" she asked, her voice hoarse even to her own ears. Why did he keep using that word or insisting they were going to get married? They weren't. And for some reason, that thought didn't make her as happy as it had before.

"Yeah. You didn't think I would mess around with a woman like you and it not be something serious."

"It can be serious. I just don't want to get married."

"Again, I say that's stupid. Just because you lost one man doesn't mean you'll lose me."

She blinked at him. "Really? You think this is about his death?"

"What else could it be?"

She drew in a deep breath, and for the first time ever, she admitted out loud just what her problem was.

"It had more to do with the way he lived."

"What?"

She didn't want to do this, to be the one to tell him. It was odd that it was more to protect Mal's feelings than the honor of her husband. But she knew he wouldn't be happy without an explanation.

"Your friend, the guy you said you could count on, was a fucking cheater."

For a moment, Mal said nothing. "Explain."

Most women would get pissed at his tone, but she dealt better with it. She had grown up with it in her house from her brothers and her father. On top of it, if he was sweet, she would never be able to get everything out, to tell him just what a disaster her marriage was.

"So, you think I had some kind of great love story. It wasn't. It was sad and it was pathetic. The man couldn't stay faithful for even two weeks from what I found out."

"You seemed so happy."

And that made her sad. Because at first, she had been so happy, so full of excitement for their future. Kyle had ruined that, ruined any chances she had at believing she could have forever with a man.

"Oh Mal, things are never as they seem."

He said nothing, and she scrubbed her hands over her face. "Okay, I'll tell you. I might as well. Someone else should know what a bastard that man was."

"He was in love with you."

"Yeah, you would think that, right? The man was such a romantic, right?" She asked but didn't expect an answer. "He always struck those wonderful cords, making sure that I knew he cared for me. But apparently, it was an act. He couldn't keep it in his pants. When I got the first credit card bill when you were deployed on that last mission, well, I was pissed. I mean, he hadn't sent me flowers, and I know damned well I hadn't gone to New York with him. Okay, so truthfully, I wanted to believe that it was a glitch. Like the other bills that he had explained away. But when he died, I had to face the truth."

"I can't believe it. I *knew* him."

She looked over her shoulder at him. Her heart hurt when she saw the expression on his face. For Seals, they thought of themselves as family. Finding this out for him was probably more like finding out his brother was a bastard who cheated. Well, she was sick of pretending.

"Your friend was a slut, or at least the male version of it. For some reason, I could never really get excited about going to bed with him, and the last time I talked to him, he blamed me. Me. So it was my fault he went looking for women. That he cheated. After he died, I figured I would just walk away and be whole at some point, but then the rest of the bills started coming in." He opened his mouth to interrupt her, but she stopped him with a shake of her head. "If you stop me, I'll never finish."

He hesitated, then nodded.

"So, there I was having to hear what a great guy he was when I was paying off his debt...paying for the fact with not only my money, but my heart. Every week brought something more horrible. I was lucky, seriously. I was worried there would be something that I couldn't pay. That a bill would come in and I would have to go take out a loan, or worse, go to my parents and have to

324

explain to them why I didn't have the money to pay it and what it was."

She couldn't stop the tears that were burning the backs of her eyes. But she blinked them away. She refused to cry over the cheating bastard again.

"I am not the marrying type. See, I couldn't keep him faithful. I know what everyone will say, but you don't know every bit of my background. I have never in my life had a man stay faithful to me. Not for an extended period of time. They all cheat. There is something broken in me. I will not be married again. I will not tie myself to a man who will just end up leaving me at some point because I can't give him what he needs."

"But you give me what I need. You're everything I want. When a Dupree marries, they marry for life."

Oh God, that sounded wonderful. And she didn't doubt it. She had seen his brother with his wife and baby, along with Shannon and Kade. But…she would ruin that. If they married, she was sure something she did would ruin it. And while he would be faithful, he wouldn't be happy. Amanda couldn't live with herself if she made him unhappy. In her head she knew it was stupid, but she had to listen to her heart.

"I made a promise. I will not marry."

The room went silent, and it seemed odd. Very odd. She wasn't used to the tension that lay in the air between them. This was something…wrong. But she couldn't change her mind.

She needed to get away, to be away from him and everything that she wanted. Did she want to marry him? Hell, with every fiber of her being, but she couldn't take that chance. Not again. She didn't think she would survive. This time.

"Please take me home."

"Amanda."

"No, please. I need…"

She couldn't come up with an explanation. He nodded.

He said nothing as he followed her out, locked the door, and then the whole ride home. Nothing. It was actually five minutes from her apartment.

She looked at him. "If you can take what I can offer, then call."

"What, sex, no commitment?"

He sounded angry, and she knew it was more about his pride than his heart. With men, it was always that.

"A commitment, but one without the ties of marriage."

"That's not what I want."

"We don't get what we want most of the time." She leaned over and kissed his cheek, but he grabbed her.

"I love you, Amanda."

The intense look on his face told her he believed it. She knew it was true without a doubt, but that didn't mean she could accept that level of commitment. When she said nothing, he pulled her to him and gave her a hot, wet, fast kiss. She felt his irritation, his need, his passion for her. Then he released her.

She couldn't say anything else. She wanted to soothe his pain. She couldn't. It was selfish, but she was in too much pain herself.

She slipped out of the car and walked up to her apartment. It was embarrassing how much she wanted him to come after her, and if he had pushed, she would have broken. She knew he waited until she closed and locked the door. She leaned back against it, hoping against hope that he would come knocking, but she knew better. He wouldn't. Mal was the type of man who would honor her request.

She slid to the floor, dropping her purse beside her as she felt the tears she'd been fighting slide down her face. Amanda had been so sure when she had given him her ultimatum, but now she wasn't so sure. She physically hurt...needed him to be there, to hold her. And that was stupid. She had just told him to leave her alone unless he did what she wanted. But she had to keep herself safe and her heart whole.

She couldn't handle losing her pride for a man all over again. At the moment though, she couldn't exactly remember why that was so important.

* * * *

Mal heard the knock at the door, but he ignored it. He wasn't in the mood. The only phone calls he was taking came from the office. It had been a long three days, but he had resisted, mainly because the woman he wanted to call hadn't called him.

"Open up, Dupree," Kade said through the door. "That's an order."

Mal snorted. "I outrank you."

"Yeah, well, I have a visitor here who is ready to kick your ass."

He rolled his eyes thinking it might be his sister Shannon, Kade's wife. But when he opened the door, he found himself face to face with a very pissed Dylan.

"What the hell is wrong with you?" Dylan asked.

"Well, that's a nice way of saying hi. I've spoken to your mother. She wouldn't be happy to know one of her kids was so ill-mannered."

Mal turned and walked away. If they wanted to follow him into his room, so be it. He didn't give a damn.

"I went to the house looking for you, but Kade said you would be here."

Mal ignored the conversation. Seeing Amanda's brother was a little too much. If he was going to deal with him, Mal figured he'd have a beer. He opened the little fridge and pulled one out.

"Good God, Dupree, it's two in the afternoon and you are already drunk," Kade said.

"Yeah, well it's five o'clock somewhere."

Kade reached over and took the bottle from Mal and then marched to the bathroom and poured it out in the sink.

"I have more."

"You will not have more. You've got to get your ass dressed and over to Amanda's apartment," Dylan said.

He gave her brother a look and opened his mouth to respond, but then the room began spinning.

"Shit." He almost fell on his ass.

"When was the last time you ate?" Kade asked.

"Uh, yesterday, I think."

"Seal, you know better than to drink that much with no food in you. Come on."

Kade sat him on the bed while Dylan called room service.

"Now, first you have to get some food in you, then you need to get yourself cleaned up."

He looked at Kade and realized there were two of him there. "Yeah, I agree on the food, but I think that I don't see the reason for getting cleaned up. It's Saturday morning. I don't have to be back at work until Monday."

The men shared a look. Kade nodded and stepped back. Dylan leaned down. "Okay, I wanted to kick your ass when we got here, but I see that Kade was right."

"Kade is never right. Ask Shannon."

Kade chuckled but then stopped when Dylan shot him a look.

"Really? Because he said you were head over heels in love with my sister, and I wouldn't have believed it if I hadn't seen what a mess you are right now."

"So I took a few days to be lazy. Shoot me."

"I was ready to. You have my sister so damned miserable, I wanted to beat the hell out of you. Kade convinced me otherwise. You have to get yourself cleaned up so you can go over there and stop her."

"Stop her from what?" Then he shook his head and felt his stomach quiver. Shit.

"From going to Capital Punishment. That ass who runs the club is letting her and Addy in again, probably because he wants to get into Addy's pants. So they are making a night of it."

His brain didn't seem to be working right. Did her brother just say Amanda was going to the club?

"She's going to the club? What for?"

"Step aside, Major," Kade said.

He did and Kade took his place. Then his brother-in-law slapped Mal upside the back of his head. "That's from Shannon. She said to use it if you were being a stupid man."

"Dammit, Kade." His head was spinning even more. "Your sister won't marry me, Dylan."

"Yeah, well, what did you do? You rented a fucking house and just assumed she would be happy with it. First of all, if you love her, you have to understand that she will never do what you want if you try to arrange it without asking."

He squinted at Dylan. "Yeah?"

He wanted to spill his guts and explain why she would never marry him, but he knew she hadn't told anyone else. He alone had been the person she had told.

"You think I don't know what that bastard Forrester did to her?"

Mal looked at him, surprised. "You know?"

He nodded, and his frown turned darker. "I would have ruined him. If I would have let him live, which was questionable."

"When did you find out?"

He sighed and settled in the chair beside the bed. "After he was dead. I was over at Amanda's checking on her. She did a lot of sleeping those days from the depression. I thought it was because of losing him. But I found out about the bills. She'd left them sitting open on her desk. I knew then what he had done. The fact of what he did was made worse by the fact that she had to pay off his bills. It took a little digging, but I even found a few people he dated in the Pentagon. Bastard."

Mal squinted at him. "Why didn't you ask her about it?"

He snorted. "Really? Are you sure you know Amanda at all?"

"Her pride."

"Yeah, her damned pride. She could never take a slight. Ever. I know friends of hers she hasn't spoken to because they weren't truthful with her. I thought it was all idiocy until I thought back on the guys she dated. She always seemed to pick guys who cheated on her. I thought Forrester was going to be good for her, but he was worse than all the others. I thought she might never date another military guy after that. Until you, she wasn't ready to trust again."

"According to her, I will at some point. Or hate her in the end."

"But she trusts you, Dupree."

He shook his head. He wished. He hoped, but he knew she didn't. "No, she doesn't."

"Really? Because the truth is, I think she does."

"Now I'm not so sure I'm the one with three days of drinking under my belt."

Dylan made a face. "Okay, I have to go where a brother doesn't like to go. But I know that you're a Dom, and that you are a member of CP. And I know that the first night you hooked up, you did it there."

"Are you spying on her?"

He rolled his eyes. "No. I know people and they know she's my sister, that's why I know. I need you to think about the one thing a truly good Dom/sub relationship has. What is the one thing that definitely makes it special? And don't even think about love. She loves you, and we both know it. She's probably already told you."

He nodded.

"The one thing you need for that relationship to really work on a level of the greatest satisfaction is trust. Shit, Dupree, she trusts you. She just doesn't trust herself."

He squinted up at her brother and shook his head.

"Being a coward, Dupree?"

"No, there are two of you."

He chuckled. "Get cleaned up and gear up. You have to go get your woman and save her from making a really big mistake tonight. I'll call Addy and make sure she's late."

"She'll be pissed if she finds out you did this."

They both knew who he was talking about. Amanda held so much in, tried to hide so much that he knew she would be pissed that her brother had shared so much. The fact that she didn't tell him until he upset her meant she hadn't wanted anyone to know.

"Yeah, well, in the end, I expect a nephew with my name."

That stopped him for a second. The idea of marriage, babies, and more importantly, Amanda in his bed every night sunk in.

Her brother nodded "Ah, he finally gets it. I'm calling Addy. You get your friend ready. If I don't help you fix this, my mother would probably kill me."

Mal stood up but the room tilted again as there was a knock at the door. He sat down. "Maybe I need to eat that food."

"Then get your woman?" Kade asked.

He smiled. "Yes, definitely get my woman."

Chapter Ten

Amanda pulled on the little leather black skirt she had worn the first time she'd gone to Capital Punishment. Had it been less than a month ago? God, it seemed like it had been a lifetime since she had challenged Mal that night.

"I think we need to stay home tonight," Addy said as she leaned against the doorjamb. "There is something telling me that this is not a good idea."

She glanced at her friend. She'd dressed in all black, except her hair was now pink. Amanda had sensed there was something else going on with Addy, but she couldn't figure it out. She had been so self-involved that she hadn't questioned her weird mood the last few days.

"Is there another reason?"

Addy fidgeted and avoided the question, which was not like her at all.

"Does this have to do with Walton?"

Her face flushed. "Not really."

"No?"

She shook her head but wouldn't meet Amanda's gaze. Another weird thing that had been happening.

"So, this guy you aren't that interested in--"

"I am not interested in him at all. I told you, I found him attractive, that was it."

Ah, so that was it. "Okay, anyway, he lets us get in, but you don't want to go because you have a bad feeling? Or maybe you're a little too tempted by him."

Addy's hands fisted by her sides, and she looked madder than a hornet. "Take that back."

Amanda laughed for the first time in days. "Oh. My. God. You're really attracted to him."

"I am not. Well, yes I am. I admitted that before. He's...well, you saw him." Amanda nodded. "But he's totally wrong for me. Worse, he keeps me off balance. I thought he would use my father to pressure me to date him, but he hasn't. And I know now he won't."

And to Amanda, he sounded perfect for Addy, but she wasn't going to say that to her. She might get a smack to the back of the head for it.

"But don't think you're getting out of the discussion. I don't think we can go to CP tonight. You're not in the right frame of mind."

She shrugged and walked to the bathroom to run a brush through her hair. "I'm not really in the mood, but I figured Walton wanted you there. Plus, it would get my mind off the problems with Mal."

Addy followed her and watched her brush her hair before answering. "Sweetie, there's a reason he hasn't called."

"Yeah, I think he saw what I had to offer and walked away."

Addy shook her head. "No. I think you both need some time, then you will get it straightened out."

She opened her mouth to respond, but the doorbell rang. Amanda frowned.

"Who could that be?"

"Hey, I'll get it, and then we'll decide about CP."

Amanda nodded but she had made up her mind. Amanda looked at herself in the mirror, realizing she had spent so much time mourning what she thought she'd had with Kyle that she had wasted her life. It was too short to worry about things that wouldn't be.

And feeling like shit wasn't going to help her. She needed people, needed a break from the pain she'd dealt with every day that Mal hadn't called.

Even as she thought it, tears filled her eyes. Dammit, she didn't need this, didn't need to deal with the pain of his decision. She had left it up to him. And he had decided. She grabbed a lipstick and started to put it on as she listened to the low murmur of voices. She couldn't make out what was being said, but she could tell that Addy knew whoever it was. Then the door shut and silence followed.

"Amanda, get your ass out here."

Mal.

She couldn't move. First of all, her brain just would not cooperate. Fear, joy, excitement wound through her system. *What was he doing here?*

"Amanda, I am not in the mood for games. I ordered you out here, and I want you out her now."

Irritation chased away all the other feelings. Wasn't that just like a man? He goes days without communicating, then shows up and expects her to hop to it.

She stomped out into the living room and was stopped by the sight of Mal in his full dress whites. He had his hat under one arm, and he didn't look happy. In fact, from the expression in his eyes, he was beyond pissed. Dammit, he looked good enough to eat.

No, Amanda, don't get sidetracked.

She crossed her arms beneath her breasts. "What are you doing here?"

"You said to come get you if I changed my mind. I decided to listen to the first half of the sentence and ignore the last part."

"I guess it's a man's prerogative to ignore what he wants." She snorted. "Of course you do. All men are that way."

"I'm pretty sure your brothers and your father would disagree with you. And do not compare me to the men you've been with in the past." He ground out every word, his temper lashing at her.

She couldn't say anything to that. He might look calm, but she could feel the barely suppressed anger simmering beneath the surface.

"I came here to take you. You're mine, so I choose to keep you."

She opened her mouth once, but no words came out. Really, she didn't know what to say to that. She counted backwards from ten...twice.

"You choose? You choose?" she asked, nearly shouting.

"I believe I said that."

His calm voice had her own temper soaring. "Just what the hell do you think you get to decide?"

"I decide that I love you, and I am not going to stop trying to convince you to marry me."

Her heart did a little jig, but she ignored it. She couldn't deal with this, with love thrown about like it was some kind of appeasement for her pride. Every man before him had done that to her, and she couldn't let him just be another man like that. He was too special in her heart.

"That will not work with me."

"What?"

"Telling me that you love me. I am not going to melt down into a gooey pool of lust for you."

"Really?" He let one eyebrow rise. "You think you're easy like that?"

"It's worked in the past."

"I don't know what you were like, but you must have changed if you used to be an easy mark for men."

"What do you mean?"

"Any man these days who tries that shit on you should know better. You might have been a doormat in the past, but you aren't one now. And woman, I swear to God, you compare me to those idiots one more time, I will take you over my knee and smack your ass red."

She tried to ignore her response. Of course her body reacted to the threat. Knowing Mal the way she did, she knew he did it on purpose. He knew how much she liked it.

"I wasn't comparing you to them."

"No? Then maybe you're just a coward."

That had her temper flaring higher, and she itched to pick something up to throw at him. From the look on his face, it would be a mistake.

"I am not a coward."

"I would have never thought so. But here you are, allowing a bastard who didn't understand your worth hold you down."

"That doesn't make me a coward."

"No? I think so. You're too afraid to even give me a chance. I wish I had known Kyle had been a bastard when he'd been alive because I definitely would have done something about it, but letting him fuck with the rest of your life is stupid."

"What is wrong with what we had?"

"Because I want more, and dammit, you deserve more."

She was stunned by the vehemence in his voice, and she couldn't stop the tears from filling her eyes.

"Oh God, don't cry," he said, panic threading his voice.

"I can't help it."

"I order you to quit crying."

Her mouth hung open for a second then she snapped it shut. "You can't order me to do that."

"Well, stop it."

That made her cry even more. "I can't. If you keep yelling at me like that, I can't stop crying."

"I am not yelling," he said in a shout.

"What do you expect me to do? You say something beyond sweet to me—the nicest thing a man has ever said to me—and then you yell at me. Of course I am going to cry."

He hesitated for a second as if trying to make up his mind, then he stepped forward, grabbed ahold of her arms and pulled her against him.

"I'm sorry, *chéri*. I didn't mean to upset you. I just…wait, you said the sweetest thing?"

She looked up at him, and she knew she was a mess. Her face was soaking wet from crying, and she was always an ugly crier.

"Yeah."

"I told you the other day that I loved you."

He didn't understand that saying the words meant little to her. She had heard them so many times that she didn't trust them. Three words didn't hold water to what he thought of her.

"No, it's that you said I deserved more. I don't think I have ever met a man who thought that, and I know they never said it."

He studied her, his gaze roaming over his face, then he laughed and pulled her back against him. "Well, darlin', I would say that you've been hanging out with the wrong men."

She chuckled.

"And I take back the coward remark."

"No, it was true." He opened his mouth to argue but she shook her head. "I *was* afraid. I love you so much, Mal, I just don't think I could bear it if you turned out like a lot of the men I had dated, and hell, the one I married. None of them meant what you mean to me and if I drove you to it, I would have broken."

"You didn't drive anyone to it. They were weak men who couldn't handle having a strong woman love them. I have no problem with that." He pulled her back and studied her face. "You *will* marry me."

He didn't ask, and how like him to do just that. "On one condition."

"What?"

"That we have a real wedding. I want it to be real this time. No running off to Vegas. No quickie ceremony. I want our families there as we say our vows."

He seemed to let out a breath. "Agreed." Then he kissed her, sweet with just a drop of heat in it.

"Where do you want to get married?"

"I don't care. Anywhere as long as we have friends there for the ceremony, and I want my dad to give me away this time."

"Yeah. I like that." Then his smile dimmed. "You sure you want to be a military wife? I mean, I know losing Kyle was bad even with your problems. Moving around, dealing with the crap that comes with it…I know it isn't easy."

"I'm not marrying the military, I'm marrying you. I know the drill, the issues we are going to deal with. And I know better than you that your time in the field is going to dwindle. They don't tap trained Seals to be over at the Pentagon for no reason. As long as we do it together, I can do it."

One side of his mouth kicked up. "Yeah?"

"Yeah, although, I would like a real proposal, a ring, and I think our audience standing outside the door is irritated with waiting."

He laughed, then surprised her by dropping to one knee. The breath clogged in her throat as she stared down at him. He pulled a box out of his pocket, opened it, and retrieved a ring. His smile faded, and he took one of her hands.

"I know you don't like convention all the time, but…you deserve romance. All the hearts and flowers, and I want to spend the rest of my life giving them to you."

Tears welled up in her eyes again. "Oh, Malachai."

"I'm taking that as a yes," he said, slipping the ring on her finger. Then he rose and kissed her, his tongue darting out to trace the seam of her lips. She opened her mouth and let him steal inside. By the time he pulled back, her heart was beating out of control and they were both breathing heavily.

She held out her hand and looked at the ring. It was a solid white gold band with a solitaire diamond.

"It's simple, but it was my grandmother's ring."

She looked up at him and smiled. "Yeah?"

"Yeah. I thought you would like it because you have a soft heart."

"Oh, I do. I really do." The fact that he understood that meant more to her than almost anything else. No man had ever realized that she had a romantic streak, which was funny because she was a florist. Until Mal. She slipped her hand around to the back of his head and pulled him down for a kiss.

They probably wouldn't have stopped except for the knock at the door.

"We *are* getting kind of sick of standing out here," Kade said through the door.

Mal chuckled as he let her go and moved to the door. Before he opened it, she laid a hand on his arm.

"I love you, Malachai Dupree."

He stepped back and gave her a quick, hard kiss. "And I love you, Amanda Forrester."

Her heart full, she waited for him to open the door so they could share the news with their friends and family— not to mention the rest of their lives.

Epilogue

Mal stepped out of the bathroom to see his bride looking out over the ocean view from their room.

His bride. His wife. He couldn't get used to hearing the thought in his head. For the first time in years everything seemed…right. She was still in her dress. It was simple, tight on top then flowing over her hips. The ivory color brought out the gold in her skin tone and deepened the green of her eyes. No ruffles, no flounces, and not much decoration, but it was…classic, just like the lady.

"Are you going to stand there all night and stare at me?"

She hadn't turned around, but he could hear the amusement in her voice. He walked forward and slipped his hand around her waist to pull her back against him.

"If I wanted to, I would."

She chuckled and leaned back against him.

"You're still okay with being married in Hawaii?" he asked. She had nixed the idea of New Orleans because she had spent her honeymoon there and she had said Texas was never home to her. When he suggested Hawaii, she had jumped at the chance, but he had worried she might have had second thoughts.

She laughed and turned around to look up at him with those green eyes. "No, I'm furious my fiancé wanted me to come to Oahu and marry. What woman wants to be surrounded by all this beauty? And to say that my parents were thrilled is putting it mildly. I didn't know they had spent their honeymoon at the Hale Koa."

"Well, if I had known that, I would have had the reception there instead of at Turtle Bay."

"Naw, they loved it. I love it here. I thought I would miss the cold weather the last few weeks, but I really don't. Actually, I am starting to love the way the air feels on my skin at night."

Now was the time for truths. He had been avoiding the issue for as long as possible. "I'm kind of glad to hear that."

"Hmm? Why?"

"I've been offered a position here at Pearl Harbor. I know it sucks and that you and Addy are starting to just explode with bookings." When she didn't say anything, he started to panic. There was no expression on her face, and for once, he couldn't really read her. "Never mind. I'll turn it down."

She gave him a small smile and shook her head. "You can't turn it down."

"I can and I will."

She rolled her eyes. "No, you won't. You will take the job. Addy and I already discussed this possibility. I knew it was going to happen, Mal."

"Yeah?"

"I told you I knew that you were on the fast track. This happened sooner rather than later, and I hate leaving my best friend running the show, but we'll work it out. I've already started to train someone to help her when I'm gone."

He smiled. "You don't mind?"

"Of course I do. I mind a lot. But…like my mother has told me before, it doesn't bother me that much knowing I will have you. It isn't about giving anything up. It's about gaining a life. And I told you I knew this would happen."

His heart expanded with more joy than he thought possible. "I love you, Mrs. Dupree."

"I love you, Lieutenant Commander Dupree."

"I rather like being called Mr. Dupree. My career isn't all I am."

She gave him a knowing smile. "I wouldn't have married you otherwise, Mal," she whispered against his lips as she kissed him.

The End

Coming this Fall and Winter, two more Military Harmless books with heroes you already know and love.

First, in November:

CRAVING: A Little Harmless Military Romance book 4

When these opposites get together, the laws of attraction go right out the window.

Jonah Berg is a man who believes in only the tangible. The Marine definitely doesn't want a woman who believes in fate and believes in things that can't be proven. Still, he can't keep his mind or his hands off Fiona Farelli. It doesn't help that the woman is sweetly submissive, or that she fills his needs on so many levels.

Fiona knows that she might be making a mistake with Jonah. The man's nickname is Diablo for goodness' sake. But she feels a pull to him like no other man before him. And when he takes her to bed, she finds herself completely and utterly enthralled.

When their relationship goes from sensual bed games to falling in love, Fiona is left with a decision to make: risk her heart on the uptight marine, or walk away from the one man who is her soul mate.

And coming this winter:

Relentless: A Little Harmless Military Romance, book 5

What happens in Vegas…

Sorry, you have to wait to find out!

More about Melissa Schroeder

From an early age, Melissa loved to read. First, it was the books her mother read to her including her two favorites, *Winnie the Pooh* and the Beatrix Potter books. She cut her preteen teeth on Trixie Belden and read and reviewed *To Kill a Mockingbird* in middle school. It wasn't until she was in college that she tried to write her first stories, which were full of angst and pain, and really not that fun to read or write. After trying several different genres, she found romance in a Linda Howard book.

Since the publication of her first book in 2004, Melissa has had close to fifty romances published. She writes in genres from historical suspense to modern day erotic romance to futuristics and paranormals. Included in those releases is the best selling Harmless series. In 2011, Melissa branched out into self-publishing with **A Little Harmless Submission** and the popular military spinoff, **Infatuation: A Little Harmless Military Romance**. Along the way she has garnered an epic nomination, a multitude of reviewer's recommended reads, over five Capa nods from TRS, three nominations for AAD Bookies and regularly tops the best seller lists on Amazon and Barnes and Noble.

Since she spent her childhood as a military brat, Melissa swore never to marry military. But, as we all know, Fate has her way with mortals. She is married to an AF major and is raising her own brats, both human and canine. She spends her days giving in to her addiction to Twitter, counting down the days until her hubby retires, and cursing the military for always sticking them in a location that is filled with bugs big enough to eat her children.

If you would like to connect with her, find her in the following places:

MelissaSchroeder.net
Twitter.com/melschroeder
Facebook.com/Melissaschroederfanpage
Facebook.com/groups/harmlesslovers
Facebook.com/groups/harmlessbookdiscussion

347

Texas Temptations
Conquering India
Delilah's Downfall

Hawaiian Holidays
Mele Kalikimaka, Baby
Sex on the Beach
Getting Lei'd

Bounty Hunters, Inc
For Love or Honor
Sinner's Delight

The Sweet Shoppe
Tempting Prudence—free on website
Her Wicked Warrior

Connected Books
Seducing the Saint
Hunting Mila
Saints and Sinners—print of both books

The Hired Hand
Hands on Training

Cancer Anthology
Water—print

Stand Alone Books
Grace Under Pressure
The Last Detail
Her Mother's Killer
A Calculated Seduction

Telepathic Cravings

Coming soon
A Little Harmless Fantasy
A Little Harmless Ride
Craving
Relentless

Writing as Kiera West exclusively for Siren Publishing
The Great Wolves of Passion, Alaska

Seducing Their Mate

The Alpha's Fall

Convincing Ethan

Shane's Need

Rand's Craving

Coming soon

Jason's Salvation

Max's Need

Claiming Their Mate